THE SWEET GOLDEN PARACHUTE

THE
SWEET GOLDEN
PARACHUTE

DAVID
HANDLER

THOMAS DUNNE BOOKS

ST. MARTIN'S MINOTAUR

NEW YORK

MYS
Handler

THOMAS DUNNE BOOKS.
An Imprint of St. Martin's Press.

www.minotaurbooks.com

ISBN 0-312-34211-X
EAN 978-0-312-34211-1

First Edition: March 2006

10 9 8 7 6 5 4 3 2 1

THIS ONE IS FOR DAVE AND JO DRAKE,
WHO'VE ALWAYS TREATED ME LIKE ONE OF THE FAM

THE SWEET GOLDEN PARACHUTE

PROLOGUE

PETE WOKE WELL BEFORE dawn and sat up in his sleeping bag and tried to remember what day it was. He had his regular morning routes and it really did matter. Knuckling his eyes, he tried to recall where he'd been the day before. The Historic District, that's where. So yesterday must have been Tuesday. And today Wednesday, which meant Route 156, upriver from the Big Brook Road business district.

There, that wasn't so hard.

Shivering, Pete reached for his pint bottle of Captain Morgan spiced rum and drank down several thirsty gulps, peering around in the dark at the dented, moldering Silver Streak that he called home. The old trailer sat out behind Doug's Sunoco in the empty lot where Doug stashed the beaters he rented out by the day to folks in need. Doug's was an old-time service station. Two licensed mechanics on duty six days a week. A twenty-four-hour towing operation. Doug even employed acne-encrusted high school kids to pump gas.

Aside from Doug, none of the guys there had anything to do with Pete, since everyone knew he was crazy and you were supposed to stay away from him. They didn't even know his real name—just called him what everyone else in Dorset called him: the Can Man.

Still swaddled in his sleeping bag, Pete shuffled his way over to the tiny kitchenette, where he kept his cans of chili and Beefaroni and the like. He kept his Crown Pilot crackers and Wonder Bread inside an old saltines tin or the mice would tear into them. He opened some pork and beans and ate them cold right out of the can with two slices of Wonder Bread. Washed it all down with more Captain Morgan and six aspirin. Then, slowly, Pete wriggled his gaunt self out of the bag, groaning from his aches. He pulled on his wool hunting shirt, heavy wool pants and pea coat, fingers fumbling from the arthritis. Stepped into his cracked, ancient work boots. Ran a hand through his iron gray hair, which he trimmed himself with shears; likewise his beard, which was mostly white. His blue eyes were deep set, his nose long and narrow. He had once been quite handsome. The girls had really gone for him. But it had been years since they'd looked at him that way. Or at all.

He was invisible.

This was perfectly okay by him. As long as people stayed away from him, Pete was fine. He just wanted to live his life his own way—no driver's license, no credit cards, no bank account, no phone, no keys. He was a free man. Didn't need the hospital. Didn't need his medication. He had his trailer, his Captain Morgan and his morning rounds. He got plenty of exercise. Kept his mind busy with his numbers. He was fine. Hell, he was probably the happiest he'd ever been.

He hobbled inside. It was barely 6:00 A.M. but Doug was already filling the till and turning on the pumps. Pete rinsed his face in the work sink and drank down a cup of Doug's strong, hot coffee. By then it was time to saddle up.

Pete made his morning rounds on a mountain bike that he'd found at the dump. It had only one serviceable gear, but it moved. His trailers, a pair of rackety grocery carts that he'd liberated from the A&P, were chained to the book rack behind his seat, one behind the other. Doug had put red reflectors on the back of Pete's trailers and installed a battery-powered headlight on the front of his bike. The beam was feeble, but it gave the early morning drivers some indication that he was there.

It was still dark out when Pete started his way along the shoulder of Big Brook Road. Pete was not quiet. People could hear him and his empty trailers coming from a half-mile away in the predawn country silence. He pedaled, wool knit cap pulled low over his eyes and ears, jacket buttoned up to his throat. It was maybe a degree or two above freezing, and the headlights on the occasional passing car revealed a dense early morning fog. It was supposed to turn warm today, maybe warm enough to melt some of the hard, grimy snowbank that the plowman had built up along the shoulder.

When he reached the river he turned right onto Route 156, a narrow, twisting country road that ran its way north of Dorset into gentlemen's farm country. He pedaled along through the foggy darkness, a half-pint of Captain Morgan snug inside his jacket pocket. His right knee still throbbed despite the aspirin. He tore cartilage in it playing rugby a hundred million years ago. And his left hip never stopped aching. He'd broken it when he flipped his Porsche late one night in the Italian Alps. The girl with him hadn't made it. Pete couldn't remember her name. Didn't want to remember her name.

He was happy that winter was passing, because the snow hadn't stopped falling last month and a lot of roads had been plain impassable. Pete got edgy without enough work to do. Mostly, he sat in his trailer all day poring over his personal bible, *The World Almanac*. Pete just loved *The World Almanac*. He had studied the bushel production of ten different agricultural products for all fifty states. Charted the distances by car between various cities. From Amarillo to Omaha it was 643 miles. From Cincinnati to New Orleans 786. Pete was very into numbers. As long as he kept his head crowded with numbers he could keep his demons shoved inside of a box, his full weight pressed down on top of the lid. The demons would try to pound their way out. But they were locked inside as long as he concentrated on his numbers. It was only when people started *talking* to him, *asking* him things, that the box would spring open and out would pop the demons.

As far as Pete was concerned, there was absolutely nothing wrong with this world that could not be solved by staying away from other people.

He pedaled. Dorset's recycling truck made its rounds by around eight. Pete would have come and gone by then. The town picked up bundled newspapers and flattened cardboard, which were of no interest to Pete. It was the empty beer and soda cans that were. The bottles, too. Each one carried a nickel deposit on it. And a lot of the rich folk put them out for the Can Man—knowing that this was how he fed himself. Some of them even bagged them separately for him.

He pedaled, steering his little vehicle onto Bittersweet Lane, a cul-de-sac of million-dollar homes that had been built a few years back in old man Talcott's apple orchards. At the foot of the first driveway he came to, Pete stopped to pick his way through the plastic recycling bins. He left the sardine cans and milk jugs. Took only the soda pop and beer empties, computing the nickel valuations in his head as he stuffed them inside his black plastic trash bags . . . *Ten, fifteen and one more that's twenty. Twenty-five, thirty.* . . .

Pete kept his cans separate from his bottles, and divided his glass bottles from the plastic ones. This saved him time when he hauled his load to the machines at the A&P. On a morning like this, he might clear twenty dollars . . . *seventy-five, eighty* . . . He'd use it to buy his groceries and his Captain Morgan. Then he'd head back to his trailer for a nap. Maybe mosey on over to the Congregational Church for the free soup kitchen lunch.

Once the weather got warmer, he'd spend his afternoons on a bench in the town green with the sun on his face, feeding the squirrels stale bread until the kids got out of school. He had to steer clear of the kids in town. Some of the boys liked to taunt him and throw rocks at him. But Pete could not defend himself or that tall black trooper lady would descend on him. The little girls were even more worrisome. Even though Pete always tried to mind his own business, all he had to do was *look* at one of them and the nice ladies in town would send him back to the hospital.

Pete made out like a bandit on Bittersweet this morning. Already, he had $5.90 worth of empties, and he was just getting started. He clattered his way back onto Route 156, heading north.

The occasional car came down the hill toward him in the darkness—workers who had themselves a long commute to Hartford or New Haven. But mostly he was still alone on the narrow, twisting road, puffing for air as he pedaled up the hill, feeling the weight of all those empties he was towing. To keep himself going, he sang his theme song—a rowdy sixteen-bar blues ode to cheap wine that he'd seen King Curtis and Champion Jack Dupree perform together at the Montreux Jazz Festival back in the summer of '71, just a few months before the King got knifed to death in New York. He remembered the instrumentals perfectly. Champion Jack's rollicking piano, King's great big sax. He could remember none of the lyrics. Only its title: *Sneaky Pete.* That was what made it his song.

"*Sneaky Pete!* . . ." he sang to himself. "*I'm Sneaky Pete!*"

As he pedaled along, singing it, hearing it, it occurred to Pete that music was the only thing he missed about having no property. A good stereo. His blues and jazz albums. He'd had an amazing collection. But the music was still up there inside his head. All he had to do was listen hard.

"*Sneaky Pete!* . . ."

Now he'd made it to the foot of *her* driveway, the compound where the old bitch and her people lived. He climbed off and filled his baskets some more, taking her bottles and cans just like he took anybody else's. He showed no prejudice. Although he did pause to spit on her mailbox.

This was a ritual he performed every Wednesday.

As Pete continued up 156 on his appointed rounds, pedaling along the shoulder, he could feel the rhythm of his song . . . *Bum-dee-dum* . . . and count it . . . *Two-three-four* . . . because music was about numbers, too, wasn't it? As he neared a stretch of wild brush and woodland, he heard a car come up behind, its headlights illuminating him and everything before him in foggy darkness. But the car did not pass him. Just stayed right there behind him, its engine making a throaty burble in the country quiet. Something about the way it sounded struck Pete as oddly familiar, but he didn't turn around to check it out. Just pulled over at the next driveway, climbed off and started to pick through more empties.

Until suddenly he heard car doors open and swift footsteps coming toward him. Now he started to turn around but before he could move he got *whacked* on the back of his head by something incredibly hard. The blow staggered him. As he fell to his knees, dazed, blinking in the headlight beams, he felt another *crack* to his head. Now there were hands. Many hands lifting him up into the air, sweeping him into the woods beyond the roadside brush. Footsteps crashed through the brambles and dead leaves. Two of them. There were two. He could hear them whisper urgently to each other, but could not make out their words. And now they'd dumped him onto the slushy mud of the forest floor and they were cracking him on the head again. He threw his hands up over his head and let out a feeble yowl of pain as he felt another blow and another and then he did not feel anything.

He could hear them running away. Hear one of them crash and fall in the brush, get back up and keep running.

As he lay there, face down in the mud, Pete felt unbelievably huge. As huge as the planet itself. He swore that he could feel the curvature of the earth under his chest. And he could hear a wounded animal moaning softly somewhere far away in the woods. Then he realized with sudden clarity that the moans were coming out of *him*. There was a rackety, jangling noise nearby. They were doing something to his bike and trailers. Now there were footsteps and they jumped back in their car and went roaring off into the darkness, leaving him behind.

But he was not alone. King and Champion Jack were still there with him.

"I'm Sneaky Pete!"

The blues stayed with him, the beat pounding in his ears. *Dee-dum . . . Bum-dee-dum.* Though it was going slower now. And slo-o-o-ower . . . *Dee . . . Dum-m-m-m . . .*

"I'm Sneaky Pete!"

Until he wasn't anybody anymore.

THIRTY-SIX HOURS EARLIER

CHAPTER 1

"MITCH, ARE YOU *SURE* you want to discard that trey of diamonds?"

"Quite sure, Rut." Mitch helped himself to another slice of sausage and mushroom pizza. He was seated across from Rut at the round oak dining table that pretty much filled the old geezer's cozy parlor. "Why are you asking?"

"You discarded the trey of clubs not one minute ago," Rut replied. "It so happens I snatched it up. A card player who wants to hold on to some of his hard-earned money might surmise that I'm collecting treys, and by discarding another one he'd be giving me a little thing we call . . . *Gin*." Rut fanned his cards out on the table, cackling with delight. "Let's see what you've got, pigeon."

Mitch had *bupkes*—for the fifth hand in a row.

"That's two dollars and sixty-three cents you owe me," Rut declared, computing the total on the pad at his elbow. "It's a good thing you excel at your profession, my pudgy young friend. Because you are one rotten card player."

"Shut up and deal," grumbled Mitch Berger, lead film critic for the most prestigious, and therefore lowest paying, of the three New York City daily newspapers. Mitch's job called for him to spend part of his time in the city. But lately he'd been spending more and more of it in Dorset, the historic Connecticut Gold Coast village that was situated at the mouth of the Connecticut River almost exactly halfway between New York and Boston. His life was here now.

"Sorry, Mitch, you said what?" Rut turned up his hearing aids. He was pretty much deaf without them.

"I said, 'Shut up and deal,'" Mitch replied, quoting that most famous of lines from *The Apartment,* his favorite Billy Wilder movie.

"It'll be a pleasure," Rut said, shuffling the cards with hands that were surprisingly deft and quick. Rutherford Peck invariably whipped Mitch at Gin Rummy. He was a more serious card player. Either that or he cheated. Mitch wouldn't put it past the sly old coot. "Care for another stout to wash down that there slice?"

"I wouldn't say no."

Rut got slowly to his feet and waddled into the kitchen to fetch two more bottles of his delicious home-brewed stout. Rut was a stocky, potato-nosed widower in his late seventies with tufty white hair, rosy red cheeks and eyes that were blue and impish behind his thick black-framed glasses. He smelled strongly of Ben-Gay, Vicks VapoRub and mothballs, a locally popular blend of scents that Mitch had come to think of as Eau de Dorset. Rut had served as Dorset's postmaster for some thirty-seven years. Had lived in this upended shoebox of a farmhouse his whole life. It was an old tenant farmer's cottage on Maple Lane, a narrow dead-end that cut in between two of the grandest colonial mansions to be found in the Dorset Street Historic District. His place was falling into weedy disrepair, like a lot of houses owned by old people. But the parlor was homey.

Mitch had gotten to know him through Sheila Enman, one of the housebound Dorset elders who he'd started marketing for over the winter. Sheila had wondered if Mitch might pick up a few things for Rut, too. "My pleasure," Mitch had assured her, especially when the retired postmaster insisted on rewarding him with bottles of his home-brewed stout. Soon, Mitch took to hanging around to drink that stout with him and catch up on village gossip. Absolutely nothing went on that Rut Peck didn't know about. When Rut's Monday night regular died a few weeks back, Mitch was promoted to a full-fledged Friend of Rut.

The Friends of Rut were a rich and varied cross section of local notables. Among the old man's roster of designated nightly visitors were Dorset's starchy first selectman, Bob Paffin, and Eric

Vickers, an organic farmer who was the son of Poochie Vickers, Dorset's most renowned WASP aristocrat. There was Milo Kershaw, a grizzled swamp Yankee who'd spent several years behind bars. And there was Mitch, a thirty-two-year-old Jewish product of the streets of New York City. Every Monday he let Rut beat his ass at Gin Rummy.

Not that he had the power to stop him. The old geezer could play cards.

Rut returned from the kitchen with two bottles of stout. He set them down on the table, wheezing slightly, and fed his wood stove with more logs. It was a cold, damp March night. Soon it would be St. Patrick's Day, which was Mitch's least favorite holiday of the year. Not because he hated parades or corned beef and cabbage, but because of something very personal and sorrowful.

Mitch poured the creamy stout slowly into his tilted mug and took a sip, savoring its rich, nutty flavor, before he dove for another slice of the pizza he'd picked up at a small family run pizzeria in Niantic. It was not Lombardi's coal-fired pizzeria on Spring Street, but it was very good.

Rut sat back down and reached for the cards, shuffling them as the logs crackled in the wood stove. "Mitch, I have a small favor to ask of you. And if this isn't your kind of thing just say so and there'll be no hard feelings. Do you happen to know Justine Kershaw? She's Milo's youngest."

"No, we've never met."

"Well sir, Justine's life is about to get a whole lot more complicated," Rut told him, setting the cards aside. "Her big brothers, Stevie and Donnie, are getting out of prison tomorrow. And it sure doesn't help that the young man who she's been seeing, Bement Widdifield, is the very fellow who called the law on them."

"So I've heard. Everyone's talking about it." The Kershaw brothers were Dorset's reigning nasty boys. They'd been behind bars ever since Mitch had moved to Dorset. Something to do with property that they'd stolen from the Vickers family. "Rut, are those two as bad as everyone says?"

Rut sat back in his chair, considering his answer carefully. "Stevie and Donnie have been boosting booze from people's houses since they were twelve years old. Fighting. Drug dealing. Getting nice girls high, stealing their parents' cars—you name it, Stevie and Donnie have done it. I think they've pissed off more people in this town than any two boys I've ever known. But I should also say that nobody's ever given them half a chance, what with feeling the way they do about Milo. He's an ornery little cuss. Has a lot of bluster in him. Plus he's been at odds with the Vickers family for years, and if you tangle with them there is no way in hell you will ever come out ahead." Rut paused to sip his stout. "But Milo's okay in my book. When he's over here, he's always rewiring a lamp, fixing a leaky faucet. Never asks for anything in return. Milo's been a real friend. And a comfort, both of us being widowers and all."

"You were going to ask me something about Justine. . . ."

"I feel bad for that girl," Rut confessed. "Let's face it, Stevie and Donnie will be furious about her being mixed up with Bement. Not just because of what happened but because of who he is." Bement Widdifield was the great Poochie Vickers's grandson by way of her daughter, Claudia, and Claudia's husband, Mark Widdifield. Claudia was Eric's older sister. "Milo's mad enough about it to spit. The Vickers are the reason he spent three years in jail himself. Claudia's none too happy either. She thinks the Kershaws are trash, every last one of them. Not that it's anyone's damned business. Bement's over twenty-one. So is Justine. Who she dates is her own affair." Rut shifted around in his chair, sighing. "Mitch, she's like a granddaughter to me. Prettiest little thing you ever saw. Has a mouth on her like you wouldn't believe. Got that from Milo, I guess. I'm real concerned there'll be a kerfuffle now that the brothers are getting out. Not that I'm asking you to get in the middle. That's more a job for your ex-girlfriend."

"She's not my ex-girlfriend, Rut."

Rut frowned at him. "Are you sitting here telling me that you and the resident trooper weren't a hot and heavy item?"

"I'm telling you she's still hot and I'm still heavy. We didn't break up."

Rut peered across the table at Mitch doubtfully. "Word is, you popped the question, she turned you down, and you two are history."

Mitch didn't know how this splitsville rumor about Des Mitry and he had gotten started, but it had taken on the weight of absolute truth—no matter what he or his exceedingly bootylicious lady love said to the contrary. "Rut, what *are* you asking me to get in the middle of?"

The old postmaster hesitated, thumbing his chin. "Maybe this isn't such a good idea, what with there being so much bad blood."

"Why don't you let me be the judge of that? Tell me about the Vickers and the Kershaws. Why *is* there so much bad blood?"

"Well, I suppose I'm uniquely qualified to answer that, seeing as how I'm the only soul in town who's kin to both families. I'm related to the Kershaws through my late wife, Helen. She and Bessie Kershaw, Milo's mother, were cousins. And I'm first cousin to Poochie on my mother's side, the Dunlop side. Poochie's mom, Katherine, and my mom, Eunice, were sisters. Dunlop is an old, old name around these parts. It was Bish Dunlop, my granddad, who built Four Chimneys."

Four Chimneys was the colossal brick mansion a couple of miles outside of the village where Poochie resided on two hundred acres of choice riverfront land. Eric's farm was there, as was Claudia and Mark's home.

"Granddad Bish put a big dent in the family fortune building that place," Rut continued. "The stock market crash took care of the rest. The family was practically bust by the time my mom and Aunt Katherine reached marrying age. Mom was no help. Married herself a science teacher. Aunt Katherine was a different story entirely. Went and married herself John J. Meier of the Pittsburgh steel Meiers. They ensconced themselves like royalty in Four Chimneys and raised Poochie just like a princess. Sent her to the finest schools in the world. She was smart as a whip, beautiful and spirited. Not to mention a world-class swimmer."

"Rut, is it true that she was kicked off the '56 Olympics team for drinking champagne with a reporter?"

"It is. And I still say that if a male athlete had kicked up his heels that way no one would have said boo. Poochie's always been ahead of her time. Never gave a goddamn what other people thought. And yet, when the time came, she married herself that big money stuffed-shirt Coleman Vickers. Or the Ambassador, as he preferred to be called," Rut added dryly. "He did serve as ambassador to France for several years. That's when Poochie took up her chef thing."

Mitch was quite familiar with Poochie Vickers's chef thing. Everyone was. She'd helped revolutionize American cooking in the 1970s by introducing home cooks to the pleasures of French farmhouse cooking, which emphasized locally grown seasonal ingredients flavored with fresh herbs, not the ones that came dried in a jar. "If they're dead then they *taste* dead!" Poochie used to exclaim on *The Country Chef,* the PBS cooking show that had made her a household name. And a bestselling cookbook author. The woman was so full of daffy charm that she'd made her mentor and good friend, Julia Child, seem almost demure.

Mitch was also quite familiar with the name Coleman Vickers. A distinguished advisor to three different U.S. presidents, Coleman Vickers had been president of Columbia University when Mitch studied there.

"A prized horse's patootie if ever I met one," Rut sniffed. "The guy's supposed to be a professional diplomat and he couldn't buy a quart of milk in this town without putting somebody's nose out of joint. Always accusing the merchants of overcharging him. Which they'd *never* do on account of Poochie. That lady is beloved. And Eric is a terrific fellow. So is Bement."

Mitch noticed that Rut did not say one word about Claudia.

"But the Ambassador was real big on leaving people nasty little notes. What the hell kind of a diplomat is that? No wonder this country's in such a mess. *He's* the reason for the bad blood between the Vickers and the Kershaws. Milo and his missus, April, used to do for Poochie and Coleman at Four Chimneys. Milo was caretaker and April kept house, same as Milo's folks before him. Until the Ambassador asked Milo to do some renovation work on the barn. Assured him he'd pay him extra for it. Or so Milo claims. Milo went ahead and did the work, and then Coleman refused to pay him. Denied saying he ever would. So Milo helped himself to a brand new lawn mower as payment. Coleman called the trooper and charged him with stealing it. In response, Milo burned the Ambassador's newly renovated barn right down to the ground."

"Are you kidding me?"

"That's the way a fellow like Milo settles things," Rut assured him, nodding his head. "The Ambassador got so apoplectic at the sight of those flames that he had a heart attack and dropped dead on the spot. Never did live to see Milo serve out his sentence. Mitch, this all happened more than ten years ago. But not a day goes by Milo doesn't curse the Vickers up, down and sideways. And not a day goes by that Claudia doesn't blame him for her father's death. So you can imagine how those two feel about Justine and Bement being in love."

"I sure can," said Mitch, his hungry gaze falling on the last slice of pizza.

"Not that Justine gives a good goddamn what her father thinks," Rut pointed out. "She and Milo have never gotten along. She doesn't much care for her brothers, either. Justine goes her own way."

"How does Poochie feel about her grandson dating a Kershaw?"

"She thinks it's nobody's business but Bement's. He's a bright boy. Still not sure what he wants to do with himself. Dropped out of Stanford one year shy of graduation, which also didn't sit too well with Claudia. Lately, he's been refinishing furniture up at Great White Whale Antiques."

Mitch knew the place well. One of his neighbors out on Big Sister ran it.

"I swear Claudia would change her mind if she just got to know Justine," Rut insisted. "That little girl can light up a whole room. She gives me a poem every year on my birthday. Writes each and every one herself. She's so gifted with words. Was always a straight-A student in high school—unless she got riled or bored. Stopped taking her college classes up at Central Connecticut because she decided her professors were stupid. Told them so right to their faces."

"Rut, what's this favor?"

Rut Peck reached for the deck of cards again and harrumphed, clearing his throat. "It seems that Justine's written herself a novel, Mitch. She hasn't shown it to a soul. Not even Bement. I told her I'd be happy to read it. She told me I'd find it too shocking, whatever that's supposed to mean. I think she ought to show it to *someone*. Get some feedback, advice. What good does it do to stick it in a drawer somewhere? Anyhow, I happened to mention that I was acquainted with a real live New York critic who's also one heck of a nice—"

"No problem, I'll be happy to read it." Mitch was no stranger to encouraging young talent. It was Mitch who'd been the first person on earth to look at Des's portraits of crime scene victims. Mitch who'd told the wary and vulnerable homicide investigator that she was supremely gifted. "Just tell her to give me a call."

"No, Justine won't do that."

"She have something against phones?"

"No, against asking anyone for help. It's the Kershaw in her. You'll have to be the one to reach out. And you've got to approach her real careful or she'll rake you with both claws coming and going."

"This keeps sounding better and better, Rut."

The old man's face dropped. "If you'd rather steer clear, I'll understand."

"Did I say that? It's just going to cost you, that's all."

Rut eyed him shrewdly. "Name your price."

"Are you going to eat that last slice of pizza?"

"You go ahead. You're still a growing boy."

"It's true, I am," Mitch acknowledged as he dove in.

Rut shuffled the cards and dealt them out, murmuring the count under his breath. Mitch picked up his cards and looked at them. *Bupkes,* yet again.

"So Des didn't turn you down, hunh?" Rut sorted through his own hand.

"She's simply in the process of thinking it over, which is a very healthy thing."

Rut nodded to himself wisely. "Well, I guess I get it now."

"You get what?"

"How the word is she's dumped you. It gives me no pleasure to say this, Mitch, but when a girl tells you she's 'thinking it over' that means 'Goodbye, Charlie.' She's just letting you down easy is all."

"Des is a woman, not a girl," Mitch pointed out, chomping on his slice. "We're both mature adults—or at least one of us is. We love each other very much. And she's going to say yes. I'm not the least bit worried."

"Are you sure you asked her right and proper?"

"Of course I did. Why, what do you mean?"

"Well, how did you put it to her?"

"I told her I wanted to get married."

"Did you show her the ring?"

"What ring?"

"*There's* your problem. Go buy her a damned diamond, you cheap bastard."

"Rut, that's totally retrosexual. Des doesn't care about diamonds."

"Baloney. She may carry a loaded weapon, but she's still a girl. Woman. Whatever. Deep down, they all want to be romanced. Where did this proposal of yours take place, if you don't mind me asking."

"In the hospital."

"You proposed to her in the hospital? Why the hell did you do that?"

"She'd just been shot."

Rut let out a short bark of a laugh. "Can't imagine why the lady said no."

"She *didn't* say no."

"When you propose to a woman, you take her somewhere romantic. Not a place where they have heart monitors and defribillators."

Mitch sorted through his cards, mulling this over. Maybe the old guy was on to something. After all, he'd proposed to Maisie on the observation deck of the Empire State Building. And he'd come prepared with a bottle of Yoo-hoo, two straws and his grandma Thelma's engagement ring. Maisie was still wearing that ring. He'd buried her with it on her finger. "It's a complicated situation, Rut," he said finally.

"While you're waiting for it to get uncomplicated, are you planning to take your shopping elsewhere?"

"If by that you mean sleep around on her, the answer is no."

"If you change your mind, my niece, Amy, just split up with her husband. Nice professional girl. A dentist. And lonely as all get-out. Not bad looking either. Mind you, she's not in Des Mitry's league. But who is?"

Mitch took a sip of his stout. "Honestly? I can't think of anyone."

CHAPTER 2

THE OLD TAN-COLORED ISUZU Trooper was sitting out in the middle of Duck River Pond with its high beams on when Des hit the brakes on her cruiser and jumped out. She could make out a driver and one passenger still in the vehicle. They were making no apparent effort to get out, meaning they might not be conscious.

Or alive.

A neighbor on McCurdy Road had called 911 at a few minutes past 10 P.M. to report that a car had just crashed through the wooden safety barrier and ended up *kersplash* in the middle of the pond, which was not quite three feet deep and not quite frozen over. McCurdy was well sanded, but there were still snowbanks along its shoulders. The afternoon sun had melted those some. Possibly, the driver had hit a patch of black ice coming around the bend.

Leaving her own high beams on, Des rolled up her wool uniform trousers, flicked on her flashlight and plunged right in, black lace-up boots and all. It had been a hard winter on boots. This would make the fourth pair she'd ruined. As she waded her way out toward the Isuzu, the icy cold water lapped up over her knees, soaking her pants, too.

The Isuzu's tailpipe was submerged. Its engine had stalled out. The water was up just above the bottom of the doors, but Des was able to muscle the driver's side door open, the better to be bowled over by the strong odor of liquor inside. Somehow, the electrical system was still operational—and the interior lights came on to reveal Poochie Vickers, Dorset's reigning white-haired aristocrat, seated there calmly behind the wheel, gazing straight ahead as if she were waiting for a traffic light to change. Her companion, an exceedingly gay old blade by the name of Guy Tolliver, was doing the very same thing. Both had their seat belts on. Neither seemed the slightest bit aware that they were sitting out in the middle of Duck River Pond.

An aging, white-muzzled golden retriever woofed at Des in greeting from behind the back seat, its tail thumping.

"Are you okay, Mrs. Vickers?" Des called out, her teeth starting to chatter.

"Hullo, Des!" Poochie exclaimed cheerily. "How's the drawing coming?"

"Just fine, ma'am. Are . . . you . . . okay?"

"Of course, I am. Why wouldn't I be? Shush, Bailey," she commanded the old dog, who obeyed immediately.

Slowly, Guy Tolliver was becoming aware of the several inches of water sloshing around at their feet. "Poochie, we appear to be somewhat wet."

Clearly, they'd been drinking. But Des was aware that more could be going on here. They could have suffered head injuries, or be in shock. Plus Poochie was over seventy. When a driver her age has a one-car mishap, a stroke can't be ruled out. Des shined her light into the old woman's eyes. They were bright blue and plenty responsive. "Do you know where you are?"

"Of course I do. I'm on my way home from the club. Tolly and I were playing bridge. What *is* it you want, dear?"

"How much have you had to drink?"

"Not nearly enough," Poochie answered airily.

The other emergency response vehicles began pulling up now, red lights flashing. Dorset's volunteer ambulance van, which was staffed by Marge and Mary Jewett, two no-nonsense sisters in their fifties. The big red fire truck, which was manned by four sturdy young volunteer firefighters in big yellow hats, yellow coats and black rubber hip waders.

"What have we got, Des?" Marge called to her as she and Mary waded out with their emergency kits, their own trousers rolled up.

"Probable DWI. Sure smells like one. They're responding to questions and way cheerful—just somewhat disoriented."

"Welcome to Dorset," Mary grunted. "We'll check 'em out just to play it safe. Then they're all yours."

Des collected Poochie's leather shoulder bag from the back seat. It had pitched over when the Isuzu hit the pond, dumping its contents—a dozen or so ten-packs of Baby Ruth bars—all over the seat.

"Getting ready for Halloween a little early, Mrs. Vickers?" she asked as Marge checked the old woman's blood pressure.

"I don't know what you mean," Poochie replied, glancing back at the candy bars. "Those aren't mine."

"This isn't your purse?"

"No, it is. But those candies aren't. Never touch the things."

Des stuffed them into her shoulder bag anyway, wondering how the old lady had come by them. An unpleasant pattern was emerging. Just a few days earlier, Poochie Vickers had strolled right out of Gene's liquor store with a gallon of vodka that she hadn't paid for. Gene's part-time clerk had stopped her in the parking lot and held her until Des got there. By then Gene had returned from the bank and smoothed the whole thing over, assuring Des that Poochie had simply forgotten to have the clerk put the vodka on her tab. After Poochie had departed, Gene confided to Des that Dorset's first lady frequently walked out the door without paying for things.

Shoving her heavy horn-rimmed glasses back up her nose, Des started for dry land with the shoulder bag. One of the firemen waded out and carried Bailey to safety. Des had him put the old dog in the back seat of her cruiser. Then she phoned Poochie's daughter, Claudia, thinking she ought to put the woman on her speed dial. "It's Resident Trooper Mitry, Mrs. Widdifield," she said, stamping her wet, frozen feet. "She's driven into Duck River Pond."

"Is she hurt?" Claudia's voice was filled with dread.

"Not visibly, no. The Jewett sisters are looking her over, but she and Mr. Tolliver both appear to be fine."

"Thank you for informing me, Trooper," Claudia said coolly. "I'll be there in five minutes."

The firefighters gently lifted Poochie Vickers and Guy Tolliver from the Isuzu and started across the pond with them toward the ambulance. By then Doug Garvey from the Sunoco station had pulled up next to Des in his big tow truck.

Doug was a large, fleshy man in his early sixties. "Thank God she was driving her Isuzu tonight," he said to Des as he climbed out, hitching up his pants.

"I hear you," she agreed. In warmer weather, Poochie Vickers drove around town in a kick-ass silver 1956 Mercedes Gullwing that she'd owned since it was new. The antique car was worth more than Des's house—which was saying something considering what they got for a starter cottage in Dorset.

Following closely behind Doug in his town-issued Ford Taurus was Bob Paffin, Dorset's snowy haired noodge of a first selectman, who monitored local emergency calls day and night. At the merest mention of Poochie Vickers's name, Bob came running. "Des, I don't suppose you have any wiggle room on this, do you?" he asked, his eyes taking in the shattered wooden safety barrier.

Des took off her big Smokey hat and ran a hand over her short, nubby hair. "I smelled alcohol, Bob, so she has to pass a Breathalyzer. That's a state law." Des brushed past him and popped her trunk. Yanked off her sopping wet boots and socks. Rubbed her frozen size twelve and a half AA feet dry with paper towels. Put on her spare socks and boots, then unrolled her soaked pant legs and grabbed her Breathalyzer.

The Jewett sisters had finished checking over Poochie and Tolly in the back of the ambulance.

"Their vital signs are normal," Marge told her. "No bumps that we can see. We'd like to run them both to the hospital for a doctor to look at, but Poochie won't hear of it. *Or* a blood sample."

"Okay if I question them further?"

"Yeah, sure. They seem fine." Mary furrowed her brow at Des. "But how are *you*, honey? Believe me, I know what it's like to break up with a man in this town."

Des puffed out her cheeks, exasperated. "Mitch and I haven't broken up, Mary."

"That's not what we're hearing."

"We heard you proposed to the Berger man," Marge chimed in. "And he said no and now you two are kaput."

"That is *so* not what happened."

"So you're not putting in for a transfer?" Marge asked.

"Putting in for a *what?* I'm not going anywhere."

"Glad to hear it," said Mary. "We both think you should stay. We've grown rather fond of you, you know."

"Back at you," growled Des, who absolutely despised the way her private life had turned into everyone else's business.

Poochie and Tolly were huddled together in the back of the ambulance, giggling like a pair of giddy little kids. Poochie Vickers had to be the most thoroughly unflappable person Des had ever come across. She was a tall, slim woman of seventy-three who'd been a champion swimmer back in her Smith College days. Still looked as if she'd dive right into Long Island Sound and swim across to Orient Point if you dared her to. Poochie wore no makeup or lipstick. Her shock of white hair looked as if she combed it with her fingers. She had on a scuffed up barn coat, a turtleneck sweater, rumpled painter's paints and Jack Purcell tennis sneakers that were so old one of her big toes was sticking out. Yet despite her dressed-down sloppiness, the lady was elegantly, effortlessly beautiful. She had good high cheekbones, a long, straight nose, strong chin and an air of indomitable good cheer.

Guy Tolliver, who had to be pushing eighty, was lanky and lantern-jawed and plenty elegant himself, although his immense ears and loose, sagging jowls did give him a more than passing resemblance to a bloodhound. Tolly's glossy silver hair was perfectly coiffed, his fingernails manicured and glossed. He wore a beautiful shearling coat over a shawl-collared burgundy cardigan, gray tweed slacks and black kid leather ankle boots.

Des crouched there in the ambulance with them and did the smile thing. "How are you folks feeling?"

"Honestly, I don't understand the fuss, Des," Poochie answered. "This road has always been poorly marked. I simply took the wrong fork."

"Could have happened to anyone," Tolly concurred, nodding.

"There is no fork. Just a curve, which you failed to negotiate."

"Now, Des, there's no need to get all quibbly."

"Mrs. Vickers . . ."

"Please call me Poochie, dear."

"The Jewett sisters say you're refusing to go to the hospital."

"That's correct. Don't believe in them. Hospitals are where people go to die. Des, what have you done with my dear young sir?"

"Bailey's in my ride, safe and sound. Are you formally refusing to give a blood sample?"

"I most certainly am. I am not some laboratory specimen."

"In that case, I have to ask you to submit to a Breathalyzer exam. You've been drinking and driving. I have to determine whether or not you're over the legal limit."

"Why, that's the silliest thing I've ever heard. May I refuse?"

"You may, but it means you'll automatically lose your license to drive for three months. That's mandatory in this state."

"So be it then," Poochie said with an easy shrug.

"That's showing 'em, girl," exclaimed Tolly, patting her on the knee. "Hell, I can drive you anywhere you want. I *think* my license is still valid. Des, is a Bahamian license valid in Connecticut?"

"I've phoned Claudia," Des said, getting up out of her crouch. "She'll be here shortly to take you home."

"Fabulous," Poochie responded gleefully. "A good, strong dose of Miss Stick Up Her Butt is just what I need right now. Seriously, Tolly, do you think she's *ever* experienced an orgasm?"

"I can't imagine our Mark has the the stamina," he replied with catty relish.

"Our Mark is out of the picture," she confided, raising an eyebrow at him.

His eyes widened in surprise. "Since when?"

"Since this morning."

"Where has he gone? Who with? Dish, you bad thing."

Des left them to their gossip only to find Bob Paffin hovering right there outside the ambulance.

"*Must* you pull her license?" he pressed when she'd filled him in.

"Bob, the nine-one-one call was logged, our emergency crews mobilized. I couldn't cut her any slack even if I wanted to—which I don't. She shouldn't have been behind that wheel."

"Sure, sure. Understood." Bob pushed it no further, but he wasn't done getting right up in her business. "Des, I think we ought to talk about your plans for tomorrow. It's an awfully big day."

"Is this the Kershaw brothers we're talking about?"

"Folks are mighty uneasy about Stevie and Donnie coming home. I don't have to tell you that."

"You're right, you don't," said Des, who knew all about Stevie and Donnie Kershaw. They were Dorset's answer to Frank and Jesse James—if the James brothers had been low-life swamp Yankee cheeseheads. Which wasn't to minimize them. The Kershaw brothers were thieving louts, and their release after a two-year stint in prison was sending genuine ripples of fear through Dorset. Everyone was wondering whether the current resident trooper could handle them. This would be a big test for Des. Not that she wasn't accustomed to being tested. Or watched. She was a single young woman of color. She was six-feet-one, broad-shouldered, high-rumped and cut with muscle. In a close-knit, uniformly white New England village with a winter population of seven thousand, she did not exactly blend. "There's no need to worry about this, Bob," she assured him. "I'm on it."

"I don't doubt that for one second," the first selectman said encouragingly. He was not patronizing her. No, he was not. "But I've been hearing from a lot of people."

"Tell them to chill. This isn't the Kershaws' town—it's mine."

Claudia Widdifield pulled up now in her black Lexus SUV and got out, looking chilly and imposing. Des excused herself and strode over to her, instantly intimidated. In Dorset, it wasn't raggies like the Kershaws who daunted her. It was vanilla ice princesses like Claudia—the poised, privileged blondes who had never wanted for anything in their entire lives. Des was not at ease around such oh-so-superior women. Mostly, she resented the hell out of them.

"Is mother okay?" Claudia demanded, her manner decidedly take-charge.

"She seems fine, although she won't let the Jewett sisters take her to the hospital."

"Of course not. That's the sort of thing sensible people do. Not mother. Never mother."

Claudia was in her late forties. Like her famous mother, she was tall, slim and strong-jawed. Unlike her mother, Claudia was very carefully put together. Her earrings were lustrous pearls. Her makeup and lipstick were fresh. The length of yarn that held her blond hair in place was color coordinated with her red quilted Burberry jacket. By profession, she was an interior decorator. One of the top decorators in New England, in fact. Claudia's specialty was English country casual. Absolutely nothing about the lady herself was casual. She was so tightly wrapped that she bristled.

Then again, Des did just hear that Claudia's architect husband, Mark, had left her that morning. So she supposed the woman could be forgiven if she seemed less than jolly.

Bailey had started barking at the sound of her voice. Des let him out of the back of the cruiser and Claudia marched the aging dog toward her Lexus.

"I'm pulling your mother's license," Des said, following her. "Which, quite honestly, might not be the worst thing in the world. How would you describe her overall health these days?"

"My mother has the constitution of an ox." Claudia eyed her probingly. "Why do you ask?"

"Because we need to have a talk," Des replied, clearing her

throat. "Our little phone calls are getting to be a habit." Des showed Claudia the stash of candy bars in Poochie's handbag. "Your mother claims she has no idea where these came from."

"Trooper, I appreciate your concern but this is a family matter," Claudia said stiffly, closing Bailey inside the back of her SUV.

"Mrs. Widdifield, look around you. Look at all these folks who've been called out of their homes on a cold night. This is not a family matter."

The Jewett sisters were helping Poochie and Tolly out of the back of the ambulance now.

Poochie immediately caught sight of First Selectman Paffin standing there. "Hullo, Bob!" she roared cheerily. "Millie kick you out of the house again?"

"Heard you were having some problems, old girl."

"Nonsense. Just missed that damned fork in the road."

"Awfully icy out, too," Bob Paffin added sympathetically.

Poochie gazed around at the emergency personnel who were gathered there, hands stuffed in the pockets of their coats. "By God, the lot of you look as if you're ready for a parade."

They laughed politely. All except for Doug Garvey, who was out in the middle of the icy pond hooking up his winch chain to the Isuzu's rear axle.

"Come along, Mummy," Claudia said, mustering a tight smile. "I'll take you home."

"Now don't be cross with me, Claude," Poochie chided her. "You seem cross."

"I'm *concerned*. You're lucky you didn't *drown*."

"Don't be melodramatic, Claude. It doesn't suit you." Poochie paused to offer Des a firm handshake. "Thank you for your help, dear."

"What I'm here for, Poochie."

Dorset's first lady let out a huge laugh. "We both know that isn't true." Then she strode regally toward her daughter's ride, Tolly trailing along behind her.

Claudia started after them, then abruptly stopped and returned to Des, car keys jangling in her clenched hand. "Mother will be visiting an old friend up at Essex Meadows in the morning." Essex Meadows was a high-end assisted living facility. "She likes to stay for lunch because they often serve fish sticks, which she insists are very hard to find these days. She particularly likes their tartar sauce for reasons that, well, God only knows. I'll be at my cottage across the courtyard from Four Chimneys. We can talk then."

"That'll be fine. Thank you, Mrs. Widdifield."

Claudia shook her head. "A thank-you is not appropriate, Trooper. Trust me when I tell you this: You are about to be very, very sorry."

CHAPTER 3

THEY WERE RUNNING THROUGH Central Park together. He was flying a kite. She was holding a great big lollipop. Her long, blond hair was flowing. It was a bright, beautiful summer day. It had never been so beautiful. . . .

A Maisie dream. Mitch was having one of his Maisie dreams. Often, there were montage sequences:

Now it was raining and they were hugging under an awning on lower Fifth Avenue. Then it was sunny and they were strolling through the West Village carrying shopping bags from stores he'd never heard of. Now they were eating ice cream cones in Washington Square. Now Maisie was feeding hers to a puppy. . . .

This montage is way sappy, Mitch couldn't help observing. Which was something he did. He reviewed his own dreams in his own head as he was dreaming them.

Now they were in their big brass bed together. Maisie was over him, her beautiful hair gently grazing his bare chest.

"You won't ever leave me, will you, Bear?"

"How could you ever think that?"

"I can feel you slipping away, that's how." She kissed his eyes, his cheeks, his chin. "You won't, will you, Bear?"

"Maisie, I'll never leave you. I'll never go."

"Yes, you will," she insisted.

Which was not at all in character for Maisie. She was never the jealous type, Mitch noted as he lay there, savoring the taste of her, the smell of her. Although she did seem a lot smaller than he remembered. Hardly weighed a thing. And her nose was cold and wet. And she was:

Purring. Maisie was definitely purring.

29

And with a startled yelp Mitch awoke to discover his outdoor hunter, Quirt, standing on his chest in the half-light of dawn, licking his face.

"Hey . . . buddy," Mitch gasped, his chest heaving as if he'd just run two miles with a forty-pound pack on his back.

He had a bitter, metallic taste in his mouth, and he was drenched in sweat. None of which was the fault of Quirt. Or of his docile stay-at-home muffin, Clemmie, who lay curled at his feet, fast asleep. No, this was one of those awful panic attacks like he'd suffered in the weeks after his beloved Maisie died. Always, they came in the night as dreams. He and Maisie would be happy. Then she'd start begging him not to leave her. And then he'd wake up with his heart galloping, convinced he was having a heart attack. His doctor had explained to him that what he was experiencing was anxiety. That the metallic taste was adrenaline. And that it would pass—which it had. Mitch hadn't had a Maisie dream since he'd come to Dorset and met Des.

So why had he had one now?

It was a few minutes past six, according to the alarm clock next to the bed in his sleeping loft. Snow was falling on the skylight above his bed. Shuddering, he got up and waddled down the steep, narrow stairs, Quirt dashing nimbly along ahead of him.

Mitch's place was a two-hundred-year-old exposed chestnut post-and-beam carriage house that once belonged to one of the grander homes out on Big Sister Island. The downstairs was basically one big room where Mitch lived and worked and made beautiful not-quite music on his sky blue Fender Stratocaster. He had a big bay window that looked out over Long Island Sound in three different directions. He had a kitchen and bath. He had his sleeping loft. He needed nothing more.

He cranked up the heat and let Quirt out. The snowfall was very light. Some of it was coating the windshield of his truck but it was not sticking to the ground. According to the thermometer outside of his bay window, it was thirty-four degrees. It was supposed to warm all the way into the upper forties by the afternoon.

Mitch had become something of a weather nerd since he'd bought his little house on Big Sister. What the weather was doing really mattered out here. Plus, he was hopelessly addicted to the Weather Channel and the daring exploits of ace storm tracker, Jim Cantore.

He built a fire in his big stone fireplace and put a pot of coffee on in the kitchen. While it was brewing he shaved. Gazing at his reflection in the mirror, he found his mind straying back to that Maisie dream. He didn't know what to make of it. Because he *wasn't* leaving her—it was she who'd left him. He'd lost her to ovarian cancer when she was thirty. Maisie was his first love. She would always occupy a cherished place in his heart. He accepted that—as did Des, the woman who he intended to spend the rest of his life with. So why had this anxiety suddenly reared its ugly head? Was it because St. Patrick's Day was right around the corner? It did so happen that March seventeenth was Maisie's birthday.

Sure, that was it. Had to be.

He dressed in a fisherman's knit sweater, baggy corduroys and his Mephisto hiking shoes. By now the snow had stopped, the clouds were breaking up in the southern sky over Long Island and Quirt was scratching to be let back in. Mitch put some kibble down for him. The sound of that brought Clemmie ambling slowly downstairs to join them, yawning hugely.

Mitch poured himself some coffee and topped it with two fingers of chocolate milk. Then he flicked on the forty-eight-inch grow lights in his bay window and spent a few good minutes doting over his tender little charges in their leak-proof modular seed trays. Tiny, bright green shoots were sprouting up out of the seed plugs. His early season lettuce, leeks and parsley. Mitch could not believe how devoted he'd grown to his vegetable garden. Not only had he sent away for a gazillion seeds but also enough gear to stock a small nursery, including propagation heating mats and a half-dozen clear plastic protective domes. These he'd taken to calling Clemmie Domes after he'd discovered that sweet, gentle Clemmie loved to dig her paws into the fragrant starter mix, gum his little seedlings and fling them around the room.

For breakfast, he put away a bowl of the Cocoa Puffs that he kept stashed in the cupboard under the kitchen sink behind the Drano. Des had no idea they were there. While he ate, he cranked up his computer and printed out the baseball stats that he'd downloaded yesterday. Mitch was in a fantasy baseball league with a gang of other film critics. Their talent draft was coming up and he was getting ready to stock his team, the Rocky Sullivans, with a roster of prime talent.

When he was done he climbed into his C.C. Filson red-and-black checked wool packer coat, grabbed his binoculars and notepad and trudged on out.

A dusting of snow still coated the meadows and trees, but the sun was starting to break out. It would melt very fast. Mitch poked around in his flower gardens and found snowdrops and snow crocus. In the slushy mud beneath some dead leaves there were daffodil shoots. The birds were returning. He could hear the cardinals, and see the robins poking at the limp, pale grass beneath the trees. Chipmunks scampered about.

Mitch filled his bird feeders, then plodded down the sandy path toward the narrow beach, feeling incredibly fortunate to be here. Mitch was the only island resident who wasn't a Peck by birth or marriage. Most of the Pecks were still down in Hobe Sound for the winter. There were five houses on Big Sister, not counting the stone lighthouse keeper's house and its decommissioned lighthouse, the second tallest such landmark in New England. There were forty acres of woods, a tennis court, a private beach, a dock where Evan Peck kept his J-24 tied up during sailing season. A narrow, quarter-mile-long wooden causeway connected the island to the mainland. It was Yankee paradise.

Spring didn't arrive gradually on Connecticut's Gold Coast—it lurched in. The giant chunks of ice that had floated downriver from the frigid north and washed ashore here still said winter. And yet those slick, shiny harbor seals that were basking out on the rocks in the morning sun positively cried out spring. Mitch watched them for a few minutes before he trained his binoculars on the osprey platforms out in the river on Great Island. He was on lookout duty for The Nature Conservancy. On this particular morning, he happily spotted his first osprey circling slowly around the raised platform. It was a blackish raptor with a white head and a wing span of nearly six feet.

Lowering his glasses, Mitch dutifully marked the date, time and location of the spotting in his notebook, tongue stuck out of the side of his mouth as he wrote. Then he noticed a long black feather stuck in the sand next to him. He reached down and picked it up. It was white on its underside. Not an osprey feather. It was the wing feather of a greater black-backed gull.

Nevertheless, Mitch tucked it carefully in his pocket for future use.

There was a big wooden bin next to the exit door of the A&P where customers could leave donations of canned goods and other nonperishables for Dorset's Food Pantry. Some guy with a truck would come by every couple of days to pick them up and deliver them to the Fellowship Center of the Congregational church. Lately, that guy with a truck had been Mitch.

He idled in the fire lane while he piled the bags into the back of his kidney-colored Studebaker half-ton. Then he headed over to The Works, Dorset's upscale gourmet food emporium, to pick up the frozen day-old artisan breads that the bakery contributed, along with dozens of those round, doughy *things* that Dorseteers chose to believe were bagels. From there Mitch rolled his way into the Dorset Street Historic District, with its towering maples and its dignified two-hundred-and-fifty-year-old colonial mansions. Anchoring the south end of the Historic District, set back behind a deep lawn, was Dorset's stately old Congregational church.

The Congo church—as most everyone called it—was the very embodiment of a small-town New England meetinghouse. It was white. It was unadorned. There were two full stories of mullioned windows to let in the sunlight. A towering steeple with a working clock and a bell tower topped by a gleaming brass weather vane. It was not, in fact, Dorset's original Congo church, which burned to the ground in the 1840s. This one had been erected in its place soon thereafter. Supposedly, it was an exact reproduction, inside and out.

The rather sterile Fellowship Center, which had been added on in the 1970s, was connected to the church by an office annex. It had a full kitchen, space for lots of long tables and folding chairs. The center was in constant use by support groups like Alcoholics Anonymous, by singles groups and senior citizens groups. The blood bank was held here. The visiting nurse gave flu shots here. And the Food Pantry was here. It was a known fact that Dorset boasted more millionaires per square mile than East Hampton. But to live here year round, as Mitch did, was to discover that there were plenty of have-nots, too. A lot of the men were in seasonal trades like roofing and landscaping. Winters were especially tough. To make ends meet, they relied on the Food Pantry. For those who wanted one, there was also a hot meal.

Mitch pulled into the gravel driveway that looped around back and parked by the kitchen entrance beside Eric Vickers's battered Ford F-150, where Eric was unloading huge baskets of his organically grown potatoes and carrots. Poochie Vickers's buoyant farmer son was in his early forties, gangly, bony-nosed and more than a little geeky. His Adam's apple always seemed too busy, and his pants invariably fell a good three inches short of his mud-caked work shoes. A big Leatherman multipurpose knife hung in a sheath from his belt. The chunky, shapeless brown sweater he wore had been made by his French-Canadian wife, Danielle, using wool from their own sheep. Eric kept his blond hair short, his beard neatly trimmed. His ears he left alone, and the man had to have the lushest ear hair Mitch had ever seen. He looked as if he were part faun. And yet Eric's ears were not his most notable feature. His eyes were. Eric's blue-eyed gaze was so intense, so *lit* with positive energy that it bordered on religious zeal. This was why many in Dorset fondly referred to him as the Green Market Messiah.

"You're looking at the last of it, Mitch," he declared as Mitch climbed out of his own truck. "Our root cellar is now officially, one hundred percent bare. But not to worry, because today's the day. As soon as I get home, I'm planting my All Blues. The soil is *re-eally* perfect today. And when the soil is perfect you do not argue with it. You get down on your knees and you *dig*. Ever eat a blue potato?"

"Uh, I've had blue tortilla chips. Do those count?"

"Those are made from corn, Mitch."

"Okay, then I guess not."

"You've got to try one. They're my fastest sellers at the Union Square green market. The chef from Savoy grabs them up the second he sees them. *God,* I love this time of year!" Eric exulted, raising his face to the sun.

The two of them started toting their loads inside for Danielle to parcel out. Danielle was heating up a vat of her bean soup for the folks who were starting to trickle in. She'd also baked several loaves of whole wheat bread. Danielle Vickers shared her husband's tireless devotion to their farm and their community, but she was much more reserved. Even a bit dour. At times, she almost seemed to have wandered in from an all-night Ingmar Bergman glumfest. Mitch had rarely seen her smile, although some of this was self-consciousness—her teeth were exceptionally crooked. Danielle had grown up poor. Her father, an itinerant Sheetrocker, had worked only sporadically. Danielle had paid her own way through Bates College, up in Lewiston, Maine, by tending bar nights. It was at Bates that she'd met Eric. She was not particularly tall but she was strongly built. Also pretty shapely, though you had to look awfully hard. She dressed in oversized sweaters and baggy overalls that hid her figure. In fact, she almost went out of her way to look frumpy. Her strawberry blond hair was always in ropy braids or pigtails. And her unflattering wire-framed glasses looked as if they'd been filled by an optician in Uzbekistan.

"How goes it, Danielle?" asked Mitch, setting his load down on the counter. Hyper Eric had already bounded back outside for another basket of potatoes.

"It goes, Mitch," she replied, stifling a yawn. She looked beat. There were dark circles under her eyes. "We're in the middle of lambing. Four of our ewes delivered last night, so I'm a little short on sleep. But, really, it's fine."

"Is the coal cellar unlocked?"

"I've already emptied out the freezers for you."

The frozen baked goods that Mitch collected were stowed in two big freezers down in the dimly lit, intensely creepy cellar under the old church. The cellar was accessed from outside by raising a pair of Bilco metal doors. Like most Bilcos, they locked from the inside. Lem, the church custodian, locked and unlocked the doors for Mitch on Food Pantry days. Mitch didn't know how Lem made it out of the cellar once they were locked, and he didn't want to know.

Mitch raised the doors and headed down the steep cement stairs, his arms loaded down with bread. It was damp and cold down there, and reeked of mold.

Eric gave him a hand—grabbing two big bags from Mitch's truck and very nearly beating Mitch down the stairs with them. Eric moved at a faster pace than most people, and possessed phenomenal energy.

"Mitch, can I get your take on something? It's kind of personal."

"Sure, what's up?" Mitch said as he stuffed the "bagels" in the freezer.

Eric squatted there on the steps, swallowing uncomfortably. "Have you noticed Danielle acting strange lately? Preoccupied, maybe?"

"She does seem a bit down."

"Has she been paying special attention to anyone?"

"I don't think I'm following you, Eric." Mitch often didn't. The trick was not minding.

"The truth is, I think she's had it with me. But I wanted to make sure before I said anything to her." Eric gazed at Mitch intently. Very intently. "That's why I'm asking *you*."

Now Mitch got it. Eric wanted to know if he and Danielle were involved. He hadn't come out and said it, but the impression was quite clear. "Eric, I'd be very surprised if she's seeing anyone else. She's devoted to you."

Eric nodded, his Adam's apple bobbing convulsively. "You think I'm being insanely jealous, don't you? That shouldn't come as a surprise, Mitch. Insanity runs in my family." Eric jumped to his feet and said, "Sorry to bother you. I'm out of here."

And he was. Jumped into his truck and sped off, leaving Mitch there to wonder what, if anything, was going on between the farmer and his wife.

When he was done down there, Mitch went up the outside stairs and lowered the Bilcos shut. Otherwise, squirrels would take up residence in the cellar. Then he grabbed the computer printouts from the front seat of his truck and went back inside. About two dozen people were gathered around the community tables, chatting as they had their soup. Seated at a table all by himself, hunched over his bowl, was Dorset's Can Man.

The gaunt old Can Man rattled around town on an old bicycle with two supermarket grocery carts chained to its back end. Spoke to no one. Guzzled rum. Dressed in filthy old clothes. A few days earlier, Mitch had noticed him poring over the NBA box scores in the *Hartford Courant* while he slurped his soup. Apparently, the guy was a stat freak.

With the fantasy baseball draft fast approaching, Mitch thought he'd try to engage him. So he ambled over, sheaf of printouts in hand, and said, "I've got my eye on Mendoza. Let me know what you think of him, okay?"

In response, the old ascetic gazed up at Mitch with a look of sheer, eye-popping terror.

Never had Mitch inspired such fear in another human being. He felt as if he'd just turned into Freddy Krueger. "Or not," he added hastily. "Entirely your choice."

But he was too late. The old guy had already jumped to his

feet, kicking over his chair, and fled the room, leaving his soup unfinished.

Chastened, Mitch helped Danielle bag up the Food Pantry donations and pass them out to the folks who were lined up waiting. In spite of her lack of sleep, Danielle worked tirelessly, the sleeves of her baggy sweater pushed up to her elbows. When they were done she helped herself to a Styrofoam cup of coffee from the urn and sat at one of the tables with it, chewing distractedly on the inside of her mouth. Danielle did seem preoccupied, Mitch observed. Behind those severe glasses, her eyes were crinkled with concern.

Mitch joined her. He and Danielle weren't especially close, but they were both outsiders. It didn't matter how long you lived in Dorset. Unless you were born and reared there, you were always an outsider. And outsiders gravitated toward each other. "Danielle, are you sure you're okay?"

She made a face, as if she'd just smelled something bad. "It's a hard time of year for us, Mitch. No cash coming in. We make our money at the green markets during growing season. Eric's in New York City at Union Square two mornings a week, I do three more out here. Our customers are crazy for our organic produce and eggs. Our grass-fed lamb, too. They can taste the difference, and they're willing to pay for it." Danielle paused, sighing wearily. "But the winters are hard. Sometimes, it all seems so *impossible*."

"What you need is a good night's sleep."

"What we *need* is to get bigger. We need at least sixty more acres, Mitch. Twice as many sheep. We're planting veggies when we should be investing in cheese-making equipment. Sheep's milk cheese is our only hope for the future," she confessed, sipping her coffee. "Unfortunately, our credit line is maxed out, Poochie is famously tight-fisted and Claudia is . . . well, Claudia. She has forty good acres of meadow out behind her cottage just sitting there. But will she let us use it? No, because that's *hers*. Claudia hates everything about our farm. Our hairy, stinky sheep. Our noisy, stinky tractor. She'd like to see us go under. And at this rate we will. I just don't know h-how much longer we can . . ." Danielle ducked her head, clutching the coffee cup in her chapped, work-roughened hands. "Eric tries to act like everything is okay. Does his yoga every morning to perpetuate his calm. Tends his flock. But I can tell he's upset about Poochie."

"I hear she drove into Duck River Pond last night."

"And didn't think a thing of it. This morning, she acted like it was a big joke. All of which means more ammunition for Claudia." Danielle's eyes met Mitch's briefly, then looked away. "Claudia has designs on the family purse strings. That greedy woman has driven poor Mark away with all of her scheming. Mark is a sweet and sensitive man. He has the soul of an artist. And now he's sleeping on his office sofa and drinking too much and . . ." Danielle broke off, coloring slightly.

Mitch couldn't help thinking Danielle seemed awfully upset about her brother-in-law. Was she involved with *him*? Could Eric actually be on to something? "Has Eric talked to Claudia about Poochie?"

Danielle shook her head. "Eric detests confrontations. And *everything* with Claudia is a confrontation. If Eric sees her coming, he walks the other way. If she phones him, he won't take the call. She doesn't speak to me at all, you know. If I answer the phone she just says, 'Is Eric there?' I don't exist. I never have, as far as she's concerned. I'm just some trash her weird brother dragged home with him from college. Eric won't stand up to her. He just says, 'If it's about money, then I don't care.' Well, I'm sorry, that's no kind of an attitude. Not when it involves your own mother—and our whole future. Only I can't say a word to him about it. He won't listen. It's very frightening."

"Why frightening, Danielle?"

"Because Claudia is strong willed but at the same time very weak. She relies on her mother more than she cares to admit. If

Claudia gets her way, she will be totally out of control. Very dangerous."

"And will she get her way?"

"Mitch, I honestly don't see how anyone can stop her."

CHAPTER 4

THE KERSHAWS LIVED IN the wooded hill country north of Uncas Lake off of Laurel Ridge, a key connector road between Nowhere and Nowhere Else. A mailbox by the side of the road marked the Kershaws' property, as did the hand-lettered plywood signs that read KEEP OUT and NO DUMPING. Des had to take it slow up the steep rutted drive that climbed and twisted its way through bleak, scrubby woodland before it finally arrived at a clearing.

There was a squat log cabin here. Wood smoke rose from a stovepipe. A Doberman was chained to the porch, barking furiously at her arrival. A mud-caked blue Toyota pickup was parked out front next to a canary yellow Ford van that had D & S PAINTING written on its side.

Near the cabin there was a lean-to where many cords of firewood were stored. The rest of the clearing resembled the salvage yard out behind a secondhand building supply center. There were piles of old windows and doors, kitchen cabinets, shutters, chimney tiles. Milo Kershaw was Dorset's most noted pack rat, famous for dragging things home from residential demolition jobs and reselling them. On occasion, some of these items didn't exactly belong to him. A few weeks back, Des had had to smooth over a dispute over some mahogany pocket doors he'd liberated from a house he was renovating. Milo insisted the owner had told him to go ahead and take them. The owner vehemently denied this. Grudgingly, Milo had coughed them up. No charges were filed.

But it was not the first time Des had dealt with Milo. Over Christmas, he'd gotten into a drunken brawl with a man half his age at the Rustic Inn, Dorset's popular in-spot for the inbred. Milo was getting the better of him, too. Again, no charges were filed, but Milo Kershaw was definitely one of those men who Des had to keep her eye on. He was sneaky, not to mention highly antagonistic.

His sons Stevie and Donnie, aged twenty-six and twenty-four, were obviously no bargains either. They'd started out with the usual playground bully stuff like vandalism, criminal mischief and unlawful possession of alcohol by a minor. Then they started boosting items from parked cars. Then they started boosting the cars. Along the way there was a string of drug possession collars. They'd been given chance after chance—counseling, community service, probation without incarceration. Until, that is, they got caught shoplifting a brand new chainsaw. For that they were deemed incorrigible and sent to the Long Lane Boys' Facility. With their most recent offense—attempted distribution of stolen property—they'd graduated to a felony and been sentenced to two years, discounted to eighteen months for good behavior, at Enfield Correctional, a medium-security institution.

Still, when it came to the Kershaw brothers the criminal record didn't tell the whole story. These boys were local legends. When they'd boosted a parked car from the lot at White Sand Beach one summer evening, for example, they'd been unaware that a couple was getting busy in the backseat at the time. And that one half of the couple was Dorset's second selectman, who was making love to someone else's . . . husband. Or take that chainsaw. They'd stolen it from Lakeside Hardware the morning after a significant snowstorm. On foot. All the resident trooper had to do was follow their footsteps home, where he found Stevie and Donnie using the stolen chainsaw on a dead, frozen deer. As for their most recent offense, some valuable items of silver were stolen from Poochie Vickers's place, Four Chimneys. Two days after the theft was discovered, Stevie and Donnie strolled right into Great White Whale Antiques and tried to sell Bement Vickers his own grandmother's silver candlesticks. Bement had politely excused himself and called the resident trooper.

Des parked next to the yellow van and got out, big Smokey hat square on her head, her boots squishing in the mud. The country air here smelled of wood smoke and of a septic tank that badly needed pumping.

Milo came out onto the porch at once and hollered at the Doberman to shut up. Milo was a feisty little whippet in his early sixties. He stood five-feet-five tops and she doubted he weighed more than one-hundred-forty pounds, most of it gristle. He wore a heavy wool sweater, jeans, work boots and a tattered orange goose down vest that was patched with silver duct tape. Milo was one of those weathered, hardscrabble workmen who seemed to be deeply tanned even in the winter. He had a suspicious, sidelong way of squinting out at the world. Just his way of letting people know that he was a force to be reckoned with.

"Morning, Mr. Kershaw," she called to him pleasantly, tipping her hat. "Thought I'd pay your boys a little courtesy call."

"Oh, is that what you call it?" he demanded, restraining the snarling Doberman by its choke collar. "I call it harassment. They ain't even been home an hour and already you're looking to put 'em back in."

"Mr. Kershaw, I'm strictly the welcome wagon. We'll have ourselves a get-acquainted chat and I'll be on my way, okay?"

Milo did not go in much for adornment. There were no pictures on the cabin's walls, no curtains on its windows. There was a wood-burning stove in the living room. A big-screen television, an old sofa with a blanket thrown over it. A spiral staircase led up to the bedrooms. The only other room downstairs was the kitchen, which smelled of cigarette smoke, cooked bacon and unwashed Kershaws. The unwashed Kershaws, Stevie and Donnie, were seated at the kitchen table knocking back cans of Budweiser and savoring their freedom. They'd just put away some bacon and eggs, apparently. There was a greasy cast iron skillet on the stove, egg shells and an empty bacon wrapper on the counter. The sink was heaped with dirty dishes.

"Resident trooper's come to bust your balls," Milo informed them sourly. "That tall one's Stevie. The short, ugly one's Donnie."

Stevie's eyes widened instantly at the sight of someone in uniform.

"Whoa, talk about a buzz kill," groaned Donnie, whose own eyes were hidden behind a pair of reflecting shades.

"I just came by to introduce myself," Des assured them, sticking out her hand. "I'm Des Mitry. Glad to know you both."

The Kershaw brothers got slowly to their feet and shook hands with her. Both wore flannel shirts and jeans. Beyond that, they looked almost nothing alike.

Stevie, who towered over his younger brother, was skinny, dark-haired and, seemingly, determined to prove to the world that the mullet haircut wasn't dead. Stevie had strikingly delicate features. His pink rosebud of a mouth was almost girlish. Perhaps to compensate for it, he'd grown a soul patch beneath his lower lip. He had a cocky smirk on his face as he eyed Des up and down. Somehow, Stevie Kershaw had gotten the idea that he was a babe magnet.

Donnie was built low to the ground like his dad, though he was a lot stockier and a whole lot hairier. He had reddish brown hair that flopped down over his eyebrows and a scraggly beard that grew right on down his neck into his shirt. Donnie Kershaw looked more like a wet cocker spaniel than any man Des had ever met.

"Would you remove your shades, please? I like to look at a man when I'm talking to him."

Reluctantly, Donnie complied, jiggling them in his hand. He had nervous, clueless eyes.

Actually, her initial impression was that neither of them reeked of being ten different kinds of nasty. Which wasn't to say they were harmless bunnies, either. Both of them projected an unsettling air of menace that she couldn't quite identify yet. And that troubled her. Des liked to be able to place people.

"So you're the new sheriff in town?" Stevie was still smirking.

"Something like that."

"Lady, how tall are you?" asked Donnie, gaping at her.

"Six-foot-one." With her boots on she was close to six-four.

"I think you must be the tallest female I ever met," Donnie marveled.

"What about Ray Ryan's sister, Lizzie?" Stevie said to him. "Played center on the girls basketball team my senior year, remember? Wasn't she over six foot?"

"Nah, she was like five-eleven. Plus, she was a major porker. This one's *sha-weet*. Wouldn't mind seeing it out of uniform."

"Not one little bit," agreed Stevie, bumping knucks with him.

"Okay, I'm standing right here, guys," Des pointed out sharply. Which seemed to startle both of them.

"You, like, want to sit down?" Stevie asked her, turning vaguely polite.

She sat, still puzzled by them. They didn't strike her as that hardened or tough. Just seemed like a couple of hapless small town skeegie boys. And yet they made the hairs on the back of her neck stand up. Why? "I understand you boys paint houses. If I hear of anybody who's looking for someone, I can let you know."

"It's still a little early in the year," Stevie said. "You need your nighttime lows up over freezing. It'll be another month before we can get going."

"We've got work though," said Donnie, scratching at his unkempt muzzle. "We start at Four Chimneys Farm first thing in the morning."

"A little hard work never hurt nobody." Milo leaned against the sink with his arms crossed, eyeing her coldly. "Not that these two have broken a sweat in their lives. Laziest good-for-nothings I ever met. Not to mention the dumbest. But if Eric's willing to give 'em a chance, I say what the hell. He's a Vickers, but he tries to do decent by people. Not like his sister. And for sure not the old lady."

"Well, I'm glad to hear that you have a plan. And I want you to know you have a clean slate with me. You've served your time, and now we're moving on."

"True or false, lady," Milo said accusingly. "If anything goes wrong in Dorset, you'll be all over them for it."

"They're convicted felons now. That's something they'll have to live with."

"But everybody's *always* blamed stuff on us," complained Donnie, his voice taking on a whiny, adolescent edge.

"All because we don't get along with the Vickers." Stevie shook a Marlboro from his pack and lit it.

"And now you show up here to do their bidding," Milo grumbled at her.

"You've got that wrong, Mr. Kershaw."

"Like hell. They tell Bob Paffin what to do, and he tells you. You call this fair? Hell, if one of us did what that drunken old bitch done to Duck River Pond last night you'd have thrown our ass in jail. Her, you just sent home. It ain't right, and you ought to be ashamed of yourself. *You* especially."

Des narrowed her gaze at him. "And you're going where with this? . . ."

"Don't play cute. You know where."

"Maybe I do know what you mean, Mr. Kershaw. A lot of people in Dorset want your boys to fail. Same as they want me to fail." She turned back to Stevie and Donnie and said, "Let's prove them wrong, okay?"

The brothers looked down at their hands. They were plenty interested in seeing her naked, but not so crazy about being put in the same boat with her.

"Ma'am, we're *not* looking to go back in," Stevie vowed. "All we want to do is get our act together. Right, Donnie?"

Donnie nodded his head. "Get our van running."

"She runs, dummy," Milo said gruffly. "Just needs a new muffler."

"So why didn't you put one in?" Stevie asked him.

"Why the hell should I?"

"As a welcome home present."

"I came and got your sorry asses, didn't I?"

"Yeah, yeah, yeah, you cheap old buzzard," Donnie groused.

"Hey, nipplehead, if you're living under my roof you'll show me some respect," warned Milo, clenching a fist at him.

Des found herself thinking that these two ought to find a place of their own, like their sister Justine had. Because their biggest problem in life, she felt quite certain, was their human hemorrhoid of a father. "I hope you guys don't bear a grudge. Justine is dating Bement Vickers these days. And he does happen to be the person who turned you in to the law."

"See?" snorted Milo. "Doing their bidding again."

"You've pretty much made that point, Mr. Kershaw. Want to move off of it?"

"I'll say what I want to say," he shot back stubbornly.

"You guys forced Bement into a situation where he had zero leeway. If he hadn't contacted the state police, he could have gone to jail for receiving stolen property."

"He didn't have to go narc on us," Stevie said. "Could have just said no."

"Not their way," Milo put in. "They want to keep us down."

"Mr. Kershaw, I'm urging all three of you to deal with Justine's relationship in a civil fashion. Are we clear on that?"

"Here's what I'm clear on, lady," Milo responded. "Every time I think about that rich bastard pawing my little girl I just about blow a gasket. And I don't appreciate you telling me how I'm supposed to feel about my own flesh and—"

"We're *plenty* clear, ma'am." Stevie raised his voice over his father's. "Who Teeny hangs with is her business. Right, Donnie?"

"Totally," Donnie affirmed, nodding his spaniel head. "You won't have any trouble from us, ma'am. Honest. We're just happy to be home."

"Are we through now?" Milo demanded angrily.

What Des really wanted to do was take aim at this snarly little man's family jewels and drop kick him right through the wall. Instead, she flashed him her sweetest smile. "I hope we are, Mr. Kershaw. I really do."

In keeping with Dorset's unofficial motto—*Above all, invisibility*—the private drive that led to Four Chimneys was not marked as such. There was simply a turn-in on Route 156 with three mailboxes and a small hand-lettered sign that read: ORGANIC FARM THIS WAY.

As Des eased her cruiser slowly up the long drive, she couldn't help notice how lush and fertile this land was compared to the stony hill country where the Kershaws lived. There were stands of towering oaks and hickories, rolling meadows that tumbled gently all the way down to the Connecticut River, which sparkled in the late morning sunlight. As she took a narrow stone bridge over a half-frozen stream, she glimpsed loamy planting fields and pastures enclosed by old fieldstone walls. She caught sight of a big, weathered red barn off to her left, along with a complex of greenhouses, and the small tenant farmer's house where Eric and Danielle lived. Another hand-lettered sign pointed to the farm's entrance on her left. There was no indication of what lay ahead on her right. Des continued on that way, came around a big tree-lined bend and found herself before a massive wrought iron gate, which was open.

She passed on through into a courtyard. And now she was face to face with Four Chimneys. It was the grandest manor house she'd ever seen, three stories of ivy-covered red brick with a slate mansard roof, two massive central chimneys and another chimney at each end. It did not look like someone's private home to her. More like a boarding school or research institute. Some of this had to do with its hugeness. But mostly it was the rotunda that the mansion was built around—a spectacular four-story glass dome framed in greenish-tinged copper.

An archway led around to a four-car garage and brick-walled service courtyard. She parked there behind Claudia's Lexus SUV, which was stashed in the garage next to her mother's gleaming silver Mercedes Gullwing.

The sun felt good on her face when Des got out. There was a

garden gate in the courtyard wall. She went through it and down a brick path that passed through a formal rose garden before she arrived at Claudia and Mark's cottage, which was so tiny and exquisite that it looked as if it were never meant to be left out in the elements. It was painted a creamy white, its shutters and window boxes bright blue. Old-fashioned tavern lanterns flanked its double Dutch front doors, which were painted that same bright blue. Snowdrops and snow crocuses were coming up in the little cottage's ornamental herb garden, which was neatly edged with manicured boxwoods.

Des used the brass knocker, feeling size huge as she loomed there in the doorway.

Claudia Widdifield swung the top door open and gazed out at her coolly. "I see you've made it, Trooper. Apparently you're serious about this matter."

Claudia did not invite her in, and Des was not about to barge in. Claudia did not inspire easy familiarity. She was more the type who made Des feel as if she had something smelly stuck to her shoe. Des did get a look at the beautifully appointed living room behind her. The grandfather clock and antique writing table. The basket full of peeling birch logs that sat beside the fireplace. Dried lavender was arranged in a battered milk pitcher on the coffee table, where a selection of art books was stacked just so. It was obvious that an interior designer lived here. Either that or the ghost of Laura Ashley.

"Perhaps we should go to the big house," Claudia said. "There's something you may wish to see."

She joined Des outside, pulling the blue door shut behind her. Claudia's shiny blond hair was held in place by a hair band today. And she was going with a lot of vanilla bling-bling. Not only pearl earrings but a pearl choker and bracelet as well. She wore a pair of taupe-colored slacks and a sweater set of white cashmere that was the sort of thing Des admired greatly but would never dare wear. Ten minutes after she put it on she'd spill something on it.

"Your house is charming," she observed as they started down the brick path. *Charming* was a word Des had never used before she moved to Dorset. Here, it popped out a lot.

"Why, thank you," Claudia said, thawing perhaps two degrees. "Mark served as project architect. I did the interior. It was actually mother's kennel in a previous life. She used to raise her golden retrievers out here. Bailey is the last of a proud line, old thing. It has only the one bedroom, so Bement is bunking in the big house with mother. It's where he grew up. Our move out to the cottage is very recent. Mind you, I'm . . ." Claudia trailed off into silence. Briefly, Des thought she might get into where Mark was presently bunking. "I'm exceedingly happy that Bement is back with us. But I'd hoped he would graduate from Stanford and pursue something worthwhile. Instead, he's refinishing furniture. That's something a man putters at in his workshop, don't you think?"

"I think we should all do what makes us happy."

"That's a very hedonistic approach to life," Claudia said disapprovingly. "I wouldn't expect to hear that from someone in uniform."

"We sworn personnel are a diverse bunch."

"I'd forgotten that you're an artist. Mother raves about your work."

Claudia chose a different path from the one Des had taken. This one led past a tennis court and Olympic-sized swimming pool. The pool had been covered for the winter. Claudia strode like a power walker, her head high, fists pumping. Des, even with her long stride, had to walk briskly to keep up with her.

"I don't mean to sound narrow-minded, trooper, but I'm also not crazy about his relationship with the Kershaw girl. I'm fully aware that she's a terribly cute thing. And when it comes to sex, well, men don't think very clearly when they're Bement's age."

"Oh, I wouldn't try to impose any age limit on it."

"I'd just hate to see him get trapped. Because I just know she's after our money. *Milo* is after our money. That insidious little man is behind this whole romance."

"Actually, he's just as upset about it as you are. Told me so himself not thirty minutes ago."

"And you *believed* him? Milo Kershaw is a *murderer*. My father dropped dead of a heart attack when Milo torched our barn. He might just as well have taken out a gun and shot Father."

"That doesn't make Justine a criminal."

"Her brothers stole from this very house."

"That still doesn't make Justine a criminal."

"I guarantee you Eric will be sorry he's hired those two. He's only done it to tick me off. Eric loves nothing better than to poke me in the eye with a sharp stick. He's been that way since we were little children."

Poochie's sleek silver two-seater was idling out in the courtyard, its exotically breathtaking doors raised, its engine burbling. Despite being nearly fifty years old, the Gullwing looked boldly modern. Also fresh off of the showroom floor. Its body gleamed, chrome bumpers and wheels sparkled. The red leather interior was spotless.

Guy Tolliver was behind the wheel, sporting a tweed racing cap, jaunty red scarf and black leather bomber jacket.

Poochie Vickers came striding across the courtyard toward them decked out in an outlandishly huge pair of yellow sunglasses, shawl-collared cardigan, paint-splattered jeans and her tattered sneakers. "Hullo, Des!" the grand dame roared as Bailey loped along behind her. "Can you *believe* it—spring has sprung!"

"That it has. Quite some ride you've got here."

"There's nothing quite like the sweet smell of excess," Tolly concurred, patting the dashboard.

"Nonsense," Poochie sniffed. "When Daddy gave it to me for graduation, it was quite reasonably priced. And I've never babied it. Machines are meant to be worked."

"There's still an awful lot of salt on the roads, Mummy," cautioned Claudia. Winter road salt was highly corrosive to the undercarriage of any car, let alone a rare antique.

"I can't help that—my clunker's in Doug's shop. What did you wish to see me about, Des? I hope it's not more to do with last night."

"I'm here to see Mrs. Widdifield, actually."

"By all means." Poochie climbed into the passenger seat and patted her lap. Bailey obediently climbed into it. Then she lowered her door shut and hollered, "Floor it, Tolly!"

As they sped off with a roar, Des could hear the old girl cry, "Wheeeeee!"

"They're just like a pair of naughty children," Claudia said, starting across the courtyard toward the main house.

"What's his story?"

"Who, Tolly? He's what's known as a permanent houseguest. Older gay men like Tolly often attach themselves to wealthy widows. He keeps Mother company. Escorts her to social functions. Makes no demands upon her. No physical ones, I should say."

"Sounds like you don't exactly approve."

"I don't care for the way she's always buying him expensive gifts. That's how he operates. He's been sponging off of wealthy hostesses for years. Plus one hears stories. It's a sad thing, really, because he was once a top photographer for *Harper's Bazaar, Town&Country,* all the best. He claims to be gathering up his old photos for a book."

They strode up the steps now to the massive front doors and went inside. Des was instantly awed as she stood there in the vast, marble-floored entrance hall, gazing first at the grand winding staircase, then up at the inlaid paneled ceiling forty feet overhead. Before her, beyond double doors of hardwood and glass, was the glass-domed conservatory, its interior bathed in the noon sunlight.

"My great-grandfather built Four Chimneys for his bride as a wedding present," Claudia informed her proudly. "It's a McKim, Mead and White home. In fact, Four Chimneys was the last project Charles McKim designed before he died in 1909. My great-grandmother loved orchids, which explains the conservatory, and she loved parties. The north wing exists entirely for the purpose of entertaining on a grand scale. There's a ballroom and formal dining room, rooms for billiards and cards, a restaurant-sized kitchen. When father was still active in diplomatic circles, he and mother threw huge functions. But mother shut down the north wing years ago. Prefers the south wing, which is much homier. And the conservatory, of course. Would you care to? ..."

"I'd love to."

They passed through the conservatory doors and into an extraordinary world. Not only was the conservatory's four-story-high domed ceiling made of glass but so was its entire back wall, which overlooked the Connecticut River. The dome was supported by a network of huge cast iron girders and trusses. Brightly colored tropical birds were flying around up there, squawking.

"You may recognize some of the structural definition from old photographs," Claudia said, following Des's gaze. "It's strikingly similar to McKim, Mead and White's long lost Grand Concourse of the old Penn Station in New York City. Architecture students from Yale make a pilgrimage here almost every semester to study it."

It was so warm and steamy in there that Des's glasses fogged up. It was also wonderfully fragrant. Poochie Vickers had a forest of edible trees growing everywhere in massive pots. There were lemon trees, orange trees, fig trees. Huge clumps of lavender, sage, rosemary and other aromatic herbs grew in planter boxes. In the midst of this indoor forest was a seating area of well-worn wicker sofas and chairs grouped around a coffee table heaped with books, magazines and game boards. There was also a badminton court and portable basketball hoop. A sturdy, chubby 1950s-era Lionel electric train chugged its way around the conservatory on a raised track.

"This was where we *lived* when we were kids," Claudia recalled fondly, showing Des a glimpse of unbridled warmth. "It was one big jungle playhouse. It's still Mother's favorite room."

Claudia led Des back out into the entry hall now and into the mansion's south wing, where the corridor walls were crowded with photos of Poochie from her glory days. So many days, so many Poochies. There was Poochie the society debutante, her blond hair swept back, face bright and animated. Poochie the Olympic swimmer, her face resolute and strong. Poochie the bride, posed on the church steps beside Coleman Vickers, a tall aristocrat with a high forehead and cleft chin. Poochie the diplomat's wife, photographed with two, three, four different U.S. presidents, with Queen Elizabeth, with Charles De Gaulle. Poochie the celebrity chef, in the kitchen with James Beard and Julia Child.

Perhaps the most striking picture of Poochie was one in which she was all by herself astride a tricycle with her long legs out in the air, her tongue stuck out and her eyes crossed.

"Tolly took that one, actually," Claudia informed her quietly. "It was on the cover of *Harper's Bazaar* in November of 1964. And that's *my* tricycle."

The parlor was a grand-sized room in a grand-sized house— although quite thoroughly lived in. Shabby even. The Turkestan rugs were threadbare. The chintz-covered sofas and chairs marked with more than a few dog pee stains. The odor was unmistakable. The parlor was also quite informal, thanks to Poochie's collection of gaudy, brightly colored sunglasses. She owned hundreds. Also hundreds of children's plastic water pistols. Her thoroughly kitschy collections were so prominently displayed that it took Des a moment to notice what was hanging there on the walls.

Once she did, she couldn't stop looking.

Poochie Vickers liked to collect informal little drawings that had been hastily sketched on things like cocktail napkins and tablecloths. Many of them looked like doodles. It's just that they'd been doodled, and signed, by the likes of Picasso, Man Ray and Miro. The more formal pieces that lined her parlor walls were amazingly eclectic. Seemingly, the lady simply displayed whatever, whomever she liked. There was a Ruscha word painting from the early '60s next to a Pollock drip painting from the late '40s. An immense Warhol flower painting hung beside a Hopper seascape. Paintings by Magritte, Mondrian and Leger were grouped with original drawings by Edward Gorey and Charles Addams.

"Mother has always befriended artists," Claudia said. "She adores them, and they adore her. I think I understand why—because she's an original, just like these works are."

Des stood there transfixed by a truly striking Alberto Giacometti self-portrait. The master sculptor had drawn it when he was a mere teenager. His face was a boy's face, hair a wild mop of curls. Yet his gaze was the piercing one of a mature artist, his command over his pen confident and bold. Des had seen this drawing before in books and admired it greatly—and now she was standing in a house in Dorset, Connecticut, staring right at the original. As an artist, she was awestruck.

As Dorset's resident trooper, she was amazed that the Kershaw brothers had walked off with silver candlesticks and left this astonishing art collection behind. Then again, Stevie and Donnie were minor league crooks. It would take someone of sophistication to know what these pieces were worth. And how to dispose of them.

"What sort of a security system does she have here?" Des asked, glancing around at the tall windows.

"You're talking to her, Trooper. Mother never so much as locks her doors."

"Are you kidding me?"

"I wish I were. I keep begging her to install a system. She won't. She doesn't think of her art as valuable. Just thinks of it all as 'stuff.' She has 'stuff' in the attic that she's never bothered to uncrate. Never even had catalogued. Individual paintings could go missing for weeks and we'd never know. I tried to install a system on my own, but she ordered the workmen to leave. Terribly frustrating, but it's *her* house. All I can do is make sure someone is around to keep an eye on it. Frankly, part of me is grateful that Bement is back home again."

"Do you have live-in help?"

"Mother doesn't believe in it. Not since the unfortunate incident with Milo Kershaw."

"Who cleans for her?"

"She does," Claudia replied. "I do. We all do."

"But this place is huge. The bathrooms alone. Why, there must be—"

"Twelve, Trooper. Four Chimneys has twelve bathrooms. But the north wing is shut down, as I mentioned. And we only use a handful of the rooms in this wing. So we manage to stay one step ahead of the cobwebs and dust. Mind you, the whole place could use a good scrubbing by a professional cleaning crew. But Mother won't go for that either. Too expensive. Mother is . . . she has her *quirks*."

"Actually, her *quirks* are the purpose of my visit," Des said. "There's no tactful way to put this: Your mother has become a chronic shoplifter, Mrs. Widdifield. And I'm not sure she even comprehends how she ended up in that pond last night. I'm becoming concerned about her safety and the safety of anyone who might get in her path. I don't wish to intrude on your family privacy, but what's going on with her?"

Claudia sighed, her proud shoulders slumping. "The short answer is, I don't know. But I'd like to show you something up in the attic."

They took the marble staircase up to the second floor, where Des caught a glimpse of a wide, well-lit hallway. More paintings and drawings lining the walls. Doors leading to at least eight bedrooms. A narrower wooden staircase went up to the attic, which was as huge as a warehouse and smelled strongly of mouse droppings and mothballs.

Claudia flicked on the overhead lights to reveal garment bags, garment bags and more garment bags. "Mother has every article of clothing she's ever owned."

There were old-fashioned hatboxes from elegant Paris shops, huge old leather steamer trunks plastered with stickers from bygone cruise lines. Everywhere, there were crates marked *Fragile*. Also dozens of stuffed and mounted animal heads. Lions and tigers and bears, things with antlers, tusks.

"My grandfather, John J., liked to display his hunting trophies in the library. Mother found them barbaric. After he passed away, she had them taken down. But she's saved them out of respect."

"For your grandfather?"

"For the animals." Claudia lifted some heavy mover's blankets from atop a steamer trunk and flung it open, her lip curling with distaste. "Have a look."

Inside, Des found hundreds of packages of candy bars. Claudia unlatched another trunk. More candy bars were hidden in there, as were bags and bags of chocolate chip cookies. The cookies had been in there a good long while. The *Use by* date stamped on the bags had expired two years ago.

"I stumbled upon all of this by accident last fall," Claudia revealed in a low, quavering voice.

Des said nothing. She'd encountered this once before on the job. It was not a pleasant memory.

"Truly, I don't understand *why* Mother is doing this. She never eats a sweet that she hasn't baked herself. Everyone knows that. And yet, she hides these thing away up here like a-a thief."

"You're sure it's she who's been doing it?"

"Who else could it be? Tolly's only been around for a few months. This has been going on for *years*." Claudia stood there wringing her hands, distraught. "Sometimes, she can't remember where she's just been or what she's been doing. She'll even drift away in the middle of a sentence. I've been doing a bit of reading on the subject. Medical encyclopedias and so forth. Apparently, hoarding things away like this is considered to be a sign of . . . paranoia. There are a number of possible explanations. The onset of Alzheimer's disease is the most obvious. Or a brain tumor. Or it may have to do with her drinking."

"How much does your mother drink?"

"A lot. She always has. Wine with lunch. Cocktails before dinner, more wine, then brandy. It's possible the long-term effects have caught up with her."

"Does she act as if she thinks someone is trying to do her bodily harm? Does she seem frightened?"

"I don't believe so, no."

"Has she experienced temporary numbness to a hand or one side of her face?"

Claudia raised her chin at her. "You're wondering if she's getting TIAs."

Des nodded. "Transient Ischemic Attacks are quite common among older people." TIAs were caused by tiny clots or plaque particles breaking away from the wall of an artery. Blood flow to the brain was temporarily impeded. "But surely her physician must have an opinion, no?"

"Now you've put your finger squarely on my dilemma," Claudia replied. "The awful truth is that Mother hasn't been examined by a doctor for more than twenty years. Calls them 'pill-pushing quacks.' I keep begging her to get a check-up. This is a woman who's in her seventies, for God's sake. But she won't do it. And you can't *make* Mother do anything. Physically, she seems perfectly healthy. I can't remember the last time she caught so much as a cold. But we have no way of verifying even what her blood pressure is."

"I'm sorry to hear this, Mrs. Widdifield."

"I'm sorry to be saying it. Candidly, I'm concerned about my family's financial affairs." Claudia moved away from the candy bars and cookies now, arms folded tightly in front of her chest. "I'm considering certain legal steps that will enable my brother and me to take control of them from her."

"This is a mighty big step."

"I realize that. And you may as well know that Eric—when I can pin him down—thinks I'm overreacting. It's his view that Mother has *always* been batty. That nothing has changed. The same goes for our family lawyer, who believes mother remains perfectly capable of making sound financial decisions. I do not. I believe her behavior in regards to money has become downright frightening. She's blown thousands of dollars on Tolly—cash withdrawals, expensive gifts, monstrous credit card bills. That is *not* my mother. I'm concerned that Tolly is preying upon her. I wish the others understood this, but they simply don't. You understand, don't you? You were there last evening. You interrogated her."

"I *questioned* her. My job was strictly to make sure everyone was safe." Des had to be very careful here. She did not want to get roped into a family dispute over money. "Have you confronted her with your concerns?"

"She won't discuss it. Just calls me vile things—power hungry, joyless, f-frigid. We've always had our difficulties. Eric, she *adores*. Me, I've never been able to please her. That's something I've had to live with my whole life."

Des nodded, thinking that this particular vanilla ice princess was turning into the Morton Salt girl—when it rained, it poured.

Claudia glanced at her uncertainly, as if realizing she'd been more forthcoming than she wanted. "Have you any experience with the legal aspects of such competency proceedings?"

"A little. When a motion is filed by a family member, the state's Social Services system gets involved, specifically Services for the Elderly. An investigator interviews family members and friends. Your mother's physical and mental condition would be evaluated by independent physicians. Eventually, a hearing before a judge would take place. Witnesses will be called. So if, as you say, other family members are not on board, then that'll present a problem. Does your husband, Mark, share your concerns?"

"My husband is much too busy flushing his life down the toilet right now to be of any . . ." Claudia broke off, her chest rising and falling. "May we go back downstairs? I find this attic overwhelmingly depressing." They retraced their steps across the cluttered attic and started back down. "My situation with Mark is very upsetting," she confessed. "I get so damned tired of being the mommy. I want a *man*. What I've got is a big baby. Mark simply won't face up to anything hard or painful. Eric is the same way. All men are. They expect us to do the emotional dirty work while they hide under our aprons, sucking their thumbs."

"I hear you," agreed Des, who was thinking she did know one man who wasn't like that. Not a bit.

"I suspect you've gotten a bit more than you bargained for today. Mind you, I've spoken with you in the strictest . . ."

"No need to even go there. What we just talked about stays with me."

"I appreciate that, Trooper. And I'm sorry if I seem a bit emotional in regards to Mother. I've never dealt with anything quite like this before."

"I have."

"How did everything turn out?" Claudia asked, glancing at her curiously.

"There were some problems."

Des left it at that. She didn't share any more details about Ellen Pitcher, a fifty-six-year-old housewife up in Glastonbury. Plastic clothes hangers had been Ellen's thing. Hundreds and hundreds of plastic clothes hangers. Ellen's hoarding had been accompanied by rampant paranoia. She became convinced that her husband, her son and her pregnant daughter were conspiring to destroy her. When they tried to take her to see a doctor, Ellen panicked and took her own life with a .38.

Before she did so, she took all of theirs, too.

CHAPTER 5

MITCH HAD ZERO PROBLEM figuring out which cashier was Justine.

Rut Peck was right—Justine Kershaw was a radiantly beautiful porcelain figurine of a young woman, no more than five feet tall and exquisitely fine-boned, with huge brown eyes and smooth, shiny jet black hair that came all the way down to her waist. She couldn't have weighed much more than ninety pounds, yet she didn't seem the least bit delicate there in her green smock as she scanned and bagged the heavy gallon jugs of antifreeze for the guy in line ahead of Mitch.

In fact, Justine was so sparkly and alive that by contrast the cashiers working there alongside her at the big box discount store seemed downright lobotomized. They stared straight ahead as they rang up their customers' purchases, jaws slack, eyes glazed. Not one of them smiled. Not that there was much to smile about. Their work environment was a cheerless, windowless cement-floored warehouse. The lighting was dim, the air heavy with the unappetizing scents wafting from the snack bar, chiefly greasy popcorn and the porky gray wieners that were sweating away on the rotating electric grill. Everywhere Mitch looked he saw surveillance cameras. And signs informing him that he was under surveillance. This place, he decided, was hell.

And yet Justine Kershaw was smiling.

"Welcome to the evil empire, sir," she chattered at him gaily when he reached her with his box of Tic Tacs. Her voice was surprisingly husky. "Did you find everything you were looking for?"

"Actually, I came to see you. Rut Peck thought we should talk. I tried to phone you here but—"

"This is the gulag, cupcake. We're not allowed to take calls unless it's a family emergency. And this is about? . . ."

"Your novel. I'd like to read it."

She glanced up at him sharply. Her large, lustrous eyes were positively piercing. "Why would you want to do that?"

"As a favor to Rut." He paid her for the Tic-Tacs. "I'm a critic."

"Okay, there's some big whoop of a critic who lives out on Big Sister."

"You're looking at him—in living black and white. I'm Mitch Berger."

"Sure, Rutty's mentioned you. You used to go with the resident trooper."

"Still do."

"Hey, whatever. Only, you'll have to buy something else if you want to keep talking to me. If I don't move you through fast enough they'll stick me in back with the warehouse apes." Justine nodded to the rack next to her register. "How about the new Britney CD? Or perhaps Jessica Simpson's more your style."

"No, and hell no." Mitch reached for a Milky Way bar.

"Well, you have *some* musical taste," she allowed, ringing it up. "But that still doesn't qualify you to read my novel. I'll need to hear a lot more from you."

"I don't mind," said Mitch, thinking that Rut hadn't exaggerated about her mouth either. Justine Kershaw came equipped with loads of attitude.

"Tell you what, I have a break coming up in thirteen minutes. Not that I'm counting. I can meet you out front on the bench."

"That's fine. I'll browse until then."

"Knock yourself out. Only, wait . . ." She shoved his receipts into his hand. "Hold onto these for dear life or the security guards will nail you. They're on monthly quotas. They don't bust enough people, they don't get promoted."

The snack bar fumes continued to follow him until he got all the way to the shoe department, where they were finally overwhelmed by the smell of synthetic leather. Next to the shoe department there were television sets. Beyond those jewelry, bedding, brassieres. You could find pretty much anything at the big box store, Mitch realized as he munched his Milky Way. You could even buy a Mossberg 500 Pump Action shotgun while you were getting a prescription filled at the adjacent pharmacy.

As a rule, he preferred to give his business to individual local merchants. In fact, a lot of people had objected bitterly when the chain store empire had announced its intention to build an outlet in Dorset. A vigorous opposition drive had been mounted. It failed, although opponents did convince the corporate planners to build the proposed outlet on a vacant tract of land *behind* the A&P, where it could not actually be seen by passersby on the street. Only a discreet, unlit sign marked its presence.

One lap around this grim discount netherworld was plenty for Mitch. He couldn't get back out to the parking lot fast enough. Blinking in the bright sunlight, he located the bench over next to the garden center, which was enclosed behind a neighborly twelve-foot fence topped with razor wire.

Justine was seated there in a scuffed leather jacket, smoking a cigarette and fending off the advances of a young security guard, who was hovering about her looking exceedingly puffed up.

"This is Trevor," she said, smiling hugely as Mitch approached. "Trevor's making sure I don't steal this bench. And now he's saying good-bye. Say bye-bye, Trevor."

Trevor eyed Mitch up and down before he started back toward the front doors, strutting just a bit in case Justine was watching him.

She wasn't. Her brown eyes were on Mitch as he sat next to her on the curved metal bench. Justine was not a calm person. She bristled with fidgety intensity as she studied him. "Buy something?" she asked mockingly.

"I didn't, no," he said, shifting around on the bench, which managed to be both ugly and uncomfortable.

"It's fairly hilarious how all of you rich people look down your noses at this place but can't stay away."

"I'm not rich."

"What*ever*," she said, as he continued to shift around. "Not real accommodating, is it?"

"It's not. And I have ample padding."

"That's intentional. They don't want us lingering out here, plotting to overthrow the empire."

Trevor had not gone back inside. He was parked outside of the front doors, scrutinizing people as they left the store.

"Do you have big shoplifting problems here?" Mitch asked, watching him.

"Yeah, although half is actually employee pilfering. Which is, like, totally understandable. We all hate the place. Check this out—we get bonus points if we turn each other in. You amass enough points, you get a whole fifty-cent raise." Justine took a final drag on her cigarette and stubbed it out. "You know how they're always telling us we won the Cold War? Look around you, cupcake. We didn't beat them. We *are* them."

"If you feel this way why don't you do something better with yourself?"

"There *is* nothing better." Justine shook another cigarette from her pack and lit it. "Besides, I'm in the belly of the beast here. The dehumanization, the grinding, hopeless despair—that just makes me stronger. It's kind of an alternative sensibility. You probably can't understand it."

"You're right, I can't. With me, grinding despair is not an empowerment thing. It's more of a misery thing."

"My girls need me here, okay?" she explained, dragging on her cigarette. "Two-thirds of our employees are women—but only one-third of us are in management. And men are paid more to do the same exact job we do. That is, like, *so* not even fair. I'm organizing our cashiers, okay? And I'm in touch with women at a whole bunch of our other New England stores. If we don't get equal pay, we're hiring a lawyer and suing their asses."

"You're a regular Norma Rae, aren't you?"

"Who the hell's *she*?"

"That's okay. Don't mind me."

"They treat us like criminals. If you treat people like criminals, they act like criminals. Believe me, I know. I have one for a father and two—count 'em two—for brothers."

"Are you happy to have them home again?"

"I'm not happy about anything that has to do with those dickheads," Justine answered bitterly. "Or with that mean old man. You know what *he* thinks I should be doing? Devoting my life to cooking and cleaning for him. I told him, 'I'm not your maid, you squirrely old bastard.' And I got a place up by the lake with Allison Mapes. We've been best buds for, like, ever."

"Is that the Allison who waits tables at McGee's? Sure, I know her." Mitch was partial to the fried oysters and spiral fries at McGee's Diner. And Allison, a scrappy fireplug of a blonde, took exceptionally good care of him. "She's my favorite waitress."

"Hey, I'll be sure to tell her you said so. It'll make her year."

A middle-aged woman pulled up now in a Ford Explorer and dropped off a pair of sullen young women. They waved lazily to Justine as they scuffed inside.

Justine waved back, then turned to Mitch and said, "I haven't let anyone read my novel. Why should I let *you*?"

"Somebody has to—if you want it to get published."

"Who says I want that?"

Seated here with this feisty, in-your-face young firecracker Mitch found himself feeling remarkably middle-aged and stuffy. Which he was not used to. Generally, he was younger and measurably weirder than most of the people he came into contact with. "We all want an audience. Otherwise, we're just muttering to ourselves."

"I could care less what other people think. Besides, I doubt it's commercial or anything. It's way disturbing. Older people won't even believe it. Because it's not about their world—it's about *mine*." Justine stuck out her soft pink lower lip, studying him critically. "How can I be sure you know what you're talking about?"

"Why would you assume I don't?"

"Well, for starters, very few people do. Especially guys."

"Have a lot of experience, do you?"

"With guys who are stupid? Duh, yeah."

"I can only give you my own opinion. Feel free to ignore it."

"So, what, you'd be doing this as a favor to Rut?"

"And because it's the best part of my job. Reviewing the latest Rob Schneider movie, that's work. Lending a hand to new talent, that's fun. But, listen, if you're afraid of the rejection . . ."

She let out a yelp of outrage. "Oh, no, you *didn't!*"

"Oh, yes, I did."

"I'm not afraid of rejection!"

Mitch smiled inwardly, pleased he'd pushed the right button.

"*If* I let you read it," she said, shaking a tiny finger at him, "can I trust you to keep your mouth shut? Because I *don't* want people knowing what's in it. It's my own private thing. And certain people might take it the wrong way."

"Certain people like Bement Vickers?"

"He's led a very sheltered life."

"What kind have you led?"

"You'd be shocked."

"I doubt it. I don't shock easily. And the answer is yes, you can trust me."

"Why should I believe that?"

Mitch sighed with exasperation. Justine Kershaw definitely required some effort. "Why shouldn't you?"

She cocked her head at him, considering this. "Well, I do trust Rut. And, who knows, it *might* be interesting to see how a guy like you reacts to it."

" 'A guy like me?' What's that supposed to mean?"

"Uh-oh, I'm out of here," Justine said suddenly, glancing at her watch. "I have to be back on the killing floor in, like, ninety seconds. Not that I'm counting. Just so you know, cupcake, there's nothing in this world that I'm afraid of. Not one single thing." She hopped nimbly to her feet and flashed him a dazzling smile. "Tell you what, I'll think it over. Cool?"

Mitch smiled back at her, liking her. "Cool."

CHAPTER 6

DES MADE SURE CLIFF cut the loin pork chops mondo-thick for her, the way Mitch liked them. The butcher was happy to oblige. He had wonderful meat. Actually, everything at Dorset's gourmet food hall, The Works, was wonderful. She gathered up fresh, beautiful mustard greens, pounds of sweet Vidalia onions. A bottle of champagne that the wine shopkeeper recommended. A chocolate cheesecake that was pure sin.

Armed with these provisions, she steered her cruiser up toward her cottage high over Uncas Lake. She needed a few more ingredients to make the meal perfect. One was the little yellow knit dress that clung to her every curve for dear life. Whenever Mitch set eyes on her in that dress he made her feel like she was the most delicious creature on the planet.

Not that she was ever able to *keep* the dress on for very long.

Bella was home. Des parked in front of the garage beside her roommate's Jeep Wrangler. There was no room in the garage for their rides since it served as their designated home for wayward kitties. Presently, they had seventeen residents of all ages, colors and religious denominations—strays that she and Bella had rescued. Some were feral, others simply abandoned. All were healthy and neutered. She and Bella had seen to that, with a kind assist from Andre the mobile vet.

Des paused on her way inside to fuss over Mos Def, their newest, baddest arrival. He immediately went into a low crouch inside his cage and hissed at her, still not happy about being warm, safe and well fed. Most were that way at first. Mos would come around. The ones who had were given free run of the garage, where they were munching or hanging together in open crates lined with hunks of carpet. Des petted them one by one. That little smudge-nosed gray guy, Carmelo, licked her nose and purred and purred. A real thief of hearts, little 'Melo was. She'd end up inviting him upstairs if she wasn't careful.

When she'd renovated the cottage, Des had opened it up so that the dining room and kitchen were all one big room. The living room, which had floor to ceiling windows overlooking the lake, served as her studio. Here, Des slashed away with a graphite stick at her fearsome portraits of the crime victims she came across on the job. It was how she survived the horror.

Right now she had an entirely different sort of portrait in progress on her easel—her own. Unfinished. Stubbornly so. Des had never tried a self-portrait before. And now she was genuinely sorry she had. Because she hated the face that was gazing back at her. Des saw self-doubt in that face. She saw the face of a woman who had no idea what she was doing with her life. As she stepped back from the easel, studying the drawing with unflinching honesty, she could not help comparing it to that Giacometti self-portrait in Poochie's parlor. His pen strokes were *alive*. Her own were so halting and timid it was as if she'd been nicking away at her own flesh with a razor blade.

Her stomach churning, Des ripped the self-portrait from her drawing pad and buried it deep under a stack of old drawings. Out of sight. *Not* out of mind.

"I didn't hear you come in, tall person!" exclaimed Bella Tillis as she barged in dressed in her ancient black ERA-YES sweatshirt and fuzzy red sweatpants. Bella was five-feet-one, totally round and truly the hardest-charging seventy-seven-year-old widow Des had ever met. "I was just on my way to my yoga class at the senior center—oy-yoy, it starts in less than an hour." Hurriedly, Bella started for the kitchen.

To many of Dorset's old-schoolers, it seemed a bit odd that the resident trooper had a Jewish grandmother from Brooklyn for a roommate. Back when Des and her husband Brandon had lived in Woodbridge, a leafy suburb of New Haven, Bella was her next-door neighbor. Bella had rescued her when Brandon dumped Des for another woman. And, eventually, became her best friend. When Des moved here, Bella sold her own place and joined her.

"Bella, it's a five-minute drive to the center," Des pointed out, following her into the kitchen.

"I like to get there early."

"And do what, cruise for booty?"

"Oh, please," Bella scoffed, filling her water bottle from a jug in the refrigerator. "Trust me, Desiree, you do *not* want to hear an old man attempt the downward-facing dog. They moan. They groan. Teddy Cavendish, you'd think some *tsotske* was sucking on his pizzle."

"Girl, do you kiss your grandchildren with that mouth?"

"Oh, please." Now Bella fetched her yoga mat from the coat closet by the front door. "If I don't get to class an hour early I don't get a good spot. Your elderly people are pathologically early."

"Okay if I steal a container of your chicken stock? I'm doing dinner for Mitch at his place."

"Of course. I put away gallons for Passover. What are you making him?"

"Um, smothered pork chops. That a problem?"

"It is not. Better you should violate my dietary laws than use something out of a can. Besides, we both know the way to Mr. Berger's heart takes a permanent detour through his tummy. *Nu,* what's the occasion?"

"No occasion, okay?" Des growled, fetching a container of homemade stock from the freezer. Also the bag of stone-ground grits her mom had sent her from a small mill in Georgia—not far from where she'd moved after she left the Deacon. Then Des went into her room for that yellow dress. When she returned to the kitchen Bella was standing right where she'd left her, a scowl on her bunched fist of a face.

"Let's have it. What's bothering you?"

"Nothing's bothering me, Bella. I'm totally cool."

"Tie that bull outside, liar mouth."

"Aren't you worried about being late for class?"

"No, I'm worried about *you*. You're still agonizing over his marriage proposal, aren't you?"

"I'm not agonizing. It's a big step, that's all."

"Indeed it is. But it's the step that two people generally take when they want to be in each other's lives. There's an old-fashioned word for it that you hipsters don't like to use—commitment. Is he bugging you for an answer?"

"Not at all. He's been incredibly patient and understanding. And, time out, but *hipster?*"

"He loves you, Desiree."

"And he knows I love him."

"So what's holding you back?"

"For one thing, I like my independence."

"Vastly overrated as a concept. We are meant to be mated."

"Yeah, well, I was 'mated' before. Didn't have such a happy ending."

"All the more reason to try again—this time with a man who, unlike Brandon, *wants* to be married to you."

There was a time when Brandon did. Back when they'd been featured on the cover of *Connecticut Magazine* under the headline: "Our State's Shining Future." She was one of the youngest Major Crime Squad lieutenants in the state. And the only one who had happened to be a woman of color. A West Point graduate. Daughter of the Deacon, the deputy superintendent and highest ranking black officer in the history of the state police. Brandon was two years out of Yale Law School and the state's top young district prosecutor. And as for eye appeal, well, Brandon was what Denzel Washington would look like if only Denzel were handsome. Except it turned out that Brandon's shiny future was in Washington with the Justice Department—and the daughter of a wealthy Philadelphia congressman. The affair had started when they were in law school together. In fact, it had never actually ended, not even after he'd married Des.

Bella was peering suspiciously at her. "You've got cold feet, haven't you?"

"Not a chance."

"Don't you flap your gums at me, missy. I'm not some beery lout you just pulled over for making an illegal left turn. Friends tell each other the truth."

"Real? Marriage opens up a whole lot of stuff that we've successfully avoided until now. There's the whole racial thing, obviously. Our two families having to deal with each other. Plus there's the issue of—"

"Children," Bella acknowledged, nodding her head.

"Whoa, flag on the play! If you have a man in your life you already have one child. Who needs another?"

Bella just glowered at her like an angry Jewish bowling ball.

"What I keep wondering," Des confessed, "is why we can't just go on doing what we're doing. Enjoying each other's company. Having fun together, great sex."

"Because that's not how a relationship works. When you're involved in each other's lives you have to keep growing together. Mitch is a centered, caring man who wants to share his life with you. In return, you cook him dinner once in a while. Show up when you feel like it, give him a good, swift shtup . . ."

"Not so swift."

"Then you jump in the shower—I trust—and out the door you go, free as a bird. You're the boyfriend from hell. It's a classic case of role reversal, if you ask me."

"You know, I'm trying to remember if I *did* ask you." Des slumped against the kitchen counter, sighing. "Want to know the crazy part, Bella? When I'm with Mitch I finally feel like the person who I want to be. I *like* myself. Brandon always had me right on the edge of panic. I couldn't eat. Couldn't sleep. I'd sob for no reason. Scream at him, throw things. Brandon and me, we fought a lot."

"You don't have to tell me. I could hear the glass breaking from next door."

"But then we'd kiss and make up and . . ." Without warning, Des suddenly remembered Brandon's body against hers, his hands on her, how he tasted and smelled. The sense memories were so vivid that she felt light-headed. "That part was so good. Except it was the only part that *was* good. With Mitch, it's *all* sweet and warm and caring. It feels so much, I don't know, *calmer.*"

"Well, it should, tattela. You're not miserable. For God's sake, don't you realize that?"

The call came in as Des was heading out the door, groceries and little yellow dress in tow. She didn't have very far to go. Just down the hill to an address on Uncas Lake Road, where two men were reportedly throwing punches out on the front porch. A neighbor had phoned it in.

High above the lake, where cool breezes blew during the summer, many of the cottages like hers had been gentrified in recent years. Down below, where dark, narrow side streets dead-ended at the oily water's edge, this had yet to happen. Here, clans of swamp Yankees remained crowded into the moldering bungalows and cinder block ranchettes that were squeezed together, shoulder to shoulder.

The address she was looking for was a dog-eared cottage that had a whole lot of beat-up cars and trucks parked out front. One of them was a canary yellow van that said S & D PAINTING on its side.

Bement Widdifield and little Donnie Kershaw were flailing away at each other out on the floodlit porch. Justine was screaming at them to stop.

Des ran up the front steps and put herself between them, her long arms outstretched. "Step back right now, hear me?" she barked. "Step back or I'm running both of you in!"

"*He* started it," Donnie protested, blood streaming from his nose down into his mustache and beard.

"I'm going to finish it, too," vowed Bement, whose left eye was blinking rapidly and watering. He'd taken a poke in it. Bement was wiry and quick-looking. Also major hunkish in a Tommy

Hilfiger boy-toy kind of way. He had blond hair down to his shoulders, a cleft chin, cheekbones to die for. "This isn't over!"

"Fine by me!" Donnie shot back.

"Both of you, *stop* this!" Justine hollered at them. She was a tiny, gorgeous thing, red-faced with rage. "Donnie, this is *my* house! And Bement is *my* boyfriend!"

"What brings you here, Donnie?" Des asked, continuing to stand between the two men.

"Me and Stevie came by to pick up Allison is all, I swear." Donnie swiped at his bloody muzzle with the sleeve of his flannel shirt. His reflecting shades lay broken on the porch floor. "Stevie and Allison started getting busy in the bedroom, so I was having a brew and watching me some tube—until *he* came over."

"And then you couldn't leave him alone, could you?" Justine smacked her brother hard in the left ear.

"Ow, Teeny, that hurt!"

"It was supposed to, you cretin!"

The front door was open. Des grabbed Donnie by the collar and shoved him inside. "You two stay put out here," she ordered Justine and Bement.

The living room was small and stuffy and reeked of cigarette smoke. There was TV, a sofa and coffee table. Not much else. A short hallway. Probably two bedrooms, one bath. The kitchen was spotless. Des found a dish towel and tossed it to Donnie for his nose.

Allison Mapes came padding barefoot out of her bedroom wearing a T-shirt and nothing more. Allison was built low to the ground and meaty through the hips, with little in the way of breasts. Her bare arms and legs were soft and pale. Allison's hair was boyishly cropped and dyed a whitish blond with streaks of maroon and green. She had six or eight ear piercings, a nose ring. Eyes that were exceptionally lifeless. Des knew her from McGee's Diner, where she waited tables when she wasn't busy rolling those eyes or scuffing around like a surly princess. Mitch maintained that Allison could be a lot of fun. Des had never seen her so much as smile.

Stevie the mullet-head followed Allison out of her bedroom, bare-chested, his flannel shirt in one hand. He was buttoning up his low-slung jeans with the other. "What's all the commotion, little brother?" he asked, eyes widening at the sight of Des.

"Donnie and Bement were mixing it up," she told him as Donnie stood with the towel pressed against his nose, not saying a word. "You didn't hear them?"

"Me and Allison were getting reacquainted," Stevie replied, leering unpleasantly.

Allison curled her lip at him. "*You* were getting reacquainted. *I* was trying to get dressed for dinner."

Stevie slouched there in the doorway with his shirt off, his bare chest hairless and concave.

"Would you put your shirt on, please?" Des asked him.

He smirked at her. "Why don't you put it on for me?"

"Not a problem." Des grabbed him by his bare shoulders, whipped him around and slammed him face-first into the wall. "Are we having fun yet?"

"Damn, lady," Stevie protested angrily. "You are crazy."

Des yanked his shirt from his hand and started to drape it around his shoulders—until she pulled back from him in horrified shock. There were dozens of raised scars on Stevie Kershaw's back. The kind of scars that come from being whipped with a belt until you bleed.

She released him, swallowing. "Does Donnie have a set of those, too?"

"None of your business." Stevie snatched his shirt from her and put it on. "Besides, it was a long, long time ago."

"Yeah, we were little kids," Donnie said defiantly. "We're not anymore."

"Did he hit Justine, too?"

"Not ever," Stevie replied. "Teeny was his little princess. And we were his dogs. But the old man couldn't hurt us. We were too tough for him. Right, little brother?"

Donnie held his fist out and the two of them bumped knucks.

Des observed them, unconvinced by their bravado. "Donnie, why don't you tell me your side of what happened between you and Bement?"

Donnie glanced uncertainly at his brother before he said, "Nothing happened. Stevie and me were gonna take Allison out to dinner is all. You know, like a welcome home party."

"So you three are old friends?"

"Growing up, me and Stevie were best buds with Lester."

"My big brother," Allison explained, her face darkening.

"Don't believe I've encountered Lester. Does he live elsewhere now?"

"If you want to call it living," she answered bitterly. "He joined the Army out of high school, and his Hummer got totalled in a roadside bombing in downtown Baghdad. He lost both legs, not to mention everything in between. He's still rehabbing at a military hospital."

"I'm sorry." Des turned back to Donnie and said, "Keep talking."

"Well, Allison said she was going to get changed for dinner—"

"And I went in to give her some wardrobe advice," Stevie interjected, grinning. "Pretty soon, the two of us were getting all kinds of—"

"Stevie, I'm planning to eat a nice hot meal tonight," Des said sharply. "I really don't want to hear what you were getting, okay?"

"I was just hanging with Teeny, getting caught up, when that Vickers bastard pulls up," Donnie went on. "And right away he gets all up in my face. Tells me, stay out of her life, go away. Hey, she's my sister, man. I'm supposed to watch out for her, know what I'm saying?"

"Damned straight, little brother."

"And I *tell* him that. So the bastard shoves me. And I shove him back, because I'm not taking that from *him*." Donnie glanced down at the towel he'd been holding to his nose. The bleeding had stopped. "And then you showed up."

"I see." Des stood there with her hands on her hips. "Why don't you three relax?"

The air outside felt bracingly cold. A frost was expected later that night. Bement and Justine were seated close together on the top step of the porch. She was stroking his face and whispering to him softly.

"Your turn, Bement," Des said. "Want to tell me what happened?"

"Donnie started it," he replied, clenching and unclenching his fists. His hands were big and rough-skinned.

"We're not in the school yard anymore. I really don't care who started it. Just talk to me, will you?"

Bement ducked his head, tucking his long blond hair behind his ears. "I stopped by to pick up Justine. We'd talked about going to a movie." He reached into the kangaroo pocket of his hooded sweatshirt, pulled out a pack of unfiltered Lucky Strikes and lit one. He got to his feet and leaned against one of the porch support beams, smoking it. He wore a tweed blazer over his hoody, baggy cargo pants, scuffed wing tip shoes. A mismatched outfit, but on him it all seemed to work. "The second I walk in the front door Donnie starts ordering me to leave his sister alone. Acting all bad-ass convict."

"Donnie was being a confrontational jerk," agreed Justine, her long black hair shining in the porch light. "Then he told Bement to step outside if he was a real man. Sweetie, I can't believe you let him bait you that way."

"I'm not afraid of those turds," Bement snapped, his blue eyes blazing.

"It's not about being afraid." Justine's voice was patient but firm. "It's about stooping to their level."

"He *shoved* me. And he called you a slut for being seen with me."

"Who cares?" she demanded. "I don't."

Des studied her admiringly. Seated there in her too-big leather jacket, Justine Kershaw looked about fifteen. And yet this dark-eyed cutie was more mature than any man in the house. "Bement, do you wish to file an assault complaint against Donnie?"

Bement flicked his cigarette butt out into the darkness. "No way."

Des went back inside. Allison was getting dressed. The Kershaw brothers were seated on the sofa together powering down beers.

"Let me guess," Stevie said snidely. "He told you Donnie started it. And you believe him, don't you?"

"Guys, I really don't care who started it. This goes down as a simple domestic scuffle in my report, nothing more."

The brothers exchanged a guardedly hopeful look.

"Does the old man have to hear about it?" Stevie wondered.

"Why, you afraid he'll take you out to the woodshed?"

"Don't joke about the woodshed, lady," Donnie pleaded, wincing.

"Your father won't hear about it from me. Really, I'm more concerned about whether or not this was a warning flare." Des took off her big Smokey hat and twirled it in her fingers, gazing at the two of them. "I've dealt with guys my whole career who couldn't stay out of jail. You guys have a decent trade. You have choices. That's why I treated you with respect this morning. I thought we had an understanding. And now I'm realizing I was wrong, because you've come here and you've dissed me. You'll get no more slack from me. You just used it all up. It's gone. I get one more call regarding you two, I'm running you right in—and making sure you're prosecuted to the fullest extent of the law. Do you want to go back in?"

"Not a chance," said Stevie.

"Then start walking the walk. For starters, why don't you find your own crib? Get out from under your father's thumb."

Donnie shook his head. "No way he'd let us."

"What do you mean 'let you'? You're grown men. The only thing that's holding you back is *you*."

And their fear. They were scared to death of that snarly, abusive little father of theirs. *This* was what had unsettled her when she'd met them that morning. It wasn't that Stevie and Donnie Kershaw were evil bad asses. It was that they were frightened. Which was definite cause for alarm bells. It was the frightened ones who you had to watch out for. The frightened ones who got in over their heads. The frightened ones who panicked and pulled the trigger.

"I saw for myself how he treats you," she went on. "The man never stops telling you how stupid and useless you are. If someone like your father keeps telling you that, pretty soon you start believing it. Maybe you two think that's just his way and he means well . . ."

"No, he doesn't," Donnie said. "He's a mean bastard. We hate his guts."

"Then stop letting him chump you."

"Lady, you know squat about us," Stevie said in a low, angry voice.

"Fine, have it your way. I've said what I wanted to say." Des glanced at Donnie. "Now you're going to bump knucks with Bement out on the porch."

"Don't do it, Donnie," Stevie warned him.

Donnie furrowed his brow in confusion. "Will you run me in if I don't?"

"Honey, you'll leave me no choice."

"You're nasty, know that?" Stevie said. "You're not a nice lady."

Bement and Justine were still seated on the top step together, holding hands. Bement's eye was starting to swell shut. He got slowly to his feet, he and Donnie staring hard at each other.

"I want to make sure there's no hard feelings," Des said.

Bement raised his chin at her before he said, "No problem." And held his fist out.

Grudgingly, Donnie bumped it with his own.

"Now leave," Justine ordered her brothers. "I want you two gone."

"We're waiting for Allison," Stevie said. "Yo, Allison!"

Justine's roommate came scuffing out the door now, clutching a denim jacket. She had on a belly shirt and ultra low-rider jeans that showed off a whole lot of skin, which might have been alluring if she was twenty pounds lighter and spent forty hours a week with a personal trainer. As it was, all she was styling were her jiggly love handles.

"Let's get gone already," Stevie huffed at her impatiently.

The three of them jumped into Stevie and Donnie's van, Stevie behind the wheel. The van wouldn't start the first three times Stevie tried it. It finally kicked over amidst a whole lot of flatulent rumbling, then stalled as they were backing out of the driveway. Stevie cranked it up again and they finally took off, leaving behind a billowing cloud of putrid exhaust.

"I'd better put some ice on this eye," Bement said, flexing his right hand. His knuckles were swelling, too. He went inside, leaving the two women alone.

"You go with Mitch Berger, am I right?" Justine asked her.

"Why, have you got some smart remark for me? Because I'm really not in the mood right now."

"No, I've got this . . ." She handed Des a fat 9-x-12 manila envelope, gulping nervously. "No big, but he's kind of expecting it, okay?"

CHAPTER 7

"Boyfriend, I'm about to pay you a huge compliment but you have to shut up while I'm doing this or it'll come out all wrong. Deal?"

"Deal," agreed Mitch, who was standing in his kitchen chopping up a mountain of Vidalia onions, a cold Bass Ale at his elbow.

Des was searing the pork chops in a cast iron skillet over high heat, a denim apron over her uniform. In the living room, a fire was roaring in the fireplace and Otis Redding was crying on the stereo. Clemmie and Quirt were dozing on the sofa. His seedlings were germinating under their grow-lit domes. Life was good.

"So don't interrupt." She stirred the stone-ground grits, which took forever to cook. "Don't make fun of me. Don't gloat. Don't do any of those other totally annoying things you always do, okay?"

"Gee, this sounds so promising I'm already getting puffed up."

"Okay, here goes," she said, taking a deep breath before the words came flooding out. "Claudia Widdifield told me today that when the going gets tough all men run and hide under mommy's apron. And I realized that *you* don't. Emotionally, you're a very brave person. You're special that way. And I just wanted to tell you that I appreciate it. Appreciate *you*." Des exhaled now. "There, I'm all done."

Mitch narrowed his eyes at her sternly. "Do you actually think you can just show up here and dump that on me? Get over here right now."

She slipped into his arms, long, lean and supple, her pale green eyes shining at him.

He hugged her tightly, grazing her lips with his, feeling that same incredible charge of electricity he always felt. "I appreciate

80

you back, Master Sergeant," he said, his lips moving northward to her ear.

She let out a little whimper. "Are you trying to get busy with me?"

"Can't help it. It's spring fever."

"I thought that was mythical. You know, like leprechauns."

"Give me your hand. I'll show you my little leprechaun."

Des slapped at him playfully. "Sir, I am making you dinner. Behave or I'll handcuff you to the refrigerator door."

In fact, dinner was unexpected. She'd arrived without warning, groceries in hand, which was not her usual deal. Not that Mitch minded. It sure beat the hell out of what he'd been planning—a big bowl of his famous American Chop Suey and a DVD of *The Three Stooges Meet Hercules*. But she usually gave him a heads-up. Not tonight. She'd simply shown up with complete dinner fixings and a bottle of Moët & Chandon Brut Imperial. Also Justine Kershaw's manuscript. Des had just broken up a scrape between Bement and Donnie at Justine's house. Apparently, the fight was nothing serious. But Mitch could tell Des was bothered by it.

"I think you should let me reimburse you for the champagne," he offered.

"No way."

"But Moët & Chandon costs a fortune. I don't like you blowing your hard-earned paycheck on me. Wait, what am I saying? Yes I do. Only, what's the occasion?"

"No occasion," she said firmly, her eyes avoiding his. "I just wanted to make us dinner. Can't I do that?"

"Any time you'd like—*if* it involves your smothered pork chops."

She rested the seared chops on a plate now and dumped the heap of onions into the pan. When the onions were good and caramelized she'd put the chops back in with them, along with some chicken stock, white wine and a sprig of fresh rosemary. This would simmer on low heat, covered, until the meat was practically falling off the bone.

"What is with you and my pork chops?"

"I had a deprived childhood."

"Your mom didn't serve them?"

"No, she did. But out of respect for the Jewish dietary laws, she made sure we wouldn't enjoy them. They were so dry they tasted remarkably like the sports section of the *New York Post*."

"Baby, I'm going to need a splash of cider vinegar."

"Haven't got any."

"Sure you have. It's under the sink—right next to your Cocoa Puffs."

"Des, is there *anything* you don't know about me?"

"God, I sure hope not."

"How was your day?" he asked as he fetched it for her.

"Way confusing. Claudia Widdifield thinks her mother is losing it, mental health-wise." Des filled him in about the candy bars in the attic, and Poochie's refusal to see a doctor. "I'm *not* a doctor, Mitch. I don't know whether the lady's in serious trouble or not. I do know this is about who controls the family fortune. And that Eric seems to think she's fine."

"Yeah, like he's a poster child for emotional security." Mitch told her how Eric had braced him about Danielle at the Food Pantry. "He practically accused me of being her lover. Can you imagine that?"

"I'd rather not, if you don't mind."

Mitch polished off the last of his Bass Ale, swallowing it thoughtfully. "You don't suppose Claudia is trying to gaslight the old lady, do you?"

"I don't take your meaning."

"Do you think Claudia could have planted that stuff in the attic herself?"

"What, to make Poochie appear crazy? Possibly, although some of it's been up there for years. And I'm still not hip to your 'gaslight' reference."

"You never saw *Gaslight*? Charles Boyer tries to convince Ingrid Bergman that she's losing it by dimming the lights on her and then telling her it's all in her imagination. She won an Oscar for that movie. I'll have to put it on top of our to-watch list, right after *The Monolith Monsters*."

Des scooped the chops back into the pan with the fragrant mound of onions, put a lid over the pan and removed her apron. "I'm going to change," she announced, starting for the bathroom. "Want to open the champagne?"

First, he lit the candles on his little dining table over by the fireplace, and put two more logs on the fire. Then Mitch fetched the champagne out of the fridge and gently worked the cork loose until it popped open. He filled two wine glasses.

By then, she'd emerged from the bathroom wearing that unbelievably sexy little yellow dress of hers. Out of uniform, the resident trooper's figure was a pulse-pounding revelation.

"You are a total hottie, know that?" he said hoarsely, unable to take his eyes off her. "What are you doing with me?"

"Right now, I'm sitting down to dinner with you. After that I intend to use you for my own selfish physical pleasure."

He held a glass out to her. She took it and they clinked glasses, gazing into each other's eyes. "What shall we drink to?"

"How about proving everyone in town wrong?"

"I'll drink to that."

And so they did. Then they ate. The chops were tender and juicy. The coarse-grained grits balanced them perfectly, as did the bitter mustard greens.

"I'm hearing you dumped me," he mentioned as he ate.

"I'm hearing *you* dumped *me*."

"Rut Peck's trying to fix me up with his divorced niece. She's a dentist."

"Marge Jewett told me the word is I'm transferring somewhere else. Now where did *that* come from? Town Hall, that's where. The powers that be want me gone."

"They do not. You've won them over, Des. And you're reading way too much into this stuff. It's just idle village gossip."

"Mitch, my life is not a reality TV show."

"To them, it is. I'm Joe Schlub and you're the sexy bachelorette. They can't wait to find out whether you'll stay with me or throw me over for some guy who looks good in a Speedo. That's life in Dorset. Ignore it. Ignore them. And, whatever you do, don't let them spoil our evening."

He got the champagne out of the fridge, refilled their glasses and sat back down.

She took a sip, dabbing daintily at her mouth with her napkin. She had impeccable table manners. In truth, she was the most innately elegant woman he'd ever met. "Mitch, do you think I play favorites on the job?"

"I think you're very fair. Why?"

"Something that Milo Kershaw said to me today. That there are two kinds of justice in Dorset—one for rich people like Poochie Vickers and the other for low-life skeegies like Stevie and Donnie."

"Well, that's pretty much true, isn't it?"

"Of course it is," she said quietly. "That's how the world works."

"So what's bothering you?"

"Milo played the race card," she confessed, staring down into her glass. "Said that *I* should know better than to be whoring for the ruling class. Not that he understands my world or me or any other damned thing."

"Exactly what did you say to the Kershaw brothers—watch your step, there's a new sheriff in town?"

"I threw in a little tough love. I hate to see people wasting their lives. Mixing it up with Bement Vickers on their first evening home is a not-good sign. What's up with that envelope Justine gave me? She a wanna-be screenwriter?"

"Novelist. I'm doing a favor for Rut Peck. He hates wasted lives, too." Mitch mopped up the last of the pan juice with his final bite of grits and sat back in his chair, sighing contentedly. "How come you haven't talked to me about it?"

"About what, baby?"

84

"This self-portrait you've been working on."

Des stared at him across the little table. "Damn, you scare me sometimes. How did you know it's a self-portrait?"

"Because you haven't talked to me about it."

She turned her gaze toward the fire, swallowing. "I'm not making things easy for you, am I?"

"Des, we really don't have to talk about this again. There's a lot for you to consider. I understand."

"Still, this hasn't been much fun for you."

"No, it hasn't. And if you'd like me to tell you you're a bad girl, throw you over my knee and spank your bare bottom, I'd be happy to."

She raised an eyebrow at him. "Are you turning kinky on me?"

"Get real. I'm a nice, clean-cut Jewish boy. I don't spank women—women spank me."

"That is *so* not going to happen."

"Then kindly allow me to tell you something else." He leaned across the table and kissed her lightly. "You've had that yellow dress on way too long."

They left the dishes where they were.

She started up to the sleeping loft with the rest of the champagne. He stopped to grab the royal blue necktie from her uniform. By the time he got up there, she had the bedside lantern lit and the covers pulled down. Her skin gleamed like burnished copper in the golden lantern light as she stretched her smooth naked self out before him, her eyes huge. He gazed at her, transfixed, before he shucked his own clothes at Warp Factor Nine.

"What are you doing with my tie?" she wondered, noticing it in his hand.

"Don't own one myself. I made a small find on the beach today, and I wanted to share it with you. Do you trust me?"

"You know I do."

He bent over and gently blindfolded her with the necktie before he opened the nightstand drawer and removed the gull wing feather. "Can you see?"

"Not really. Why, what are you going to? . . ."

"Go exploring," he replied, wafting it gently across her belly button. Her stomach muscles fluttered instantly. Then he delicately grazed her tender nipples with it, teasing them. "You okay with this so far?"

"G-Gaaaah. . . ."

"I'll take that as a yes." He headed due south with it—toward the back of her knees, between her toes. Then, ever so slowly, he began caressing his way up the soft flesh of her inner thighs. "Oh, hey, you're not in any hurry tonight, are you? Because this particular expedition may take a while."

"B-Boyfriend," she gasped, wriggling beneath him. "You take all of the time you need."

And so he did, igniting a passion that burned so deeply into the night that Mitch became convinced that it was inexhaustible, *they* were inexhaustible. It seemed as if he'd only just collapsed into a deep sleep when Quirt woke him at four-thirty to be let out. Yawning, Mitch waddled downstairs and let him out, then got back into bed. Des hadn't so much as stirred. He snuggled up against her, his face buried in her satiny smooth warmth. Instantly, he was asleep again.

He dreamt. Another Maisie dream.

They were hiking a trail together high above Lake Mohonk. Maisie was already on chemo. She had that silk scarf on over her balding head, and those dark circles under her eyes. Her complexion was sallow. And she was so tired she could hike no farther.

She stopped and grabbed him by both shoulders. "It's too late, Bear. You're already leaving me. I can feel you leaving me."

"I'm not, Maisie. I swear."

"Don't go! Please, don't go!"

"I won't go. I'll never, ever go."

But she didn't believe him. She was still clutching him by the shoulders, shaking him and shaking him and . . .

With a startled yelp he realized it wasn't Maisie who had him by the shoulders—it was Des. It was daylight now, and she was standing over him wearing her uniform and her game face. He lay there panting, his heart racing, that same metallic taste in his mouth.

"Damn, what *were* you dreaming about?" she asked, holding a cup of hot coffee out to him.

"I-I don't remember. Why?"

"You were jabbering in your sleep."

He sipped the coffee gratefully, glancing at his alarm clock. It was just past seven. "What was I saying?"

"Sounded like it had something to with Bosco."

"Sure, I remember Bosco. Used to drink that when I was a kid. It was chocolatey good. I'll bet it still is."

"Mitch, you're a very weird man," she informed him, kissing him on the forehead. "But as long as you keep your magic feather around you will never, ever get rid of me. If you change your locks, I'll break down the door. If you move, I'll track you down—and break down the door."

"So why are you all dressed?" he wondered, reaching for her.

"Got to run. I just got paged."

"What's up?"

"Grand theft auto. Somebody has stolen Poochie Vickers's Mercedes."

CHAPTER 8

IT HADN'T TAKEN ANY kind of master thief to make off with Poochie's prized Gullwing. There was no security system at Four Chimneys to bypass or disarm. The garage door was unlocked. So was the Gullwing itself.

In fact, Poochie's keys had been in the ignition.

"You're kidding me," Des responded in disbelief when Claudia Widdifield told her the key thing.

"I wish I were," Claudia snapped, her cheeks mottling with anger as they stood in the courtyard outside of the garage. It was a damp morning. Four Chimneys was shrouded in the dense fog that hugged the Connecticut River. "Mother *always* leaves her keys there."

"Mr. Tolliver is supposed to be doing the driving now," Des reminded her.

"And he is. But Tolly does as Mother asks." A sheaf of insurance paperwork was clutched in Claudia's trembling right hand. "She chooses to keep her keys there so she won't lose them—or so she claims."

Claudia was the one who'd phoned it in. She'd provided the 911 responder with the five-digit license plate number that Connecticut issued to antique cars. The particulars would be out to all troopers and municipal police departments by now. If the thief tried to drive it anywhere in the state, it would be spotted soon enough.

"I keep *telling* her she needs proper security," Claudia said, gazing into the vast four-car garage. Her own Lexus SUV was in there. Nothing else except for a stack of firewood and an old red Radio Flyer wagon. "Maybe now she'll listen to me. What am I saying? She *never* listens to me." Claudia wore a pale blue cashmere sweater set and navy pin-striped slacks today. Des wondered if she ever tumbled out of bed and threw on a pair of jeans. Or if she even owned a pair of jeans. "By the way, Trooper, can we keep this out of the media? Because I don't wish to advertise to every criminal in the northeast that we're running an all-you-can-eat buffet here."

"We can try."

"Thank you." She glanced at Des uneasily. "Perhaps now you can understand why I feel it's so imperative to have more legal control."

"I understood you just fine yesterday, Mrs. Widdifield. Right now, I'm here to file a stolen car report."

Claudia handed over the paperwork she'd been clutching.

"Who discovered that it was gone?"

"Mother did."

"Any idea who might have taken it?"

"Those damned Kershaw boys did. You know that perfectly well."

Des didn't touch that. Just wrote down the information she needed.

"Eric was expecting them to show up for work this morning," Claudia went on. "Instead, they took off in mother's Gullwing. It's painfully obvious."

"Let's not get ahead of ourselves, okay?" Des handed the paperwork back to her. "May I speak with your mother now?"

Claudia led her inside through the laundry room. A stereo system was blasting Mel Tormé backed up by a big band of at least eighty trumpets. Claudia immediately darted into the parlor to shut it off.

"Hey, who turned down my morning music?!" roared Poochie from the kitchen, where she was filling up the entire house with the aroma of frying bacon.

"The trooper's here!" Claudia called in response.

"Get your body in here, Des—breakfast's on!"

It was a huge kitchen with a long farmhouse table parked in its center. There were two ovens, a six-burner range, cupboards and counters everywhere—plus a walk-in butler's pantry with its own sink and counters. A bay window looked out across a meadow to the river. Bailey was dozing in the window seat. Poochie had two cast-iron skillets going. One had four thick slices of bacon sizzling in it, the other hash browns with sauteed onions.

As Des walked in, Poochie snatched a third skillet from the hanging rack overhead and lit a burner under it, her movements swift and expert. She seemed amazingly peppy and chipper under the circumstances. Almost defiantly so.

By comparison, Guy Tolliver looked positively comatose slumped there at the table in his maroon silk bathrobe and striped pajamas. Tolly was unshaven and uncombed. His color was not good, not unless gray was considered good.

"How do you take your eggs, dear?" Poochie slapped a pat of butter into the third pan to melt. Here she differed from Des's mom, who always cooked her eggs in bacon fat.

"I'm a little tight for time, Poochie."

"Nonsense. They're fresh from Eric's chicken house. Danielle just brought them over, dear thing. She's *so* sweet."

"I don't trust her," Tolly muttered, sipping his coffee shakily. "Sure, she's got that earthy, sheep manure between the toes thing going on, but the woman is too good to be true."

Poochie lifted the cooked bacon from its pan and laid it on a paper towel. "Des, I don't mean to throw my weight around but you *will* eat. Now sit!"

Des sat. Clearly, Poochie wouldn't cooperate with her otherwise. Besides, Poochie Vickers did happen to be a great American chef.

"My Smith classmate, Maddie Barnes, sends me one of these every month from her farm in Putney, Vermont." Poochie whacked a brisket-sized slab of bacon down on the massive butcher block next to the stove and hand-cut four more slices. "It's honestly smoked from her very own hogs. Best I've ever had. Now how would you like your eggs, Des?"

"Sunny-side up. Two, please."

Poochie cracked a pair of eggs into the hot pan and started the strips of bacon she'd just sliced. Then she spooned some of the crisp hash browns onto a plate along with the bacon that had been draining. By then, Des's eggs were done. She slid them onto the plate and put it in front of her. "Dig in, dear."

Not surprisingly, everything tasted amazing. "You run a pretty fair diner here, Poochie."

"God, I'd love nothing better," she laughed, delighted by the compliment. "We could call it Pooch's. Have tons of marvelously ghastly dog art everywhere. Claudia could wait tables. Wouldn't you like that, Claude?"

"Mummy, *please,*" protested Claudia, who stood before the window with her arms crossed.

"You're not eating, Mrs. Widdifield?" Des asked.

"Claude never eats my cooking," Poochie said as she turned the sizzling bacon. "Afraid I'll poison her. I have four best-selling cookbooks to my name. Why, they've even called me a *doyenne.* And, trust me, not just anyone can be a *doyenne.* You have to be very knowledgeable and *very* old."

"I'm watching my cholesterol," Claudia explained tightly.

"You keep on watching it, dear. Believe me, no man is."

Tolly let out a hoot at this.

"Trooper Mitry is very busy," Claudia said between gritted teeth. "She is trying to get your Gullwing back."

Poochie waved her off. "Not to worry, it'll be returned by nightfall. This community is filled with good, honest people."

"You should really think about upping your security around here, Poochie."

"Nonsense. I won't live in a high-security prison. And I assure you that my Gullwing *will* be returned. There's really no need for you to get involved. Not that I'm not glad to see you on this fine morning."

"Were you awake when it happened?"

"I was," Poochie acknowledged. "I'm up doing my calisthenics at five-thirty every morning. And Bailey needs his morning constitutional, or he'll turn into an arthritic lump."

"Were you up, too, Mr. Tolliver?"

"God, no. I haven't been up that early since I was a Marine in Korea."

"Golly, I bet you looked cute in your uniform," Poochie teased him.

"As butch as all get-out."

"Today's recycling day," Poochie said. "Bailey and I marched our cans and bottles for old Pete down to the road in my Radio Flyer. Claude's as well, since she doesn't like to go out in public that early. Afraid someone will see her in her curlers."

"Mummy, I haven't worn curlers since the seventies."

Tolly brightened considerably. "Gawd, did she have big hair?"

"She looked just like Ivana Trump," Poochie said giddily. "I have photos."

"About the cans and bottles? . . ."

"Claude leaves hers in my wagon," Poochie went on. "I've had that red wagon since she and Eric were babies, you know. I keep it garaged and oiled and it's still very serviceable. Bailey and I returned it to the garage by six-thirty. I noticed the time when I came in here to put the coffee on."

"And the Gullwing was still in there?"

"Yes, it was."

Des got up and put her empty plate by the sink. "Did you see anyone on Route 156 when you were down there?"

"Not a soul. It was still quite dark. I needed my flashlight. I fed Bailey and planned my dinner menu while I drank my coffee, same as I do every morning. And that's when I heard my car start. There's no mistaking the roar of its engine. I went and looked outside and there it was, speeding down my driveway."

"Could you see who was behind the wheel?"

Poochie shook her head. "Some local youth, I'm willing to wager."

"Did you hear anyone coming up the drive prior to that? An engine idling, footsteps, anything like that?"

"I'm afraid not, Des."

"How about Bailey—did he bark or growl or anything?"

"Young sir's been deaf as a post for the past two years," Poochie said sadly. She got down on all fours and crawled her way over to him. "And who is this handsome young man?" she cooed, bumping the old dog's head with hers. He opened an eye and snuffled at her, his tail thumping gamely. "Des, the boy who took it will return it. I'm quite certain."

"*Nobody* is going to return it, Mummy," Claudia said heatedly. "It's *gone.*"

"Not possible." Poochie knelt there on the floor petting the dog. "That car was a present from Daddy. It's mine. Everyone in Dorset knows that. Why would someone take it?"

"It's worth a fortune, that's why," Des explained.

"Any idea how much?" Tolly tried to sound casual about it. Almost succeeded, too.

"Not offhand, no."

"Daddy will be so upset if no one returns it," Poochie said fretfully. "And, believe me, you do *not* want to make that man mad because he will . . ." She broke off, an alarmed expression on her strong, lovely face. "Heavens, did I just say Daddy *will* be upset?"

"You did, Mummy," Claudia said, not unkindly.

Poochie got up and returned to the stove, where she cracked two eggs for herself. "I meant to say *would.*"

"Of course you did, old girl," Tolly assured her.

Des turned to Claudia, who was staring right back at her, eyes narrowed. "Did you hear anything?"

"Not a thing. I must have been in the shower."

"And how about Mr. Widdifield?"

Claudia bit down on her lower lip, reddening. "Must we involve Mark?"

"Absolutely. When a theft of this magnitude occurs we need to ascertain the whereabouts and backgrounds of everyone who routinely has access."

In response to which Tolly released an audible sigh.

"Was Mr. Widdifield here when it happened?"

Claudia lowered her gaze to the floor. "He's spending his nights at the office. It's at the marina, upstairs from the Mucky Duck."

"I didn't see Bement's truck outside. Has he already left for the day?"

"Bement didn't come home last night. He hardly ever sleeps in his own bed anymore."

"And why should he?" Poochie demanded, sitting down with her breakfast. "He's young and gorgeous and he can have his pick of any girl in town."

"Not just the girls," said Tolly, winking at her.

"I think the trooper has heard just about *enough* of this," Claudia blustered.

"Don't yell at Tolly, Claude."

"That wasn't yelling, Mummy," Claudia shot back, her voice getting shrill. "But if you want to hear me yell, just keep on needling me. You'll hear such yelling you'll wish you never got me started."

Des heard footsteps outside on the gravel and Danielle came shlumping in the kitchen door from the courtyard in denim overalls and green rubber mud boots, her hair in pigtails. She was toting a baguette fresh out of the oven, still crackling and fragrant. "Morning everyone," she murmured.

"Your timing is impeccable, dear. Bless you!" Poochie promptly tore a hunk from the warm loaf and used it to mop up the egg yolk on her plate. "Such a wonderful crust," she exclaimed, smacking her lips with pleasure. "But you *must* stop spoiling me this way, Danielle. This is me not being serious."

"I'm just sorry it wasn't out of the oven sooner—our lambs needed me." Danielle studied Des's face with concern. "Is everything okay?"

"No, everything is *not* okay." Claudia was staring daggers at her frumpy, dentally challenged sister-in-law, clearly resenting the way her mother doted on her. "Someone has stolen the Mercedes."

"Not your car, Poochie!" Danielle gasped.

"They'll return it," Poochie assured her. "By God, Danielle, you're a miracle worker. And I don't just mean this bread. Every time I look at Eric I thank my lucky stars he met you. That boy used to be afraid of his own shadow. He stammered, had asthma. Girls hated him. He's come such a long way, my dear."

"I've done very little, Poochie," Danielle demurred, blushing furiously. "Do we know when the car was taken?"

"Shortly before seven this morning," Des said to her. "Did you happen to see or hear anything?"

Danielle pondered this carefully. "I'm afraid not. We were bottle-feeding our lambs in the barn."

"Have the Kershaw brothers shown up for work yet?"

Danielle shook her head. "No sign of them, and they were supposed to be here a half-hour ago. Why do you ask, Des?"

"Pretty damned obvious, isn't it?" Claudia interjected. "What amazes me is that those two thieves were *invited* here."

Danielle shrank away from Claudia, cowed by her harsh rebuke.

"Stay for coffee, dear," Poochie said, ignoring Claudia completely.

"No, I must get back," Danielle said uncomfortably. "So much to do."

"One cup." Tolly pushed out a chair for her obligingly. "Stay and sit."

Des heard someone pull into the courtyard, gravel crunching under tires.

"Here's Bement," Claudia said, peering out the window.

Des thanked Poochie for breakfast and started out the kitchen door.

Claudia stayed with her, stride for stride. "Now do you see what I'm up against? Half the time she thinks my grandfather is still alive. You heard her."

"I also heard her correct herself."

"Hey, what's up?" Bement asked as he climbed out of his Ford pickup, looking rumpled and battered. His eye was swollen nearly shut, with a purplish shiner under it.

"What *happened* to you?" cried Claudia, reaching for his face.

Bement recoiled from her. "Nothing. Stop fussing over me, will you?"

"I'm your mother," she reminded him, deeply stung. "I'll never stop fussing over you."

To her own great surprise, Des was starting to feel sorry for Claudia Widdifield. Because absolutely nobody seemed to want her love. That sort of thing could turn a woman into a nagging, desperate loon. Des knew something about this. Brandon had turned her into one. "Your grandmother's Gullwing has been stolen," she informed Bement.

"Get out! Any idea who? . . ."

"I've just started to collect information," Des replied, although she did know this much: Four Chimneys was several miles from town. And the private drive down to Route 156 added at least another half-mile. No one would have walked that distance in the dark. Whoever had taken the Gullwing must have been dropped off here—which made it a two-man job.

"Collect all you want, Trooper," Claudia sniffed. "We all know the Kershaw brothers did it."

"Might be payback," acknowledged Bement. He lit a Lucky and leaned against his truck, smoking it. "I did chump Donnie last night at Justine's."

"Exactly what did happen?" Claudia demanded.

"I punched him in the nose," Bement told her, fingering his tender eye. "He hit me back. Des didn't charge us or anything."

"You *knew*?" she said to Des accusingly. "Why didn't you tell me?"

"It's not my business to do that, Mrs. Widdifield."

Claudia heaved her chest, one foot tap-tap-tapping on the gravel. "Bement, I really wish you'd stop seeing that girl."

"Justine, Mom," he said testily. "Her name is Justine."

"No good will come from you mixing with her crowd."

"Is that right? Tell me, what's so damned special about *my* crowd? Are you and Dad all happy together in *my* crowd? Have you two got life all figured out? No, hunh? So let me live my own damned life, will you?"

Claudia's lower lip quivered, but she didn't cry. Wouldn't cry. Instead, she stormed off toward her cottage, slamming the garden gate shut behind her.

Bement cursed under his breath. "Sorry, she just gets to me sometimes."

"Not a problem. I come from a family, too."

"This is why my dad left. Because she just won't leave you the hell alone." He flicked his cigarette butt off into the damp gravel, watching it smolder and sizzle. "They'll trash Nana's car, if I know them."

"It's worth way more if it's in one piece."

"Do you honestly think they're smart enough to know that?"

"You stayed over with Justine last night?"

"Yeah. We stayed in, watched some old Eddie Murphy movie on TV."

"Were you awake when Stevie and Donnie brought Allison home?"

"She didn't stagger in until this morning."

"She partied all night with them?"

"I guess. We didn't talk. She just went straight to her room and crashed."

"What time was this?"

"Right around six o'clock. I could hear their van idling outside."

The kitchen door opened and closed and Danielle came tromping across the gravel toward them in her rubber boots. "Morning, Bement," she said, smiling at him faintly.

"Hey, Danno. Listen, Des, I have to hit the shower and get to work." He headed inside, his stride lithe and athletic.

"I should be off, too." Danielle made no move to leave. "My chores await me."

97

"So do you bring Poochie eggs every morning?" asked Des, anxious to keep her talking. The woman had something for her, she sensed.

"And bread when I have time to bake. She seems to appreciate it." Danielle hesitated, clearing her throat. "Des, Mark Widdifield is in a very dark place right now. He's lost the clients he had and isn't trying to find new ones. He doesn't even seem interested. The man's in terrible pain. So frightened. He needs Claudia's support, but she only sees his failure."

Des nodded her head, patiently waiting Danielle out.

"H-He said something to me yesterday," she continued haltingly. "He'd been drinking. And sobbing his heart out about how Claudia doesn't care about people, only *things*. I don't know if he really meant this or not. . . ."

"Exactly what did Mark say to you, Danielle?"

"He said he'd do just about anything to make Claudia understand how desperate he is."

Stevie and Donnie's van was parked outside of Milo's log cabin in the woods when Des got there. Honestly, it wouldn't have shocked her to find Poochie's Gullwing parked there, too. But she didn't. There was no sign of Milo's pickup. Nor, happily, his Doberman. Wood smoke rose from the stovepipe in the cabin's roof. And she could hear the deep, steady *tha-thump . . . tha-thump* of heavy metal music coming from inside. Otherwise, it was quiet. An unsettling kind of quiet. As she stood there looking at the cabin, Des shuddered involuntarily.

She laid a hand against the van's front grill. A bit warm, but not a lot warm. The van hadn't been driven in the past couple of hours. She peeked through the driver's window and saw fast food wrappers, rumpled drop cloths. Nothing more.

She started toward the cabin. It was nearly nine-thirty now. On her way over here she'd checked all of Dorset's beach and state forest parking lots for the Gullwing. No sign of it, but they'd have been fools if they didn't look. There was always a chance Poochie was right—that some kids really had taken it for a joyride and then ditched it. On this point she and Luke Olman, the investigating detective from Troop F barracks, had been in total agreement. It was Luke's case now. She was assisting with the interviews while he canvassed the neighbors and school bus drivers, and logged some computer time back at the barracks.

She knocked. No one answered. The door was unlocked. She called out "Hello? . . ." Heard no response. Only the music, which was "Whole Lotta Love," a Led Zeppelin paleo-metal favorite. She went inside.

They were passed out in the living room—Stevie sprawled out on the sofa with his mouth open, Donnie face down on the floor beside the coffee table. Donnie's legs twitched busily in his sleep.

Des thought she detected a whiff of marijuana smoke in the air, but she didn't see any joints lying around. Besides, the house smelled so foul it was hard to be sure. The kitchen sink was heaped full of dirty dishes and several inches of dark, oily water. There were more dirty dishes on the table, greasy pans on the stove. Something was moving around in one of the pans. It was a mouse, she realized.

The stereo was over next to the big screen TV. She flicked off the music, knelt next to Donnie and rapped him sharply on the side of the head with her knuckles. "Knock-knock!" she shouted into his ear. "Anybody home?"

Little Donnie rolled over onto his back, groaning, his eyes bloodshot, his nose looking fat and tender from his bout with Bement. He smelled strongly of alcohol and sweat. "Wha' the? . . ." Breath wasn't real fresh either.

Over on the sofa, Stevie began to stir, blinking up at her, his pallor vaguely greenish, mullet damp and stringy. Actually, the two of them looked as if they needed to be hosed off and deloused.

"Morning, guys!" she exclaimed brightly. "Had yourselves a real welcome home celebration, didn't you?"

Stevie staggered over to the kitchen sink and stuck his head under the cold water tap, somehow managing to overlook the dirty dishes and disgusting water. He wiped his face with the sleeve of his flannel shirt, took two cans of Miller out of the refrigerator and came back and flopped back down on the sofa, handing one to Donnie before he popped open his own and drank deeply from it. He belched hugely, then lit a cigarette, holding the cold can against his forehead.

Donnie popped open his beer and drank deeply from it. And belched. And lit a cigarette. And held the cold can against his forehead.

"What did we do *now?*" Stevie finally asked her, his voice raspy.

"You tell me," Des replied, standing there with her arms crossed.

"Is the old man still here?" Donnie wondered, peering around nervously.

"I didn't see him, or his truck."

"Oh, yeah, he split," Donnie recalled, scratching at his reddish beard.

"When was that?"

"Right after we got home," Stevie replied, squinting at her.

"And when was *that?*"

"Lady, I ain't no clock."

"You got to help us out here," Donnie said, gulping his beer. "Because we got zero idea what you're stepping on our nuts about."

"You didn't show up for work this morning."

"So we're a little late," Stevie said. "We'll get there."

Donnie stuck his chin out. "Yeah, since when is being late a crime?"

"It's not. But grand theft auto is."

They stared at her in blank silence.

"Poochie Vickers's Mercedes Gullwing is gone. Are you trying to tell me you don't know anything about it?"

"You've got the wrong guys, lady," Stevie told her. "We didn't have nothing to do with that. No way."

"Account for your time. Where have you two been?"

"With Allison at the Yankee Doodle," said Donnie. The Yankee Doodle, a fading motor court on the Boston Post Road, was Dorset's designated hot sheet motel. "We stayed the night."

"All three of you? What did you, take turns?"

Stevie smirked at her. "You want details?"

"Now that you mention it, I really don't."

"Allison will back us up," he said. "Go ahead and ask her."

"Believe me, I will. Is she at home now?"

"That's where we dropped her."

"Can you remember what time that was? And don't tell me you're not a clock again or I *will* step on your nuts."

Stevie shrugged his narrow shoulders. "We left the Yankee Doodle before dawn. Ran her right home, then started for Four Chimneys. Figured we'd just crash there in the van for an hour or two before work. Right, Donnie?"

Donnie nodded his cocker spaniel head. "But then we got the munchies so we came home to eat. Only we must have crashed."

"We didn't get a whole lot of sleep last night," Stevie explained. "Neither did Allison, if you know what I mean."

"Yeah, I'm hearing you, Stevie," she said. "You've got the hugest johnson in Southern New England. She bounced, she hollered, she screamed for more. Does that about cover it?"

His face tightened. "Lady, you're just plain evil."

"Honey, if I were evil I'd be looking at the contents of that ashtray a lot closer. Know what I'm saying?"

"Not really," Donnie replied, frowning.

"Shut up, Donnie."

"Your father was here when you got home?"

"He was just leaving for work," acknowledged Stevie, his tone considerably cooler since she'd made light of his johnson. "The old weasel's demolishing a house on Whippoorwill. Had his truck all loaded up with stuff for the dump. He likes to make his dump runs when they first open, because when the guy on the gate's half-asleep he's not so particular. The old man's always trying to lay off asbestos on him. Has no conscience when it comes to the ecology."

"So you think he was going straight there?"

"Couldn't do nothing else until he dumped his load."

During the summer, the Dorset landfill opened at 7:00 A.M. This time of year it didn't open until eight o'clock. It was a fifteen-minute drive there from here. Which meant that it was entirely possible the boys didn't get home until after seven-thirty.

"What I'm hearing you tell me," she informed them, "is that you have no one to vouch for your whereabouts at the time when the Gullwing was taken."

"We can vouch for each other," said Donnie, nervously licking at his lips with a rather brownish tongue. "We were together."

"You'll have to do better than that, sunshine."

"But we didn't *do* it." Donnie was starting to get his whiny on again. "Why does everyone always blame us for everything?"

"You bring that on yourselves. A man like Eric holds his hand out to you and you slap it away. Don't show up. Don't keep your word. Instead, I find you here passed out and smelling, well, not so good. Don't you see how this looks? Like you *did* show up for work. Saw Poochie tottering down the driveway with her recyclables, got to talking about that *sha-weet* Gullwing of hers and decided to rip her off. Beats shoveling manure all day."

"And we sure could use the bread," Stevie acknowledged sourly. "For the sake of talking, let's say we did jack it. Where's it at now, lady? What'd we do with it, hunh?"

"That's the million-dollar question. If the Gullwing is returned today, intact, I'm willing to bet Poochie will say she loaned it to you and just plain forgot. The lady's a bit nutty that way. Thinks the best of people. But you've got to get out in front of it right now. An investigator is busy working this case, as am I. Not that I don't enjoy hanging with you two, inhaling your rich, musky scents."

"How come you keep talking about the way we smell?" wondered Donnie.

"Wait for it—it'll come to you. But first, take me to the Gull-wing."

"For the fortieth time, lady, we don't know nothing about it," Stevie insisted. "We didn't jack any car. We're not about that stuff anymore. We're workingmen." He climbed to his feet unsteadily, reaching for his smokes. "And right now we're splitting for work. That okay with you?"

"More than okay. But there is one other thing . . ."

"*Now* what is it?"

"Don't you dare leave town."

The Dorset Marina was situated in a horseshoe-shaped cove at the mouth of the Connecticut River a half-mile upriver from the Peck's Point Nature Preserve. As she drove there Des reached out to Allison Mapes, who answered her phone on the sixth ring, sounding even less with it than the Kershaw brothers had. After considerable prodding, Allison allowed that Stevie and Donnie had dropped her home from the Yankee Doodle some time around six in the morning, thereby confirming what Bement had told her. And the brothers as well—their version vaguely coincided with the truth, as far as it went. Which wasn't very.

The marina was still completely shut down for the winter, its floating docks pulled from the water. The yachts and power boats were in storage, the boatyard's parking lot crammed with their shrink-wrapped hulls. More were stacked inside the immense storage shed, where some sanding and sawing was getting going. Des could hear the whine of power equipment through the open shed doors as she eased her cruiser over near the commercial promenade that wrapped its way around the marina. The tourist-oriented businesses—T-shirt and postcard shops, ice cream parlor, the galleries that sold regrettable seascapes and shell art—were shuttered from Thanksgiving through Easter. The Clam House, a family-oriented seafood restaurant, stayed open year around, as did the Mucky Duck, a British-style pub. Neither had opened yet for the day.

The Mucky Duck was located in the ground floor of a white-shingled two-story building. Upstairs were the offices of a yacht broker, a marine insurance agent and Mark Widdifield, noted local architect. Des parked in back next to a smart blue Morgan Plus 4 roadster and got out, making her way around front to the promenade. It was very quiet. She could hear the water lapping against the pilings, the thwack of her own footsteps on the boardwalk.

Mark Widdifield's office door was unlocked. She went in. Found herself in a small outer office. There was no secretary, nor a secretary's desk. Just a sofa that was presently doubling as an unmade bed. A pair of suitcases lay open on the floor next to it, heaped with wadded-up laundry. A coffeemaker sat half-full on the counter of the kitchenette along with an open box of Entenmann's doughnuts. A doorway led into a big, bright office with windows facing the marina. There were drafting tables for two in there. One of the work stations also had a computer with a big-screen monitor and an immense printer. Anchoring the center of the room was a work island heaped with books and documents and a pair of elaborate architectural models.

Mark was seated there, X-Acto knife in hand, fashioning Foamcore walls for one of the models.

"Excuse me, I need to have a word with you, Mr. Widdifield."

"Some other time," he said distractedly. "I'm really quite busy."

"I'm afraid it can't wait, sir. Someone stole your mother-in-law's Gullwing out of her garage this morning. Do you know anything about it?"

Mark didn't respond for a long moment. Just continued to measure out another piece of wall. "Such as? . . ."

"Such as who took it?"

He sat back in his swivel chair, regarding Des with an air of profound defeat. Claudia's husband was around fifty and very likely had once been quite handsome in a dashing sort of way. These days, he merely looked dissolute, flabby and sad. His strong jaw was melting into a puddle of chins and jowls. The upturned ski-jump nose was blotchy. He needed a haircut. He needed a shave. Mostly, he needed to do something about the lost little boy look in his eyes. "Haven't got a clue who might have taken it," he told her, sitting there with his feet up. He was dressed in a yellow Izod shirt that hugged his swollen gut, worn chinos and broken down Bass Weejun loafers. His bare arms seemed uncommonly thin and pale to her. "Why, do I look like a car thief to you?"

"Not at all. The investigating detective asked me to touch all of the bases. This is me touching them."

"Did Claudia accuse me of taking it?"

"Absolutely not."

"Well, *somebody* put a bug in your ear. Otherwise you wouldn't have dragged yourself down here."

"I'm told you've been making noises about teaching her some kind of a lesson."

"You got that from Danielle, didn't you?" he said, blushing at the mention of his sister-in-law's name. *Something* was going on between them. "That was nothing more than barstool talk. I'm all hot air, as Claudia will be only too happy to confirm."

"Where were you earlier this morning, Mr. Widdifield?"

"Right here. I haven't been out."

"Can anyone vouch for you?"

"There's no one to vouch for me," he confessed, gazing mournfully across the room at the computer work station. "I had to let Phillip go. There was no money to pay him." He turned his attention back to Des. "You may tell your detective that we've spoken. Now if you don't mind . . ."

Des stayed right where she was, studying those models on the work island before him. One appeared to be an apartment house built around a central courtyard, the other a detailed replica of a two-room apartment, complete with furniture, kitchen appliances and even little models of people—four people, to be exact. "What's this you're working on?" she asked him curiously.

"It's the holy grail, Trooper. The greatest unsolved mystery of modern American architecture. There isn't an architect worth his salt who hasn't tried to solve it. *I'm* the one who is going to succeed." He gazed at the replica of the two-room apartment, warming to her slightly. "You see, this is the apartment at 328 Chauncey Street."

"Which should mean something to me because? . . ."

"Why, because Ralph and Alice Kramden lived here, of course. Surely you've seen *The Honeymooners.*"

In fact, Mitch had recently made her watch Norton's sleepwalking episode, which he considered one of the four or five funniest half-hours in the history of television. Des had found the show overwhelmingly bleak and depressing. Just another one of those things that made her wonder if men were, in fact, mutant beings.

"It would not be an exaggeration to label it as a tenement, actually." Mark pointed out. "It's *supposed* to be located in the Bensonhurst section of Brooklyn. The problem is the show's creators took artistic license—Chauncey Street isn't in Bensonhurst. It's in Bushwick. So we really can't say for sure *where* we are, which makes the truth that much more elusive." He swung the two-room model around to face her. "The camera is always pointed toward the fire escape, remember? Anchoring the center of the room is this round wooden table and four chairs." He'd built little replicas, right down to the checkered tablecloth. "We have the icebox here on our right, next to the old stove and sink. Straight ahead is the window overlooking the airshaft. To the left of the window is the hall door. Next to it is the dresser where Ralph always deposits his lunch pail when he comes home." Mark demonstrated by moving one of the little figure people around the apartment. "Next to the dresser is the doorway into the mythical bedroom, which we never, ever see. Nor do we ever see the wall *behind* the camera—which presumably faces Chauncey Street. My objective is to ascertain in a systematic, architecturally grounded fashion precisely what the Kramdens' bedroom would have looked like. Where the closet was. Which way the window would have faced. Was the toilet out in the hall or did the Kramdens have their own? Where was their bathtub? We don't know these things, do we?"

"No, I suppose not."

"When I'm done with this project we will. I've written away to the Brooklyn Department of Buildings. I'm reaching out to architectural historians, archivists. I'll determine, once and for all, the exact age and design of the actual buildings that were on Chauncey Street at that time."

"So they've all been torn down?"

He frowned at her. "I'm afraid I'm not following you."

"If any of the apartment houses are still standing, you could go check them out. Knock on some doors, take photographs. That way you wouldn't have to guess what was where. You'd be laying your own two eyes on it."

Mark Widdifield looked at her with an unbelievably hurt expression on his face. She'd crossed over a line, apparently. Thrown a bucket of ice cold reality all over his little pipe dream. Because none of this was real. The man was strictly hiding in his room playing with dolls. Mark Widdifield was exceedingly fragile, she now realized.

"You damned women are *so* negative," he snapped.

"No, we're not. I'm certainly not."

"Yes, you are. I can see the disapproval in your eyes."

"Sir, you're seeing what you want to see."

"From time to time, a man *needs* to set sail for distant shores. Why can't you see that?"

Des didn't respond. He wasn't really talking to her.

He got up now and shambled into the kitchenette to pour himself coffee. He went over to the windows with it and stared out at the water. "I'm in a bit of a slump right now," he said hopelessly. "No one likes my ideas. Quite simply, I've lost it."

"That renovation you did on your cottage is lovely."

"Thank you, but that was mostly Claudia's doing. She's thrown me out, you know. Tired of my self-pity is what she told me. In

Claudia's world, if you pause for one second to take stock of your life, then you're a leper. And she wants you far, far away."

"Have you folks thought about counseling?"

Mark let out a short laugh. "She won't hear of it. The idea of sharing her private fears with another human being is abhorrent to Claudia. She's pathologically desperate for her mother's approval, in case you haven't noticed. The sad thing is that she doesn't understand Poochie. Never has. The old girl's strength comes from her simple, uncomplicated love of life. Poochie Vickers is the single happiest person I've ever met. All she's ever wanted is for Claudia to be happy. But Claudia doesn't enjoy life. I honestly can't remember the last time I saw her laugh. And that's a terrible thing, Trooper."

"Her mother's extreme behavior lately has Claudia worried. She's looking to gain power of attorney over the family finances."

"The old girl's had some lapses," Mark acknowledged cautiously.

"Is Claudia prone to extreme behavior herself?"

"Not in my experience. Claudia isn't wired that way. Why are you . . . Hold on, are you wondering if *she* stole the Gullwing herself just to prove how irresponsible Poochie is?" Mark tugged at his ear thoughtfully. "Boy, that's an interesting notion."

"What do you think, Mr. Widdifield?"

"I think," he replied slowly, "that I really don't want to get caught in the middle of this."

"But you *are* in the middle. You're a member of the family."

Mark made his way back over to his little models and sat down. "Trooper, I am in no mood to say anything nice about Claudia. I harbor so much anger toward that woman that I can hardly stand it. However, I do believe she's genuinely worried about Poochie. It's just that there's heavy family baggage here. Eric has always been Poochie's favorite. The old girl dotes on him. Claudia takes more after the Ambassador. Very big into proper decorum. She never shucked her panties and went skinny-dipping on a hot summer day. Never picked up some guy in a bar somewhere and screwed herself silly." Mark grinned impishly at such an unlikely thought, showing Des a glimpse at the sly charm he'd once possessed. "If you want my opinion, this power of attorney business is about Claudia trying to prove to Poochie that she, not Eric, is the one who really cares. And she does care, whether Poochie knows it or not."

"Claudia's not very happy about Bement being involved with Justine Kershaw. How do you feel about it?"

"I envy him," Mark said softly, gazing out the window again. "He's happy. To hell with the rich bitches his mother wants him to date. To hell with Stanford. None of that will make him happy. Believe me, I know what I'm talking about. I'm just hanging on by my fingernails. If it weren't for Danielle, I'm not sure I'd be making it at all." Mark shot a quick look at her. "We're not involved, if you're wondering. Danielle's like the sister I never had. She lets me talk. She believes in me." Mark trailed off, his eyes puddling with tears. "I fell in love with a woman of great beauty and privilege. Eric married a Sheetrocker's daughter who absolutely no one would mistake for Angelina Jolie. And yet I'd trade places with him in a second. He has work that gives him great satisfaction. And a good-hearted woman who is truly there for him when he . . ."

Des's pager beeped at her now from her belt.

"I'll have to take this," Des said, grateful for the interruption. She was starting to feel suffocated by the man's warm, wet blanket of self-pity. "You've been real helpful, Mr. Widdifield."

He shrugged his soft shoulders, sorry to be losing his audience. "I hope I didn't go on about myself too much."

"Not at all. You did good."

"Trooper, you're a terrible liar."

She reached for her cell phone as she darted out the door. It was Luke Olman who'd paged her. She got through to him while she was heading back down the promenade toward her cruiser. "What do you know, Oly?"

"How much that Gullwing is worth, for starters," the investigating detective replied. "The Hemmings Motor News website has one listed for—get this—$325,000. This isn't a car. It's a high-end antique. Nobody's going to return that thing by nightfall. Or ever. It's gone."

"Color me down with that. Pick up anything on canvass?"

"One tidbit from the guy who drives the recycling truck. Know that commuter parking lot on Old Shore Road next to the I-95 on-ramp? When he was on his way to the town garage early this morning he saw a huge tractor-trailer idling there. This was at maybe a quarter past six."

"The long-haulers pull in there sometimes to catch a few zees," Des told him as she reached her cruiser and got in. "As long as they're gone by rush hour, I leave 'em be. Did he notice any markings on it?"

"He didn't, no. Think it might connect up?"

"It might," Des said, mulling it over.

"Des, I ran that criminal background check you asked for. How did you know?"

"I didn't." She felt her pulse quicken. "Just had a hunch."

"Well, this is something we definitely need to pursue. I'm heading back up there now. Would you mind sitting in? You know these people."

She rang off and started her cruiser back toward Four Chimneys, thinking she wouldn't mind stopping by Eric's farm to see if the Kershaw brothers had shown for work. If they hadn't, it would lend a whole lot of credence to the idea that they'd suddenly gotten a few thousand ahead.

The sun was starting to burn through the morning fog as she eased her way back up through the gentlemen's farm country. The trees alongside the road were still iron gray and bare, the wild lilacs and blackberries nothing but brambles. But the sunlight on her face felt warm through the windshield, hinting tantalizingly at spring for the second day in a row.

As Des slowed down to make a left into the driveway of Four Chimneys, she noticed a ray of that sunlight glinting off of something shiny in the roadside brush. Her first thought was that it was an empty beer can that a thoughtless passerby had tossed in there. Her second thought was that it looked like something bigger. More like a bicycle. She didn't have any current stolen bike reports. Wrong time of year. Still, she pulled onto the shoulder and got out for a closer look.

It was a beat-up old mountain bike with two grocery carts chained to its rear rack. She recognized this odd little conveyance at once—it belonged to Dorset's Can Man. Although why old Pete would ditch it in the brush near the driveway to Four Chimneys she could not imagine. The grocery carts were empty. Typically, he'd have himself a pretty full load by the time he made it this far up Route 156. Yet there was no sign of his haul. Or, for that matter, of Pete himself.

Des was standing there in the ditch, trying to puzzle it out, when she noticed the trampled, slushy mud beyond the bicycle. Someone, it appeared, had dragged something deeper into the woods. She stepped her way carefully through the thicket for a better look.

And that's when she found Pete.

CHAPTER 9

Last winter, on the night I turned fourteen, my two older brothers got me high on Jose Cuervo and weed and took turns raping me. They raped me pretty much every night after that. At first, I tried to fight them. But I was much better off if I didn't resist or cry for help. Because if I did stuff like that they'd beat me so bad I could barely get out of bed the next day. So I would just lie there and let them do what they wanted. They had me outnumbered. And there was no one to answer my cries for help. My mother was dead. My father was always passed out drunk pretty. And it wasn't like he cared anyway.

Besides, I could take it.

That's one thing I can do like nobody else. I can take it.

After a few weeks, when the thrill of banging me wore off, they started passing me around. Every day after school, their friends would come by the house and do me in my room. Sometimes a half-dozen or more of them would line up outside my bedroom door. Before long, I'd done pretty much every guy in their class. My not-so-secret nickname around school became She'll Do Ya. That's what they called me.

Me, I stayed high pretty much all of the time.

My brothers did this to me for the coolness of it. And they did it for the money. They collected off of me, all right. If the guy was a friend of theirs, I cost twenty. If he was some rich jerk, and believe me there are lots of those in this town, I was fifty. Condoms were mandatory. I got none of the money they collected. Not one cent.

This town is really small and proper and New Englandy. You would die if you saw how pretty it is. Anyway, it didn't take long before word about me got out. One of the rich jerks told his father, who is this big-time state judge. The judge didn't get in my father's face about it. He went right for my brothers. And now here's the part that shouldn't have surprised me but totally did. The judge didn't come down on them. He just wanted in on it for himself and his own friends.

So now I'm doing the dads.

I'm trying to think if there's a single upstanding do-gooder in this town who I haven't done. Nope, can't think of one. Not unless you count my pediatrician because that would be even too weird. I've done every big shot in town government. I've done my minister, whose whole thing is preaching Moral Values. I've done my history teacher, who's always lecturing us on how we all have to stay vigilant against terrorists and other such evildoers. Guess what? The evildoers are already here. They're passing themselves off as upstanding, freedom-loving citizens. Which they're not. I can tell you that they're not.

A lot of them own boats. One of their favorite things is to take me along on their fishing trips. Maybe four men go. All of them rich and important. My brothers collect a hundred apiece from them. Even more for overnighters. I don't like the boat trips very much. I'm always afraid they'll throw me overboard and leave me out there to drown. They all trust each other. But me they aren't so sure about. I'm the one they fear. If I ever decided to out them, I mean. Actually, it amazes me they haven't thrown me overboard by now. But I'm still here. I guess the reason I am is they'd miss doing me. Plus, they probably figure no one would listen to me anyway, right? Why would they? I'm just some underage skank. If I did try to make trouble they'd probably just shove me in a hospital somewhere for drugged-out teen nymphos. Absolutely no one would believe me.

You believe me, don't you? The reason I'm asking is that there's more I want to tell you. I've been kind of afraid to tell anyone this because I'm, well, ashamed to admit it. So you have to promise you won't think less of me when I tell you. Do you promise? Okay, then here goes:

Lately, I've started to enjoy it.

So began Justine Kershaw's raw, brutally frank short novel entitled *She'll Do Ya*.

Mitch took a peek at it over his Cocoa Puffs after Des left for Four Chimneys. He'd intended to sample the first few pages, then tackle it in earnest after he'd filed his Sunday column on *Safety Last!*, a forgotten Harold Lloyd slapstick classic. Instead, he spent his entire morning reading *She'll Do Ya* from start to finish as the fog hung heavy outside over Long Island Sound and the foghorn sounded from the Old Saybrook lighthouse. Not that reading it was easy. Mitch was so shaken by Justine's novel that he felt outright physical revulsion. But he could not put it down. Never before had he encountered a voice quite like that of her unnamed fifteen-year-old storyteller. It was pure and piercingly honest—the voice of a tough, savvy young girl who has suffered so much emotional and physical cruelty that she is beyond all illusions, all hopes, all dreams. Mitch found her stubborn will to survive inspiring. Also heartbreaking. Because somehow, in spite of everything, she is still a child who wants nothing more than to be loved:

Doing them is pretty much the only attention I ever get. Otherwise, I'm invisible. My teachers never call on me. The other girls don't like me one bit. Can't imagine why. And it's not like a boy wants to ask me out for real. I own a mirror. I know I'm not much to look at. But if I do a boy then I've pleased him, right? Especially if he's this one boy, Tommy, who I totally like. And who knows? Maybe Tommy likes me, too.

I promise I won't lie to you. I'll tell you everything that happened. Or as much as I can remember. Some of it's still a haze. I kind of like it that way. That's why I stay high a lot of the time. If I'm straight I think too much. Listen, I hope I don't shock you too much. But I'm telling you this so you can learn something

about the world you live in. I'm real. I'm walking among you.
I'm your daughter, okay? And, hey, whatever you do, don't take
it too hard. Because it's not so bad. Really, I don't feel that bad.
I don't feel anything at all.

Mitch could barely get up out of his chair when he'd finished reading *She'll Do Ya*. It was easily the most disturbing thing he'd read in years. Somehow, Justine's confessional novel was more than one girl's visceral cry for help. It was a cry from a million confused, rudderless young people all across the land. She had a remarkable gift, especially considering that she was a twenty-three-year-old college dropout with no advanced writing training. Not that *She'll Do Ya* was without its flaws. The subplot involving that one particular boy, Tommy, went nowhere, for example. But the talent was there. All she needed now was a good editor. Truly, Mitch believed this was the work of a major new voice in American fiction. Assuming, of course, that it was a work of fiction.

Was it true?

As he turned the pages, Mitch couldn't stop asking himself this. Was he, in fact, reading Justine's autobiography? Had Stevie and Donnie raped her when she was fourteen? Had Dorset's leading male citizens plundered her, one by one? Had her father tolerated it? Or had Justine dreamt this all up? How could *anyone* her age dream up such morally depraved stuff? How could she tap into such pain?

It had to be true.

Mitch found it hard to conclude otherwise—which made *She'll Do Ya* even more disturbing than it already was. Mitch was so bothered that he couldn't work, couldn't think. All he could do was plug in his beloved sky blue Fender Stratocaster—the same make Stevie Ray Vaughan had played—and sit in with Taj Mahal on *The Natch'l Blues*. Jesse Edwin Davis's tasty riffs on "Corinna" left Mitch plenty of room for his own brand of soaring, high-decibel blues. And so he jacked up the power and he played, reaching for that high note, finding it, squeezing it as Clemmie hid upstairs under the bed. Mitch had no talent. None. But he had the juice. And the love. And, right now, he had the feeling.

It had to be true.

Which made *She'll Do Ya* more than just a compelling read. It was a blistering one-hundred-fifty-page statutory rape indictment against her twisted warpo brothers and a whole lot of Dorset's leading male citizens. Seemingly, Justine had kept quiet until now because she didn't think anyone would believe her. After they'd read *She'll Do Ya,* everyone would. And Dorset would no longer be that quaint, beautiful Yankee Eden on the Connecticut Gold Coast. It would be the ugly little town with the ugly little secret about those dirty men who had done unspeakable things to a young girl.

No wonder she hadn't wanted Bement to read it. No telling what the hotheaded love of her life would do to Stevie and Donnie when he got full wind of this. Assuming, that is, Bement didn't already know about it. But how was that even possible? In a town this size, how could Bement *not* know? What about Rut Peck? Did *he* know? Mitch figured not, because if the old postmaster had any idea what *She'll Do Ya* was about then he wouldn't have encouraged Justine to pass it on to him. But she had. And now Mitch was sitting on pure dynamite.

It was true. It had to be true.

Or did it?

Mitch needed to find out for certain. He just needed to take care of a personal matter first. Something that wouldn't wait. So he snatched up his cell phone and speed-dialed the number in Vero Beach, Florida.

And when he heard that familiar voice at the other end, he said, "Hi, Mom . . . Nothing's wrong, I'm fine . . . I do not have a cold. My voice sounds perfectly normal. I just have a somewhat weird favor to ask of you. . . ."

Honestly, she looked so innocent and bug cute seated there on that uncomfortable metal bench that it was hard to believe Justine Kershaw had ever *done* anyone.

She'd smiled at Mitch with genuine delight when he'd shown up at her cash register. Told him she'd meet him outside in, like, eleven minutes—not that she was counting. "So what do you want to talk to me about?"

"Your novel. I've read it."

"Is that right?" Justine's left knee began to jiggle convulsively. And Mitch swore she'd just sucked down half of that cigarette in one drag. "And? . . ."

"I have to ask you something. Did those things really happen to you?"

Justine looked at him in bewilderment. "Why does that matter?"

"People will want to know. Your editor, your readers, the media."

"The *media?* Whoa, cupcake . . ."

"Not to mention the police. Terrible crimes were committed, Justine. Someone has to pay."

"Okay, I definitely don't care about *that.*"

"Exactly how much does Bement know?"

Justine stubbed out her cigarette, her dark eyes scanning the crowded parking lot. "Bement is very sheltered. But we love each other and we're together in every way possible. That's all I feel like saying about him right now, okay?"

"*Not* okay. Justine, did it really happen to you or didn't it?"

"It happens to young girls like me every day, and no one ever gets in trouble. I'm surprised you even mentioned the P-word. Did you already tell your girlfriend about it?"

"I haven't told anyone. I came directly here. I need to know whether—"

"Oh, hell!" Her gaze had fallen on a mud-caked Toyota pickup that was sputtering its way across the parking lot toward them. "That mean old bastard's *always* checking up on me, bugging me . . ."

The pickup drew up before them in the fire line, its engine clanking, its back end crammed with black plastic trash bags that seemed to be full of empty bottles and cans. An angry looking Doberman was barking out at the world from the passenger seat.

Milo Kershaw got out, snarled at the dog to shut up and sidled over to them. He was a chippy little runt in his sixties, with shrewd eyes and a down-turned mouth that gave his face a decidedly nasty expression. "What do you think you're doing out here, little girl? Supposed to be working for a living, not flirting with the boys."

"I'm on a break," she answered coldly, lighting another cigarette. "And I told you to leave me the hell alone."

"Don't care what you told me. I'm still your father. Besides, I was on my way over to them machines at the A&P."

"Since when are you such a big recycler?"

"Never mind since when." Milo pointed his chin at Mitch. "Who's this?"

"I'm Mitch Berger, Mr. Kershaw. Pleased to meet you."

Milo shook a finger at him. "You got one hell of a lot of nerve sniffing around my girl, considering where you been dipping *yours* lately."

Mitch stiffened. "I'm not sure I understand what you mean."

"Oh, I think you do," Milo said fiercely. "I'm talking about you and that high and mighty *afro-disiac* of yours."

Mitch climbed slowly to his feet, clearing his throat. He had at least six inches on the little man, not to mention a solid eighty pounds. "I don't think you want to take this conversation where you're taking it, Mr. Kershaw."

"Get lost, old man," Justine ordered him. "You're embarrassing yourself."

"That's how you talk to your father now?"

"That's how I talk to ignorant racists who don't know when to shut up."

"I should slap your face for saying that to me."

"I'd like to see you try," she responded, flicking her lit cigarette at him.

Milo swatted it away. "Tell your black bitch to stay away from me and my boys," he said angrily. "Or there's no telling what might happen."

"You'd better get back in your truck right now, Mr. Kershaw," Mitch said to him as calmly as he could. "You'd also be wise to steer clear of me in the future, or I may have to beat the crap out of you."

Milo let out a harsh laugh. "Who are you kidding, you marshmallow? I could take you apart in sixty seconds."

Mitch moved in a step closer, towering over him. "Get back in your truck."

Something in Mitch's voice convinced the little man to scurry back to his pickup and jump in, slamming the door behind him. He drove right off, his engine sputtering.

Justine watched him go. "Do you hate your parents?"

"Not at all."

"God, that must be weird." She studied Mitch curiously now. "When you tell people about my book, what are you going to say?"

Mitch considered his next words carefully, because he felt certain that *She'll Do Ya* was about to become a major literary sensation. High school girls across America would devour its explosive contents. This lovely, fearless young woman would become their literary idol. Tremendous controversy would surround *She'll Do Ya*. Talk radio pundits would condemn it. Religious groups would want it banned from libraries and big box outlets like this very store. "I'd like to show it to a literary agent I know," he said finally. "If that's okay with you."

Justine stuck her lower lip out, confused. "Are you saying you think somebody might want to *publish* it?"

"I'm saying I think it's sensational."

She let out a gasp. "Oh, no, you *didn't!*"

"Oh, yes, I did." Mitch smiled at her. "You're a very gifted young writer, and I'm honored to know you."

She let out a high-pitched adolescent shriek and jumped right into his lap. "I can't *believe* this!" she cried out, hugging him, kissing him. "I *must* be tripping!"

"No, no, this is totally real. Only slow down, because we still have to—"

"You can't *imagine* what this means to me!" She was squirming around in his lap like an excited kindergartner. Which Mitch was acutely aware she was not.

"I think I can. But you still have a lot of questions to answer. So go back to your neutral corner, will you?"

"Sure, absolutely. Whatever you say." She climbed out of his lap and sat back down, rubbing her little hands together eagerly. "Fire away."

"For starters, what do you hope to gain from this book?"

Justine frowned at him. "I'm not sure what that means."

"Do you want justice?"

"There's no such thing, cupcake. That's a twentieth-century term."

"Okay, then I'll put it to you this way: What's your dream?"

"I don't really have dreams. What's the point, you know? Bement wants to buy a boat and sail around the world for the rest of his life."

"Would you go with him?"

"In a heartbeat. All we have is each other. Both of our families suck beyond belief. His happens to be rich, but he won't be until they all kick off, which won't be for years. It wouldn't have to be a huge boat. He thinks a thirty-six-footer would do. He's crewed to Bermuda and stuff. I know jack about sailing, but I can learn if . . . Why are you looking at me that way?"

"His grandmother's Gullwing was stolen this morning. You could swap that for a pretty nice boat, I'd imagine."

"Probably so," she acknowledged. "But we didn't steal it. That would be unbelievably stupid."

"Justine, did these things really happen to you or not?"

She rolled her gleaming dark eyes at him. "Why do you keep obsessing on that? Why does it even matter?"

"Because if this is a true story then things could get really messy around here. For that matter, even if it *isn't* a true story things could get messy—because people are going to *think* it's true. And a lot of them won't want you to publish it."

"Screw them."

"Your character thinks that her life might be in danger. Is *your* life in danger? Are you afraid?"

"Of what, dying? Why should I be? Take a look at my world." She gestured out at the parking lot full of avid shoppers who were rushing headlong into the joyless discount emporium. "Check out all of these people who are so desperate to max out their credit cards on meaningless crap. Say hello to total despair at bargain prices. Being dead can't be any worse than this, can it?"

Mitch had no response. Absolutely could not fathom this talented young woman. Justine possessed so much sensitivity, heart and passion. Yet she could also seem as dead inside as her burntout heroine. Was this her life story or wasn't it? Was she someone who'd been plundered by half the men in town or wasn't she?

Would the real Justine Kershaw please stand up?

She was gazing at him. "You really think somebody will publish it?"

"I really do, Justine."

"Then you could do me one more huge favor, if you don't mind." Justine lowered her eyes and swallowed. "Would you tell Bement for me?"

CHAPTER 10

HER FIRST THOUGHT WAS hit and run.

Old Pete was always pedaling his funked-up contraption right along the edge of the road in the predawn darkness. It was entirely possible that some half-awake commuter had accidentally clipped him and sent him flying into the ditch. Wouldn't be out of the question for the driver to keep right on going, afraid to phone it in, afraid of trouble, *afraid*.

Except that Des could find no skid marks of any kind. Nor any fresh dings in the bike or carts.

And then there were all of those shoeprints in the muddy forest floor. Enough shoe prints for two people. Also a deep toe gouge in the moist earth, as if someone had tripped and fallen. A number of the bare branches in the deep thicket had gotten trampled and broken. Whoever accidentally hit Pete may have dragged him deeper into the woods—out of sight, out of mind. Or, a struggle of some kind may have taken place here.

He was lying face down. Smelled strongly of liquor. What she could see of his face was weathered and grimy. There were no obvious wounds to his body. Not that there necessarily would be if he'd been struck by a car. His innards could be completely crushed and it wouldn't be apparent until he was laid out on an autopsy table. As she looked at him lying there on the cold ground, discarded and dead, Des realized that Pete bore an uncanny resemblance to roadkill.

She didn't even know what his last name was.

He wore an old pea coat, stained wool trousers, cracked and oily work boots. The toes of his boots were not caked with mud. A knit stocking cap lay on the ground next to him. Des crouched down for a closer look at the back of his head and, just like that, her hit and run scenario flew right out the window. The man had suffered multiple skull fractures from a linear object of some kind, such as a baseball bat. His hands were crusted with dried blood. There appeared to be numerous broken bones in both of them. No doubt he'd been trying to shield his head from the blows—at least some of which he'd suffered right here. His scalp wounds had bled down into the moist ground beneath him. He was ice cold. Rigor had begun.

Des glanced around her for a possible weapon. Nothing was immediately apparent to her, and she was not about to search any further. She did go through his pockets. Found a broken half-pint of Captain Morgan in his coat, which explained the smell. Found no wallet. No identification of any kind. All Pete had on him were two rumpled dollar bills, a handful of change and a pen knife.

The uniformed troopers from Troop F barracks got there first and began rerouting traffic north and south of the crime scene onto alternate roads. Then the forensic nurse from the medical examiner's office arrived. Des took her to the body. Soon, the white-and-blue cube vans had shown up and the crime scene technicians in their blue windbreakers were unloading their gear.

Lastly, a pair of slicktops pulled up onto the shoulder of the road, one behind the other, and out popped Soave and Yolie, who were two people Des knew very well. Back when she'd been a lieutenant on Major Crimes, Lt. Rico "Soave" Tedone had been her stumpy young bodybuilder of a sergeant. Smart enough, but seriously lacking in the maturity department. Also major insecure, due to his short stature and overbearing, higher-ranking big brother. Thanks to family juice, Soave was now a lieutenant. And somewhat more mature—although still a work in progress. He'd revamped his look since the last time Des saw him. He was experimenting with that goatee and shaved head thing. Plus the wardrobe was new. For as long as she'd known him, Soave had always dressed like a pallbearer for hire. Today he had on a very nice gray pinstripe with a powder blue shirt and a bold pink and yellow patterned tie.

"Let me guess, Rico," she said after they'd done the hello thing. "Has Tawny started dressing you?" Tawny was the high school sweetheart he'd finally married after the longest courtship in recorded history.

"She took me shopping for my birthday," he answered defensively. "Why, no good?"

"It's all good, Rico. Especially the tie. Did Tawny talk you into that clean head, too?"

"This was all my own idea." He ran a hand over his smooth, shiny dome. "How does it look?"

"Seriously pigment challenged."

"I *hear* that," agreed Yolie Snipes. "You need to get you a tube of bronzer, Rico. Right now, your head glows in the dark like one of those plug-in night lights." Yolie flashed Des a huge smile. "Miss Thing, it is *so* good to see you again." Yolanda Snipes, Soave's brash young half-black, half-Cuban sergeant, had grown up in a hurry in Hartford's Frog Hollow section, and owned a knife scar on her cheek to prove it. Yolie had a Latina's gleaming, liquid brown eyes. Her lips, nose and braids said sister all the way, as did her hour (and a half) glass figure. The guys in Meriden called her Boom Boom because of what she had going on up inside of her sweater. She wore slacks with it, and a pair of boots with chunky heels that had her towering over Soave. "And how's that cute teddy bear of yours?" she asked Des warmly.

"Mitch is fine. We're fine. Everything's fine."

"You two set a date yet?"

"Feel free to move on to the next question any time."

"Suits me," said Soave, who couldn't fathom Des and Mitch at all. "So what's going on here this morning in your nice, quiet country hamlet?"

"We've got ourselves two noteworthy events, Rico. Possibly related. Happily, that's your job to decide, not me."

"Big thanks for the procedural pointer."

"One is the theft of a slammin' '56 Mercedes Gullwing from the house right up that driveway over there—estimated Kelley Blue Book value north of three hundred thou. Belongs to Poochie Vickers, who is our most notable of notables. A true grande dame. Not to mention a television celebrity and best-selling author."

"No need to tell me that," Yolie said. "I've got all of her cookbooks."

"The lady is highly beloved and way trusting. She left the garage unlocked and the keys in the ignition. They just drove it away. I say *they* because it was most likely a two-man job, given how far we are from town. Our other event is the murder in these woods of Dorset's resident recycling bin scavenger, old Pete. Ready to have a look?"

"Tell us about him," Soave said as they followed her into the brush toward Pete's bicycle.

"Pete was an odd soul. Spoke to no one. Avoided people like poison. But he was harmless enough, and folks looked out for him." Des recalled that First Selectman Paffin had urged her to keep an eye on Pete when she first came on the job. "Today is recycling day in this neighborhood. Chances are, he was making his rounds at about the same time the Gullwing was taken."

"Sounds like he witnessed it and they shut him down," Yolie put in.

"Sounds like," Soave said. "You agree, Des?"

Des came to a stop before Pete's ditched bike and grocery carts. "I'm on board, except that you'll notice his cans and bottles are gone. If this was just about silencing him then why did they make off with his haul?"

"Maybe somebody else came along later and took them." Soave, tugged at his goatee with his thumb and forefinger. "Maybe they didn't see his body in there."

"There appears to have been a struggle over here. Note the deep toe mark in the mud."

A techie was snapping pictures. The death investigator was crouched over Pete's body, dictating her notes into a tape recorder.

"He received several blows to the back of his head," Des said. "The weapon was some sort of club or crowbar. There are defensive wounds to the hands. Also, he bled-out here."

"What do you think in terms of time?" Soave asked the death investigator.

She flicked off her recorder and stood up. "He hasn't been here all night, if that's what you're wondering. Three or four hours is more like it."

"Which fits with our time frame," Des said, glancing at her watch.

"Yolie, have these woods searched but good. I want that weapon." Soave started back through the brush toward the road.

"Totally whack idea," Yolie offered as they followed him. "Any way these two crimes are completely unrelated? Like, could this one just be a straight robbery gone bad?"

"I don't buy it," Soave replied. "Too coincidental. It's not like this is a high crime area. It's a *no* crime area. Am I right, Des?"

"This is Dorset," Des agreed. "Not many people around here are so desperate for pocket cash that they'd beat a scavenger to death for his empties." As they made it back to the road, she noticed that the troopers had waved in several television news vans from the local Connecticut stations. "The Vickers family is looking to low profile this if at all possible, Rico."

"No problem. We can put a cruiser at the foot of the drive. Keep talking, Des. Give us the big picture here."

"Big picture? You've walked into an old-school family feud." Des filled them in on how the Kershaw brothers had just been released from Enfield for stealing from the Vickers. On how their father, Milo, had gone to jail for torching the Vickers's barn. On Justine Kershaw, who was dating Poochie's grandson, Bement Widdifield, the very person who'd called the law on her brothers. On his mother, Claudia, who was estranged from her cash-strapped architect husband, Mark. And how Claudia was also at odds with her brother, Eric, not only for hiring the Kershaw brothers but for failing to help her take control of the family purse strings. Des told them all about Poochie's worrisome be-havior of late—fishing her out of Duck River Pond, that hoard of candy bars in the attic, Claudia's assertion that the congenitally frugal Poochie had started showering expensive gifts and sums of cash on Guy Tolliver, her companion.

Which was when Soave stopped her. "Time out, he's her *what?*"

"Her companion, Rico."

"I grew up in Waterbury, remember? I don't know from 'companion.' "

"The man lives with her but he's gay," Des explained patiently. "Get it now?"

"Yes," he replied firmly. "But no."

"Neighborhood canvass has turned up squat so far on the stolen car. But before this got bounced to you, Detective Olman did learn that an unmarked tractor-trailer was idling in the com-muter parking lot early this morning. He also dug up a sheet on one of our principals that you'll want to run with. I have the print-out in my ride. And he's available if you need backup."

"Why would I need backup?" demanded Soave, bristling. He did not play well with others. Felt threatened. "You saying I can't handle this on my own?"

"Not at all, Rico."

"Sure sounded like it."

"You know, I really don't think it did."

"Freudian therapy, little man," Yolie chided him.

"What *about* it?"

"You really need you some."

He shot Yolie a withering look. "See what I have to deal with, Des? Nothing but lip, day in and day . . . what are *you* smiling at?"

"Not a thing, Rico. I just miss the two of you, God help me."

"I want you with us up at the house. Can you stick around?"

"Be happy to. Just prepare yourselves. You're about to get all tangled up in weird."

"*Damn,* girl!" Yolie cried out as she stood there inside the fragrant warmth of the conservatory, gazing up, up at its four-story dome. "Somebody *lives* here?"

"Wait until you see what she's got hanging on her parlor walls."

Soave was speechless as he took in the highlights—the brightly colored tropical birds perched up there among the cast iron trusses, the vintage Lionel train that was *chuff-chuff-chuffing* its way around on its raised track.

Decked out in a pair of outlandish hot pink shades and a straw hat big enough to bathe in, the mistress of Four Chimneys was vigorously trimming back one of her Meyer lemon trees. "Why, it's an entire contingent, Tolly!" Poochie exclaimed merrily at the sight of them.

Guy Tolliver was seated on the wicker sofa reading a copy of *Vanity Fair* and looking considerably more together than he had earlier that morning. His silver hair was neatly brushed, his loose-jowled face clean shaven. He wore a soft yellow flannel shirt with a gold silk ascot and a pair of green moleskin slacks. Beside him on the sofa, Bailey lay asleep. Tolly stood to greet them, a hopeful smile on his face. "You've found the Gullwing, have you?"

"I knew you would!" Poochie came charging toward them, yanking off her garden gloves. "Where was it, Des, at the beach?"

"Poochie, there's been a new development since the last time we spoke. I'd like you to meet Lieutenant Rico Tedone and Sergeant Yolanda Snipes. They're with the Major Crime Squad."

"Surely a joyride doesn't constitute a major crime in this state."

"This isn't about that, Mrs. Vickers," Soave said.

"Please call me Poochie. And that good-looking home wrecker is Tolly."

"Absolutely love your tie, lieutenant," Tolly said pleasantly.

"Thanks," Soave grunted, reddening.

Poochie removed her pink shades, the better to examine Yolie. "My, *my,* you're a strongly built young lady. Do you lift weights?"

"Three times a week, ma'am."

"I like the prideful way you hold yourself. Too many full-bosomed young women develop slumpy shoulders. Are you drinking plenty of milk?"

Yolie glanced at Des in bewilderment. "Um, not really . . ."

"You must start," Poochie ordered her. "I myself drink four glasses of farm-fresh milk a day, and my height hasn't changed a fraction of an inch since I was twenty-one. Now, Des, what *is* all of this?"

"We've found Pete the Can Man in the woods down near the foot of your driveway. Somebody bashed his head in."

Poochie's blue eyes flickered, as if her entire body had been zapped by an electrical current. "Do you mean . . . he's *dead*?"

"It appears likely that it happened right around when your car was stolen."

"Oh, my lord, they're going like hotcakes . . ." Poochie sank into a wicker armchair, ashen-faced. Her voice sounded hollow, shaky. In fact, her entire edifice of peppy optimism seemed to have crumpled from within. "That's what mother said when everyone . . . when they all started to die on her. Poor Pete. Such a dear soul."

"You didn't happen to see him when you took your wagon down there this morning, did you?" asked Des, surprised by how hard she was taking it.

Poochie didn't answer Des. Didn't seem to hear her.

"Des wants to know if you saw Pete today," Tolly prodded her gently.

"Why, no . . ." she replied after a long moment. "He hadn't come yet. Not until around seven, usually."

Des heard footsteps now. Claudia was crossing the conservatory toward them.

"Who's this?" Soave murmured at Des.

"The daughter, Claudia Widdifield."

"Am I going to like her?"

"You could always surprise me."

"Have you arrested the Kershaw boys?" Claudia asked.

"It's old Pete, Claude," Poochie said, her voice still quavery.

"*He* took your car? Mummy, I told you he wasn't that harmless."

"We've found his body near the foot of your drive," Des explained. "Somebody murdered him."

Claudia stared at her in surprise. "Why would someone do that to an old wino?"

"Pete was *not* a wino," Poochie said indignantly. "He was a sensitive human being who did the best he could under very difficult circumstances. He didn't complain. And he never harmed a soul."

"Fine, have it your way." Claudia turned back to Des. "About the Gullwing? . . ."

"We're making good, steady progress, ma'am," Soave told her. "Nothing we're prepared to go into just yet."

Claudia looked at him and Yolie rather doubtfully. "How can you be making 'good, steady progress' when you're all standing around here?"

"Claude, dear? . . ." Poochie had a pained smile on her face. "Don't you have someone's interior to make over?"

Claudia flared instantly. "You don't want me here, is that it?"

"I'll keep you posted, dear," Poochie assured her.

Claudia stormed off, her black pumps clacking sharply on the quarry tile.

"Please pardon my daughter, officers. The poor thing got brains and looks but no heart whatsoever." Poochie retrieved her sunnies and gardening gloves from the coffee table. She'd already recovered her composure, it seemed. "Is there anything else I can help you with?"

"Actually, we were wondering if we could have a word in private with Mr. Tolliver," Soave said.

"Why, of course," she said. "I want to finish my cassoulet, anyway. You'll stay for lunch?"

"I don't believe so, ma'am," Soave said. "But thanks."

"Very well. I shall be in the kitchen if you need me. Come along, young sir!" she roared, smacking her ancient dog on the rump.

Bailey stirred, yawning, and padded slowly along behind her.

"Do join me, please," Tolly said, smiling at them graciously.

The three of them sat—Des beside Tolly on the sofa, Soave and Yolie in facing armchairs.

"Mr. Tolliver, exactly how do you support yourself?" Yolie asked him.

His smile slipped a bit, though he quickly recovered. "No small talk with you new generation types, is there? You just go right ahead and stick the knife in."

Yolie didn't respond. Just gazed at him steadily. With her big shoulders and battle-scarred street face, she could be very intimidating when she chose to be.

Tolly swiped at some invisible lint on his moleskin slacks. "Obviously, you've checked to see if I've ever run afoul of the law. Obviously, the answer is yes. You've asked me how I support myself. The short answer is that I don't. I have a checking account in a New York bank with a small cash balance. No income. No investment portfolio. No retirement plan. I've been a gypsy my entire adult life. Mostly, my friends are kind enough to take me in."

"Are you sure *they're* not the ones being taken in?"

"I'm not following you, young lady," he responded politely.

"Is that right? Because trouble sure has an amazing knack for following you around, sir." Yolie glanced down at the computer printout that Des had passed her. "In '94 you were charged with passing forged checks belonging to your hostess, a Mimi Overmeyer of Old Westbury, Long Island. The charges were later dropped by Mrs. Overmeyer, but similar charges were leveled the following year in Aspen, Colorado. This time your hostess was a member of the Ford family. In '96 some valuable jewelry disappeared from your hostess's horse farm in Jackson, Wyoming. A Degas disappeared six months later in Palm Beach. This list just goes on and on, Mr. Tolliver—a Cartier watch in Maui, a Tiffany diamond bracelet in Montecito. In Beverly Hills we've got credit card fraud—"

"Eva *loaned* me that card," Tolly objected, after having suffered the rest in composed silence. "Besides, what you've failed to mention is that not once have I been *convicted* of any crime."

"True that," Yolie conceded. "But the sheet doesn't lie. Wherever you've stayed some wealthy lady has wound up paying for it. You're quite the smooth operator, aren't you?"

"You make me sound like a gentleman thief out of an old Hollywood movie."

Des was thinking the same thing herself. Didn't know which movie, but she had a pretty fair idea who would.

"I didn't say anything about you being a gentleman," Yolie pointed out, raising her chin at him.

"Young lady, that was not a nice thing to say."

"We're just trying to be thorough," Soave interjected soothingly. "Mrs. Vickers has lost herself a pretty valuable car, and a man is dead."

"I'm neither a murderer nor a car thief," Tolly said. "I had nothing to do with any of this."

"Why did you leave the keys to the Gullwing in the ignition?" asked Yolie.

"Poochie told me to."

"Sure it wasn't your idea?"

"Positive."

"We can subpoena this house's phone records. Find out who you've been in contact with."

"Go right ahead. You won't get anywhere. Not regarding *me* you won't."

Soave peered at him. "You have some idea who is behind this?"

"I have my ideas," Tolly acknowledged. "None I care to share with you."

Yolie kept right on coming. "I understand Mrs. Vickers has her some mighty tasty artwork around here."

"Sergeant, this is not you being thorough, merely insulting," Tolly said to her calmly. "But you're wasting your breath. I am impervious to insults. You see, I've been a queer my whole life."

"Have you got a man in your life right now?" she inquired.

"I haven't, no," he replied wistfully. "In recent years, it's been my pleasure to befriend a handful of great, kind ladies. Lonely ladies who make me a part of the family. Mind you, other family members tend to have it in for me—witness Claudia."

"What about her?"

"She despises me, simply put. I'm a rival for her mother's affections. I've encountered this before. If something goes amiss, I'm the fellow they try to pin it on, and you people are only too happy to see it their way. I'm just the sort who you classify as 'the likely suspect.' I'm a lone wolf, and I've never owned things. As if *things* legitimize you. The most disreputable people I've ever known owned *things*—multinational corporations, banking empires. Trust me, *they're* the criminals in this world. But the law always picks on me. You people are so compliant in that regard. Besides which," he added pointedly, "Poochie knows all about what's on that sheet of yours. I've told her. And she trusts me completely. She also needs me. Not just because I'm her friend, but because I pull my weight around here. I help out in the yard, shop for her, wash dishes. She has no maid, you know."

"Claudia told me you're putting together a book of your photos," Des said.

Tolly brightened considerably. "My photos are my legacy. Before I go, I want to show your generation what real style was about. What *they* were about. I was Babe Paley's favorite, you know. She'd let no other photographer near her. I shot all of the great ones—Jackie Kennedy, C.Z. Guest, Slim Keith. They had such elegance, such breeding."

"You were a fashion photographer?" asked Yolie.

"I never shot fashion," he replied crisply. "Although that's a common misconception, Sergeant, so don't get too down on yourself for making it. I shot fabulous ladies going about their daily lives. I shot them lunching with friends. I shot them riding horses, throwing charity galas. I was their chronicler, and now that I'm closing in on eighty I want to publish my chronicle. Those ladies are a part of our heritage. They speak to a wonderful bygone era when sophistication and grace ruled our society. Who are our standard bearers now? Paris Hilton? Britney Spears? The Olsen twins?" Tolly let out a discreet snort of disgust. "They're all gone now, except for Poochie. She's a national treasure, really. And she's grown even more beautiful as she's gotten older. Because of her spirit. She savors every single day of her life."

"Do you still take pictures, Mr. Tolliver?" Yolie asked.

"Haven't touched a camera in years. These days, I'm nothing more than a remarkably well-preserved relic."

"Which brings us back to the subject of how you support yourself."

"I haven't a cent, Sergeant, as I've already told you. Could I use one of those sweet golden parachutes that the corporate titans are awarded for running their companies into the ground? Absolutely. Instead, I'm relying on Poochie for the roof over my head, for my pocket money, for my everything. I adore that woman. She's good to me, and I'm good to her. We laugh an awful lot. We're happy to-gether. I have peace here. I have security. And I *didn't* steal her Gullwing. Not worth it to me at this point in my life. Which is not to admit that it ever was. May I be excused now?"

"You can stay right here if you want," Soave told him. "We're leaving."

As soon as they were outside Soave undid his flowered necktie and ripped it from around his throat. "I *knew* this thing made me look light in the loafers," he fumed. "I should never have listened to Tawny."

"You don't look gay, Rico," Des assured him.

"You trying to tell me that old guy wasn't hitting on me?"

"He was simply paying you a compliment. That wasn't gay code."

"That there is one sly old boots," Yolie mused aloud as they crossed the gravel courtyard toward their rides. "Did you believe anything he said?"

"Not a single word," Soave replied, scowling.

"Dig, how do we know he doesn't have a young stud on the side?" she suggested. "A partner who does the heavy lifting while he's being all lovey-dovey."

"We should definitely check his phone records," Soave said. "Also his bank account. His and everyone else's. Maybe we'll turn up a funky deposit or withdrawal. And, Des, you ought to nose around at your quaint local inns. See if any unattached male guests came and went recently."

"I'll get right on it, Rico."

"So who are *you* liking for this, the Kershaw brothers?"

"My mind's still open. But my gut hunch is Pete's killer wasn't some out-of-town leather boy who's hooked up with Guy Tolliver. We're looking for people who Pete knew. People who were afraid he might blab their identity to someone."

"Girl, you told us the man barely spoke," Yolie pointed out.

"I know I did. Just walking it around. Sorry if I'm muddying the water."

"That's okay, don't ever hold back. I had a wise lieutenant once who taught me that." Soave flashed a grin at Des as they arrived at their cars. "Let's cowboy up, ladies. Yolie, grab some uniforms and recanvass the neighbors and school bus drivers. Find out if anyone saw Pete on his rounds this morning. And we need to go after the Gullwing hard. If we find the car we find our killers. They had to unload it somewhere. And we're not talking some chop shop in Bridgeport. We're talking high-end operator, which rhymes with m-o-b."

"I know a task force Fed in New Haven I can reach out to," Yolie said.

"You also might want to contact the supervisor of the guard detail up at Enfield," Des suggested. "The Kershaws are strictly small time, but they may have hooked up while they were there. Maybe one of the guards saw them hanging with a guy who has a background in car theft."

"That's good, Des," Soave said. "I'll get right on that. Could you—?"

"You want me to notify Pete's next of kin, am I right?"

"Any idea who that might be?"

"Rico, I don't have a clue. But I do know where to start."

CHAPTER 11

"*WOULD YOU TELL BEMENT for me?*"

Mitch could not believe what he'd just gotten himself into. As he steered his high-riding Studey pickup toward Great White Whale Antiques up in Millington, he asked himself exactly how he'd let Justine Kershaw rope him into being the go-between with her boyfriend. In his own defense, Mitch could think of several reasons. Her book was remarkable. He wanted to see it published. And he had to find out how much of it was based in reality. All good, sound reasons for taking on such a sensitive mission. And all bull. There was only one reason Mitch was running this fool's errand and he knew it—because Justine Kershaw was a wily, adorable little manipulator who'd maneuvered him into it.

As he rolled his way through the bare, muddy late winter countryside, Mitch found himself wondering who else she'd been moving around lately, and what sort of things she was capable of making them do.

Millington was a tiny rural hamlet in the rolling farm country about ten miles inland from Dorset. Great White Whale Antiques was housed in an old barn across the road from a family-owned garden center. One lone car with Massachusetts plates was parked out front of the shop. It was still pretty early in the year for tourists and antique hounds to be out browsing. Evan Peck, the shop's owner, shut it down completely in January and February. Evan was one of Mitch's neighbors out on Big Sister. He was still wintering at the family compound down in Hobe Sound. His cousin, Becca, was running things with Bement until he returned.

The shop was cluttered, its merchandise eclectic. There were colonial armoires and bedsteads alongside weathered Victorian garden ornaments. An art deco living room set was displayed right next to a slender Danish-style one. There was sterling silver and crystal, quilts, paintings. Some of the pieces were very high end. Others were borderline garage sale material, although absolutely none of it was cheap.

Becca was behind one of the glass cases showing flatware to a pair of elderly ladies. Mitch waved to her and mouthed Bement's name. She motioned to a door marked *PRIVATE*. He went through it into a workshop that smelled strongly of turpentine and linseed oil. Here, he found dressers without drawers, chairs without seats, tabletops, table legs. A carpenter's bench was laden with saws and drills and a dozen different kinds of clamps.

Bement Widdifield was taking a roaring handheld power sander to a gently aged white kitchen table, exposing an old coat of blue paint underneath, as well as some bare pine. A can of paint stripper and a scraper were at his elbow. Bement wore a protective dust mask over his mouth and nose. It was chilly there in the workshop, but he was stripped down to a frayed red pocket T-shirt and cargo pants. A fine white powder clung to his bare arms, which bulged with muscle.

When he spotted Mitch standing there he immediately turned off the noise, yanked off the mask and started toward him with a welcoming smile on his face. "You must be Mitch. Teeny called me on her break. Told me you might stop by."

"Glad to meet you," Mitch said, gripping Bement's dry, strong hand.

Bement had the sort of easy physical confidence that Mitch had always admired in other men. He did not look like any effete rich kid. The day-old beard and purplish mouse under his eye gave him a rugged, scrappy air. He was not particularly tall, but he had the lean, coiled athleticism of a guy who would excel at any sport he tried. Standing there with him, Mitch felt like a different species of animal—a plodder who'd been bred for towing heavy wagons through mud.

"So this is your office?" he asked him, glancing around.

"Evan's a much better wheeler-dealer than I am," Bement acknowledged. "He also knows where to find stuff, so he goes on most of the buying trips. Unless he can't get away, in which case I'll go. But I'm much happier when I'm working with my hands. It's good, honest work. I'm not trying to fool anyone."

Mitch studied the farmhouse table with intense interest. He'd furnished his own cottage mostly with castoffs, and was still learning the refinishing ropes. "Will you strip this down to bare wood?"

"No, I'll leave a lot of this paint on. People are into the 'distressed' look right now. Lends the piece a patina of age. A decorator like my mom will pay top dollar for a table like this, even though it's a factory-made piece from the 1930s—not really an antique at all."

Mitch nodded his head in agreement, even as it occurred to him that Bement *was* trying to fool someone. He'd just admitted so.

"Actually, I'm still pretty new to furniture. I know boats way better. Did donkey work down at the boatyard every summer when I was a kid."

"Justine told me you two would like to buy a boat and sail away together."

"All we have to do is win the lottery."

"Actually, it may not have to come to that. Can we sit somewhere and talk?"

A hooded gray sweatshirt was draped over the back of a chair. Bement flung it on over his head and started toward the back door, pausing at a work sink to wash the white sanding powder from his hands. Next to the sink sat a table with an electric coffeemaker on it. He poured some coffee into a Styrofoam cup and dumped sugar and creamer in it. Mitch did the same. Then they went out the door to a weedy, muddy area behind the barn that served as a boneyard for rusted-out patio furniture and garden gates. Becca's Honda Civic was parked back there next to a pickup that Mitch assumed was Bement's.

A wooden picnic table sat invitingly in the winter sunshine.

They flopped down there, the rays feeling nice and warm on Mitch's shoulders. The land out behind the barn fell off sharply into a deep, tree-shaded gorge. The stream down there was still frozen. Bement pulled a pack of unfiltered Lucky Strikes from his sweatshirt pocket and lit one, eyeing Mitch guardedly. The more Mitch studied him, the more aware he became of the intensity that lurked beneath Bement's apparent physical ease.

"You hear about our latest local crime news?" he asked Mitch, dragging on his cigarette.

Mitch nodded. Des had called to tell him. She always called him when something broke. He liked it that she did. "I tried to talk to Pete just yesterday at the Soup Kitchen. The guy ran from me in sheer terror."

"When I was in high school he used to sit out on the town green every afternoon," Bement recalled. "The Kershaw brothers would throw rocks at him on their way home from school. I had to tell them to cut it out."

"Sounds like you've been messing with those two for years."

"To know them is to mess with them."

"I guess the poor guy was in the wrong place at the wrong time."

"I wouldn't be so sure, man."

"What do you mean by that, Bement?"

"I mean he wasn't necessarily killed because of what he saw."

"Well, why else would he? . . ."

"I can't say anything more because I'm not supposed to know." Bement gulped his coffee, staring across the table at him. "Did you ever hide behind the sofa when you were a little kid? Overhear what the grown-ups were saying to each other when they thought you'd gone to bed?"

"Sure, but all they were ever talking about was my Aunt Esther's gall bladder. I never heard any good stuff."

"Well, I did. In my family we had lots of secrets. But I don't talk about them. Besides, that's not why you're here. You've read

Teeny's book, or as much of it as you could stand, and you don't know how to tell her it stinks. You're afraid you'll hurt her feelings. Am I right?"

"Not even close. You haven't read it yourself?"

"She won't let me near the thing. Keeps saying it's private, like a diary. Which is fine. I can respect that." Bement cocked his head at Mitch curiously. "So why are you here?"

"To tell you I think it will be published to great success."

Bement drew his breath in, flabbergasted. "You're . . . kidding me, right?"

"I'm absolutely not kidding you."

Bement sat there in stunned silence, absently massaging the skinned, swollen knuckles of his right hand. "Collided with Donnie's face yesterday," he explained, flexing the hand. "A guy's cheekbone is a hell of a lot sturdier than your fist is. They never mention that in the old westerns, do they?"

"The sound effects are usually wrong, too. It should be a dull thud, not a smack." Mitch sipped his coffee, studying Bement. "Do you have any idea what her book is about?"

"I really don't, Mitch. Teeny never works on it when we're together. Don't ask me why."

"I'm going to tell you why, actually. And you'd better brace yourself, because this may be a bit hard to take. It's about a small-town New England teenaged girl who is brutally raped by her two older brothers, who then turn her out. First she takes on half the boys in town, then their fathers."

Bement pulled on the last of his Lucky and flicked the butt off into the weeds, his face revealing nothing. Until suddenly he lunged across the table and grabbed Mitch by the front of his jacket. "Are you trying to say my girlfriend was the town bang?"

"This is a very good question you ask," Mitch responded hoarsely. "Want to let go of me?"

"*Not* until you tell me what you're getting at." Bement's eyes were narrow slits.

"Let go of the material, Bement."

Bement abruptly released him and sat back on his bench, a blue vein throbbing in his forehead.

Mitch straightened the collar of his jacket. "Freak out much?"

He ran a hand through his shoulder-length hair and reached for his coffee, his hands shaking. "I just love her so damned much that I lose it sometimes. I apologize, man. Really, I do."

"No harm, no foul."

"I couldn't stay away from her, you know," he confessed miserably. "I was out there in Palo Alto, starting my senior year at Stanford, and I was a total nut job. I can't make it when we're not together. I begged her to join me out there, but she wouldn't. I guess she's more attached to this place than she lets on. That's why I dropped out. *She's* why. I had to be with her. It was like she *controlled* me." Bement shook his head slowly. "Whatever love is, it's sure not about being smart. Me getting my degree from Stanford? *That* would have been smart."

"You're not enjoying what you're doing?"

"No, I am. And the two of us are real happy together. But my mom's pissed at me *all* of the time. Hell, the whole town's pissed at me. They watched me grow up. They act like I've let them down."

"You can still get your degree, Bement. Plenty of colleges around here would take you."

"I don't see the point anymore." Bement gazed across the gorge at the bare winter hills beyond. "I don't even know who I am."

"Again, that's why they invented college."

"What are you, a campus recruiter?"

"You just don't strike me as the kind of guy to sail off and hide from the world, that's all. I happen to know a little about hiding. I spent twenty years in darkened movie theaters doing just that."

"And what are you doing now, exactly?"

"Trying to understand people, I guess. We're a lot more screwed up than I ever realized."

Bement let out a short laugh. "Now you're talking about my

142

parents. My dad's totally lost. Which for me is way weird, because your dad's the one who's supposed to have the road map, you know? They've always had to work at their marriage, but he doesn't even want to try anymore. My mom's freaking, as you can imagine. And totally pretending that she's not. It's just a huge mess. My dad's a good guy, too. I love him to death. Hell, I love both of them." Bement drained the last of his coffee, glancing at Mitch coolly. "You wanted to tell me about Teeny's book. Is there more?"

"There is. And I mean to be as tactful as I can, but it's still going to come out blunt. Justine won't tell me whether it's a true story or not. Frankly, it's so detailed and explicit that I find it hard to believe it's not at least partly based on personal experience."

Bement's nostrils flared slightly. "Mitch, who my girlfriend may have banged is not my idea of a legitimate topic of conversation between us, okay? I barely know you. And even if we were blood brothers, I still don't know if it's any of your damned business."

"I don't disagree."

"Then why are you sweating me?"

"Because once this book is published it'll become everyone's business. If there's one thing I do understand, it's the media, and I'm telling you right now that Justine is about to get one hell of a lot of attention. And so are you."

"*Me?* Why me?"

"Because you're the man she's seeing. Total strangers will want to know everything about you. You'd better prepare yourself, Bement, because if you can't handle it, then your life will become a special kind of hell."

"I didn't ask for any of this," he pointed out hotly.

"I know that. But I'm here to tell you that it's what you're looking at."

Bement Widdifield stared at Mitch long and hard. Not so much with anger now. He had a solemn look on his handsome face. "Fine, if it's an answer you want then I'll give you one. But I won't discuss this with you or anyone else ever again. This is it.

Teeny was never raped by her brothers. She never did their friends. She never did their fathers. None of those things ever happened to her."

"How do you know this, Bement?"

"I know it, okay?"

"Not okay. *How?*"

"Because we've been going together a lot longer than most people know. Since we were in high school. We had to sneak around so our parents wouldn't find out. Teeny was seventeen the first time we slept together. That was the night of our senior prom and I . . . I was her very first. She was a virgin, okay? Teeny was still a virgin." Bement crumpled his Styrofoam cup angrily in his fist. "*Now* do you believe me?"

CHAPTER 12

POOCHIE'S MUCK-SPLATTERED ISUZU TROOPER was up on the lifter in one of the service bays, where a mechanic was working on it. Doug was on the computer in his glassed-in office ordering parts from a catalogue. He got off of it quickly when he saw Des standing there in his doorway.

"How's that working out for you?" she asked him, gesturing at the Isuzu through the glass wall.

"She's a hurting girl, but we'll get her right soon enough." Doug Garvey was big and balding, with an easy-does-it small town air. More than a few of Dorset's high school boys over the years got their first paying work pumping gas for him here at his Sunoco. A lot of them bought their first ride from him, too. Doug moved a lot of cars on consignment. Also rented them out by the week. The man was no easy-does-it businessman. He owned summer rental cottages in several shoreline towns. A piece of the boatyard at the Dorset Marina, a car wash in Old Saybrook, convenience stores in Branford and New Haven. "Have a seat, Des. How can I help you?"

She sat in the chair across the desk from him, twirling her hat in her fingers. "I'm sorry to tell you that Pete's dead."

"Aw, hell, that's a damned shame. He seemed perfectly fine this morning, too. What was it, heart attack?"

"No, somebody bashed in his head."

Doug's eyes widened in shock. "Where did this happen?"

"Near the foot of the driveway to Four Chimneys. The Major Crime Squad is up there investigating it right now, along with the theft of Poochie's Gullwing. We figure the two are related."

"Pete saw it happen, is that it?"

"That's our working theory."

"He'd never have told a soul."

"An outsider wouldn't necessarily know that."

"So you don't think it was someone local?"

"Doug, we don't know."

"I was just beginning to wonder about him. He should have been home from his rounds by now." Doug ran a scarred, meaty hand over his face, knuckles permanently etched with grease. "Any sign of the Gullwing yet?"

"Not yet."

"Poochie will need something to get around in. I'd better run the Jeep up there later."

Des nodded her head, thinking that everyone saw life through the prism of their own priorities. For Doug Garvey, this represented an opportunity to rent Poochie a car. "The state is legally obligated to notify Pete's next of kin. Can you help me out?"

"Des, I'm happy to do whatever I can," he replied, although he seemed uneasy now. "Just don't expect much in the way of answers. It's not like Pete opened up to me or anything."

"You let him stay here," she pointed out.

"I did," he allowed, rocking back in his chair. "I felt responsible for him. He was one of ours. And he wouldn't go into a facility. That crazy son of a gun jumped right out of my truck when I tried to take him up to Connecticut Valley Hospital. Took off running down the center divider of Route Nine, almost got himself killed. I'm no miracle worker, Des. Just an old grease monkey. I found Pete sleeping under the I-95 overpass one winter, must be five, six years ago. I was afraid he'd freeze to death, so I let him use the old trailer out back. Figured it was the decent thing to do. No different from what you and Mrs. Tillis would do for a stray cat. Speaking of which, I've got a ton of mice nesting up in my storage loft."

Des treated him to a huge smile. "Stop by any time. Happy to fix you up. Doug, you mentioned that Pete was 'one of ours.' Does he have family in Dorset?"

"Well, you always heard stories . . ."

"What kind of stories?"

"Crazy stuff. You know how people are. One time, I heard that he was the illegitimate son of Ted Williams, who'd kept himself a mistress here in town. Your Yankee fans were floating that one. Then I heard he was a Kennedy cousin who'd been disowned because he was loco. Your Republicans were behind that one. I also heard he was a Swamp Yankee from up in the hills, whose parents had been, well, brother and sister. Mind you, folks say that about pretty much anyone in Dorset who's a little slow or off or whatever. In plenty of cases, it's not so far off the mark either. I'm a Swamp Yankee myself, so I can say it."

"Would you happen to know what Pete's last name was?"

"Des, that's not something I can help you with."

"Then can you point me to someone who was related to him?"

"That's not something I can help you with either."

Des shoved her heavy horn-rimmed glasses up her nose, studying Doug carefully. He was acting all amiable and cooperative, but he wasn't being the least bit forthcoming. Which wasn't to say that he was lying. He was being scrupulously careful not to—so careful that she could swear he'd been coached. "Doug, was there anything unusual about Pete's routine this morning?"

He shook his head. "He came in and washed up about six, had himself a cup of coffee and took off on that bike of his. I was getting ready to open up when he left."

"Were you here all morning?"

"Pretty much. I took the truck out a little after seven to jump a dead battery for Mrs. Bingham up on Old Ferry Road."

"You have to go past Four Chimneys to get to Old Ferry. Did you see Pete making his rounds?"

"Sorry, I'm afraid not."

"Doug, how long did you know Pete?"

"Since we were little guys—eight, nine years old."

"Is that right?" Nothing he'd said so far had even hinted at this. "So Pete grew up in Dorset?"

"Well, yes and no. Pete was one of those kids who didn't seem to belong to anybody. For a couple of years, he lived next door to me with the Millers. They were both schoolteachers, had a whole mess of kids. Some their own, others foster kids they took in. Although that kind of thing seemed a lot less formal back in those days. We three used to play together in the woods behind my house."

Des frowned. "You three?"

"Me, Pete and Milo Kershaw. Milo lived right across the street. We were always getting into mischief together."

"Are you and he still good friends?"

Doug lowered his gaze. "I run a business. I try to get along with everyone. Milo can be difficult. He's always searching for villains in his life."

"Did Pete seem at all strange to you when you were boys?"

"Not at all. He was a fun-loving little guy. And a real chatterbox, if you can believe that."

"You say he lived next door for two years?"

"Until they sent him away."

"Who sent him away, Doug?"

"No idea, Des. I don't know where he went either. I never saw him again. Not until I spotted him camped out under the overpass, like I said. I hadn't seen the guy for almost fifty years, but he had that same long, bony nose he had when we were kids. So I pulled over and said, 'Holy Christmas, Pete, is that you?' He just shrugged at me. I threw his duffel bag in my truck and brought him here. Thought maybe Pete could pump gas for me. But that didn't work out. He got too frightened by the customers. I did what I could for him—not that he'd let me do much."

"Did Milo reach out to him as well?"

"Milo thought he was crazy. Wanted nothing to do with him."

"Pete had no identification on him. May I go through his personal effects?"

He led her out back through the service bays, moving none too swiftly. Doug had the ponderous duck waddle of a big man with a bad back. There were half a dozen clunkers parked out there in the mud alongside of the dilapidated old Silver Streak. The trailer was unlocked. Doug showed her in. Long ago, it had been all tricked out with a kitchen sink, propane stove and electric refrigerator. There was a dinette, a built-in bed. No doubt it once was very nice. Not anymore. The appliances were history, and it reeked in there of mildewy carpeting. There was a rumpled sleeping bag on the bare, stained mattress. A few canned goods on the counter next to the sink. Some dirty laundry. Newspapers in a pile. A dog-eared copy of *The World Almanac.*

"My dad used to take this baby up to Maine on fishing trips," Doug recalled fondly, his bulky frame filling the dank little trailer. "It's seen better days, but it suited Pete's needs. Mostly, he just kept to himself out here. The ladies in town would drop off old clothes for him. If he wanted anything he'd take it." Doug shook his head sadly. "Not much for a man to leave behind, is it?"

Des searched the trailer for personal papers, letters, anything that would provide a key to Pete's identity. The storage cupboards were empty. She looked inside the pockets of his soiled, stinky clothing. Under the mattress. She found nothing.

"Doug, did you ever get mail here for him?"

"Not once, Des. He wasn't in contact with the outside world at all."

"Then I guess I've hit a dead end. You can't help me at all." She stood with her hands on her hips, staring at the big man. "Is that how it is, Doug?"

He cleared his throat, his eyes avoiding hers.

"Doug, I'm not trying to get in your face here, but I'm sensing you're not telling me everything you know."

He kicked at the moldy rug with his heavy work boot. "I just don't want to stir up a hornet's nest, that's all."

"There's absolutely no need to worry. I'll be the one doing the stirring."

"Well, okay," he said reluctantly. "Awhile back I was given instructions about what to do in case Pete's condition ever took a serious turn for the worse."

"By whom?"

"By Bob Paffin."

"Is that right? Now why did the first selectman take such an interest in our village scavenger?"

"Des, I don't know. I only know that he told me who to contact under extreme medical circumstances."

"The man is dead, Doug. This qualifies as an extreme medical circumstance. Now just exactly who in the hell did Bob tell you to contact?"

Glynis Fairchild-Forniaux worked out of a stone cottage on Turkey Neck Road that had originally served as the town icehouse. It was built right into the granite ledge next to her riverfront center-chimney home, which had been a tavern back in the 1700s when Turkey Neck was a commercial district serving the ferry passengers who were crossing over to Old Saybrook. Des knew all of this because Glynis had represented her at the closing when she'd bought her house. Hers was the oldest and bluest of Dorset's blue blood legal practices. Glynis had taken it over from her late father, Chase Fairchild, who'd taken it over from his father before him.

Glynis had three kids, two dogs and a veterinarian husband, Andre Forniaux, who she'd met while she was on a college ski trip to the French Alps. Dr. Andre was out in the driveway loading veterinary supplies into the drawers of his specially outfitted pickup when Des pulled in alongside of Glynis's Dodge minivan. Dorset's mobile vet was a tall, slender Frenchman in his early forties, with thinning sandy hair, a narrow face and a long nose with rather pinched nostrils. He cared for hundreds of Dorset's dogs and cats by driving from house to house just like an old-time general practitioner. Dr. Andre was totally on board with the feral stray rescue program Des and Bella had undertaken. He inoculated and neutered the healthy cats at no cost, and humanely put down those too sick to be saved. He was a good vet who cared about animals. He was not so in sync with their owners, some of whom called him Andre the Drip due to his dismissive bedside manner.

"How goes it, Andre?" Des called to him as she started inside.

He puffed out his cheeks—the classic Gallic shrug for which there is no American equivalency. "It goes, Des. Round and round it goes, eh?" Andre had studied veterinary medicine at the University of Tennessee in Knoxville, so in addition to his French accent he had a slight drawl. "And how are your wards?"

"Doug Garvey may adopt one. If you hear of anyone else who's interested, please let me know, okay? We've got to move some of those kids out."

Aside from the elderly secretary who she'd inherited along with the practice, Glynis Fairchild-Forniaux worked on her own. Her office was very old-timey. There was a huge oak rolltop desk. Legal books in glass-doored walnut bookcases. Clubby leather armchairs. A potbellied stove. There was also action. The phone in the outer office rang constantly from the moment Des walked in.

Glynis was a snub-nosed, fluffy blonde in her late thirties, with a trim figure and a lilting voice that could fool people into thinking she was a dippy airhead. She was not, and had the framed diplomas from Smith College and Harvard Law School to prove it. Glynis was also a highly dedicated runner who was training for next month's Boston Marathon, which would be her seventh. She was dressed casually in a turtleneck and jeans. As she showed Des into her office, she appeared to be limping.

"Girl, what did you do to yourself?" Des asked, noticing the Ace bandage wrapped around her right ankle.

"Absolutely nothing serious. I just slipped on some ice this morning while I was running on Route 156."

"What time was this?" Des asked, settling herself into a leather chair.

"Early. I usually get my road work in by dawn."

"You weren't up near Four Chimneys, were you?"

"No, I wasn't." Glynis hobbled over to her desk and sat in her tall-backed chair, wincing.

"You are really hurting, Glynis. Have you seen a doctor?"

"I see one every morning across the breakfast table."

"Andre's a vet," Des pointed out.

"And an ankle's an ankle. I slapped some ice on it and I wrapped it. It'll be fine. And there is absolutely no way I'm not running tomorrow."

"Spoken like a true fanatic," said Des, who had a jumble of feelings about Glynis Fairchild-Forniaux, attorney at law. Glynis was gen-next—a modern, open-minded career woman who Des could vibe with better than most. But she was still a purebred member of Dorset's inner circle and a careful keeper of confidences. Also very shrewd politically. Des had heard that Glynis might challenge Bob Paffin next election.

"Doug Garvey just alerted me that you'd be coming by," she said in her fluty little voice. "This is an official visit regarding the death of old Pete, correct?"

"Correct." Des pulled out her notepad and pen. Whenever the phone stopped ringing, it got real quiet there in Glynis's icehouse office. She could hear the ticking of the wall clock, the firewood sizzling in the stove. "Did you know him well?"

Glynis did not choose to answer her. Just leaned back in her chair, bandaged ankle propped up on the desk, and said, "His full legal name was Peter Ashton Mosher. "Date of birth—March thirtieth, 1943."

"Place of birth?"

"Dorset, Connecticut."

"Can you provide me with a next of kin?"

"By contacting me you've fulfilled your legal obligation under the laws of the state of Connecticut."

Des looked at her in surprise. "You represented Pete?"

"I had that privilege," Glynis confirmed. "And I wish I could tell you more, but I'd be violating my responsibility to my client."

"Even though he's dead?"

"Especially because he's dead. According to the terms of his will, I'm also executor of his estate."

"There's an estate?"

"A considerable one."

"Glynis, are you telling me that our Can Man was an eccentric millionaire?"

"I didn't say he was a millionaire. I said there is a considerable estate."

"May I ask *how* you represented him?"

"By managing his portfolio." Glynis gestured at a fat file on her desk. "His financial statements came here to the firm. I kept track of his income and reinvested it for him as I saw fit. Also dealt with the IRS on his behalf."

"How often were you in contact with him?"

"I was never in contact with him. I never even met Pete. We were retained by a third party."

"Whose identity is? . . ."

"Confidential, Des."

"You said 'we' were retained."

"My father was the attorney of record before me. This arrangement goes back quite some time."

"So you basically inherited Pete as a client?"

"I did."

"And would this third party you spoke of also be a client?"

Glynis smiled at her faintly. "Again . . ."

"Confidential, right." Des took this to mean yes. "Who do I contact regarding the disposition of Pete's body?"

"I'll arrange for his burial. His plot at Duck River Cemetery was purchased some time ago."

Des sat there soaking this in. "Glynis, is this all just a bit not normal?"

The blonde attorney relaxed her guard somewhat. Des doubted she ever completely lowered it. "From my end it's not so unusual. I perform precisely this kind of service for a number of wealthy widows in town. Their late husbands have seen to it. It's strictly Pete's lifestyle that makes it seem odd."

"You mentioned you're his executor."

"Correct."

"Doug Garvey has been watching out for him for several years. Does he have an expectation of some money coming his way?"

"You'd have to ask Doug what his expectations are. I wouldn't know."

"How about First Selectman Paffin?"

"Bob merely served as an intermediary. There's nothing more to that."

"Well, who *does* get Pete's money?"

"Des, you know perfectly well I can't disclose the contents of my client's will. The names of his beneficiaries are strictly confidential. You'll have to convince a judge that this information is vital to your investigation. I'm sorry to make you jump through hoops, but those hoops are there for a purpose."

"Okay, let me put it to you this way," Des persisted. "Who else besides you was aware that Pete had money?"

"You're merely asking me the same question with different words," Glynis replied patiently. "We can't have this conversation. Not until you come back with a signed warrant."

Des thanked Glynis Fairchild-Forniaux and headed out the door, her head spinning. Because they might be looking at a whole new scenario now. Because that morning's events may have had squat to do with Poochie's Gullwing and everything to do with the Can Man. Because if Pete Mosher did have a considerable fortune then it was entirely possible that someone had murdered him for it—and stolen Poochie's Gullwing to throw them off.

Because it was entirely possible that they had this whole damned thing backwards.

CHAPTER 13

Des was frowning at him as she came through the door of McGee's Diner in her uniform and Smokey hat. "You okay?" she asked, sliding her slender frame into the booth. "You have a funny look on your face."

"It's nothing serious," Mitch assured her. "My heart just skips a beat every time you walk into a room."

She drew her breath in, her pale green eyes growing soft. "Mitch, you can't say such things to me when I'm on duty. My toes get all wiggly and I'm no good to anyone."

"Oh, I wouldn't say that," he said, squeezing her knee underneath the table.

"Sir, that there's a class-two IPG." When Des was in uniform she had ironclad rules regarding Inappropriate Public Groping.

"How about we skip lunch and head straight for my palatial island getaway? You can show me your tattoo. I can show you my feather."

"Baby, I would love nothing better. But I'm up to my eyeballs in a murder."

In fact, she'd told him she could only give him a few minutes when he'd phoned her to meet him at his favorite greasy spoon. McGee's was known throughout New England for its fried oysters and its view of Long Island Sound. During the summer, the place was packed with beachgoers. This time of year, it was downright sleepy. A couple of local carpenters were chowing down on cheeseburgers at the counter. Four old geezers were hanging in a booth, nursing cups of coffee and listening to Perry Como on Dick McGee's cutting edge jukebox.

One of those geezers kept sneaking glances their way. Mitch

was used to being stared at whenever he and Des showed up in public together. But this wasn't the usual look. This was more along the lines of intense nosiness. After all, the critic and the resident trooper had split up—everyone in Dorset knew that. Or thought they did.

Allison Mapes scuffed her way over to their booth with his order, her waitress uniform stretched a bit tight across her generous hips. Justine's streaky-haired roommate looked a bit on the trashed side today. There were dark circles under her eyes. But she still managed a big smile as she approached. "Here we be, Mr. Movie Guy," she declared, setting his fried oyster hero down before him. "I slipped a few extra spiral fries on your plate when Dick wasn't looking."

Des ordered coffee. Allison nodded curtly, filled her cup, then moseyed off toward the kitchen. Des watched her go, a rather stony expression on her face.

"You're not eating?" Mitch asked, diving headfirst into his lunch.

"I had a huge breakfast. Besides, you're already eating for two."

"Go easy on me, thinnie. I've got a lot on my mind."

"So you said on the phone. What is up?"

"You first. How's the case going?"

She told him what she'd learned. That the Can Man had actually been a wealthy eccentric named Peter Mosher. That he, not the Gullwing, may have been the intended target all along.

"So the car theft was like a staged misdirect?"

Des nodded. "To provide cover for the real crime. It's a theory, anyway."

"And it jibes with something Bement Widdifield just told me—that Pete wasn't necessarily killed because of what he saw. It seems that Bement overheard something when he was a little kid. He wouldn't tell me what."

"Lot of that going around today. Glynis wouldn't tell *me* how much money Pete had or who he left it to. Not until a judge signs off on a warrant."

"Is that going to happen?" Mitch asked, munching on his sandwich.

"Soave's on it as we speak. I just hate the waiting, is all."

"So go at it another way. Reach out to someone who isn't constrained by official procedure."

"Such as who?"

"Such as your sweet baboo," he replied, grinning at her.

"I *knew* this was where your twisted mind was going. Mitch, you can't go messing in a murder investigation. How many times do I have to tell you?"

"Des, you have to admit that I've been of immense help to you in the recent past."

"What I have to admit is that you've almost gotten yourself killed in the recent past. Not to mention me fired off of the job. We are not going to do this again. *You* are not going to do this. Talk to me about Guy Tolliver. Was he the real deal?"

Mitch popped a fry in his mouth and said, "Sure, Guy Tolliver was a major name back in the Fifties and Sixties. His specialty was slick magazine spreads full of rich, goyish people hanging out at home looking rich and goyish. Actually, he's kind of retro-chic these days. The style mavens at my paper are ga-ga for him. Why are you asking?"

She told him how Tolly had been relying on the kindness of rich widows like Poochie Vickers for years. And how jewelry and other valuables seemed to disappear whenever he moved on.

"No way!" Mitch erupted excitedly. "This is straight out of E.W. Hornung's *The Amateur Cracksman*—better known to filmgoers as *Raffles*. Very cool stuff. The 1930 version with Ronald Colman is the best, although the 1940 David Niven isn't bad. I'll have to put that on our to-watch list."

"Mitch, I have to admit something—my own first thought was that Tolly seemed straight out of an old movie. That *never* used to happen before I met you. I was strictly a reality-based individual. God, how ill is that?"

"I don't think it's the least bit ill," he replied, cramming the last of his sandwich into his mouth. "It's romantic. Tell me, has Tolly ever been involved in anything violent?"

"No, that part doesn't sound like him. Mind you, he may keep a partner on the side—someone who plays rougher than he does. I just checked around at our local inns for any stray male guests. No likely candidates in the past few days, which doesn't necessarily mean—" Her pager started beeping at her. She glanced down at it. "I'll be back in a sec."

"I'll be here," he promised, smiling contentedly as he watched her stride out the door.

Allison came over to clear his plate and fill his coffee cup. "Kind of surprised to see you and her together again."

"Don't believe what you hear. We're doing fine."

"Justine told me she thinks you're cute. Know what I told her? Hands off, I saw you first."

"If you don't watch out I'm going to take you seriously one of these days."

"How about *today?*" Allison's eyes gleamed at him invitingly.

Mitch poured cream into his coffee, no longer sure whether she was kidding around or not.

She lingered, a hand on her hip. "Are you just going to leave me hanging? You're supposed to say, 'Awesome, Allison, want to get together for a drink?'"

"I just told you—I'm still with Des."

She shrugged her soft shoulders. "Some things I believe. Others I don't."

The door opened and Des strode back inside, her Vulcan Death Stare trained directly on them. Allison immediately headed back toward the counter.

Des folded herself back into the booth. "That was Yolie. Crime scene techies found the murder weapon in the woods a hundred feet from Pete's body."

"What was it?"

"A two-foot length of one-inch black iron pipe. Pig iron, they call it. Nothing special about it, aside from the fact that it has blood, scalp tissue and hair on it—which will, presumably, turn out to be Pete's. No fingerprints on it. None they could find on preliminary examination, anyway."

"The killers wiped it clean?"

"Wore gloves, more likely. We have some partial shoe prints in the mud. No slam dunks, but they're making impressions. Might prove helpful."

"Des, when you found Pete's body did you notice any blood or tissue under his fingernails?"

She smiled at him. "Now *I'm* rubbing off on you—this I am digging. He sustained wounds to his hands. To me, they looked like defensive wounds. But he may have struggled with his assailants. We can determine whether any of the blood belongs to someone else. The state has Stevie and Donnie's DNA on file. If it's one of them, we'll know right away."

"Did Yolie have anything else?"

"Recanvass turned up nothing," she replied, glancing down at her notepad. "But a Fed who she knows schooled her about Poochie's ride. There's only a select handful of Mercedes Gullwings on the U.S. market at any one time. The experts know each car's pedigree. You can't just unload one somewhere. No reputable dealer would touch it."

"What about a disreputable dealer?"

"Well, here's where it gets interesting. The Feds landed hard last year on an operation that was cherry-picking high-end vehicles from Gold Coast towns up and down the I-95 corridor between New York and Boston. They paid low-level hoods a flat fee—maybe five grand—to deliver the ride to a nearby locale, where they'd whisk it into a big rig. The truck would then transport it to a container ship docked in New York. Within twenty-four hours, the ship's on its way to Saudi Arabia, loaded to the gills with rare, valuable sports cars. Those royal boys love their toys, and they don't care how they come by 'em. A black market Gullwing like Poochie's will fetch a cool million in cash over there. And did I mention that an unmarked tractor-trailer was spotted in the commuter parking lot early this morning?"

"I thought you said the Feds shut that operation down."

"Doesn't mean someone else hasn't taken their place. Yolie's man is sure someone has. There's been an uptick of thefts lately. And there's never a shortage of raggies looking to make a quick buck. Speaking of which, Rico reached out to the guard at Enfield Correctional who was in charge of Stevie and Donnie's cell block. The guard says they pretty much kept to themselves. Doesn't mean they didn't hook up with a guy while they were in. The guards don't see everything. But hey . . ." She closed her notepad, raising her chin at him. "Enough about my job. You wanted to talk to me about something."

"I did. I do." Mitch drained his coffee and sat back. "But this has to stay between us. Strictly off the record, okay?"

"Okay . . ."

"Hypothetically speaking, what are the legal obligations of someone who might be in possession of information regarding adult males having sex with a teenaged girl without her consent?"

Des regarded him with cool, professional detachment now. "How old a girl are we talking about?"

"Fourteen."

"A girl that young it's statutory rape even with her consent. Does this hypothetical girl want to reach out to the law?"

"Not necessarily. In fact, I'd say no."

"Then I mustn't know her identity—not even off the record. I'd be legally obligated to pursue a criminal investigation. And you should be aware that in Connecticut we have a Mandatory Reporting Statute. If a teacher or coach gets wind of this type of situation then he or she is obligated to pass the information on. The statute extends to any adult who's serving in an advisory role. A tutor, even a mentor."

By invoking the m-word Des was signaling that she had a

pretty fair idea where he was skating, and that the ice was not safe. "Even if she's an adult now?"

"Doesn't matter. I'm still obligated to investigate."

"Okay, but here's the truly strange part. There's a decent chance that she made it all up."

"Why would she want to do that?"

"I really can't go into the specifics."

"What makes you even think it?"

"Because she's presently in a long-term relationship with a man who insists it never happened. He's quite vehement. I just don't know if I believe him. He's got a temper, Des. I'm concerned he might go after someone."

"Such as who?"

"Once I tell you that we're past the point of no return."

Des puffed out her cheeks, exasperated. "Mitch, I don't like this. I don't like it at all. If someone gets hurt, then it's on you."

"I know that, and I promise I'll tell you everything just as soon as I can. Give me today, okay?"

She stared at him hard. "Okay," she allowed, signaling for the check.

"One sec!" called out Allison, who was topping off the four geezers' cups for about the eleventh time.

As they sat there waiting for her, Des impulsively reached over and put her hand on top of Mitch's, squeezing it.

He glanced down in surprise. "Master Sergeant, are you aware that your uncommonly delectable fingers are in direct, public contact with mine own?"

"I am," she replied, her eyes twinkling at him.

"Here we go, folks . . ." As Allison put their check down on the table her gaze fell on their hands locked together there. And lingered a second before she added, "Have a good one." Then she scuffed back toward the kitchen.

"Why, you sly vixen," Mitch said, beaming at Des across the table. "You're feeding the village gossip mill, aren't you?"

"Just playing the game according to house rules," she said, pulling her hand away. "I'm out of here. Have to go canvass the bottle return centers to see if anyone brought in an unusually large load this morning."

"Oh, is that right? . . ."

Des narrowed her gaze at him. "Do you know something?"

"Let me put it to you this way—you're about to be reminded, yet again, why I'm what's known on Wall Street as a blue chip investment. I pay dividends."

"Mitch, tell me what you know right now or I swear I'll rearrange your facial features with that ketchup bottle."

So he told her.

CHAPTER 14

THE PLACE ON WHIPPERWILL Road that Milo Kershaw was demolishing wasn't hard to find. It was the one that looked as if it had just taken a direct hit from a Texas twister. The walls were standing, but its roof, roof joists and ceilings had vanished, along with the windows and front door. It reminded Des of extreme storm footage that she'd seen on the Weather Channel, which was the only channel Mitch kept his television tuned to anymore. If her doughboy wasn't watching an old black-and-white movie then he was glued to Jim Cantore. The fact that she found this trait endearing—as opposed to crashingly boring—was just another measure of how into Mitch she was. Although she could have sworn that he and Allison Mapes had been vibing at McGee's. Unless it was just her own paranoia. After all, Mitch was not Brandon. Mitch would never two-time her. Mitch was true blue, wasn't he?

Well, wasn't he?

The house was sided with cedar shingles. Milo was stripping them off and loading them into his truck, which was parked on the lawn right about where you'd expect to find a rental Dumpster. No such Dumpster for Milo Kershaw. Dumpsters cost money. The little man worked alone and was salvaging pretty much everything he could crowbar out of the place. The kitchen sink and cabinets were piled on a tarp next to the truck, along with a heap of lumber and copper pipes. His snarly Doberman was tied up to a tree, standing guard over these secondhand treasures.

When he saw Des pull up and get out, Milo muttered sourly under his breath and kept right on prying the cedar shingles loose. The dog barked at her furiously. Milo hollered at it to shut up. It obeyed him, cowering.

"Taking her down to the ground?" she asked him, looking the place over.

Milo waited a long moment before he answered her. When he did, his voice was low and hostile. "I *got* me a demolition permit. It's posted right there next the doorway, signed and legal."

"Not why I'm here, Mr. Kershaw."

He paused from his labors now, his jaw clenching. "I'm trying to do an honest day's work, lady. Why can't you leave me alone?"

"I enjoy our little chats so much that I just can't help myself. You're like a tonic, Mr. Kershaw."

He kept working on the shingles. His hand on the pry bar was deeply scratched, oozing blood.

"I've got a first aid kit in my cruiser. Be happy to slap a butterfly on that."

"It's *nothing*."

"Mr. Kershaw, we need to talk about those returnables you took to the market this morning."

"So your fat boyfriend ran and told you, hunh?"

"He's not fat, he's *thick*." And that wasn't all Mitch had told her. He'd also shared that Milo had gone racial on him. "Besides, this has nothing to with Mitch Berger. I stopped at the A&P in the routine course of my investigation. You were there, Mr. Kershaw. The returns machine gave you a printout that you redeemed for cash at the courtesy desk."

"*Courtesy* my eye. Nastiest bunch of people I ever seen."

"That very nice lady on the desk commented on your own sunny disposition. Described you right down to that duct tape on your vest, too. She checked her register tape for me. At 9:53 A.M. you collected on $23.20 worth of returnables."

"Yeah, so what?"

"I was wondering how you came by them."

"Saved 'em up."

"Is that so? Then how come Justine was so surprised that you had them?"

"She don't know everything about me," Milo replied, peering at her shrewdly. "You did talk to Berger. I knew it."

"What makes you think it wasn't Justine?"

"Because I brought her up to spit at the law, same as my boys."

"And we know you did a good job with them."

"You got no cause to get snippy with me, young lady."

"Mr. Kershaw, we couldn't find a trace of Pete's haul at the murder scene. Somebody took off with it."

Milo shook his head at her disgustedly. "You really think I'm fool enough to kill that old bum for a lousy twenty-three bucks?"

"Poochie's Mercedes is worth a lot more than that."

"Don't know nothing about it."

"Okay, then let's try this on for size. Let's say you were driving past Four Chimneys this morning, spotted the stuff lying there by the side of the road and helped yourself. Is that how it went down?"

Milo didn't answer. Just kept on working in surly silence.

"If it is, I won't come down on you for it, Mr. Kershaw. All we're interested in is who killed Pete Mosher."

"*Mosher?* Where'd you come by that name?"

"Why, does it mean something to you?"

"Not a damned thing. Just never knew it is all."

"But you knew Pete. Doug Garvey told me you three were pals back when you were kids."

"He lived with them do-gooder schoolteachers for a while. Miller was their name. She always hated me."

"Pete's body wasn't visible from the road, Mr. Kershaw. It's totally credible that someone stopped to liberate his load and didn't see him lying there. If that's how you came by it then you'll be doing us a huge solid if you just say so."

Milo grimaced at her. "Lady, I been through the system, remember? If I admit to that, then I've placed myself at the murder scene. Not a chance. I'm not the village idiot. And I'm done answering questions. I got work to do, so just shove off."

"Mr. Kershaw, I still have a few more questions. And if you don't cooperate then I'll have to take you in."

"You and who else?"

"I won't require any backup."

"You try mixing it up with me and you'll be seeing me in your nightmares until you're old and gray."

Des treated him to her sweetest smile. "If you want to find out who has the bigger cojones we can go around back of the house and throw down right now."

"Sure, you with a gun on your hip. I lay one finger on you you'll shoot me dead and call it self-defense."

"Fine, I'll take it off." Des took off her entire belt, actually. Removed her holstered SIG Sauer from it and set it on the hood of Milo's truck along with her pager. She stood there holding the belt by its buckle. It was a wide belt made of rugged black bridle leather. "Now we're even," she said, snapping it in the air like a whip. "Unless, that is, you're afraid to get it on with an unarmed *afro-disiac*."

"You stay away from me," he ordered her.

"Or what, you'll call a cop?" She moved steadily toward him. "Or maybe you'd like to take off your own belt and try whipping *me*."

Milo backed away from her, glowering fiercely.

She kept on coming. "Still whaling on your boys in the woodshed?"

"Those nippleheads needed discipline when they were young, same as I did."

"If you ask me, you still need it." She snapped her belt in the air again, moving in closer.

His eyes widening, Milo scampered around behind his truck, where he tripped over a piece of lumber and tumbled to the grass. She immediately put her lace-up boot on his chest and pinned him there, the belt dangling loosely from her hand as the Doberman strained against its chain, snarling ferociously.

"Kids who are treated violently by their parents tend to resolve conflicts violently themselves when they grow up," she said calmly, the little man squirming around on the grass under her foot. "Considering how you used to beat on Stevie and Donnie, and still enjoy telling them how worthless they are, it makes perfect sense that they'd cross the line with some poor, defenseless soul like Pete."

"They had *nothing* to do with it," he insisted, his face twisting with fury and indignation.

Des raised the belt high over her head in a distinctly threatening manner. "What about *you?*"

Milo Kershaw had felt the lash himself. He knew how much pain it inflicted. The likes of Des standing over him this way was enough to make him tremble in terror. "I don't *know* anything. And you better let me up or I-I'll file charges against you."

"For what? I haven't laid a finger on you, Mr. Kershaw. We're just talking. Tell me where those returnables came from."

"I found 'em!"

"Found them *where?*"

"None of your damned business is where, bitch!"

Des used the belt now—savagely whipping the grass less than an inch away from him.

Milo let out a strangled yelp. "Okay, okay! I found 'em at my place. Somebody dumped 'em there."

"When?"

"How should I know? Besides, how do you even know they're Pete's?"

Milo was right. Des didn't know for certain if it was Pete's haul he'd come into. Except that in her heart she did know it. "*Where* had they been dumped?"

"Lady, what do you *want* from me?"

"The truth!" she roared, whipping the grass next to him a second time.

"They were at . . . at the foot of our drive," he gasped. "Practically ran the damned bags over when I was . . . I was heading out for work. I deal in building supplies. People drop crap off . . . I got out for a look, saw they were empties and t-took 'em with me."

"What time did you leave for work?"

"Seven-thirty . . . maybe," Milo panted, his chest heaving.

She eased off a little. She wanted him to talk, not have a heart attack. "And where were your boys at the time?"

"Won't . . . help you put my boys away."

"It's not me you're helping. It's them, if you can give them an alibi. Were Stevie and Donnie home by then or weren't they?"

"Ain't . . . ain't saying a-a word." His face contorted as if he were straining mightily. "Whip me, I don't care."

"You can't be sure, can you? It's possible that your boys brought Pete's load home this morning after they killed him. Is that right?"

"I don't *know* who left 'em there! I just . . . I just told you . . . I just . . ." Milo's eyes flickered and then, suddenly, the resistance went right out of him. He untensed, his breathing returning to normal. Lay there in defeated silence, glaring up at her. Not so much with hate in his eyes. Hate wasn't what she saw.

She saw humiliation.

As Des looped her belt back onto her uniform trousers a sharp, acrid smell tweaked her nostrils. She recognized it instantly but did not acknowledge it. Did not say another word. Just fetched her weapon and pager from the hood of Milo's truck and started back toward her cruiser, knowing that from this day on whenever she ran into Milo Kershaw he would flee, his eyes avoiding hers.

She would never forget the look on that nasty little man's face when he wet his pants.

CHAPTER 15

RUT PECK WASN'T DRESSED for company. He had on an ancient, food-stained wool robe, long johns and carpet slippers. Still, the old postmaster seemed happy to see Mitch as he led him into the cozy parlor, where a daytime return of *Gunsmoke* was blaring away on the TV.

"You've stumbled onto my dirty little secret, Mitch," he confessed as he flicked it off. "I'm a Marshal Dillon man. He treats people with respect. Doesn't act tough. Just *is* tough. That's my idea of a lawman. But I guess I'm dating myself, aren't I? It's my idea of a *resident trooper.* Our Des has a lot of Matt's quiet confidence."

"That she does, Rut."

Rut turned up his hearing aids. "What's that you say?"

"She knows how to handle herself."

"Say, I'm not being much of a host. What can I get you?"

"Nothing, thanks." Mitch took his usual seat at the round oak table.

"Kind of thirsty myself," Rut said, smacking his dry lips. "Just might pour myself a glass of my stout."

"In that case, I just might join you."

Rut waddled into the kitchen and opened the fridge. A moment later he returned with two glasses of stout topped with creamy foam. He handed one to Mitch, eased himself slowly into his worn armchair and put his feet up on the footstool. "You come here to lose more money at cards?"

"I wanted to tell you that Justine's novel is quite good. I think I can help her get it published."

"Hey, that there's a piece of good news." Rut took a celebratory sip of stout, studying Mitch over the rim of the glass. "And yet I'm sensing you're uneasy. What's on your mind, son? This about you and Des?"

"It does involve her. It seems her decoder ring is malfunctioning."

Rut frowned. "Sorry, you'll have to trot that by me again."

"She's in the middle of a case that's giving her trouble. I told her I'd try to help out if I could. I suppose you've heard about old Pete?"

"I have," Rut confirmed sadly, resting his half-empty glass on his tummy.

"Rut, how much do you know about him?"

"Why are you asking?"

"Because you're more up on local family history than anyone else I know."

"I guess I do know a little, being related to so many folks like I am." Rut scratched at his chin thoughtfully. "What does Des know?"

"For starters, that his last name was Mosher."

"And how did she come by that?"

"Pete had a lawyer, believe it or not."

"Young Glynis?"

"Why, yes."

Rut sipped his stout, nodding to himself. "Folks here in Dorset take an indecent amount of pleasure in swapping tales about each other. But no genuinely decent person takes pleasure in gossiping about someone who's suffered through no fault of his own. No sir." Rut's phone rang on the end table next to him. He reached over, lifted the receiver an inch and hung it back up again, then gazed down into his glass in silence for a moment. "I can tell you some things that Des ought to know. She'll be hearing bits and pieces soon enough. May as well get the real story—not some pack of lies the village hens cooked up over at Town and Country beauty salon. But you didn't hear this from me, and it's not for spreading around. Strictly to help your lady friend catch a killer.

Maybe earn herself a pay bump. Not that she needs one. Already has a rich boyfriend."

"You don't know much about the newspaper business, do you, Rut?"

Rut Peck got up out of his chair and fetched them two more glasses of home brew. Then he sat back down, shifting around in his chair. "To begin with, Mosher was the maiden name of Milo Kershaw's mom, Bessie. Bessie was a Mosher. So was my dear wife, Helen, who was first cousin to her. Used to be Moshers all over Dorset. They're an old, old family. Swamp Yankees, every last one of them."

"Are you telling me that Pete was related to Milo's mother?"

"Mitch, this takes some telling, so drink your stout and let me yammer, okay?" Rut paused to sip his own. "Back in the Roaring Twenties there was a big, puffy-chested fellow name of Mr. John J. Meier. Heir to a huge Pittsburgh steel fortune. John J. was the youngest of three boys. His older brothers took over the family business from the father. And a fine job of it they did. John J. was sent off to Andover and Yale to improve the family's social standing. A strutting, handsome fellow he was. The ladies went for him in a big way. Well, you put that all together and it spells a career in politics. That was the plan, anyhow. Trouble was, John J. couldn't sell a pair of mittens to the Eskimos. Became the family playboy instead. Cut himself a wide swath through the young ladies of New York, London, Paris. Eventually, he latched on to beautiful young Katherine Dunlop of the Dorset Dunlops."

"This would be your aunt?"

Rut nodded. "John J. spent buckets of money refurbishing Four Chimneys. Hired a young local couple, Ed and Bessie Kershaw, to be caretaker and cook. And then he and Aunt Katherine settled in at Four Chimneys to start themselves a family. At least, they tried. She lost the first baby at birth, then miscarried. She wasn't a strong woman. She finally gave John J. a daughter, Poochie, in '33. But after that Aunt Katherine couldn't have any more kids, so Poochie grew up an only child." Rut paused to collect his thoughts. Mitch could hear the old man's breath wheeze in and out in the warm, airless silence. "I can still remember John J. tearing around the village in that block-long Duesenberg of his. You never saw so much chrome in your life. Nor a more dashing fellow, with his slicked-back hair and waxed mustache. Bought himself one of those forty-five-foot wood-hulled speedboats they made up at the Dauntless shipyard in Essex. He'd go roaring up and down the river in it. Take his lady friends out on the Sound for a little you-know-what. John J. had his way with any number of other men's wives. Any gal he felt like." Rut's apple-cheeked face tightened. "A fella of that sort, it can really get to bothering him as the years pass."

"What can, Rut?"

"Me, I've got three beautiful daughters and I love them to death and I've never, ever cared that not a one of them was a boy. But John J. was the sort who did care. Anyhow, along comes World War Two and John J. gets himself declared 4-F. Bum knee, supposedly. Though it never kept him off of the squash court. The man kept right on living the high life at Four Chimneys while other good men fought and died. His family's steel mills didn't make out too badly, either, but don't get me started on that. Ed Kershaw got sent to the Pacific. Bessie stayed on as maid and cook. She gave birth to Milo just before Ed shipped out in '42. Me, I was in high school during the wartime years. I can remember Bessie well. She was no raving beauty, but she was a healthy young woman. Her husband was overseas for two years. And she was alone in that big house with John J. whenever Aunt Katherine went into New York to visit friends." Rut let out a long, regretful sigh. "Mitch, there's two different versions of how it happened. One's that he got drunk and forced himself on Bessie. The other's that the two of them were romantically involved. I'm inclined to believe the latter myself. Anyhow, I don't have to tell you what happened next, do I?"

"I guess not. You're telling me that Pete Mosher was the son of John J. Meier and Bessie Kershaw."

"Their bastard child—to use a not-so-quaint old expression."

Mitch sat there turning this over. "So that would have made Pete . . ."

"Poochie's brother," Rut said, snuffling through his nose. "Half-brother, to be technical. But if you swivel around and look at it another way, he was also half-brother to Milo. Pete was related to them both. He belonged—or I should say, *didn't* belong— to both families. Next you'll be asking me if Poochie and Milo knew about this."

"Did they?"

"Of course they did. That's why Milo nurses such a grudge toward that entire clan. Mind you, he also took an intense personal dislike to Poochie's husband, Coleman Vickers, who wasn't even on the scene yet. But the roots of Milo's animosity go back to John J. and what he did to Bessie. Give Milo half a chance and he'll still curse that man up, down and sideways."

"What happened once Bessie got pregnant?"

"When she got big enough to show, Bessie went away for several weeks to tend to a sick aunt up in Glastonbury. That was the cover story, anyhow. She did have an aunt up there. A Mosher who was a retired nurse. Bessie stayed with her until little Pete was born. Milo, who was still a toddler himself, went along with her. After she gave birth, Bessie came right back to work at Four Chimneys. The aunt agreed to raise the baby for her. John J. made sure Pete's financial needs were seen to. And nobody was any the wiser. By nobody I'm referring to Bessie's husband, Ed, when he came back from the war a year later."

"What about your Aunt Katherine, Rut? Did she know?"

"In those days, women like Aunt Katherine didn't ask any questions they didn't want to know the answers to."

"Meaning she looked the other way?"

"Meaning there was an unspoken understanding that men like

John J. kept a private life. And what was private stayed private. He'd wanted a son. Aunt Katherine couldn't give him one. Knowing her like I did, she more than likely took it as a failing on her own part that John J. bedded Bessie. Katherine was always inclined to doubt herself." The old postmaster drank the last of his stout, crossing his chubby ankles on the footstool before him. "Ed Kershaw put away his uniform and came back to work at Four Chimneys. Bessie's aunt raised the baby. And everything was fine. Until, that is, Bessie's aunt upped and died a few years later. Little Pete turned up here in town with the Millers. They took in a lot of charity cases. They also happened to live right across the street from Bessie and Ed. Hell, Pete and Milo even became playmates. But then Milo started hearing all of the whispers. Little kids repeat what they hear their parents saying, and they were saying that Bessie had had another man's son during the war. Apparently, somebody saw her up in Glastonbury while she was showing. Wasn't too hard to figure out who this other man was either—Pete was the spitting image of John J. Same blue eyes. Same long, bony nose. Poor Pete heard the whispers, too. He knew that his own mother was living right there across the street from him and wouldn't so much as acknowledge him."

"Ed must have heard the whispers, too, right?"

"You bet. He wouldn't believe them at first, not until some friend or another set him straight."

"And what did he do?"

"First, he took it out on Bessie," Rut recalled sadly. "Beat that woman until she was black and blue. Then he went looking for John J. with a shotgun. Our local lawman headed him off and locked him up until he'd cooled off. Ed had no choice but to cool off. John J. was a rich, powerful man. Ed was the hired help. So he swallowed his pride and kept on working for him and kept on beating Bessie senseless. Never, ever forgave her. When little Milo tried to stop him, Ed beat him, too. Which should tell you something about why Milo turned out the way he did. Mitch, I've always felt a special kind of sorry for that woman. Not once was she allowed to show Pete a mother's love. You can't tell me that didn't have something to do with Pete's troubles later on. It certainly destroyed her. All she was left with was her shame and the beatings that Ed gave her. Poor woman took her own life in, let's see, I think it was '52. Drank a whole bottle of insect poison. Milo found her on the kitchen floor one day when he came home from school." Rut shook his head disgustedly. "Awful business. After that, Ed had to raise Milo on his own. And live with his own shame."

"What happened to Pete?"

"John. J shipped him off to an English boarding school. That's where Pete did his growing up."

"Where did he spend his adult life?"

"Haven't a clue, Mitch. I never heard another peep about him."

"Did he and Poochie have any kind of a relationship?"

"None, as far as I know. Poochie was a good ten years older than Pete, don't forget. She was already away at Smith by the time he came to live with the Millers. But she was aware of the gossip from the get go, if that's what you're wondering. Not that the two of us have ever discussed Pete. My mom's the one who told me this."

"Did she say how Poochie handled the news?"

"Poochie never felt quite the same way toward her father after that. Steered plenty clear of him once she was old enough to. Settled in New York, not Dorset. When she married the Ambassador they lived in Washington, Paris, London—again, never Dorset. Not until John J. and Katherine had retired to Hobe Sound fulltime. Only then did Poochie and Coleman move into Four Chimneys. Claudia was a teenager by then. Prettiest thing you ever saw. Quite the little flirt, too, though you'd never know it now. Eric, he was a scrawny little bookworm."

"Did the two of them know Pete's real identity?"

"Don't believe so. I'm good friends with Eric and he's never seemed the slightest bit curious about Pete. And I've never raised the subject. Don't believe a man has any business telling a son about the sins of his father. Besides, this whole thing between John J. and Bessie happened over sixty years ago. It's ancient history."

"Maybe not so ancient, Rut," Mitch said quietly.

Rut shot a glance at him but left it alone. Just sat there, clutching his empty beer glass.

"Did Milo ever come to feel any kinship toward Pete?"

"None," Rut answered. "And it bugged the living hell out of him when Pete showed up here again a few years back. Every time Milo saw him peddling that bicycle of his down the street he'd see their mother lying dead on the kitchen floor. Milo told me so himself."

"I understand that Pete left quite a bit of money behind."

"Wouldn't surprise me. John J. probably laid a trust fund on him."

"Would Milo know about that? I'm asking because as Pete's half-brother he'd be in a position to inherit. Or at least think he was entitled to."

"You can bet he'd think that," Rut said. "If Milo knows, he's never said so to me. But I can guarantee you it would drive him nuts if Pete had himself a bag full of John J.'s money. Milo still feels that family owes him something after the set-to he had with Coleman Vickers. Only, there's one thing I'd like to say on Milo's behalf—the man's nine-tenths talk. He was a loud-mouthed little yipper growing up, and he's never changed. Sure, he's made his mistakes. But he's not nearly as bad as people think. Neither are Stevie and Donnie. Okay, they're not the sharpest knives in the drawer. But cold-blooded and rotten to the core? I don't think so."

The low March sun passed behind the trees, darkening the parlor significantly. Rut reached over and flicked on the lamp next to him.

"You don't think the brothers are behind Pete's death, is that it? What *do* you think happened to Pete?"

"I think this'll turn out to be what this kind of business is usually about."

Mitch found himself leaning forward in his chair. "Which is? . . ."

"Somebody wanting something more than they ought to. Get you another glass of stout, Mitch?"

"I'm good, thanks. But there is one other thing I need to ask you about. And you have to promise me it won't get back to Des."

The old man's face broke into a grin. "You want my niece's phone number after all. Sure you do. All it takes is that first whiff of spring to make a man—"

"Rut, I'd never do that to Des. Not my style. Which is not to say I *have* a style, but that isn't what I wanted to talk to you about. Was there a time a while back, maybe seven or eight years ago, when there were whispers about a certain girl in town?"

"What sort of a girl, son?"

"A girl who used to party with groups of men out on their boats."

Rut grew a bit more guarded. "Well, sir, there used to be a bar up on the Post Road called the High Life that always had a couple—two, three—of them kind hanging around. Yankee Doodle Motor Court was right next door. Mighty handy arrangement. But the High Life shut down a good fifteen years ago."

"Rut, I'm not talking about a pro. At least, not in the usual sense. This was a girl whose own family was making money off of her. She was very young. Too young. And drugs were involved. It's not a nice story."

The old postmaster shifted in his chair now, eyeing Mitch with intense suspicion. "Where's it coming from?"

"I'd rather not say."

"Can you tell me what kind of men were having their way with her?"

"The very best kind, Rut."

"I believe I'm reading you now," Rut said, rubbing his chin thoughtfully. "You're asking me if there was a teenaged girl here a few years back who was so messed up on drugs that she'd take on anyone, no questions asked."

"Was there, Rut?"

"I do remember hearing a little something about this," he conceded, a look of profound sorrow creasing his face. "But you'd better have that glass of stout, Mitch, because you're absolutely right about one thing. It's not a nice story."

CHAPTER 16

"GIRL, ARE YOU SAYING you *believe* Milo Kershaw just stumbled on those cans and bottles?" Yolie asked as they strode toward Eric and Danielle's weathered red barn. The Kershaw brothers' van was parked there next to Danielle's Subaru. "What did you do, see into the man's soul or something?"

"Or something," Des said. Although it turned out that she hadn't broken Milo completely after all. Not according to what Mitch had just reported to her over the phone about Milo and Pete having shared the same mother, Bessie Mosher. Milo had denied any knowledge of the name Mosher.

A wire enclosure adjoined the barn where twenty or so sheep were munching on hay from a trough. Dozens more dozed away on the ground inside the barn itself, which was stacked with bales of hay. A half-dozen new mothers were inside the birthing stalls, their lambs huddled around them for warmth and nourishment. Some of the floppy-eared little lambs had nestled together the same way Des's stray kittens did, using each other as pillows. Danielle was on her knees in there milking a newborn with a bottle. A pair of middle-school girls were gently bottle-feeding two other lambs, their cheeks flushed with pride.

"Some of them don't take to their mother right away," Danielle explained when she spotted Des and Yolie standing there.

"Aren't they just the sweetest things?" one of the girls cooed, stroking the cuddly little lamb.

"They sure are," Des said softly, thinking there was absolutely no way she could ever send these adorable lambs off to be slaughtered. She could never farm. "Danielle, Sergeant Snipes and I were looking for Stevie and Donnie."

"They're turning over the soil in the east meadow," Danielle said, kneeling there in her baggy overalls. "Mostly, they just complain a lot. I've never seen such a pair of big babies in my life."

Des thanked her and she and Yolie headed back outside past the chicken house in the direction of the greenhouses. The chickens were roaming around in the yard outside their house of sun-bleached boards and shingles. Within the ramshackle greenhouses, seeds were germinating in seed trays by the hundreds.

"So who do you think left Pete's haul at the foot of Milo's driveway?" Yolie asked as they walked, her braids glistening in the slanting sunlight. "His boys?"

"That makes the most sense. Then again, if they were behind all of this you'd think they'd be halfway to Mexico by now, wouldn't you?"

"Could be they're more calculating than you give them credit for."

"Check them out for yourself. Maybe you'll spot some hidden talent that I haven't."

The Kershaw brothers were out in the fieldstone-walled meadow slowly forking heaps of composted chicken manure into the raw, ready planting beds. The air was fragrant with the smell of the manure, the meadow underfoot moist and spongy. Stevie and Donnie were showing the effects of their night of drinking and carrying on. Both were slumped over their forks as they toiled away, their faces ashen, limbs heavy.

"How's it going, guys?" Des called to them.

"We're pushing chicken shit is how it's going," Stevie responded wearily.

"You'd think a dude with Eric's money would have one of those earth movers or something," Donnie grumbled, panting for breath.

"Man doesn't need no powerized equipment, little brother. He's got us."

Donnie leaned against his fork and peered at them, his red-rimmed eyes bleary. "Whoa, I'm seeing double—or I'm tripping."

"You're not tripping," Stevie said, looking Yolie up and down.

"Gentlemen, I'd like you to meet Sergeant Yolanda Snipes of the Major Crime Squad. Yolie, give it up for Dorset's own kings of cruel, the Kershaw boys. That tall stud is Stevie. The hirsute one's Donnie."

"What's hirsute mean?" Donnie demanded.

"I was referencing your beard," Des said to him.

Stevie wasn't saying anything. He was too busy ogling Yolie's super-sized boobage. Actually, both brothers were.

"Yo, I'm up here, guys," she said to them pleasantly. "Keep going north . . . *here* I am. Hi, nice to make eye contact with you."

"How would you two ladies like to go on a double-date with us some time?" Stevie asked.

Yolie studied him, hands on her hips. "Honey, you don't mess around with the get-acquainted thing, do you?"

"I'm no good at hiding my feelings," Stevie said, smirking at her.

"You say that like you *are* good at something."

"We don't look so hot right now. But we clean up real good."

"Well, I sure believe *half* of what you just said."

"Guys, this isn't a social call. Sergeant Snipes is looking into Pete's death."

Stevie fished a cigarette from the pocket of his flannel shirt and passed the pack over to Donnie. They lit their cigarettes in silence, all playfulness gone. They'd retreated into their prison shells.

"Know anything about it?" Yolie asked.

"We heard about it from Eric when we got here," Stevie replied, his face a blank.

"Did you know the victim?"

"We used to goof on him back in high school."

"You used to throw rocks at him," Des said reproachfully.

"We never hurt him or nothing," Donnie insisted. "Just having fun."

"I hear you, sure," Yolie said easily. "Does the name Mosher mean anything to you?"

"Our grandma on the old man's side was a Mosher," Stevie said.

"Do you know how your grandma died?" Des asked.

"How would we know that? We weren't even born yet."

"Your dad never mentioned it to you?"

"Nope," Stevie said, pulling on his cigarette.

"If I told you Pete's last name was Mosher what would you say?"

The brothers exchanged a guarded look before Donnie said, "There's tons of Moshers around here."

Des said, "Your dad claims he found some black trash bags full of returnables at the foot of your drive when he left for work this morning. You told me you were home by then from your night out with Allison, right?"

"Uh, okay . . ." Donnie said uncertainly.

"You do remember we talked this morning, don't you?"

"So what?" Stevie demanded.

"So did you guys notice those trash bags there at the foot of your drive when you made it home?"

"I don't remember seeing 'em," said Stevie.

"Me neither," said Donnie.

"Maybe you boys left them there yourselves after you killed Pete," Yolie suggested.

"It wasn't us, lady," Stevie said. "We weren't even there. And if you ask me, somebody's goofing on *you*. This is all some kind of a frame, this stuff going down as soon as we get out. Don't you think it's even a little weird?"

"Not really," Yolie replied. "Not if you did it."

"But we didn't," Donnie protested.

Quite possibly someone *had* fitted the Kershaw brothers for a frame, Des reflected. Using their release from prison as a convenient cover for a crime that they'd been planning for a good long while. Then again, quite possibly Stevie and Donnie were the culprits. Sometimes, the most obvious explanation was obvious for a reason.

"Oh, no-o-o . . ." Donnie groaned, his bloodshot eyes focusing across the meadow. "Please tell me I'm not seeing what I'm seeing."

A battered Ford F-150 pickup loaded down with more manure

was bumping its way toward them. Eric was behind the wheel, waving to them excitedly.

"Big brother, I will pass out in my own vomit if I have to fork one more load."

"That man is beyond crazy," Stevie concurred glumly. "He should be kept away from other people."

Eric cozied the truck up close to the bed the brothers were working and hopped out, a lanky, hyperkinetic bundle of geekiness in his shapeless sweater and too-short jeans, a he-guy Leatherman multipurpose knife sheathed to his belt. "Afternoon, Des!" he called to her. "Isn't this a *great* afternoon?"

"It's a fine one," Des said, thinking he needed to take sheep shears to all of that hair growing out of his ears. "Eric, I'd like you to meet Sgt. Yolie Snipes."

"*Re-eally* pleased to meet you." Eric dropped the tailgate of the truck, jumped in back and began shoveling the manure out onto the ground. The man was positively raring with bright-eyed vigor. "Sergeant, you are one lucky lady."

Yolie stared up at him with her mouth open. "Is that right?"

"Oh, absolutely. This is *the* most exciting day of the year to visit Four Chimneys Farm, right, boys?"

"Don't ask us, man," grumbled Stevie. "We're just spreading manure."

"It's not manure, it's gold!" exulted Eric. "By spreading it you are helping to create life. Honestly, if you can't get excited about this, what *can* you get excited about?"

"A hot bath," Donnie answered promptly. "A cold beer. A nice, soft place to lie down."

"You guys had it too soft up at Enfield," Eric scoffed, scooping the chicken manure out of his truck with manic energy. "Just sat around all day doing nothing. Not here. Here, we are taking on The Man."

"We're doing what?" asked Donnie, puzzled.

"Big corporations *control* the agribusiness now. It's all multinational this, genetically engineered that. Here we grow things the way nature intended them to be grown. No artificial anything. We're fighting the system here. This is right up your alley, don't you get it? You have a problem with authority and so do I."

"Man, are you like a farmer or some kind of cult leader?" Stevie wondered, shaking his mullet head at him wearily.

Des heard a car door slam. Danielle's Subaru was pulled up at the meadow gate and she was trudging her way toward them with a Thermos and two big plastic tumblers.

"I made some cold lemonade," she called out. "Thought you might be thirsty."

"Wow, thank you, ma'am," Stevie said gratefully.

"Real nice of you, ma'am," echoed Donnie.

Danielle filled the tumblers for them. The brothers gulped down their lemonade so fast that some of it streamed down their chins.

Danielle poured them more before she glanced somewhat meekly up at Eric in the truck. "I'm heading out for a few minutes, okay?" she said, twirling one of her pigtails around her fingers.

"Where are you off to?" A slight edge had crept into Eric's voice.

"I made a big pot of stew. I thought Mark might eat some."

"Yeah, okay," he said disapprovingly.

"Eric, if I don't take him food he doesn't eat."

"I said it was okay, didn't I? I just don't like him taking advantage of you."

"He's not."

"Fine, he's not," Eric snapped, effectively closing down the conversation.

"Big thanks for the lemonade, ma'am," said Stevie.

"You're quite welcome. I'll make some more for you tomorrow."

"We'll be here."

"Unless we're in jail," said Donnie, glancing at Des and Yolie.

Eric watched Danielle scurry back across the meadow, a concerned look on his face. Then he shook himself and said, "How about you guys start working that other bed over there? If you get moving, we can still mix this in before dark."

The brothers glanced unhappily at the broad swath of raw, untilled soil that awaited them fifty yards away.

"You're the boss," Stevie said defeatedly.

They slunk off, trailing their forks along behind them on the ground.

"Des, I still can't get over what happened this morning," Eric confessed, hopping down out of the truck. "That's my land down where Pete was found. It's upsetting, knowing that a murder was committed there. I feel responsible."

"You're not responsible for what somebody did to Pete."

"I know that, but it's going to take me a while to process this. Maybe I should plant some new trees down there."

"That'll have to wait," Yolie said. "It's still an active crime scene."

"When you're done with your investigation, I meant." Eric glanced over at the Kershaw brothers, who'd begun poking at the new planting bed with a tremendous lack of enthusiasm. "I just need to do *something*."

"Can you tell us anything about Pete?" Des asked him.

"Not a whole lot," he replied, blinking at her rapidly. "I did get the impression that there was something special about him. The old-timers at the soup kitchen would whisper to each other when he came in. Almost with a kind of awe. I asked Doug once whether Pete was a Vietnam War hero . . ." Eric left off, his eyes on a vehicle tearing its way up the gravel drive. It was Claudia's black Lexus SUV, and it was slowing up now, stopping.

"And what did Doug say?"

"He said no," Eric replied distractedly, his buoyant spirit deflating as Claudia got out of her Lexus and marched her way across the meadow toward them, her clenched fists pumping furiously.

"This don't look jolly," Yolie observed.

"When it comes to my sister there is no such thing."

In fact, Claudia looked exceedingly hostile. "Officers, *how* can you allow those criminals to work here!" she demanded, her eyes icy blue slits.

"The matter doesn't fall under our jurisdiction, Mrs. Widdifield," Des said as the Kershaw brothers stood there over in the planting bed missing nothing. "Stevie and Donnie were invited here."

"By m-me," Eric stammered, his eyes fastened on the soil at Claudia's feet. "I have to start field planting soon. I need the help. What's the big deal?"

"What's the big deal?" Claudia's voice dripped with scorn. "Eric, do I have to remind you what's happened here today?"

"You don't," he mumbled, his Adam's apple bobbing up and down. "And you don't need to talk to me that way either. I happen to be a full-fledged adult."

"Then why can't you act like one?"

"Why can't *you* let other p-people alone?" he sputtered angrily. "Those guys aren't hurting anybody. They're just slinging manure. If you want to pitch in, grab yourself a fork. Otherwise, go home."

Claudia stood her ground. "I *am* home."

"This is *my* farm, not yours. So just back off!"

"Eric . . ."

"And let people live their own lives, will you? Maybe then you'll actually have one of your own. And Danielle won't have Mark crying on her shoulder about what a cold-hearted *bitch* you are!"

Claudia drew her breath in, stung. "My marriage is *my* business."

"Oh, I see." Eric nodded his head up and down convulsively, blinking, blinking. "And my business is your business, too."

"It is when it threatens everyone else's health and safety."

"Get your own house in order, Claude. Stop trying to control mine. And mom's. And everybody else's." Now Eric flung himself into his truck, started it up and went roaring *bumpety-bump-bump* back across the meadow.

Claudia was left standing there, speechless, her face etched with strain. She was a deeply frightened woman, Des observed. And yet she hadn't been able to share her fears with Eric. Couldn't, wouldn't admit them to him. And so they butted heads. Again, to her surprise, Des felt sorry for this vanilla ice princess.

Another car door slammed shut. Soave had nosed his slicktop up behind Claudia's Lexus. He started toward them, his weight-lifter's chest puffed out, shaved head shining in the sunlight. Claudia immediately charged her way across the meadow toward him. Soave froze in his tracks, eyes widening as she got closer.

Yolie let out a sigh. "Maybe I'd better get his back for him."

"And maybe I'd better get yours," Des said, tagging along with her.

The Kershaw brothers just kept right on turning over their planting bed, taking in every bit of this.

"Lieutenant, these are convicted felons." Claudia was chest to chest with Soave. "*How* can they be permitted to be here?"

"We have no proof that they were involved, Mrs. Widdifield," he said soothingly. "We're still collecting evidence. These things take time."

"I don't mean to be difficult, Lieutenant, but I don't *have* time. I have a mother who is not in complete control of her faculties. I have a brother who is a dangerously naïve fool. I need results."

"And you'll get them, ma'am. Just give us a chance to do our job, okay?"

"Now you're trying to pacify me," Claudia sniffed. "Let me give you a word of advice—don't." She marched back to her Lexus now and got in, slamming the door behind her.

Soave exhaled with relief as she headed up the drive toward Four Chimneys. "Next time I see *that* coming I'm staying in the car with my doors locked."

"How'd you make out with that judge in New London?" Yolie asked him.

"Got it," he exclaimed, yanking the folded warrant from his

breast pocket. "Des, why don't you roll on back to that lawyer's office with this. Yolie and me will have ourselves a talk with Mrs. Vickers about her long-lost brother, Pete."

"Sounds good, Rico," Des said, reaching for the warrant.

He snatched it back from her; his goateed chin stuck out belligerently. "How come it feels like me and her are just along for the ride? You've generated every single productive lead so far."

Des sighed inwardly. Rico could do this—get all competitive and turfy. It was his insecurity showing. "Not even close, wow man. You've pretty much nailed down what happened to the Gullwing, haven't you?"

"Which would do us some good if we actually *had* the Gullwing. Guess what? We don't."

"Rico, I'm not trying to bogart your investigation. All I'm doing is taking direction from you."

"So kindly stuff your male ego crap, little man," Yolie agreed.

Soave shot a scowl at her before he turned back to Des. "How did you come by all of this family history, anyhow?"

"Got it off of the local gossip mill."

"By way of who, Berger? Because this has his jumbo-sized shadow looming all over it."

"My man does not loom."

"What is he, your unofficial deputy now?"

"Rico, I've got no agenda here. If we close this out, you're the one who gets the props, not me. It's your investigation. If you want me off of it, just say so and I'm gone."

"God, I hate it when you act all accommodating and reasonable. Bugs the hell out of me."

"Do you want me in or don't you?"

"In," he barked. "Go talk to that lawyer lady about Pete Mosher's will."

"Fine." She pocketed the warrant, Yolie standing there grinning at her.

"You want to know something?" Soave fumed. "My life was way simpler before there were so damned many *women* in it."

"Maybe so, Rico. But you dressed like a chump."

"Plus you never, ever got any touch," Yolie added.

"Are you ladies quite through?" he demanded, glowering at them. "Des, reach out to us soon as you have something."

Des was about to say she'd do just that when things suddenly got a lot simpler. A Dodge minivan was bouncing its way up the gravel drive toward Four Chimneys. And behind the wheel was Glynis Fairchild-Forniaux, attorney at law.

"In answer to what will doubtless be your first question, I'm present for this interview in my capacity as Mrs. Vickers's attorney," Glynis announced once she'd examined the judge's warrant carefully. She limped on her bandaged ankle over to a chintz armchair and sat, a batch of thick files in her lap. Glynis had traded in her jeans for gray flannel slacks. Her fluffy blond hair was pulled back in a ponytail. Her manner was brisk and confident. "As previously requested, I come bearing the last will and testament of Peter Ashton Mosher. I also have a copy of John J. Meier's will, which was filed in Probate Court in New London some thirty years ago and is therefore a matter of public record."

They'd gathered in the parlor, with its faded, pee-stained furniture, its priceless art and Poochie's bizarre collections of sunglasses and water pistols. A couple of lamps were on, since dusk was fast approaching. Poochie sat in an armchair with Bailey asleep in her lap. She had poured herself a generous jolt of brandy from the decanter on the side table and was sipping from it. Soave and Yolie faced them on the sofa.

Des had started out there, but found it so hard to keep her eyes off of Giacometti's self-portrait that she'd moved over to a chair. "When you and I spoke earlier," she said to Glynis, "you didn't tell me you were Poochie's attorney."

"I'm under no obligation to divulge the identity of a client. You'd been tasked with notifying Peter Mosher's next of kin of his death. I told you that by speaking to me you'd dispatched your official responsibility. And you had."

"We can talk like regular people, can't we, dear?" Poochie chided Glynis, glancing down into her brandy snifter. The great lady wore her sadness like a mask. Her lively, lovely face was expressionless. "Des, I *am* Pete's next of kin and Glynis *is* my lawyer. We Smithies stick together, after all. Besides, her father was our family attorney, as was his father. We place great stock in continuity." Poochie sipped her brandy, stroking Bailey absently. "I told her that you'd requested another interview, and she'd insisted upon being here—assuming that's all right with you."

"Absolutely, ma'am," Soave assured Poochie. "It's your legal right."

"Will Mr. Tolliver be joining us?" Des asked.

"No, Tolly's cutting back my rosebushes," Poochie replied with a wave of her hand. "Got his gloves and pruners and off he went. He's been upset ever since you three spoke to him this morning."

"We have to look at everyone," Yolie said. "It was nothing personal."

"I don't wish to be rudely contradictory, Sergeant, but it was very personal. Also hurtful. You've completely failed to grasp our situation. Tolly would never, ever steal from me." Poochie gazed out the window at her view of the river. Her face had a fond, faraway look on it. "Funny, him wanting to garden all of a sudden. When we were first married, he wouldn't go near it. Ladies' work, he called it."

Soave looked at Des, puzzled. Des kept her own expression neutral, though she could feel her stomach muscles flutter.

Glynis smiled gently at her client. "Poochie, it's Tolly who we were discussing."

"And your point is? . . ."

"You just said that when you two were first married he disliked gardening."

"No, dear, you're mistaken. Tolly and I have never been married. But I do wish he'd sit in on this conversation. He ought to be here."

"Would you like us to go get him?" Des offered.

"No, leave him be. He needs to work out his creative tensions." Poochie reached for the brandy decanter and poured more of it into her snifter.

"Poochie, we've been told that Peter Mosher was the offspring of your father, John J. Meier, and the family maid, Bessie Mosher," Des began. Soave wanted her to get it rolling. "Can you confirm this?"

"I can," Poochie said forthrightly.

"We've requested access to Mr. Mosher's will so that we might learn who he'd named as his beneficiaries."

"I have his most recent financial statements as well." Glynis opened one of the files in her lap, scanning it. "The income from Mr. Mosher's trust fund was more than adequate for him to live on comfortably. In point of fact, we hadn't even touched his interest income for more than twenty years. Consequently, his assets have . . ." Glynis, cleared her throat. "At the time of his death, Peter Mosher was worth somewhere in the vicinity of eighteen million dollars."

"Shut up!" Yolie immediately clapped a hand over her mouth. "*So* sorry. Didn't mean for that to . . . are you *sure* about this?"

"Quite sure, Sergeant," Glynis replied tartly.

"But why does a man worth that kind of green live like he was living?"

Glynis looked to Poochie for an answer.

Poochie was staring down at Bailey in her lap, stroking the old golden retriever with so much focused intent that she seemed not be listening. "I wish I could give you a decent answer, Sergeant," she replied softly. "But Peter and I hardly knew each other. That was father's wish. For mother's sake, he didn't want the two of us to form an attachment."

Soave's cell phone rang. He answered it and listened a moment before he glanced up at Poochie and said, "Doug Garvey's here."

"Send him through."

"He can pass," Soave said into the phone, flicking it off. "Go ahead, Des."

"Poochie, did your mother ever speak to you about Peter?"

"Absolutely never," Poochie replied. "Mother wasn't one to share her secrets. Mind you, she knew the truth about him. How could she not? There were *so* many whispers around town. I was only a girl, yet I can still remember them. I can remember the shame as well. And father *did* feel shame, so young Peter had to go and young Peter did go—off to boarding school." Poochie sipped her brandy, swirling it around in the snifter. "He wrote father regularly from England. Father kept a post office box for that sole purpose. He would read each letter carefully, then burn it. He burned all of Peter's letters. He confided this to me over martinis one evening when I was home from Smith. Father told me things he could never tell Mother." Poochie's face had a faraway look on it again, though this one was not especially fond. "I was his confidante, his pet, his plucky little pard."

Des heard the flatulent rumble of a vehicle arriving out front, a car door slamming, heavy footsteps on the gravel. Then the front door opened and a husky male voice called out, "You around, Pooch?!"

"In here, Dougie!"

Doug Garvey lumbered into the parlor jangling a set of keys. "Brought you that Jeep of mine to get around in."

"Bless you, dear. Need a lift back to the station?"

"Not necessary," Doug said, his eyes flicking around at everyone curiously. "I'm meeting one of my boys down at the foot of the drive in a minute. I'll leave these keys by the front door."

"Don't people ring doorbells in this town?" Soave wondered as Doug tromped back outside.

"Doug is a friend. Why would he do that?" Poochie hesitated now, frowning. "Sorry, where was? . . ."

"Peter was away at boarding school," Glynis reminded her.

"And giving every appearance of being a bright, outgoing young man," she continued, nodding her head. "He played soccer and rugby, was a fine horseman. An excellent shot, too, all of which made father exceedingly proud. But Peter didn't much care for university life. He left Cambridge during his second year and settled in London, where he fell in with a rather wild crowd. That 'mod' scene was all the rage, and Peter embraced it fully—no cares, no worries, nothing but one big party. Father did keep him comfortably provided for, after all. Winters, he'd ski in Gstaad. Summers, he'd head for St. Tropez. He took lots of girlfriends. Dropped them when he felt like it. Was seldom sober. Eventually, when Coleman was posted to Paris, I had him to the residence for lunch." Poochie paused, her face darkening. "It was not easy for either of us. I was a good little diplomat's wife. Peter was a full-time hedonist. Exceedingly hostile to me. High on pot, I might add. He offered to smoke some with me. He'd recently been up to the Montreux Jazz Festival, where he'd seen a group that he wanted to manage. Champion somebody and . . ." She shook her head. "I can't remember their name. It came to nothing. None of Peter's plans ever amounted to anything. They were drug-induced fantasies. He went on who knows how many LSD trips. I can't say for certain whether it was the drugs that triggered the . . . change in him. I only know that Peter became uncontrollable, given to fits of wild, schizophrenic rage. In 1971, he attacked a policeman and had to be put in restraints in a London hospital. A friend of his wrote Father, who saw to it that Peter was transferred to a highly regarded psychiatric institute in Lausanne, Switzerland. Not that they actually helped him. Mostly, they just kept him sedated. If they didn't he'd try to escape."

"Did your father think about hospitalizing him closer to home?" Soave wondered.

"Switzerland *was* Peter's home," Poochie answered in a strained voice. "I heard very little about him after that. Coleman and I were posted back to Washington. And then, of course, Father passed away."

"After John J.'s death in '74 our firm took over guardianship of Peter's financial affairs," Glynis stated. "We paid for his long-term care by drawing on the income from his trust fund. In 1983 Peter was transferred to another institute, in Livorno, Italy. Their experimental treatments were showing promising results. Their security, however, left a great deal to be desired. Peter was able to discharge himself two months after he arrived, at which point he slipped under the radar. Wandered God only knows where for years. Had no known means of support. Apparently, he was able to get a passport, because he did make his way back to America eventually."

"Back to Dorset," Poochie said. "He just showed up here one day, filthy and homeless. Doug phoned me after he'd found him. I drove straight down to the filling station, hugged him and said, 'Welcome home, Brother.' He just looked away and said two words to me: 'Sneaky Pete.' Those were the only two words he ever spoke. I brought him back here, set him up in a room, ordered him some clothes from the men's shop. But he ran away that very night. Turned up back at Doug's like a stray animal. Doug brought him back here but the same thing happened again. Finally, Doug was kind enough to put him up. But it was all so incredibly heartbreaking. I couldn't help thinking Peter *wanted* his family's love. He could have gone anywhere in the world and he chose to come *here*. And yet he wouldn't speak to me or let me . . ." Poochie's eyes filled with tears. They spilled down her cheeks. She swiped at them with her hand. "I'm sorry to be so emotional. But this is very hard for me."

"I was rebuffed as well," Glynis put in. "He wouldn't touch a penny of his money."

"Poochie, what did you tell Eric and Claudia when you brought Peter home?" Des asked.

"That he was an old childhood chum fallen on hard times. Eric was fine with that, chiefly because he smelled a cheap, useful field worker. Claudia told me I'd lost my mind. I've never fit her idea of a suitable mother, I'm afraid. I didn't tell them who Peter was. But I intend to this very evening. They deserve to know, and I believe I'm free to speak the truth now. Is that all right, Glynis?"

"As far as I'm concerned, it's fine."

"Father didn't want them to know. He made it very clear to me on his deathbed. Mother was in failing health herself. She died less than three months after father."

"How was Peter provided for in his will?" Des asked Glynis.

Glynis scanned John J. Meier's file folder before she said, "He'd already seen to Peter's needs when he set up the trust fund. Initially, it consisted of shares in the Meier Steel Corporation equal to but not exceeding the sum of five million dollars—which over the past thirty-some years has grown into the eighteen-million-dollar figure we discussed. The vast majority of John J.'s holdings, including Four Chimneys, he left to Poochie."

"Was anyone else provided for?"

"Bessie Mosher was long dead, if that's what you're wondering."

"By her own hand, I'm told."

"Yes," Poochie said. "Father felt no financial obligation toward Ed or Bessie's other son, Milo. He provided only for Peter."

"With certain safeguards," Glynis pointed out. "Peter had been institutionalized by this time, after all. Legal guardianship was granted to my father, who subsequently signed it over to me when he retired from the firm."

"Did Peter ever marry?" Des asked.

"There was a brief misadventure with a German fashion model back in, oh, '66," Poochie recalled. "Apparently, they ran off and got hitched in Marbella, both of them high as kites. A week later it turned out she was still legally married to another man, so her marriage to Peter was annulled or voided or whatever it is they do. She didn't get a penny off of him."

"How about children—did he ever have any?"

Poochie gazed at Des blankly. "Why, no."

"None that we are presently aware of," Glynis hedged, going legalese. "To the best of our knowledge, Peter died without issue."

"But you're not sure?"

"As sure as we can be. No one has come forward to make any such claim."

"Say someone does. What happens then?"

Glynis studied the Can Man's last will and testament, her lips pursed primly. "No provision was made for heirs. And with good reason, I might add. Peter's doctors kept him in a drugged state. There was genuine concern that an unscrupulous nurse might try to get herself pregnant by him, produce an heir and make a claim to his fortune. Such things have been known to happen. John J. made sure that it could not by spelling out unequivocally that upon Peter's death the entirety of his trust fund passes to Poochie and no one else. You're correct to suggest that an unknown heir could come forward and try to contest it, thereby throwing the ball into a judge's court, but John J.'s wishes were quite clear. Absolutely no one else is provided for."

No one like, say, Pete's half-brother Milo. Or his old friend Doug Garvey. Neither man had a financial upside in seeing Pete dead. At least none that was apparent to Des. "Forgive me if this sounds morbid, but who would his trust fund have passed to if Poochie had predeceased him?"

"It would have gone to her heirs, Eric and Claudia," Glynis replied.

"Poochie, may we talk about your own estate for a moment?"

Poochie didn't respond. Didn't even seem to be listening to Des. She was too busy gazing at Yolie. "You have such a sad aura, sergeant," she observed. "A healthy girl like you ought to have a man in her life."

Yolie swallowed uncomfortably. "What makes you think I don't?"

"Because I know you're lonely. You've never been so lonely."

"I-I don't know what you're talking about," responded Yolie, seriously weirded out.

"Poochie, we seem to be straying a bit," Glynis put in tactfully. "Des wants to know who stands to inherit from you. You're under no legal obligation to respond, The judge's warrant applies to the contents of Peter's will, not your own."

"I don't have anything to hide, do I?"

"No, of course not."

"Then tell Des what she wants to know."

"As you wish," Glynis said deferentially. "In fact, there *is* one slightly unusual wrinkle. John J. was very particular about this house and land, all two hundred and seven acres of it. As his sole male issue Peter stood to inherit Four Chimneys upon Poochie's death—*not* Claudia and Eric."

"Did that include the house's contents?" Des asked.

The attorney shot a quick glance at Poochie before she said, "The contents of the house are considered separate. As are Poochie's own financial assets, which are hers to distribute as she sees fit. But as to Four Chimneys itself, John J.'s wishes were quite specific."

"So, in a sense, Poochie and Peter have owned Four Chimneys together all of these years, am I right?"

"You are," Glynis replied. "But now that Peter has predeceased her, it will pass to Claudia and Eric—and from them on to Bement. Should Eric and Danielle have a child, then he or she would share title with Bement until one of—"

"Stop this horrid nonsense!" Poochie erupted suddenly. "I cannot abide it!"

"We're trying to help, Mrs. Vickers," Soave said. "Sorry if this is upsetting to you."

"It's *very* upsetting!" Poochie had grown highly agitated. "I feel as if my cold dead flesh were being picked apart by turkey vultures. I *hate* talking about money. I *won't*! Glynis, you're on your own. I'm starting dinner." She scrambled out from underneath Bailey and charged off toward the kitchen.

The snoozing dog remained where he was. In terms of alertness, Bailey was only slightly keener than a napa cabbage.

Soave watched Poochie go, tugging at his goatee thoughtfully. "How big an estate are we talking about?"

"I'm not going to talk specifics," Glynis answered, hands folded neatly in her lap. "I will say that Poochie was born into great wealth, married great wealth and has amassed a considerable amount through her own hard work." She glanced at her wristwatch. "Now, if you'll excuse me, I have to return to soccer mom mode. Number two daughter needs picking up."

"Glynis, there's something else that's staring us right in the face," Des said.

Glynis returned the files to her briefcase and snapped it shut. "Which is? . . ."

"Poochie herself. She's been acting a little strange lately."

"I heard that," Yolie agreed. "What *was* that about my aura?"

"That was just Poochie being Poochie, Sergeant. She's apt to say the oddest things." Glynis hobbled her way across the parlor toward the front hall, the three of them joining her. "When I was fourteen she pulled me aside and told me to focus my intellectual energy on science. Geology, specifically. Why? Because I was obviously destined to become the first woman in history to reach the planet Mars."

They headed out into the front courtyard. Doug's Jeep was parked there alongside their Crown Vics and Glynis's mini-van.

"Poochie is also very upset about Peter," Glynis added. "Perfectly understandable under the circumstances."

"Perfectly," Des allowed. "Except I've been getting her out of a lot of jams lately. And Claudia wants power of attorney over the family's financial affairs. She's told me so. Given that we've been talking about estates worth millions of dollars, it's hard not to wonder if it all connects up."

Glynis opened the door to her minivan and set her briefcase inside. "I regret that Claudia spoke to you about this matter. I've tried to discourage her from pursuing it. As far I'm concerned, Poochie remains perfectly capable."

"Glynis, there are a whole lot of candy bars squirreled away in that attic."

"What of it?" Glynis said mildly. "When I cleaned out my father's attic I discovered that he'd stolen ashtrays from seemingly every saloon, nightclub and restaurant he'd been to since his undergraduate days at Harvard. There were *thousands* of them. This was a man who didn't smoke. And he was practicing good, solid law right up until the day he died."

"Claudia wants Poochie to see a doctor."

"As do I. Poochie hasn't had a checkup in years. But do you nuke the entire family in order to force her hand? You do not, as I've told Claudia again and again." Glynis climbed in and started the engine, rolling down her window. "I've also told her that if she chooses to pursue this she'll have to retain another attorney. *Poochie* is my client."

Glynis put the minivan in gear and took off down the drive. The three of them stood there in the courtyard watching her go, the setting sun casting a golden reflection off of her back window.

"We should be bearing in mind that Pete was ten years younger than Poochie," Des said quietly.

Soave furrowed his brow at her. "Meaning what?"

"That our Can Man stood a better than decent chance of coming into this whole place. Or I should say his trust fund did—with Glynis Fairchild-Forniaux running the show."

"You've got your eye on her, is that it?"

"She's a lawyer, Rico, and therefore has to be considered not above reproach."

"Me, I keep chewing on the Gullwing. So what if it was stolen to provide cover for the murder? It's still the key. If we find our thieves, we find our killers."

"Could be that somebody local hired a pair of outsiders to jack it while they killed Pete themselves," Yolie pointed out. "Even so, I'm with you. We nail our jackers they'll give us the killers."

"Your money's on Claudia, am I right?" Soave asked Des. "You think Claudia's got a full-blown case of the grabbies."

"It sure does play," Yolie agreed. "Only, who's in on it with her?"

"She and Eric don't get along," Des said. "She doesn't get along with her husband, Mark, either."

"What about Guy Tolliver?" Soave asked.

"Him she can't stand."

"No, I mean, is there any chance *he's* behind it?"

"Rico, I honestly don't see why he'd bother."

"What if the old lady asked him to?"

Des studied him intently. "Are you just spitballing or what?"

"Or what. We know that Poochie took her recyclables down to the road right around the time of Pete's death. Where was Tolliver?"

"Asleep in bed. Or so he claims."

"What if he wasn't? What if *they* killed Pete? Christ, you want to talk motive? She inherits eighteen mil. How do we know that batty old lady didn't hire somebody—say, the Kershaw brothers—to steal her very own car? How do we know she hasn't engineered this whole thing herself? How do we know she isn't crazy like a fox?"

"We don't, Rico," Des answered, shivering. The sun had fallen behind the bluffs over Essex, and she suddenly felt cold without her jacket. She popped her trunk and grabbed it and put it on, burying her hands deep in her pockets. "We don't know anything."

"Seems to me," Yolie said slowly, "Milo Kershaw's hatred for this family runs way deep. Could be he feels entitled to get in on some of their riches. Are you with?"

"With," Des said, nodding. "We can't ignore that all of this went down as soon as Stevie and Donnie got home from Enfield. We also can't overlook that Pete's haul somehow turned up at the foot of their drive. What we don't know is what it means. Were those two bad boys waiting behind bars all of this time for another go at the Vickers? Or was someone else just waiting for them to get out so they could pin it on them? Also, let's not forget that their sister, Justine, is seriously involved with Poochie's grandson, Bement."

Soave considered that for a moment. "You have any idea how they—?"

"Rico, *please* don't ask me how their romance factors into this. Because I really, really don't know."

He looked at her in surprise. "Are you okay, Des?"

"No, I'm not okay. I'm pissed as hell. This is my place, Rico. I don't like it that somebody has been moving me around like a fool. I don't like it at all. Whoever the hell they are, they are going down. Because nobody punks me in my own home, understand? *Nobody.*"

Chapter 17

During boating season, boisterous young sun-kissed singles crammed their way into the Mucky Duck's narrow barroom to drink up and hook up. There were forty-five different kinds of beer, at least a dozen on draft. There were dartboards. The sound system blared good time rock 'n' roll.

On a chilly weeknight in March, the dockside pub was still home to a singles crowd, but nobody rocked and absolutely nothing rolled. These regulars were older and gloomier, not to mention exclusively male. By unwritten accord, this was Dorset's designated haven for divorced men. It was their place. Night after night, they parked their tartan-slacked selves at the bar and drank their martinis and watched the business news wrap-up on CNBC, eyes hollow, shoulders slumped. Most were professional men between forty-five and sixty. Most knew each other. But they didn't converse. And they didn't go home. Those belonged to their ex-wives now. So they came here and they sat at the bar and they drank, night after night.

There was a name in Dorset for these men. They were called Mucky Duckers.

Mitch had to pass through the bar to reach the dining room. During the summer, this could be something of a battle. Tonight, hardly anyone blocked his path. Just one rather pouchy man in an Izod shirt and rumpled khakis who was paying his tab at the cash register. It was Mark Widdifield. Mitch only knew him from around town to smile and say hello to.

In response, Mark instantly turned bright red and fled for the door. The man just took off. It wasn't quite so extreme a rejection as the one that Mitch had received from the late Pete Mosher. But it wasn't exactly a warm fuzzy either.

The Mucky Duck's dining room served burgers, fish and chips, a pretty decent clam chowder. It was a small room, no more than twenty tables. Only two couples were eating in there. Seated at a table in the corner, over a nearly empty glass of red wine, was Danielle Vickers. She'd called his house ten minutes ago and asked him if he could meet her there. She'd sounded quite frantic.

As Mitch sat down across from her, he sensed that something serious was up. Danielle looked rattled. Not to mention tousled. Her hair and clothing seemed unusually disheveled. And she smelled sweaty. Behind those smudged, unflattering wire-framed glasses, her eyes seemed puffy. To Mitch, she came off like a guilt-wracked married woman who'd just had a furtive tumble upstairs on the office sofa with her lover. This would certainly explain the way Mark had bolted out of there.

"Are you okay, Danielle?"

"W-Why, yes," she stammered, tongue flicking at her lips nervously. "I just . . . needed to talk. Hope I didn't drag you away from Des."

"No, she needed to spend some alone time in her studio. This case is getting to her. What about Eric?"

"Tonight's his night to watch pro hockey on TV with Rut," replied Danielle, glancing up anxiously as the waitress approached.

Mitch had already hoovered up two immense bowls of his world famous American chop suey, so he settled for a Double Diamond on draft. Danielle asked for another red wine. When the waitress left he said, "Danielle, I just bumped into Mark in the bar. He was not happy to see me."

She lowered her eyes, swallowing uncomfortably. "You have some ideas about us, haven't you?"

"I don't, but Eric does. He asked me if you were mixed up with someone. I got the feeling he actually thought it might be me."

"Is that so hard to imagine?" Danielle squinted across the table at him, her gaze slightly unfocused. She was quite tipsy, he now realized. "Do you find me that unattractive?"

"I wasn't suggesting that. I just meant that you and I know we're not involved."

"We know that, but Eric doesn't," she said, gripping the wine glass in her work-roughened hands. "And it so happens he's insanely jealous. He's so upbeat and positive. Hates negativity of any kind. And yet he's prone to unfounded jealousy. He was a tongue-tied nerd when we met at Bates. He'd never even kissed a girl before. He's still deeply insecure when it comes to women. And he feels threatened by Mark, who he thinks is very dashing."

The waitress returned with their drinks. Danielle reached for her wine and tossed back half of it right away. Mitch sipped his beer, watching her carefully.

"We did have a drink together just now," she admitted. "An innocent drink. Mark wouldn't let me leave this afternoon unless I promised to come back for one. Then I told him I needed to speak to you and he'd have to go. That's why he took off in such a huff when he saw you. Mark has . . ." Danielle let out a jagged sigh. "Mark has problems. I'm beginning to think there's no such thing as a man who doesn't."

"Well, we are people, after all."

Her eyes met and held his. "I've given Eric no reason to be jealous, Mitch. You do believe me, don't you?"

"Sure, I do," he said, because she needed to hear the words.

"This afternoon, I found Mark sitting up there in his office weeping uncontrollably. I'm holding out a lifeline to him. If I don't, I'm afraid he'll crawl into a deep black hole and Claudia will never get him back."

"Does she want him back?"

"In her heart, I believe she does. She's just so intolerant of weakness. She probably thinks I'm meddling. Maybe I am. But I can't stand to see Mark lose hold of himself this way. He's acting so crazy. Today he . . ." She leaned across the table toward Mitch, lowering her voice. "He withdrew the last five-thousand dollars he had left in his account. He wants to run away with me to St. Kitt's. He has a friend with a house where we could stay."

"Danielle, you just told me you two weren't involved."

"We're *not*. Nothing has happened between us, Mitch. And nothing ever will, as far as I'm concerned. But Mark is so starved for affection that I'm afraid he's taken my feelings for him the wrong way. It's insane, I know. He's married to a glamorous, accomplished beauty. I'm a Sheetrocker's daughter who smells of the barnyard. Why on earth would he want me?"

"Strange things happen," Mitch said, reflecting on the unlikely-hood of himself and Des. Himself and Maisie. Himself and, well, anyone.

"He thinks I'll make him happy. That's what he keeps saying." Danielle tapped her wine glass distractedly with a chipped fingernail. "Maybe it's my fault. When he kissed me goodbye yesterday, I-I let it go a bit farther than I should have. But I was caught by surprise, and flattered. Maybe I gave him the idea that we . . . that something is going on between us. I'm concerned that Des and her people may think so, too. They'll get around to examining the banking records of everyone in the family, won't they?"

"Most likely."

"By withdrawing his money like that, Mark has invited speculation that he used it to pay someone off. They might even think he's behind the whole thing. I'm so afraid they'll jump to that conclusion. Mark is deathly concerned about it."

"Why doesn't he just put the money back in the bank?"

"He's being juvenile, that's why. He thinks that by casting deep, dark suspicion upon himself this way he's proving how much he loves me." She drank down what was left of her wine. "Like I said, he has problems."

"What do you want me to do, Danielle?"

"Tell Des. Tell her quietly, so there won't be any fallout. This mustn't get back to Eric or Claudia. It would be needlessly hurtful." Her eyes searched his face imploringly. "Can you do that?"

"I can try. Only, are you sure Mark *isn't* involved in Pete's death?"

"Mitch, this is a man so paralyzed by depression that he can barely dress himself, let alone arrange a car theft and a killing." Danielle snuffled, her eyes filling with tears. "He wants to run away to an enchanted isle with *me*. How screwed up is that?"

"Stop running yourself down, will you? I'll talk to Des. I'm sure she can keep it confidential. God knows Eric and Claudia already have enough on their plates." He reached for his beer mug and took a sip. "Pete's identity must have come as quite a surprise to them."

"Oh, it absolutely did," Danielle acknowledged. "I was just putting supper on the table when Poochie called and told Eric to meet her at Claudia's right away. And as soon as we sat down Poochie dropped this bomb on them about old Pete." A slight smile lifted Danielle's downcast face. "I don't know which upset Claudia more—finding out she had a homeless man for an uncle or that she shares a blood link with the Kershaws."

"How did Eric take it?"

"Eric never lets on if something has gotten to him. He just sticks out his chin and says, fine, okay."

"Is there any chance that he's known the truth about Pete all along?"

"I doubt it, Mitch. Eric's notoriously bad at keeping secrets. One sip of wine and he just blurts them out. I'm almost certain he didn't know. Besides, this situation doesn't affect us one bit. Pete's fortune goes to Poochie, and she's already rich, and we're already not." Danielle let out a brittle laugh. "The more things change, the more they don't."

Mitch studied her. Despite all she'd gotten off her chest, Danielle was still giving off an edgy, animal vibe. Something was roiling her. Talking wasn't helping. The wine wasn't helping. "Can I give you a ride home?"

"I'm going to sit here a while longer." She signaled the waitress for another glass of wine. "And put away your money. I'm treating."

"Thanks. Will you be okay to drive?"

"Not to worry. I'll have a coffee before I leave, okay?"

"Sure, okay." Mitch saw no point in pressing the issue. Danielle wasn't driving anywhere. Not for a while anyway. As soon as he walked out that door she'd be heading right back upstairs to Mark's office for another sweaty round of inside-the-family boinkage. He was positive. "Take care of yourself, Danielle."

"Mitch, am I a huge disappointment to you?" she asked suddenly.

"Who am I to judge you?"

"I don't know," she confessed, her lower lip quivering. "I just wondered."

"We all do the best we can, Danielle. Sometimes we do better than others. But I'd never sit in judgment of you. You'll get only friendship from me. And a ride home if you need one. Call if you do, okay?"

She reached for Mitch's hand and pulled it to her weathered cheek. "Okay, Mitch," she said softly, grazing his knuckles with her lips before she let go.

Then the waitress brought Danielle her wine and she took a sip and gazed off into space, somewhere else. Mitch left her there that way as he trudged his way past the legion of the lost and lonely at the bar and back out into the cold March night.

McGee's was shutting down for the night. The diner's illuminated sign was off, most of the inside lights out. Two cars were left in the parking lot. Mitch idled there in his pickup and waited.

She came scuffing out of the kitchen door at a few minutes past ten, a denim jacket thrown over her waitress uniform. He pulled up next to her, rolling down his window.

Allison peered at him with a hopeful smile on her round, freckly face. "Hey there, Mr. Movie Guy," she exclaimed, resting her forearms on his door. "Didn't expect to see you back here tonight."

"You did say you wanted to have a drink some time, didn't you?"

Allison weighed this, her lower lip stuck out. "I dunno, it looked to me like you and the trooper lady were getting along pretty good this afternoon."

"Is that a problem?"

"You want to get into some trouble, don't you?" Allison shook her head of short, streaky hair at him. "Try another waitress. Try another diner."

"This is the only diner in Dorset."

"Then try screwing yourself," she snapped, starting away from his truck.

"Wait a minute, will you? Can I please get a do-over?"

She didn't say yes or no. Just stood there in the empty parking lot with a distrustful expression on her face.

"I've got a lot on my mind tonight, and I didn't feel like being alone. Sometimes, it helps to talk things out. I was driving by and I thought of you, okay?"

"Mitch, I appreciate the offer or whatever this is, but I've been on my feet for like twelve straight hours. All I want to do is go home and soak them."

"I have a perfectly good bathtub at my place. Also a fresh box of Epsom salts."

"What kind of a guy keeps Epsom salts around?" she said in disbelief.

"You don't have much experience with Jewish men, do you? Believe me, once you've gone Semite you'll never go back."

"So, what, you're inviting me over?" she asked him shyly.

"I'll make a fire. We'll have a glass of wine. I'm harmless."

"No way you're harmless. But sure, why not?"

He waited for her to start up her Volkswagen Jetta before he pulled out of the lot and headed down Old Shore, Allison following a cautious distance behind him. When he pulled into the Peck's Point Nature Preserve he flicked on his brights, startling three deer right there before him. They pranced off into the darkness and disappeared. At the end of the dirt road Mitch used his access card for the security gate. It lifted up and he went thumping and bumping slowly across the narrow quarter-mile-long wooden causeway out to the island, Allison tailing him as the gate lowered after her.

It was a good ten degrees colder out here than on shore. The light of the rising three-quarter moon shimmered on the calm waters of the Sound.

He opened the front door and flicked on a light. Allison followed him inside, looking very wide-eyed and uncertain. Clemmie moseyed over to check her out. Decided she didn't like the smell of her and darted upstairs to the sleeping loft. Mitch took off his jacket and started building a fire in the fireplace.

Allison stood there in her waitress uniform gazing around at the exposed chestnut beams, the pieces of found furniture, stacks of books, papers, DVDs. "This is not what I was expecting at all," she told him, her voice hushed.

"You were expecting a mansion?"

"God, no, it's just . . . it's like a fantasy, you know?"

"I absolutely do." Mitch lit a match to the crumpled newspaper under his kindling and took a bellows to it. Right away, the wood began to crackle. "Sometimes I look out the window and I can't believe I'm living here."

Her gaze fell on his Stratocaster. "Can you play me something?"

"I'm not that kind of guitar player."

"What kind?"

"The kind who can play you something." But he did pop Neil Young's *After the Gold Rush* into his CD player and crank it up. "Have a seat in front of the fire, Allison. Wait, what am I saying? I really do have Epsom salts if you—."

"Naw, I'm good right here." She flopped her plump self down on his love seat, yanked off her sneakers and ankle socks and put her feet up on his coffee table, which he'd made himself by bolting a discarded storm window onto an old rowboat. Her bare legs seemed kind of stubby. Compared to Des, all women's legs seemed stubby.

Mitch uncorked a bottle of Gabbiano in the kitchen and returned to the living room with it and two glasses. He filled them and handed her one. "I'm glad you could make it out, Allison."

"Me, too." She took a sip. "Hey, son, this is good wine. What is it?"

"A Chianti Classico." He sat next to her on the love seat and patted his lap. "Park 'em here. Time for your massage."

Allison narrowed her eyes at him. She wore altogether too much eye makeup, in his opinion. He wondered whether she'd look younger or older without it. "Mitch, are you the answer to my prayers or just a perv?"

"Does that matter?"

"Not really." She swiveled around and plopped her pudgy feet in his lap. "I just don't get why you'd want to."

"Please don't take this as a rebuke," he said, kneading the ball of her left foot with his thumbs. "But I don't think you're accustomed to being treated very well."

"Damn, I could get used to *this* in a hurry," she groaned, squirming with animal pleasure. "Do all Jewish men do this or is it your own special thing?"

"I don't like to brag, but I possess certain skills."

"I guess our resident trooper would know about that."

"That's not fair, the way you keep mentioning her. I haven't said anything about the Kershaws."

"Ker*shaw,*" she corrected him, gazing into the roaring fire. "I went out with Stevie for a while before he got sent up. He wrote me some letters from prison. When they got out, he wanted to get together. But it's nothing serious between us. And I do *not* do both of them, if that's what you were thinking. That would be skanky and disgusting. And, Mitch, my other foot is feeling really lonely over here."

Mitch went to work on it. Allison let out a soft moan, grinding her hips into the sofa cushion.

"So you three didn't spend the night together at the Yankee Doodle?"

"No, we did. I'm just saying that squirrely Donnie crashed in a chair, not in bed with us." Allison glanced at him curiously. "Trooper Des thinks they did it, doesn't she?"

"What do *you* think?"

"I can only go by what Stevie's telling me, which is he really wants to clean up his act, get out of the old man's house. He'd like to move in with me. I told him I've already got a nice, clean roommate who pays her rent on time. Besides, wherever Stevie goes Donnie goes. But I told him, hey, if you're trying to stay straight I'm all for that. Not that I've made him any promises or whatever. I have to be kind of careful, because I have this habit of letting guys use me. You seem nice enough, and you sure have good hands. But tell me, Mitch, are you using me?"

Mitch gazed gloomily into the fire. "I sure hope not."

"Wow, you sound bummed all of the sudden. How come?"

"I can't stop thinking about my wife. I've started dreaming about her all over again, and it's making me crazy."

"She died, didn't she? That's why you moved here. You're still hung up on her?"

"I can't let go," Mitch confessed, wondering why on earth he was sharing his most private feelings with Allison Mapes. Maybe it wasn't so strange. He did need to talk it out with someone. Allison was here, and she did ask. "Maisie won't let me go. In my dreams, I mean. I'm always leaving her, and she's always begging me not to. I guess I'm feeling, deep down inside, that by being happy with someone else I'm abandoning her."

"You're *not,*" Allison said vehemently. "You're just living your life, son. If you were moping around the house all day going boohoo *then* you'd be abandoning her. Because you'd be giving up. No way she'd want you to do that. Enjoy it while you can. That's what I say. Not that I'm any kind of genius."

He sipped his wine in brooding silence, staring into the fire. "It's *your* life story, isn't it? Justine's book is about you."

Allison totally freaked. Scrambled up off the love seat away from him. "Is that why you invited me out here?" she demanded, her eyes darting wildly about. "To talk about *that?*"

"I'm the one who's been doing all of the talking. I've just confided something very personal to you. I'm hoping you'll do the same for me."

"Why should I?"

"Because a man is dead, Allison."

"What does that have to do with me?"

"This is what I'm trying to find out."

She stared at Mitch in hurt, angry silence. "Justine told you?"

"Not a chance. She keeps trying to make me think it's her story. I just didn't buy it, that's all."

"Hey, thanks for the wine . . ." Allison snatched up her sneakers and jacket and fled for the door.

"Please don't go, Allison. We have to talk about this. I'll make it easier for you, okay? I already know that your older brother, Lester, was heavy into dope back in high school. I know he's living in a VA hospital now, minus the limbs and genitalia that he left behind in Baghdad."

"He got what was coming to him," she said savagely.

"I know what's in the book, okay? I know all of it."

She let out a derisive snort. "You know jack."

"So tell me the rest. Please. This is your chance."

"My chance for *what*?"

"For something good to come out of it. You can even the score now, and get on with your life. Just like you were saying I ought to do."

"Okay, do not try lumping us together, Mitch, because compared to yours, my life totally sucks."

"Grab hold of this chance, Allison. If you don't, you'll regret it for as long as you live. Trust me. Please, trust me."

Slowly, she returned to the sofa and sat, still clutching her jacket and shoes. She wouldn't look at him. Only into the fire. He got up and fed it with two more hickory logs. Refilled her wine glass. Then sat back down, waiting her out.

"Justine's book pretty much says it all," she said finally, in a voice that was flat and emotionless.

"So you've read it?"

"I wasn't . . . I'm not as bad as the girl in her story," she said, swallowing hard. "Justine bigged it up some. It happened a few times is all. And, believe me, I never *liked* doing it. I may have said that to her once, like I was bragging. There's a lot I don't remember. I was stoned all the time in those days. *That's* what I liked—being stoned. Mitch, I was fourteen and stupid. My mom had split on us. My dad's a long-haul trucker, and he was always on the road. Mostly it was just me and Lester. And his friends. And their dope. They were major, major stoners. I'm talking coke, meth, oxy. Once they started getting me high things just got out of control, okay? But after a few months my mom moved back in with us, and as soon as she found out what was going on she got me right into a drug program, and they set me up with a shrink. I was fine after that. I *am* fine. I smoke a little pot now and then, but I'm good." Allison turned and gazed at Mitch steadily now. "Justine asked me if she could write about it and I said sure—as long as she changed the names and everything."

"It doesn't bother you that she's done it?"

"I think it's cool, actually, because it's not about me. It's about them. The phony assholes who are always lecturing us about family values and personal responsibility. I did a few of those fine, upstanding hypocrites, Mitch. That part's all true. I did our high school principal right in his office. I did the resident trooper. He was the one who had the fishing boat. And, yeah, I did my minister. Once they found out about me they all wanted to 'help' me. They're all just a bunch of horny married bastards who can't wait to get over on a messed-up fourteen-year-old girl. Hell, I wasn't even cute. I'm not cute. Not like Justine is. I know that." Allison trailed off, hugging herself in morose silence. "I know too damned much."

"Did you know that you could still file criminal charges against them?"

"I don't even want to go there. That's all behind me now. These days, I try real hard to see the good in people. I work hard. I pay my bills. I stay healthy. And I let no one into my heart."

"You can't live that way, Allison."

"You totally can. I do it every day."

"Justine's book mentions a boy named Tommy who her character is madly in love with. *Was* there a Tommy?"

"He wasn't any boy," she replied woodenly. "He was a married man. And, yeah, I was crazy about him. He was crazy about me, too, in his own sick way. Kept telling me I was too sweet and wonderful to treat myself like I was. That I was his princess. Pretty weird thing for a guy to call you when he's banging you in a motel room, don't you think? He took me with him on his business trips. He never traveled far. Just York City, Boston, Vermont a couple of times. We'd stay overnight in a motor lodge along the turnpike. He'd get us a bottle and we'd smoke a joint together and he'd just go and go all night long. I don't think his wife ever let him have any. He did like to brag. Kept telling me he'd be really rich someday. And when I turned eighteen he'd leave his wife and marry me. I believed him, too. But he turned out to be as big an asshole as the others. Once he'd had his fill he dumped me. That's when I really hit bottom. I won't lie—I even thought about doing myself in. God, I was *so* into him. I still am. Every time I see him my little heart goes pitter-patter."

"He's still around Dorset?"

"Yeah, I bump into him all of the time. When he sees me he panics and runs." Allison flashed a quick, uncertain smile at Mitch. "I guess we don't have any secrets from each other now, do we?"

"Except for one—his name. I think it might be important, Allison. Will you tell me?"

She hesitated a moment. "I might. But there are certain conditions."

"Name them."

"You have to pour me some more of that wine."

"Done," he said, reaching for the bottle. "What else?"

"You have to play me something on your guitar."

"It won't be a pleasant experience for you, Allison. Everything I play comes out sounding like "Purple Haze" and not in a good kind of way. But, okay, I can do that, too. What else?"

"You have to let me spend the night with you."

CHAPTER 18

WHEN THE CALL CAME it was just past three in the morning and Des was finally getting somewhere in the studio. Not on her dreadful damned self-portrait. Hell no. Tonight, she'd thrown herself headlong into a portrait of Pete Mosher. This was her life's mission, after all—illuminating the victims she encountered on the job. Them, not herself. Sometimes, the job had a way of bringing that realization home to her with startling clarity. Because she was feeling it again. Wielding her stub of graphite stick like a sword as she slashed away at the drawing pad, all of her energy and passion harnessed in pursuit of the only goal that was worth going after.

The truth.

What was Pete Mosher's truth? Why had this bright, handsome bastard son of great wealth, a multimillionaire in his own right, dissolved into someone who picked through other peoples' garbage? Why could he find no peace? As she stared at the crime-scene Polaroids of Pete that she'd clipped to her easel, Des kept thinking that he already seemed at one with the forest floor. At long last, Peter Ashton Mosher had found his peace. But he hadn't exited peacefully. Somebody—make that two somebodys—had been determined to get even, get rich, get what? Was this about the money, or was there more to it?

And so Des drew. A few hours back, Mitch had called to say goodnight and to tell her that Mark Widdifield had withdrawn the last five thousand dollars in his checking account that day. Supposedly, he wanted to run off to St. Kitts with Danielle. Mitch had gotten this from Danielle, who he felt was in way over her head with her troubled brother-in-law. Which Des could believe. But she wasn't so sure whether Mark was as interested in Danielle as he claimed to be. Could be Mark was just playing Danielle—using her as a convenient cover for his cash withdrawal. True, he did appear to be a helpless soul in the midst of a genuine midlife meltdown. Yet he was also an intelligent, creative man who was still legally married to Claudia and therefore had a vested interest in the family's financial affairs. How deep into this murder might Mark be? What had he gotten himself into? What had *Mitch* gotten himself into? Des wondered, because there had been an edge in his voice on the phone. There was something the doughboy wasn't sharing with her. To do with what? That statutory rape business he'd dropped on her at lunch? She had her concerns. Mitch had a great big heart but he was a product of the MGM golden age. He had no idea just how far real people could go to get what they wanted. And his phone voice had sounded so strange that, well, she could have sworn someone else had been there with him. Which had to be her imagination.

Didn't it?

She drew, feeling Pete's madness and his sadness as Al Green cried about his own pain on the stereo. She was barefoot, clad only in the ancient, tattered West Point T-shirt that was almost long enough to cover her tattoo. The big fire in the studio fireplace kept her warm, as did The Balvenie twenty-one-year-old single malt scotch on the stand next to her. She'd set one spot beam on the drawing pad. Lit some candles. Beyond the studio, her house lay in darkness.

Des drew, feeling weightless on the balls of her feet. Dancing like Ali danced back when he was still Cassius slaying the mighty Liston. She floated like a butterfly and stung like a bee, the tendons popping in her arm, her skin tingling. There was her and there was the page. Nothing else. She hadn't felt this *connected* in weeks. And she owed it all to the Can Man. Des would give the man his props. She would find out who killed him. She would.

She paused now to catch her breath and sip some scotch. Step back and take in the entirety of the page. Step back and . . .

Bounce right off of Bella, who was standing right there behind her in the candlelight, scowling at her. Bella Tillis could be a bit of a jolt at 3 A.M. in her quilted pink bathrobe, hair net and plush, oversized bear-claw slippers.

"Sorry if I woke you, girl," Des gulped. "My music too loud?"

"No, it's all of that stomping around. Are you drawing or doing the polka?"

"If you're going to unleash the inner beast, you've got to use your whole body."

"And does your whole body have to be nine-tenths naked?"

Des looked down at herself, frowning. "I'm dressed."

"You are not. That T-shirt has so many holes in it your twins are staring right at me. You're not staging a nutty are you?"

"Everything's cool, Bella. I'm just feeling the—"

"Wait one second." Bella shook a stubby finger at her. "You're stewed, aren't you? How much have you had to drink?"

"Half of that." Des nodded toward the scotch on the stand.

"Half of that bottle?"

"No, half of the glass. Which I fully intend to finish."

"Did you have any dinner?"

"I don't remember."

"Come, I'll make you a sandwich. And, for pity's sake, will you throw something on? You look like a porn star."

Des fetched a hoody, still seeing Pete's long, gaunt face before her eyes. She washed the shiny graphite stick residue from her hands in the kitchen sink while Bella carved breast meat off of the remains of a roast chicken. Bella had visited a friend in New Haven yesterday and brought back a challah from a Jewish bakery. She cut four thick slices, then began slicing up cucumbers, tomatoes and radishes, her chubby hands working with rapid-fire precision.

"Now in the old days back on Nostrand Avenue," she recalled, slathering the bread with mayonnaise, "you'd go with a generous schmear of schmaltz. Much tastier than mayo. On the down side, you used to keel over dead of a heart attack by age forty-eight. I'll have milk with mine. Would you pour me a glass, please?"

Des poured each of them a glass and leaned against the fridge, sipping hers.

"I know what you're afraid of, Desiree," Bella informed her as she finished assembling their sandwiches.

"And we are now talking about? . . ."

"Marriage to our Jewish gentleman, of course. Why you won't say yes."

Des sighed inwardly. "Okay, what is it that I'm afraid of?"

Bella handed Des her sandwich. "At first, I thought it was that whole independence thing of yours. How you're in charge of your own life, your own career, your own orgasms—"

"No, the big guy pretty much sees to those."

"But that's all bull. Want to know what really scares you?"

Des took a huge, starved bite of her sandwich. She hadn't eaten since breakfast. "I'm just standing here waiting for you to tell me."

"That you're still in love with Brandon."

Des put the sandwich down on the counter, her appetite instantly gone. "Bella, Brandon came *this* close to destroying me," she said softly, her stomach knotting. "It took me so long to get over him, but I did."

Bella glanced at Des's discarded sandwich. "Are you sure about that?"

"I'm *sure* that I love Mitch."

"And Mitch loves *you*. Brandon didn't, you know. Brandon never loved you." Bella said this with such cold certainty that it was like a hard smack in the face.

Des drew back from her, stunned. "How can you say that to me?"

"I can say it because it's the truth. Brandon never loved you. If he had, he wouldn't have broken your heart that way. Desiree, I saw what that man did to you. Trust me, people don't do that to people who they love."

Des's mouth had gone dry, but she did not want to reach for her milk glass. Not the way her hands were shaking. "Girl, I am *over* Brandon, okay? I do not still love him."

Bella shrugged her round shoulders. "If you say so."

"You don't believe me, do you?"

"I believe that you want to believe it. I just don't think it's true."

Now was when the phone rang. Des reached for it at once. She was a first responder. Often took emergency calls in the night.

"I'm so sorry to awaken you, dear." It was Poochie Vickers, sounding utterly cordial and gracious.

"Not a problem. I was still up doing some drawing. Don't have any news for you, if that's why you're calling."

"It's not, dear. It's about Tolly. I can't seem to find him. The plain truth is he's gone."

It took Des thirty minutes to jump into a fresh uniform and drive up to Four Chimneys in the utter blackness of Dorset in the middle of the night, her headlight beams on high and her defroster blasting.

She found Dorset's first lady seated at the kitchen table before a mug of coffee and a plate of chocolate biscotti. Poochie wore a bulky red turtleneck sweater, painter's pants and an anxious expression. Bement was seated there with her, his long blond hair uncombed, broad shoulders hunched inside the wool shirt he had on over a T-shirt and sweatpants. The bruise under his left eye was turning a gaudy shade of yellow.

Bailey was helping himself to some kibble before he climbed up onto his window seat cushion and stretched out, groaning like an old man.

"Why don't you walk me through it, Poochie?" Des suggested as she stood there drinking coffee and stamping the two blocks of ice formerly known as her feet. The kitchen was barely heated. "You said on the phone that you spent the evening with Claudia?"

"I did, yes." Poochie swiped distractedly at some biscotti crumbs on the table. "Claude asked me over for dinner. The orderliness of cooking is something that calms her. She was terribly upset. Didn't take my news about Peter at all well." Poochie glanced over at her grandson, smiling faintly. "I've told Bement, too. He's an adult now, and deserves to know."

"I'm hearing you already had some ideas about Pete," Des said to him.

"Sort of," he grunted.

Poochie seemed taken by surprise. "How?"

"I overheard you and Grandpa talking once. I was hiding. You didn't know I was there."

"You don't still do that, do you?" Poochie demanded. "Tiptoe around trying to catch people doing and saying awful things?"

"No, Nana."

"Good, because there's a nasty name for such people. They're called *congressmen.*"

"How did Eric take the news?"

"Eric was fine with it," Poochie answered. "I swear, if it's not about his animals or his crops, Eric couldn't care less. But Claude was very angry with me. I tried to explain to her that the secrecy wasn't my doing. I'd merely been honoring Father's dying wish."

"Did she accept that?"

"Eventually," Poochie said slowly. "Claude's not a secure person. She needs a good deal of reassurance, and Mark's not around to provide it anymore."

"Mr. Tolliver was working in the rose garden yesterday afternoon when I left with Lieutenant Tedone and Sergeant Snipes, is that right?"

"It is. After you'd gone, I called Eric, and he and Danielle met me at Claude's." Poochie glanced fondly at her old dog. "Bailey and I strolled over there together."

"Did you encounter Mr. Tolliver in the rose garden?"

"I saw tools and a tarp. I did not see him. I assumed he was in the shed or somewhere. But really, my mind wasn't on Tolly. I was thinking about how I was going to tell my children about Peter."

"Of course."

"Afterward, Claude asked me to dinner, as I mentioned. She's exceedingly self-conscious about cooking in front of me, so I moseyed back here while she was preparing it."

"By now it was what time?"

Poochie sipped her coffee. "I don't know, some time after six. It was quite dark out. Tolly's bedroom door was closed, and his light was off. He often likes to nap before dinner. I didn't wish to wake him, so I left a note here on the table instructing him to join me over at Claude's. But it was just us two girls. And an absolutely vile duck breast swimming in a tureen of *something* pale green. It makes me ulp just to think about it." She reached for a biscotti, nibbling at it. "I got back here by around ten. His door was still closed. I tapped on it to ask if he'd like me to fix him something, but there was no answer. I figured he'd just overdone it in the rose garden and needed his rest, so I went to my own room and got into bed. Ordinarily, I sleep like a field hand. Tonight, I couldn't seem to relax. I just felt a tremendous sense of unease. Finally, at around two, I got up and knocked on Tolly's door again. That's when I discovered he was gone."

Des wondered if there was anything here for her. It was entirely possible that the old photographer had simply decided it was time to move on. He did float around, according to his sheet. Then again, taking off right on the heels of Pete's murder could not be considered a wise travel plan. It was the act of a man who was either foolish or desperate. She'd checked with the trooper posted at the foot of the drive. At no point in the past twenty-four hours had Guy Tolliver left the premises. Not by way of the front drive anyhow. So wherever he'd gone, he'd been careful about it. "How about you?" she asked Bement. "Were you with Justine last evening?"

"I wasn't up for any company. Had some things on my mind."

Bement lit a cigarette, dragging deeply on it. "I came straight home after we closed the shop. Well, not straight home. I stopped off at the liquor store to pick up some brews, got here around six. Had to show some trooper my damned ID to get in."

"Your mother requested that," Des explained. "Otherwise, you'd have media people swarming around right outside your door."

"The Kershaw brothers were leaving right when I was stopped there at Checkpoint Charlie. Probably just as well, too. If I'd run into those turds farther up the drive I might have had a few more things to say to them. I'm not real happy about them hanging around here."

"You need to do a better job of managing your temper," Des said, her eyes on his scraped knuckles.

"That's what Teeny keeps telling me. I can't change how I feel."

"You can change how you respond."

"When I got here Nana was about ready to head back over to Mom's for dinner. I just jumped in the shower and stretched out and watched some hoops on TV. Drank my six. Heated up some leftovers."

"Did you encounter Mr. Tolliver at any time during the evening?"

"I didn't. But I stayed mostly in my room. And I crashed early, maybe ten-thirty." Bement got up and refilled his mug from the electric coffeemaker on the counter. "Next thing I know, Nana's waking me up and asking me to look around for him."

"And did you?"

"Absolutely. Tolly's an old guy. I thought maybe he had a heart attack or something. I've searched this place from top to bottom. I even looked in the north wing, which is closed off. The man's not here, believe me."

"Did you check around outside?"

"With a flashlight. There aren't any floodlights in the rose garden. Those tools are still out there, collecting frost. He didn't put them away. I looked around in the shed. Nothing. That's when Nana called you."

Poochie's bright blue eyes moistened. "I'm terribly concerned. I can't believe he'd just up and leave me this way. Not so much as a note."

Des turned it over in her head. Her guess was that Guy Tolliver had cleared out yesterday under the cover of dusk, which would give him a solid twelve-hour head start by the time daylight hit. Someone—a partner—could have picked him up out on Route 156. Or, for that matter, a taxi could have. It played. The trooper at the foot of the drive could be avoided by hiking through the woods and coming out a half-mile up the road. Tolly was no kid, but he was plenty mobile. She could phone the three area cab companies. Show his picture around at the train stations in Old Saybrook and New London. Also the car rental agencies. Someone might have seen him. It played, all right. But it didn't answer the question that kept nagging at her: *Why on earth would Guy Tolliver murder Pete Mosher?*

"Bement, when you looked around the house for him, did you notice anything missing?"

Bement's eyes widened. "You mean like a painting or something?"

"Tolly would never do that to me," Poochie said heatedly. "How dare you even suggest it?"

"I'm not suggesting anything, Poochie. But when you call a trooper, you get a trooper asking the kind of questions I have to ask."

"Didn't notice anything missing." Bement thumbed his jaw reflectively. "But I was looking for *him*. Besides, I'm not even sure I'd be able to tell."

"Let's go have a look, shall we?"

The lamps were already lit in the parlor. Des stood in the middle of the cluttered room scanning Poochie's breathtaking collection. The Picasso and Toulouse-Lautrec drawings were still there.

So was the Giacometti. The Magritte, Mondrian, Leger—all of it was intact. There were no blank spaces on the walls. No empty frames.

"You see?" Poochie said defiantly. "Tolly would *never* take anything of mine. Besides, there would be no point in it, would there?"

"Why not?" Des asked, glancing at her curiously.

Poochie didn't seem to hear her. Her mind was elsewhere now. Somewhere that bothered her greatly. "He wouldn't leave me this way," she sobbed, wringing her hands. "Go look in his bedroom if you don't believe me."

Tolly's bedroom was more Des's idea of a luxury suite, complete with dressing room and private bath. There was a seating area with a pair of leather club chairs set before a fireplace. A huge walnut desk. An antique four-poster canopy bed, its covers neatly folded. It hadn't been slept in. His clothes were still hanging in the dressing room. Tolly was quite fastidious about his wardrobe. His suits, sports jackets and slacks were all pressed and ready to wear, his shoes evenly spaced on the floor, all of them stuffed with shoe trees. Des pulled open the drawers of the built-in dresser one by one. She found cashmere sweaters and fine dress shirts by the dozen, silk scarves, socks, underwear.

"Look in the top drawer." Poochie's voice quavered slightly.

Des found a slim jewelry box filled with cuff links made of silver and of gold. There were jeweled rings and tie pins, a gold Rolex dress watch. Des also discovered Guy Tolliver's passport in the drawer, along with his checkbook from Citibank in New York. His account carried a balance of $843.67, assuming his records were up to date. His last check, in the amount of $125, had been written in January to Salon Fodera.

All of these things Guy Tolliver had left behind.

She flicked on the bathroom light. He'd left his toiletry items behind, too. Razor and cologne, toothbrush, hairbrush. She opened the medicine chest. Very little was in there besides Band-Aids and aspirin.

"Is Mr. Tolliver currently taking any prescription medications?"

"He is not. His health is perfect."

Des followed Poochie back into the bedroom to the walnut desk. Inside its deep drawers she found stacks of old slick magazines individually bagged in plastic for safekeeping, file folders full of contact sheets, metal strong boxes stuffed with negatives, scrapbooks, journals.

"You're looking at the work of Tolly's lifetime," Poochie informed her quietly. "He'd never leave it behind. I swear he wouldn't."

Des nodded in agreement, all the while thinking: *Not unless he had to.*

"Maybe he just split for a day or two, Nana," Bement said gently. "He could be visiting old friends in the city or whatever."

Poochie smiled at her grandson fondly. "Bement, I know you're trying to make me feel better, and it's very sweet of you, but something's happened to Tolly. That's why I awoke in the night. I *feel* it."

"Does he usually carry a lot of cash on him?" Des asked.

"Hardly any, why?"

"How about credit cards?"

"We use mine."

"I don't mean to pry but did you issue him cards of his own for your accounts? Because if he's using them, we can trace his whereabouts."

Poochie considered this carefully. "You're demanding my account numbers, is that it?"

"I'm not demanding anything, Poochie. It might prove helpful, that's all."

"Very well," she conceded. "But I won't freeze my accounts. Tolly may need a hotel room or a hot meal. I won't deny him that."

"Then that's how we'll handle it. Have you got a recent snapshot of him?"

"In my room. I'll get my purse as well." Poochie strode out the door and down the hall.

Bement remained there with Des. "You think he killed Pete, don't you?"

"They don't pay me to think. I'm just taking it all in." She shoved her heavy horn-rimmed glasses up her nose, studying him. "That idea you were pitching about how he'd be back in a day or two. Where did that come from?"

Bement shot a quick glance at the hallway door, lowering his voice. "Tolly has it good here, but that doesn't mean he hasn't jumped the reservation. Just before Christmas, he told Nana he was spending the night in New York with one of his old Park Avenue lady friends. Next afternoon, he shows up back here totally trashed and stinking of cheap aftershave. He couldn't get out of bed for two days. Told Nana he had the flu, but I knew better. Some young Puerto Rican guy kept calling him night after night."

"What was his name?"

"He never said. Just called himself a 'friend.' Tolly told me he did not want to talk to him. I made sure I answered the phone for the next couple of weeks, until he stopped phoning. Nana never found out."

"Why were you so willing to cover for him?"

"I like the old guy. I think he's cool."

"Your mom thinks he's nothing more than a con man."

"Maybe she's right. But he makes Nana happy. And that's worth something, isn't it?"

Poochie returned now clutching her wallet and a color photo of her and Tolly clowning by the swimming pool on a bright summer day. They'd swapped hats. Her straw number fit too high and tight on his head. His porkpie flopped way down over her eyes and ears.

"Nothing is missing from my own jewelry box. I assumed you'd wish to know." Poochie opened her wallet and jotted down her credit card numbers on the lined yellow pad on the desk, then tore off the sheet and handed it to her. "You'll file a missing persons report?"

"Mr. Tolliver hasn't been gone long enough, Poochie. There's

also no concrete reason to believe he's missing, as opposed to simply gone."

"He's not gone. *Why* won't you believe me?"

"I'm hearing what you're saying. But we had a murder here yesterday, and his disappearance does raise some serious questions."

Poochie's nostrils flared. "You intend to arrest him, is that it?"

"Let's not get ahead of ourselves, okay? I'm going to leave you
folks now. I'll be back in touch."

"When?" Poochie's hand gripped Des's arm tightly. "When
will I hear from you?"

"Soon. We'll get to the bottom of this, I promise."

As they started down the grand marble staircase, Des could see
the sun rising through the east-facing windows, bathing the entry
hall in an orange glow. With the arrival of daylight, a thorough,
professional search of Four Chimneys was called for. She was particularly interested in the rose garden.

"Thank you for not treating me like a crazy old lady," Poochie
said as Des headed for the kitchen door.

"I don't think you're any such thing. I'm going to look around
a bit before I leave, if you don't mind."

Bailey padded his way over to the kitchen door to be let out.
Poochie obliged, venturing out into the courtyard with him while
Des passed through the wrought-iron gate into the walled rose
garden.

The day was dawning clear and frosty. The bare, dormant
winter garden was blanketed by hoarfrost, the icy brick path slick
underfoot.

Bailey tagged along with her, his nose to the frozen ground.

The rose garden scene was as Bement had described it. A heap
of thorny branches laid out on a green canvas tarp. A battered old
garden stool, a pair of loppers, pruners, work gloves, a small saw.
All of it was finely dusted with frost. In a matter of minutes, that
frost would thaw into dew. Right now, it looked like something
Van Gogh might have painted.

There was another gate here, an open one that led down brick steps and out into several untamed acres of meadow. Across the meadow, alongside the bank of the Connecticut River, a broad swath of swamp maples shielded the lower reaches of the property from the prying eyes of boaters.

Bailey ambled his way slowly through this gate, snuffling at the ground. Then, suddenly, he started barking excitedly and tore his way across the frosty meadow like a young pup.

"Bailey, you come back here!" Poochie hollered after him from the courtyard. "Leave those squirrels alone, you bad boy! Bailey? . . ."

The old dog ignored her—galloped all the way across the meadow and into the swamp maples, barking and barking.

"Bailey, come back here, you senile old thing!"

But Bailey wouldn't come back. Or stop barking.

Des, who'd taken basic K-9 training at the academy, thought she knew why. And it had nothing to do with senility. She wasted no time dashing her way across the meadow after him. The dog came out of the woods to greet her, his tail wagging furiously.

"Show me what you've got boy," she encouraged him, breathing heavily.

He took off down a muddy path that snaked into the woods. She followed him, stepping carefully, until she reached a small clearing among the trees.

Here was where old Bailey had found Tolly.

CHAPTER 19

THEY WERE OUT ON the Sound together, cutting smoothly through the water in his trim little sailboat, the one that had been built especially for him at the Dauntless Shipyard in Essex. He was manning the tiller. Maisie was expertly raising and lowering the sails, catching the breeze, running with it. It was a beautiful day. The sky was blue, the background music exhilarating and yet oddly menacing, too.

Mitch recognized it as Bernard Herrmann's score from Hitchcock's *North by Northwest*. An odd creative choice, he reflected as his amazing Technicolor dream unfolded before him. Because they were sailing in such perfect harmony out there, so in tune with the boat and the wind and each other.

Except, wait, that wasn't Maisie working those sails at all. It was Des, nimble as a cat in her yellow tube top and crisp white shorts. Pretty amazing since she did not know how to sail. Nor did Mitch. Come to think of it, this was not his sailboat. He had never owned a boat. He could barely even swim. Yet there they were—sailing with such joyful expertise it was as if they'd been doing it their whole lives.

It's about time, Mitch noted approvingly. Enough already with those dreams where Maisie was feeding ice cream cones to puppies. This was nice, him being out on the water with the new woman in his life.

Only now, it wasn't so nice. They weren't sailing with the wind— they were running smack into it. It was whipping up their sails, pitching the little boat violently from side to side. The sky had turned stormy. There was lightning and thunder. And now he was remembering that Jim Cantore had warned him to stay off of the water today. It was getting incredibly choppy, huge swells washing over the deck, threatening to capsize them.

"*Come about, Des! We have to come about!*"

"*Mitch, help me!...*"

But he was alone on deck. Des had been washed overboard. He jumped into the roiling sea after her, calling to her as his mouth filled with foamy salt water and the sharks began to circle. At least four sharks, moving in closer.

"*Des!...*"

"*Mitch, help me!...*"

"*Des!...*" *There she was, bobbing just out of his reach, her eyes wide with terror. Mitch reached his hand out to her in vain, sinking underwater himself, gasping.* "*Des!...*"

"*Don't leave me, Mitch!*"

And now he was going down and staying down. And she was the one reaching out to him and shaking him and shaking him and...

With a yelp Mitch was suddenly awake in the morning light, his heart thudding, mouth tasting metallic. She was kneeling there on the edge of his bed, rousing him from his nightmare.

He reached for her, hugging her tightly. "I won't ever leave you," he promised. "I swear I won't."

She pulled away from him, having none of it. "What is *up* with you, son?"

Because it was not Des. Allison Mapes was sitting there on his bed clad in his beloved No. 56 Lawrence Taylor New York Giants jersey. With her face scrubbed clean of makeup, she looked about thirteen. She also looked as if she thought he was insane.

"You were shouting in your sleep," she informed him. "You having a nightmare?"

"I was drowning." Mitch rubbed his eyes, gasping. Part of him felt as if he were still underwater, still fighting for breath. It had been such a vivid dream. A *Des* dream. He had moved off of Maisie and on to the master sergeant. This was significant, Mitch sensed, though he couldn't yet grasp why. He sat up in bed, slowly recalling that second bottle of Chianti he and Allison had gone through. Also his ear-splittingly, inspired rendition of Leslie West's *Mississippi Queen*.

"You got any flip-flops I could borrow? One of your cats peed in my sneaker."

"Which one?"

"The right one."

"No, which cat?"

"The skinny one."

"That's Quirt. He's very loyal to Des."

"Kind of getting that. He spent half the night circling the sofa and glowering at me."

She'd been too tipsy to drive home, so he'd made up the sofa for her. It was the responsible thing to do. It was also the bargain they'd struck. And Allison had proven to be a stubborn little negotiator.

"I really like your terrarium thingies. Didn't notice them last night."

"Those are my seedlings. The domes keep Clemmie out. Otherwise, she tears them to pieces."

"No offense, but your life seems pretty much ruled by your cats."

"Well, yeah. We all need strong authority figures in our lives."

"Whatever. I made coffee. You take yours with cream, right? I should know that by now."

"Today I think I'll go with two fingers of chocolate milk."

"Yum, I may try that myself."

"I'd better get a fire started. It must be freezing down there."

"I can do it," she said, starting down the narrow steps to the living room. "Least I can do after making you listen to my sob story for half the night."

Mitch lay there and listened to her rattle around downstairs, remembering what she'd told him about the drugs, the boys, the men. Clemmie jumped up onto the bed with him, padding at his belly determinedly before she curled up there, purring. Allison returned with two mugs of coffee and handed him one. It was hot and strong. He gulped it gratefully.

She perched on the edge of the bed with hers, smiling at him uncertainly. "I had a really good time last night. I feel really safe with you. Like I can say anything and you'll understand. I just wanted to say thanks, and tell you if you ever feel like, I mean, if you want to . . ."

"Actually, I'm the one who should be thanking you."

"Really, for what?"

"You helped me through something that's been bothering me."

She studied him curiously. "You're my first, you know. The only guy I've ever stayed over with didn't try to do me. I guess what you and Des have must be different from what I have with Stevie."

"It's different," Mitch acknowledged, stroking Clemmie.

"Otherwise you would have, right? If you weren't with her, I mean."

"In a New York minute."

"Kind of what I thought." Allison's round face glowed with satisfaction. "I'd better get going, hunh?"

"Wait, you promised you'd tell me his name, remember? The married guy who took you with him on his business trips."

She scrunched up her face, chewing nervously on the inside of her mouth. "You're not really going to hold me to that, are you?"

"I totally am. A deal's a deal. I was straight with you, wasn't I?"

"I guess," she allowed. "Only, how come you're so interested?"

"Because Justine's book is based on real people. Whoever publishes it has to know from the get-go if someone might cause problems."

"So it's important?"

"Very."

"Am I going to see you again?"

"Are you kidding? I must be in McGee's five times a week."

"I mean can we do *this* again?" Her eyes twinkled at him. "I could make you happy."

"I believe that."

"But it's not going to happen, is it? Story of my life, I guess."

Mitch was about to tell her that she was much too young to

have a story. But she did have one. Justine had put it down on paper. "We can be friends."

"Friends. I'm trying to think if I've ever had a guy as a friend. Nope, can't think of a single one. You have girls as friends?"

"Absolutely. My editor at the paper is a woman, and we're very tight. We go to dinner together all of the time when I'm in town."

"And you don't want to do each other?"

"We're friends."

"I don't see how that could possibly work."

"It's just understood, that's all."

Allison sat in silence for a long moment. "You have to promise me you won't spread this around town."

"I give you my word."

"If you tell *anyone,* it'll get back to me. And I'll hunt you down and I'll hurt you." She shifted around on the bed, gazing at him with a sadness that bordered on bottomless despair. "You really want his name, hunh?"

Mitch took her soft, pudgy hand and squeezed it. "Listen, how about if I say it? Because I'm starting to think I know where this is going and—"

And then Allison blurted out the married man's name and Mitch realized he didn't know where it was going at all.

CHAPTER 20

IN DEATH, GUY TOLLIVER was nowhere near stylish.

The jaunty old society photographer lay on his back, his head against a granite fieldstone, his left hand still wrapped around the empty bottle of lye that he'd drunk down. The human body instinctively wants to regurgitate a powerful corrosive such as lye—even in the death throes. So there were heavy burns around Tolly's mouth. The skin was eaten away, tissue underneath red and goopy. Lye had come foaming up through his nasal passages, too.

Des stood over the body with Soave and Yolie, their breath steaming in the chill, dry air. It had taken them nearly an hour to get down to Four Chimneys from their nice warm beds in their nice warm Hartford suburbs. The forensic nurse had beaten them, as had the crime scene techies. Everyone was hushed. It was barely seven in the morning, and this was an exceptionally not cheery way to start the day.

"What are you thinking, Des?" Soave asked, breaking the silence.

At first glance, Tolly's death cried out suicide. It appeared he'd come down to these woods from the rose garden, chugalugged the lye and keeled over, hitting the back of his head against that granite. A scalp wound had bled down the back of his neck.

"Des? . . ." Soave tugged at his goatee as the techies hovered around them, snapping pictures. "What are you thinking?"

"It's your case, Rico," Des responded, thinking that she could have, should have prevented this. But she hadn't. They hadn't.

And now Guy Tolliver lay dead on the cold, muddy ground. The forensic nurse believed that he'd been there for about twelve hours, placing his time of death at around dusk—the same ap-

proximate time when they'd been interviewing Poochie and Glynis in the parlor.

Soave began humming tunelessly under his breath, which was
a thing that he did whenever he was shook. He had reason to be.
Rico Tedone would have a lot of explaining to do in Meriden.
"How about you, Yolie? Run with it."

"No way in hell this is a suicide," she declared, shivering in her
belted leather jacket. Yolie was strictly a warm weather girl.
"Someone whacked this man on the back of his head, okay? And
while he was semiconscious forced him to drink down that lye."
Yolie crouched next to Tolly, studying him closely. "We have finger marks on his neck and jaw here and here," she added, using her
Bic pen as a pointer. "Somebody pried his mouth open. And there
was a struggle. His scarf thing . . . girl, what do you call these
again?"

"It's an ascot," Des said softly.

"Yeah, the knot's yanked halfway around his neck, see? And
check out these bloodstain patterns on his neck. They're all wrong."

"He bled *down* his neck," Des agreed. "Which means he was
either standing or sitting when he incurred the head wound. He
was positioned here after the fact. There's a bit of blood under his
head, but no soak pattern, no drainage. The scalp injury didn't
happen here." Des knelt next to Tolly's grotesque body for a closer
look at his left hand. "I see no lye on his wrist or sleeve. If he'd
been holding that bottle himself when he drank the lye it would
have streamed down his hand like a melted ice cream cone. Somebody positioned it in his hand after they killed him." She stood
back up, swiping at her muddy knees. "One more thing, and I
can't emphasize this enough—Tolly *lived* for style. Absolutely no
way does he leave such a vile-looking corpse behind. Not even
within the realm of possiblity."

"So we're all in agreement," Soave concluded. "What we're
looking at here is a staged crime scene."

"I'm betting he got it in the rose garden," Yolie said. "The
man's bent over, working away at his pruning. Somebody bops

him from behind, then carries him down here—out of sight, out of earshot—and forces him to drink that lye."

"We'll search the ground up there," Soave said. "If that's how it happened, we'll find the blood."

"This man was plenty good-sized," Yolie went on. "One person couldn't have horsed him all of the way across that field. And I'm seeing no wheelbarrow treads or whatever in the mud. That makes this another two-man job. We're looking for the same pair who took out Pete Mosher, am I right?"

"That's a slam dunk."

Des said nothing. She was too busy playing it out.

"What's wrong with it, Des?" Soave asked, studying her warily.

"It's tight, Rico. I've got nothing."

"Yeah, you do. Something's still bugging you."

"Nothing I can put my finger on. But this all just feels *clanky* to me. Too obvious. Too clumsy. Too . . . I don't know, as if someone smart wants us to think they're really stupid. Does that make any sense?"

"Not so much."

"It *appears* to be a clumsy attempt to mask a murder as a suicide—the kind of thing somebody small time might try to pull off. Somebody like the Kershaw brothers. Except that whoever pulled this had to be calculating and cool. Check it out: If they'd waited until pitch dark they would have needed flashlights or lanterns. Way too risky. So that means they killed Tolly no later than six, six-thirty. For all we know, we three may still have been on the premises at the time. Plus we've got a cruiser stationed at the foot of the drive. And yet, somehow, they murdered this man right under our noses."

"I'm with my girl," Yolie said. "We are not talking lame-assed raggies."

"What we *are* talking is desperate," Des said. "They took an enormous chance. Tolly must have known something."

"This one's on us, isn't it?" Soave's shoulders slumped defeatedly. "We let it happen."

This was not something that a younger Soave would have admitted out loud, Des reflected. "We're dealing with some serious customers here, Rico. And they're totally messing with our heads again. But we'll nail them."

"Who had access to this site? Run it for us, will you, Des?"

"Claudia was around, as were Eric and Danielle. Bement got home by six, so he's in play. And he made a point of telling me the Kershaw brothers were leaving for the day when he got here. So they're in play, too."

"Don't forget Glynis," Yolie said. "*And* the old lady."

"So we know where to focus our attention." Soave rubbed his hands together briskly. "We'll go at them, one by one."

"Pull over to the curb, wow man," Des cautioned him. "I didn't know this until a half-hour ago, but there's more."

She continued down the footpath through the trees, Soave and Yolie trailing along behind her, until she emerged at the hard, frozen shallows where the Connecticut River met its eastern bank. Here, all was icy winter calm. And here, things got considerably more complicated. Because the footpath didn't end at the water. It hugged the bank for as far down river as the eye could see.

"I discovered this while I was waiting for you to get here," Des explained to them. She'd also phoned Mitch on her cell to tell him about Tolly. Things weren't real until she'd shared them with him. He'd sounded upset by the news. Also strangely preoccupied. "After a half-mile or so it comes out at a state-run boat launch at the foot of Kinney Road. During the summer, people put in their kayaks there. This time of year, it's pretty much deserted. Someone could have parked there yesterday afternoon and hiked in and out, totally unseen."

"There's no fence to keep people out?" Yolie asked, stamping her feet against the cold.

"It's posted to keep the hunters out, but no fence."

Soave shook his head disgustedly. "Who'd know about this?"

"Anybody who's ever spent time here. Claudia's husband,

Mark, for one. And Milo Kershaw used to be caretaker here. They're in the mix, Rico."

Soave tugged at his goatee. "What's the link, Des? Why have Pete Mosher and Guy Tolliver both turned up dead in the last twenty-four hours? Why did they have to die? What did they have in common?"

"Rico, I honestly . . ." She broke off, her memory suddenly tweaked by something that had bothered her earlier. "I have no idea. But I think I know who will."

Poochie's KitchenAid power mixer was in high gear, roaring away on the counter like a jumbo jet as it creamed together butter and brown sugar.

Dorset's first lady was in high gear herself. "I *crave* gingerbread this morning," she exulted as she raced around the kitchen, flinging flour and baking soda into a bowl, followed by ground ginger, powdered mustard, coarse ground pepper, cinnamon, cloves. "Tolly *loved* my gingerbread. The secret is adding one cup of hot, strong coffee for moisture. And good molasses, of course. God, how I love the smell of molasses!"

Glynis Fairchild-Forniaux sat at the table with her briefcase before her, looking very somber. Claudia sat there with her, as did Bement and Danielle.

"Mummy, please sit down, won't you?" Claudia said anxiously.

Poochie pulled a pair of loaf pans out of a cupboard. "I *can't* sit."

Eric couldn't either. Or wouldn't. The gangly farmer was pacing around the kitchen like a restless, petulant teenager, heaving his chest and making it abundantly clear that he wanted to be somewhere else. Pretty damned juvenile, Des felt, considering how upset his mother was over Tolly's death.

Danielle was well aware of this. Her eyes repeatedly made contact with his, silently pleading with him to park his geeky self at the table.

He refused, clomping back and forth in his work shoes. "We've got soup kitchen detail," he complained over the whirring mixer. "How long will this take?"

"Not long," Soave said, standing there with Yolie and Des.

"Eric, would you kindly show some basic human consideration?" Claudia said reproachfully.

"Would *you* kindly buzz off?"

Claudia abruptly got to her feet and shut off the mixer, leaving them in blissful silence. She took Poochie firmly by the shoulders and steered her toward the table. "Mummy, these officers need to speak with you. Sit down for a minute, will you?"

"There's no need to manhandle me, Claude," Poochie said indignantly, perching next to Bement. "What is it, Des?"

"Poochie, something you said earlier this morning struck me as a bit peculiar. Mr. Tolliver was missing, and at that point we were operating under the assumption that he'd skipped town."

"*You* were operating under that assumption. I never was, as you and Bement will recall."

"She's right," Bement acknowledged, hands gripping his coffee cup.

"I asked you if any works of art were missing," Des went on. "You insisted that Tolly would never take anything of yours. I believe you said, 'There would be no point in it.' What did you mean by that? Have you made specific provisions for him in your will?"

"I don't wish to discuss it," Poochie said dismissively. "Ask Glynis."

"Poochie did amend her last will and testament in November to provide for Mr. Tolliver," Glynis offered guardedly.

"Provide for him how?"

"Poochie, you're under no legal obligation to answer this," Glynis advised her. "The contents of your will are confidential."

"Lady, we will be right back here in an hour with a warrant and you know it," Yolie huffed at the lawyer. "Right now, all you're doing is impeding an investigation into two murders."

"*Two* murders?" Poochie gaped at them in astonishment. "But I thought . . . you told me Tolly swallowed poison."

"We believe he was struck on the head and forced to drink it," Des said.

"Oh, I am so relieved to hear that." Poochie's blue eyes puddled with tears. "Not that I mean to suggest I'm *happy* Tolly was murdered. I simply refused to believe he was despondent. He was *happy* with me."

"Of course he was." Claudia reached a hand out to her mother's. Poochie instinctively pulled away. Claudia's face tightened, a mask of anguish.

Poochie was unaware of it. Or appeared to be. She got up and went back to the counter and began greasing the two loaf pans with a stick of butter. "Four Chimneys is for my children," she said in a firm voice. "Father wanted it that way. The house and the land will be theirs. Likewise my stock holdings. Poor Peter's as well. But I did what I could do for Tolly. And there you have it."

Des shook her head at her. "*How* did you do what you could for him?"

"Why, by leaving him the contents of the house, of course. Those are mine to distribute as I choose, and I chose to leave them to Tolly."

Des's jaw dropped in disbelief.

Soave looked at her blank-faced, still not grasping the hugeness of this.

"She left him her art collection, Rico," Des explained.

"And do not overlook the furniture," Claudia added in a muted voice. "Some of those antiques are priceless."

"You knew about this?" Des asked her.

"Of course she did," Poochie said. "Both of my children did."

Eric had nothing to say. Just lurked there by the back door like an impatient kid who couldn't wait to go play ball with his friends.

"I wanted them to understand how much Tolly meant to me," Poochie explained.

"Tolly told me about it himself," Claudia said quietly. "He hoped it would bring the two of us closer together, I believe he said. I just thought he was lording it over me."

"You had no cause to feel that way," Poochie chided her.

"Well, I'm sorry, Mummy."

"And what did *you* think?" Soave asked Eric.

"About what?" The farmer's attention seemed elsewhere.

"Poochie leaving Tolly her art collection," Danielle said in a patient voice.

"A bunch of meaningless adornment," Eric responded, shrugging his shoulders. "Who cares?"

"Know what strikes me as odd?" Soave said. "Mr. Tolliver made zero mention of this when we interviewed him. All he did was cry poverty."

"Because he was afraid you'd think exactly what you're thinking, Lieutenant," Poochie said. "That he was nothing more than an aging gold digger. I told him to hell with what other people think. But Tolly was terribly sensitive. Surely you can understand that."

"I guess. Only, why didn't *you* tell us?"

Glynis answered, "We complied with you fully yesterday, Lieutenant. We granted you access to Peter Mosher's last will and testament. We answered your questions regarding the estate of John J. Meier. My client's own bequests were outside the scope of your inquiry."

"*Damn,* lady," Yolie fumed. "If you weren't being such a nitpicky lawyer that man might still be alive. Don't you get that?"

"I was doing my job."

"Girl to girl, your job stinks!"

"You have *no* call to speak to me that way, Sergeant," Glynis responded coldly. "It's highly unprofessional, and I resent it. Lieutenant, I do not care for the adversarial tone this conversation is taking."

"Duly noted. Can we please move on?"

Glynis continued to glare at Yolie.

"I'm no art expert, Mrs. Vickers," Soave said. "Can you give us a ballpark figure on how much your collection is worth?"

"Why, I would have no idea. I've never placed a dollar value on it. That's not what art is about, is it, Des?"

"Poochie, I'm afraid that's very much what it's about right now."

"Well, that's just fine then," the grand old lady declared. "If you people insist upon being so vulgar I shall be in the conservatory with my plants and other living things."

"Mummy, please don't go," Claudia protested.

But Poochie had already barged out of the kitchen, leaving them and her unfinished gingerbread behind.

"If she's gone, I'm gone." Eric flung open the back door. "Come on, hon."

Danielle got up from the table and followed him, mustering an apologetic glance at Des.

"I've got to open up the shop," Bement said as he, too, headed out.

Only Glynis and Claudia remained there at the table.

"In response to your question, Lieutenant," Glynis said crisply, "the value of Poochie's art collection has been placed at one hundred million dollars. And that is a very, very conservative estimate, considering the prices that modern pieces have been fetching at auction lately. It could easily be worth four or five times that much. A representative of Sotheby's phones me regularly to convey how anxious they are to get their hands on it."

"Correct me if I'm wrong," Soave said to her. "You're telling us that the 'contents' are worth more than the house, the land, the stock and everything else put together, am I right?"

"Unquestionably," Glynis confirmed.

"So *this* explains it," Des said to Claudia. "Why you've been so anxious to gain power of attorney over your mother's business affairs."

"I was concerned," Claudia conceded coolly. "And why not? Some of those pieces belong in a museum. There's no telling what Tolly might have done with them. If she wanted to leave the man a chunk of money, fine. But the family's art collection? I couldn't accept that. Because I love my mother and I'm worried about her." Claudia trailed off, her eyes cast down at the table. "Is that so hard to believe?"

"Not at all. You're not the only one who's worried."

"Meaning what, Des?" Glynis asked, frowning at her.

"Would you ladies please excuse us?" Des was already on her way out the back door. "We'll be leaving you now."

"Certainly," said Glynis, saving one final glare for Yolie.

"That blonde ball of fluff better hope she never tangles with *me* again," Yolie growled as Des led them across the courtyard toward their Crown Vics. "I will kick her skinny pink ass."

"Don't mess with Glynis, girl. She's got major juice."

"Not to mention some shifty moves," said Soave. "Yesterday she fails to disclose Guy Tolliver's *huge* windfall on a technicality. Today the man turns up dead. Was she just doing her job, like she said, or was she doing a job on us? How do we know she's not a part of this thing herself?"

"We don't know, Rico," Des acknowledged as they arrived at their cars. She leaned against hers, gazing up at the magnificent brick hugeness of Four Chimneys. "What we do know is someone is after the grand prize—this place and all that comes with it. A calculated, systematic master plan is taking shape. And they aren't done yet. There's still one more step. Mighty big one, too."

"The old lady," Yolie said in a hushed voice.

"You think her life is in danger?" Soave asked.

"I know it, Rico," Des said. "Poochie's bound to be their next target. They won't have everything they want until she's dead, too. And these are not patient people."

"We're putting an armed guard on her right now," Soave said with grim determination. "She needs protection around the clock."

"I'm guessing she won't like the idea much," Yolie said.

"Count on it," Des agreed. "But if she wants to stay alive, she'll do what we tell her."

"We can keep her safe, Des," Soave promised. "But you've got to help us out here. Haven't you got *any* idea who we're after?"

"I wish I did, Rico. But I'm still a million miles from nowhere, and getting more damned frustrated by the—"

Her cell phone rang. She glanced down at the home screen. It was Mitch. She took his call.

"Your troubles are over, Master Sergeant," he said to her excitedly. "I've just figured out how we can blow this whole thing wide open."

CHAPTER 21

"KIND OF BUSY HERE," Des said back to him over the cell phone.

"That's what I figured," Mitch responded as he sat behind the wheel of his truck, sipping hot coffee. "But I need face time with you. I'm parked out on Route 156 about a hundred yards from the driveway." He and a crush of TV news vans. "I tried to get inside, but the trooper told me to am-scray. And it's been a long time since I've heard anyone use pig latin, let me tell you."

"Mitch, I can't give you any time right—"

"Wait, have you guys figured out yet that Poochie's the next victim?"

Silence from her end. Until she said, "We're putting a twenty-four-hour guard on her."

"No, you don't want to do that. This is what I need to see you about. I have fresh doughnuts."

"Mitch, I can't just pick up and . . . did you get any jelly?"

"Do I know you or do I know you?"

He heard her sigh. "Okay, the trooper will let you through. I'll met you at the fork."

Eric's fragrant sheep farm seemed uncommonly peaceful in the morning sunlight after the hubbub down at the road. It was so quiet Mitch could hear the bleating of the denizens as he waited there.

It took Des ten minutes to stride her way down the private drive to him, looking ultra-stressed. When the master sergeant was tightly coiled she developed a yen for jelly doughnuts. Absolutely her only junk food vice—unless you classified carrot sticks as junk food, and Mitch did.

She hopped in next to him and lunged for a football-sized jelly doughnut, attacking it ravenously. "Tell me how you figured out that Poochie is next in line. I'm a trained homicide investigator and I just got there. What makes you so damned smart?"

"I watched a great deal of Larry, Moe and Curly in my formative years. And I know how you can cut through all of the procedure and nail your killers. In movie parlance, it's known as cutting to the chase."

"That's funny, we call it that in real life, too."

"Okay, now you're being pointy."

Des stuffed the last of the doughnut in her mouth, dabbing at her face with a napkin. "Mitch, tell me why we don't want to put a guard on Poochie."

"Because if she has police protection then she'll never be attacked."

"Well, yeah, that's kind of the whole idea."

"No, it's not. You have a golden opportunity here to smoke them out. But our killers have to think she's alone in the house when she calls them up. Otherwise, they won't come over."

"Slow down. Who is she calling?"

"We'll get to that in a minute."

"Keep talking." She reached for another doughnut.

"You set up a video camera in Poochie's parlor. Wire the whole room for visuals and sound. Then, at your behest, Poochie calls up the suspects and says, 'I know it's you. We need to talk about this. Please come over right now.' And so they do. Meanwhile, you're in the next room watching the whole thing on the monitor. She gets them to incriminate themselves on tape. And you swoop down on them and, bam, case closed." It occurred to Mitch that Des had not stopped staring at him for the longest time. "Okay, I know exactly what you're going to say next."

"No, I really don't think you do."

"It smacks of entrapment, right? I'm well aware of that particular problem, and I have a way around it—Soave's on board from the get-go. He can run it by the district prosecutor. Get proper authorization for the video camera. It'll all be aboveboard." Mitch dug a cinnamon cruller out of the bag and bit into it. "I'm done. Say what you were going to say."

"First of all, it's not my case. Second of all, no. Third of all, that's not a plan—it's a Hail Mary pass from the last reel of one of your dumb-assed old *Saint* movies."

"The *Saint* movies were not dumb-assed. And it so happens the police were *happy* for Simon Templar's help. Especially when George Sanders played him. He was a highly undervalued leading man."

"Mitch, there is absolutely no way any of this can happen."

"Sure it can. You own Soave."

"Tawny owns him. I just rent him out by the day."

"You think he won't go for it?"

"Baby, we can't possibly endanger a civilian's life that way. They could just come right through the door, guns blasting. Meanwhile we're sitting in the next room going 'Uh-oh, what just happened?' Besides, you're assuming they'll confess everything in great detail. That's strictly Hollywood. Out here in the reality-based community the bad guys just deny, deny, deny. Only way we can ever get one to admit he's done anything is by offering him a deal to rat out his partner. And the only way we can do *that* is if we know who the hell they are."

"So let's use our heads." Mitch paused to collect his thoughts. "Back story, we're looking at two families who share a history of hostility and, it now turns out, common blood—in the person of Pete Mosher. Both Poochie Vickers and Milo Kershaw knew about it and kept it to themselves, correct?"

"Correct. Poochie because she was told to by her father. Or so she claims. Milo because he was ashamed that John J. Meier had gotten his mother pregnant."

"Cut to the present. We have one missing Mercedes Gullwing and two dead guys. One is the very same Pete Mosher, who it turns out was worth a fortune, and the other is Guy Tolliver."

"Who stood to inherit a fortune," Des put in. "We just found out that Poochie left him her entire art collection."

"No way! I mean, that's good. Now we don't have to ask ourselves why he died. We know why. Are you still looking for a pair of killers?"

"That's our working theory."

"Then let's put a few potential alliances out there. People who share an interest in what's been happening. Like Milo and Doug. They were childhood buddies with Pete, right? Doug gave Pete a place to stay. Milo was Pete's half-brother. Pete was way rich."

"Milo wasn't provided for in Pete's will. Neither man was."

"Which Milo was bound to resent. Doug, too, maybe."

"The *Jeep* . . ." Des said suddenly. "Doug delivered an old Jeep to Poochie while I was there yesterday. He was around Four Chimneys at the time of Tolly's death. *And* he was out in his tow truck when Pete was murdered."

"Meanwhile, Milo's also allied by blood to that twosome perennially voted Dorset's least likely to succeed . . ."

"Stevie and Donnie." Des picked up this ball and ran with it. "Fact: These crimes occurred as soon as they got out of jail. Fact: The Kershaw brothers were supposed to show up for work at Four Chimneys Farm at the same time the Gullwing disappeared and Pete got whacked. Fact: They were on the premises, finishing up work for the day, when Tolly got it. Fact: They're lying, scummy bad boys."

"Then we've got their sister, Justine, whose boyfriend happens to be the sole living member of Four Chimneys' gen-next. And therefore has a huge stake in how the financial future shakes out. Bement has a temper, and no one but Justine to vouch for his whereabouts when Pete was murdered."

"No one to vouch for him period yesterday. He got back from work well within our time frame of when Tolly died. Claims he was home alone at Four Chimneys."

"And where was Justine?"

"Good question." She jotted that down in the notepad she kept in the left breast pocket of her jacket. "Let's look at Poochie's two heirs, Claudia and Eric."

"We know they can't stand each other. We know Claudia's not getting along with her husband, Mark."

"And now we know why she's been trying to seize control of the family purse strings," Des added. "Because Poochie recently amended her will to leave Tolly her art collection. Which Eric claims he could care less about."

"I can believe that." Mitch bit into another doughnut, sorry he'd settled for a half-dozen. "Eric is way too wrapped up in his farm to care about anything else. The man is over-the-top intense about it. And, let's face it, madness runs in the . . ." Mitch trailed off, swallowing.

She looked at him. "Were you going somewhere with that?"

"Not really." His head was suddenly spinning. Something had just clicked. Something he'd forgotten.

"We also have to look at their respective spouses, Mark and Danielle, who may or may not be involved with each other."

"Mark's definitely into her," Mitch said, chewing on his doughnut. "Danielle's the iffy one. She may be a caring, good-hearted sister-in-law. Or she may be a scheming slut."

"She hardly seems that type, does she?"

"Why not? Where is it written that scheming sluts have to be sex kittens in tight skirts and Jimmy Choo stiletto heels?"

"They make for an awfully unlikely couple," Des said doubtfully.

"Have you caught a look at us in the mirror lately, slats?"

"Good point," she admitted. "But what's their motive for mowing down Pete and Tolly?"

"On paper, their respective spouses end up a whole lot wealthier. That could translate to much heftier divorce settlements should they choose to opt out and marry each other."

"They may have signed prenups. That would cut your argument right off at the knees. Worth looking into, though." This Des jotted down, too.

Mitch beamed at her. "You've come to depend on these skull sessions, haven't you? Just between us, where would you be without me?"

"Still on the Major Crime Squad, for starters."

"Okay, now you're just being outright nasty."

"We've also got to consider Glynis Fairchild-Forniaux, official keeper of secrets. She's known the truth about Pete's identity and wealth all along. The details of his will, Poochie's bequest to Tolly—these are things that she's had inside knowledge of. And she's a player, our Glynis. Someone with political ambitions. A thriving law practice. An amazing home, kids, a veterinarian husband who's handsome and . . ." Des drew her breath in.

Mitch studied her curiously. "Handsome and what?"

"Plus there's her ankle. She told me she twisted it yesterday morning while she was training for the marathon. There was a toe skid in the mud near Pete's body. Someone tripped and fell. Possibly that someone sustained a minor ankle injury. Plus Yolie dislikes her intensely. I've never seen Yolie take such an intense personal dislike to someone. That's worth something, don't you think?"

"I do," Mitch said, nodding his head.

"Mitch, is there something else you haven't told me?" she asked, her eyes locking onto his. "Because on the phone last night I had the feeling you were holding something back. Is it to do with that hypothetical statutory rape?"

"I've told you everything I can without putting you in an awkward position."

"To hell with awkward," she said angrily. "We're trying to solve two murders here. Why are you holding out on me?"

"Because I gave my word. I'm a working journalist, Des. If I'm told something in confidence then it has to stay in confidence. It's a matter of ethics."

"Know what? I hate it when you invoke your holy journalistic calling this way. It's like you have a bubble of moral superiority around you and if I try to burst it I'm being all evil. It's not fair, Mitch."

"I don't disagree, but here we are. Doing any better on that self-portrait?"

"Much better. I drop-kicked it."

"Good."

"Why good?"

"Because you obviously weren't enjoying it. That's a clear sign that you should be doing something else. I had a dream about you last night."

"What was I doing?"

"Drowning in Long Island Sound. We both were, actually."

"Did you rescue me?"

He took her hand and squeezed it. "No, you rescued me."

"Glad to be of service," she said huskily, her eyes softening.

"I believe in you, Des. This is a tough case, but you'll crack it open."

"Right now, I don't see how."

"Well, I do have another idea."

"Somehow, I knew you would."

"We go with my plan but we don't tell Soave. I've got a tape recorder back at my place. We can stash it somewhere in the parlor with Poochie while she braces the suspects."

"Mitch, we both know that's not going to happen. I'd lose my job, my pension, my . . ." She drew back from him, stiffening. "You know who Poochie places that first call to, don't you? That's why you're so sold on this."

"Not really. But it wouldn't surprise me if Poochie has her suspicions. She might even be protecting them out of family loyalty."

"And you think she'll give them up if we hold her feet to the fire?"

"The thought did occur to me."

"You may not be wrong," Des conceded. "But it's Rico's investigation, and we move the ball downfield his way. That's how it has to be. And now I'd better get back." She started to get out, then stopped, staring at him intently. "Will you promise me you won't pull anything suicidal the minute my back is turned?"

"Why would you think I'd do that?"

"How about because you always do?"

"You make it sound like I have a death wish."

"No, never. I think you're a good-hearted man who sometimes does truly hose-headed things."

"That's one of the nicest things you've ever said to me."

"Mitch, promise me you won't do anything crazy. Otherwise, I swear I'll handcuff you to that steering wheel right this instant."

"You're serious about this, aren't you?"

"*Promise* me."

"Okay, okay. I promise."

CHAPTER 22

DES SPOTTED HIM OUT in front of the white farmhouse on Frederick Lane where the Jewett sisters lived. Marge and Mary absolutely doted on their Jack Russells, Huey and Dewey. Des often saw the sisters walking the feisty little dogs on Dorset Street, all four of them wearing the matching kelly green turtleneck sweaters that the sisters had knitted.

Dr. Andre had just finishing calling on them. When Des pulled up, the tall Frenchman was depositing used syringes in a medical waste bin in the back of his red truck, his appointment book and medical bag set before him on the tailgate.

"How goes it, Andre?" she called to him as she climbed out of her cruiser. "Are Huey and Dewey well?"

"Just needed their booster shots," he responded in his Tennessee-tinted French drawl. "And the sisters needed a talking to, eh? They spoil those two beasts rotten. Sauteed sirloin tips for breakfast, can you imagine?" A hint of a smile crossed his lean face, which was about as much warmth as Andre the Drip ever displayed. "And what may I do for you?"

"Just passing by," Des replied. Actually, she'd called his answering service to find out where he was. "Andre, there's something I need to ask you."

Andre immediately held up a warning hand. "I know precisely where you are going, and the answer is no." He glanced down at his opened appointment book, then began restocking his medical bag from the supply drawers. "Believe me, Des, I always ask if anyone wants to adopt a cute kitten. Particularly when I visit families with young children. But I have no takers. Which reminds me, I've heard that there is some activity by the Dumpster out behind the Rustic Inn."

"Ferals?"

"Full grown, I'm afraid."

"Damn . . ." For rescuers, adult feral strays were almost always a source of heartbreak. They were the hardest to catch and most likely to be diseased. "We'll check it out right away, Andre, but that wasn't what I wanted to ask you about."

"What is it then?" A slight edge of impatience crept into his voice. "Not that I mean to rush you, but I have many stops to make this morning."

"You do make your share of rounds, don't you? You must travel these roads a lot."

"I do, yes."

"Early in the morning?"

"Quite often."

"Did you develop any kind of relationship with Pete Mosher?"

"Who, The Can Man?" Andre puffed out his cheeks. "I would wave to him. And he would sometimes acknowledge my existence by nodding to me. He accepted that I was making rounds of my own, and therefore was no threat to him. But I did not try to speak to him. There was no point."

"I imagine Glynis saw him pretty often, too. Training early in the morning the way she does."

"She did. We both did. When it's warmer out I often run with her. But my knees act up in the cold, and the footing is terrible. She twisted her ankle on a patch of ice just yesterday."

"I noticed. Looked pretty painful."

"Not too bad, no. The hard part is convincing Glynis to rest it for two or three days. When my wife sets her sights on a goal, forget it." Andre looked down his nose at Des. "Why do you ask me about Pete?"

"It's a funny thing, actually," she replied, feeling a slight uptick in her pulse. "I know so much about Glynis's family history. How she took over her dad's law practice. How he took it over from his dad before him. But I don't know a thing about yours, beyond the obvious fact that you were born and raised in France. I don't suppose you had any further connection with him, did you?"

Andre closed the supply drawers and set his medical bag in the front seat. "We're still talking about Pete?"

"We are."

"I'm afraid I don't understand. What kind of further connection?"

"By blood, Andre."

"By *blood?* How in God's name have you gotten such a crazy idea?"

Honestly, that's how. Because if Dr. Andre Forniaux's arrival in Dorset had not been a chance occurrence, if it was all part of a calculated plan, then everything added up.

"Pete did sow his wild oats in France in the Sixties," she said to him. "Which would make you about the right age."

"The right age for what? I truly don't . . ." Andre halted, turning six different kinds of chilly now. "My God, you think Pete was my *father,* don't you? You think that I'm the bastard son's bastard son, come to claim my rightful share of the treasure. This is beyond preposterous, Des. It's truly insulting!"

And yet it made so much sense. After all, Andre was married to a woman who enjoyed detailed inside knowledge of John J. Meier's will and the wills of his two children, Poochie and Pete. Who better to secretly help him contest those wills than the family's own lawyer?

"I mean no offense, Andre. From time to time, this job compels me to ask even my friends some very unpleasant questions."

"It does indeed," he shot back, his jaw clenching. "And here I thought my job was unpleasant. Telling a lonely widow that I have to put down her beloved poodle, that's something awful. But *this* . . . Des, you are grossly underpaid."

"You won't get any argument from me."

"Still, we do what we have to, you and I," Andre conceded grudgingly. "And we get up every morning and we do it again, eh? So I will not sputter at you like an angry headwaiter. I will honor your professionalism by granting you a civil reply."

"I appreciate that, Andre."

"I never met Pete Mosher before I moved here," he said, his voice calm and quiet. "I have no dark secrets in my past. Merely a conventional middle-class upbringing in a suburb of Paris. My father was a civil servant. When I was sixteen I came to America as a foreign exchange student. I lived in Scarsdale, New York, with John and Diane Alterman and their three children. The Altermans ran a veterinary clinic. From them I learned to love animals and America. I went home to finish my schooling and be a ski bum for a while. Then I met Glynis and followed her back here. After veterinary school, I never returned home. Dorset is home."

"Are your parents still living?"

"They've retired to Collioure, a small fishing village on the Mediterranean coast near the Spanish border. You'd enjoy Collioure, Des. The likes of Picasso painted there in their youth. There is a restaurant called Les Templiers where many fine paintings still hang—the starving young artists paid for meals with their work, you see."

"Sounds great," she said, barely hearing his words. She was too busy sagging inwardly. She'd thought for sure she'd nailed it. Had felt it down in her gut. Now where the hell was she?

Her cell phone rang. Glancing down at it, she saw that it was Mitch yet again. "*Still* kind of busy here," she growled into the phone.

To which he blurted out: "I know, I know. And I'm sorry to bother you again. But something *slightly* urgent has come up. . . ."

CHAPTER 23

THE SNUG LITTLE PACKAGE from Vero Beach, Florida, was waiting for him at the post office, tightly bound in a manner reminiscent of the wrap job on Boris Karloff in *The Mummy*. It was the only way Mitch's mom knew how to wrap packages. While he was at the post office, Mitch express-mailed Justine's manuscript to his literary agent. The note he attached read simply: *Am I crazy or is this great?*

From there, Mitch picked up a load of nonperishables at the A&P and frozen day-old bread from The Works. Then he toodled his way through the exquisite calm of the Historic District to the Congo church. It was not yet eleven o'clock, but two dozen or so people were already lined up outside the door to the Fellowship Center. He parked around the back. Lem the custodian had unlocked the Bilco cellar doors for him. Mitch raised them open and stashed the loaves of bread in the freezers down in the old coal cellar. Then he lowered the doors and toted the rest of the load into the kitchen, where a pigtailed Danielle was at the stove heating up a vat of soup.

"Morning, Danielle. How are you today?"

"A bit ashamed," she confessed, blushing. "I was feeling sorry for myself last night, and I needed to unload on someone." She stirred the soup pot, chewing on her lower lip. "Thanks for being such a good listener."

"No need to thank me. Friends talk to each other. It's what they do. Not a big deal."

"Yes, it was," Danielle insisted, her eyes avoiding his. "And I'm grateful. I want you to know that, okay?"

"Okay," Mitch responded, glancing around. The long dining tables were set up for the soup kitchen regulars, but they were shy at least a dozen folding chairs. "Where are all of the chairs?"

"I've sent Eric off to find them. You could give him a hand."

Mitch tried the parish offices but found no sign of the chairs there. Or Eric. But he did hear sounds coming from inside the meetinghouse itself. The connecting door was propped open. And the missing chairs were arrayed up on the horseshoe-shaped dais behind Reverend Sweet's pulpit. Eric was folding them up.

Mitch had to pause there in the doorway to gather himself. He hadn't set foot inside a church since Maisie's funeral.

The Congo Church was not nearly as grand inside as he'd expected from its towering profile out on Dorset Street. Its ceiling was barely high enough to accommodate the wraparound balcony. And the décor was spare and unadorned. Bare, polished wooden pews. Whitewashed walls. Wide-planked oak floors. There were windows everywhere. Two stories of windows. The low March sun flooded the sanctuary with sunlight.

"Ah, an extra pair of arms," Eric remarked, spotting him there.

"That's me." Mitch started toward the dais. "How goes it?"

Eric snapped the folding chairs shut and leaned them against the wall. "Just had to do a sucky family thing this morning," he replied a bit edgily. "Mother's all freaked out because her 'friend' is dead. Like we're supposed to care about some old fairy who was sponging off of her. Hey, if Tolly made her happy, I was all for it. But now that he's dead I'm supposed to care? Sorry, that's something I've always had trouble with."

"What is, Eric?"

"Being a phony. Can you grab half of these?"

"Absolutely. I just have a quick question. Did you pay the Kershaw brothers to kill Pete and Tolly or did you actually kill them yourself? I still can't figure that part out."

Eric froze, his eyes widening at Mitch. *"What? . . ."*

Mitch's powerful microcassette tape recorder was stuffed in the pocket of his wool jacket. He flicked it on, convinced that he was not breaking his promise to Des. He'd told her he wouldn't do anything crazy, and he wasn't. What he was doing was very sane. And necessary. "You offered Stevie and Donnie work on the farm when they got out of prison. You had them start the same morning that Pete would be pedaling past Four Chimneys on his rounds. They were still around the place when Tolly was killed. Did you arrange it that way because you'd hired them to do the killings or because you wanted people to think they had?"

Eric continued to gape at Mitch, his Adam's apple bobbing up and down. "Are you hallucinating? This is *me*."

"And you're the single most amazing scam artist I've ever come across," Mitch said. "I've been schmoozed by big-time Hollywood studio bosses, producers, agents. I'm talking world-class talent. But they can't even touch you, Eric. You present yourself as the ultimate American hero—the small farmer, an idealist who wants to grow things honestly. You perform good works in the community. You're a loving husband. To know you is to look up to you. Except no one knows you, do they?"

"Mitch, they need these chairs in the fellowship room," Eric said tightly. "And I *re-eally* don't think this is funny."

"Who actually did the killings, Eric? Who kept bashing Pete in the head with that pipe until he was dead? Who poured that lye down Tolly's throat? I'd *re-eally* like to know."

Eric blinked at Mitch rapidly, saying nothing. He'd grown extremely pale.

"Give it up, Eric. Just admit what you did. I can help you."

"Guys, what's taking so long?" Danielle called to them from out in the hall. She appeared in the doorway, looking harried. "Come on, will you? People will have to eat standing up."

"Lock that door behind you, hon," Eric blurted out.

Danielle stared at him, bewildered. "But why?"

"Mitch knows everything, that's why."

"Well, not everything," Mitch pointed out. "A whole lot of blanks still—"

"Danielle, lock that damned door!" Eric barked. "Do what I tell you!"

"Don't do it, Danielle," Mitch cautioned her. "That would be really stupid, and we both know you're not stupid."

Danielle seemed frozen, so paralyzed by fright that she could hardly breathe. Mitch could actually hear her gasp for air. And then he heard something much closer to him.

He heard Eric whip open his Leatherman knife.

Before Mitch could react, the gangly farmer had a strong left forearm wrapped around his throat and the three-inch razor sharp blade held to his jugular vein, its tip pricking his skin.

"Don't move a muscle," Eric warned Mitch, hugging him tightly against his own body. "Lock it, Danielle. And go make sure the front doors are locked, too. Hurry!"

She flew into action. Locked the hallway door behind her, then dashed up the aisle and pushed open one of the foyer doors. Mitch could hear her throwing the bolts on the church's three big double doors out front.

"Don't do this, Eric," he said hoarsely, feeling the man's hot breath on the back of his neck. "It will end badly, believe me."

"I don't want to hurt you, Mitch," he growled in response. "But I will. So just shut the hell up."

"Eric, what are you *doing?*" Danielle protested as she scurried back down the aisle toward them.

"Tie his hands with my belt," he ordered her. "*Now,* Danielle."

She obeyed, yanking Eric's worn leather belt from the loops of his pants, her eyes goggly with fear as she bound Mitch's hands tightly behind him. As soon as she'd finished, Eric shoved Mitch roughly to the floor. The microcassette recorder tumbled from his jacket pocket. Eric promptly stomped on it hard with his work shoe, then removed the tape and stuffed it in his pocket.

Mitch lay there with his hands bound awkwardly behind him, his shoulders screaming in pain. "You'll be so much better off if you just turn yourselves in," he said, squinting up at them in the sunlight that streamed through the church's windows. "You can't get away."

"Yeah, we can," Eric assured him. "We have a bargaining chip. We have you." He rummaged in Mitch's pockets for his cell phone. "What's Des's number?"

"Just hit redial."

Eric did, then held the phone to Mitch's ear.

Mitch heard her say, "*Still* kind of busy here."

To which he said: "I know, I know, and I'm sorry to bother you again. But something *slightly* urgent has come up. . . ."

Chapter 24

Here's what Des did after she got the call that would change her life forever:

She thanked Andre Forniaux, mobile vet, for his time and she ran like hell for her cruiser, cursing the day she ever met a pigment-challenged New York widower by the name of Mitchell I Am a Big, Fat Fool Berger. From the front seat of her ride she called Soave to scream at him that Eric and Danielle Vickers were holding Mitch hostage inside the Congregational Church and would slit his throat unless they got exactly what they wanted.

Eric had snatched the cell phone from Mitch to tell her what that was: A private jet with enough range to fly them nonstop to "somewhere like the Cayman Islands." A car to deliver them to that jet, and a briefcase filled with $1 million in cash. Once they arrived at their destination, safe and sound, Mitch would be freed.

"Otherwise, your boyfriend dies," Eric had promised her, his voice sounding alarmingly high-pitched. "Understand?"

Des had responded, "I'll have to get back to you, Eric. Just be cool, okay?"

Quickly, she alerted her troop commander of a life-threatening hostage situation. He'd send cruisers to secure the area. Also notify the district commander, who'd bring the state's high command into the loop. Soave, meanwhile, reached out to Emergency Services for a hostage unit. There would be a negotiator to try to talk them into giving up. There would be a SWAT team. If Eric and Danielle refused to back down then snipers would take them out—assuming they had a clean shot. If they didn't, the team would have to storm the church with overwhelming force. Although that would be a last resort. This was a house of worship, after all, and these were not hardened gangbangers. Just an organic farmer and his pigtailed wife who happened to have gone nutso.

This was Mitch.

Des floored it down the center of Dorset Street with her siren blaring and her lights flashing, pounding the wheel as she drove. Mitch had *promised* her he wouldn't do anything crazy. She should have known better. Should have stopped him while she had him.

The fool. The big, fat fool.

She was the first to arrive on the scene. Immediately ordered the Food Pantry patrons from the area. Answered no questions, told them no lies. Simply said that there was a public safety situation and they would have to leave. She combed the parish offices, which were mostly staffed by volunteers. None were present. The offices were deserted. The hallway door to the church was shut. And no doubt locked from the inside by Eric and Danielle.

She heard the sirens as half a dozen troopers from the Westbrook Barracks pulled up. Their job was to close off every intersection within two blocks of the church. While they did that Des undertook her own personal recon by pacing all the way around the outside of the church, stepping quietly on the gravel. She checked out the service driveway around back, where Mitch's truck was parked next to Eric's. The back door to the Fellowship Center kitchen. The handicapped ramp, which provided wheelchair access to the old church by way of the Center. There was no other back way into the church. No rear windows. Just a pair of Bilco cellar doors, presently shut.

She circled back around to the front of the church, crossed Dorset Street and stood there on the opposite sidewalk, trying to take it all in as her heart pounded and her knees trembled. She was absolutely frantic. But absolutely no one could know this. Des had to keep it together. Stay focused on what she was looking at:

The stately church faced east from behind a hundred feet of pale winter lawn. Two huge old oaks framed its entrance. Six steps led up to the three double doors. The church's north and south sides were made up mostly of windows, upstairs and down. The downstairs windows were at least twelve feet up off the ground, so there was no chance of her catching sight of them in there. Maybe from a second-floor window in one of the neighboring houses. The church's upstairs windows were roughly even with the rooftops of those three-story colonials. Above the sanctuary there appeared to be an attic space—the roof beneath the clock tower was slightly peaked, and there was a fanlight there beneath the two-story-high clock. Atop the clock sat the bell tower, and above that the gracefully tapered steeple that soared some ten stories up into the blue sky, where she could make out a chopper approaching from off in the distance.

A slicktop pulled up out front with a screech and out jumped Soave and Yolie. They immediately marched across the street toward her.

"What did that bozo get himself into now?" Soave demanded angrily.

"The worst kind of trouble, Rico."

"He means well," Yolie spoke up in Mitch's defense.

"He's a total pain in the ass," Soave shot back. "And when I see him I'm going to punch him right in the nose."

"You'll have to wait your turn," Des said. "I've got dibs."

Reverend Cyrus Sweet, a calm, red-bearded man in his fifties, showed up next, accompanied by Lem Procter, the gnarled old church custodian. Lem was trembling with fear.

"I've known Eric since he was a boy," Reverend Sweet informed them in his resonant voice. "I could try to talk to him if you'd like."

"It might come to that," Soave said. "Right now, we're still trying to figure out what's what."

"They've secured the front doors," Des said. "Also the connecting door to the parish offices. Are there any other ways in?"

"No, ma'am," Lem replied, his voice quavering.

"Talk to us about that fanlight window. Is there an attic up there?"

"Yeah, that's how we get at the clock works. The attic stairs are up in the balcony, next to the organ."

"Is there any other way to reach the attic?" Yolie was thinking the same thing Des was: If they could get up there then that would put them in the balcony. "Back stairs? Fire stairs?"

Reverend Sweet shook his head. "The balcony is our only access."

"I noticed a set of Bilco cellar doors," Des said.

"That's the old coal cellar." Lem scratched his ear with a wavering finger.

"Does it run all the way under the church?"

"It does, but it's mostly wiring and pipes. Some storage."

"Can you access it from inside the church, Lem?"

"Sure can. Cellar door's in the cloakroom out in the foyer."

Des shot a glance at Soave and Yolie, her pulse quickening. "Lem, I didn't see a padlock on those Bilcos. How do you lock them?"

"From the inside. All your Bilcos are that way. I have to go through the cellar from the cloakroom to unlock 'em."

"We have ourselves a situation here, Lem. Is there any nice, quiet way we can pry those Bilcos open from the *outside?*"

"No need to. Today's a Food Pantry day—I unlocked 'em first thing this morning. Only reason they're down is to keep the danged squirrels out of there."

Des tried to picture the layout of the church's foyer. Just inside the front doors there were two staircases up to the balcony—one on the left, the other on the right. The cloakroom was adjacent to the stairs on the right. "That cellar door in the cloakroom," she said. "Do you keep it locked?"

"You bet. Need a key to get down there. Otherwise the kids sneak down, get into mischief."

"Okay, now here comes the million-dollar question, Lem . . ." Des breathed in and out. "Can that cloakroom door be unlocked from *inside* the cellar?"

"Not a problem. Just have to turn the thumb latch."

Des grabbed the old custodian by the shoulders and kissed him on the forehead. Then she charged off in the direction of the church.

"Slow down, Des," cautioned Soave, trotting to catch up with her. "The hostage unit will be here in ten minutes."

"I'm not waiting for this situation to harden, Rico." She paused at her cruiser for her flashlight.

"Look, I know you're worried about Berger but we got proper procedure to follow here. We need risk assessment, authorization. You can't just go cowboy."

"Rico, I'm *not* waiting around for some jarhead with a bullhorn to hammer out a deal for Mitch's life. That fat fool in there is the man I'm going to marry."

"Since when?" Yolie erupted.

"Since I heard his voice on the phone just now. He's my soul mate, Yolie. I'll die if I lose him. We belong together. And we're getting married. And, damn it, it would be nice if he lived to find that out. Which is why I'm going in." She started her way around back of the church, both of them striding along with her. "And why you two are staying out here. You had no prior knowledge of my play. We never even had this conversation, understand?"

"Des, I really, really don't like this," Soave said.

"Deal with it, Rico."

"I'm going in with you, girl," Yolie insisted. "You'll need back-up."

"Big thanks, but I won't let you risk it. It's my man and my career."

They'd reached the rear of the church. Quietly, Des raised the Bilco doors, throwing sunlight on the steep cement steps down to the coal cellar. She removed her big Smokey hat. Unlaced her boots, slipped them off and started down the narrow steps in her stocking feet, pausing to glance back up at Soave and Yolie as they stood out in the driveway.

They both looked worried sick.

Des flashed a reassuring smile at them. Took a great big deep breath. Then plunged her way into the deep, dark recesses of the basement below the old church.

CHAPTER 25

INSIDE THE CHURCH, THEY could hear the first siren approach, coming very fast.

Des, most likely, Mitch reflected as he lay there on the floor, his arms lashed together beneath him. Not a very comfortable position—especially with Eric holding that sharp, cold blade against his throat. Eric was behind him on the floor with his back resting against the edge of the dais and his left arm wrapped around Mitch's chest, hugging Mitch against him. Mitch felt powerless, utterly terrified. And, yet, strangely comforted. Being held this way reminded him of when he was a little boy and his dad would read him *Bartholomew and the Oobleck*. Although Nathan Berger had smelled much better than Eric Vickers. And he'd never held a knife to his only son's tender young throat.

Danielle sat before them in the front row of pews, wringing her hands. Her eyes darted wildly with fear behind those wire-framed glasses.

Mitch heard the cruiser pull up outside with a screech. A car door open and shut. Footsteps. *Her* footsteps. A voice. *Her* voice.

"She'll clear all of the Food Pantry people out of here," he said hoarsely as he lay there, quaking with fear. "In a few more minutes the others will get here from Westbrook. They'll close off this intersection and reroute the traffic. It'll take another twenty minutes for the big boys from Meriden to show. We have some time, is what I'm trying to say. We could use it productively."

"*Or* you could shut the hell up," Eric growled.

"Don't think I can, Eric. I chatter when I'm nervous. I know this about myself. I also know it's not too late to make the best out of this situation. Why don't you tell me how it happened? Maybe I can help you turn things around."

"You can't even save yourself. What makes you think you can save us?"

"Oh, what does it matter now, Eric?" Danielle demanded hotly. She wasn't merely scared. She was pissed at him. Why, because it was *his* plan? "Tell Mitch how it happened. What can it hurt?"

In the distance, Mitch could hear the wail of the other sirens.

"Fine, then *I'll* tell him," Danielle snapped, heaving her chest. "It was just supposed to be about the Gullwing, I swear. We needed the money, Mitch. The farm is . . . we're *so* strapped for cash. But the more we talked about it, the more it all grew into something . . ."

"Bolder," Eric spoke up.

"That's what you call it?" asked Mitch.

"Absolutely," Eric replied, his voice brimming with pride. Which Mitch found incredibly bizarre—not that any of this wasn't bizarre. "Let me tell him, hon. It's *my* story." Eager to share it now, Eric shifted himself around so that he was kneeling directly over Mitch, looking right down into his eyes as he held that knife to his throat. "See, I got to talking with this teamster-type guy at the Union Square green market last summer," he began, blue eyes burning bright with intensity. "He drove a truck in from Long Island every Wednesday and Saturday for one of the old farmers out there. And he started telling me his brother had just gone to jail for stealing exotic cars for some shady dealer who'd sell them overseas. I immediately thought of Mom's Gullwing, right? He put me in touch with them. At first, they only offered me a few grand for it. I dickered with them all winter. Held out for twenty thou. They finally caved since the Gullwing's such a collector's item. Gave me my choice of delivery dates. I picked one that coincided with the Kershaw brothers' release from prison. That way absolutely everyone would figure Stevie and Donnie were behind it—especially if they had a reason to be at Four Chimneys Farm that same morning."

"They were ideal fall guys," Mitch suggested as more cruisers pulled up outside, car doors opened and closed. "Congenital bad boys who have a real grudge against your family."

"They were perfect. And it was *even* recycling day."

"Which gave you the perfect opening to take out Pete. Anyone investigating his death would assume that Stevie and Donnie bashed the guy's head in so he couldn't identify them to the police. But it was you and Danielle who stole the Gullwing, wasn't it? You and Danielle who went looking for Pete. You didn't have to go far either—you encountered him as soon as you pulled out of your driveway. If he noticed the Gullwing, he probably figured it was Poochie. Had no reason to think otherwise. Not until you two beat him to death with that length of pipe. One of you took a tumble in the process."

"I tripped in the dark," Danielle said miserably, seated there with her shoulders slumped. "I wasn't hurt. It was nothing."

"Once Pete was dead you delivered the Gullwing to the truck that was waiting in the commuter parking lot."

Eric nodded. "I did that while Danielle ran back up to our house, quick as a bunny, for my truck. She grabbed up Pete's returnables, then picked me up at the commuter lot. It was still dark out. No one saw us."

"On your way home, you dropped Pete's bottles and cans off at the Kershaw place, the better to incriminate them. Then you returned home to your morning chores and no one was the wiser. Everyone figured Stevie and Donnie were the culprits. Everyone except for Des. She never fell for it. Not that she had the slightest idea it was you. No one did."

"How did *you* figure it out?" Eric demanded, crouching over him with that damned knife.

"You told me," Mitch replied, swallowing carefully. "The other day in the coal cellar, when you were being all jealous and paranoid about Danielle and Mark."

"What did I? . . ."

"You said that madness runs in your family. A very odd admission for you to make, considering how you won't side with Claudia's attempt to have your mother declared legally incompetent. You won't even acknowledge that your mother has a problem. So what was I to make of that remark? I didn't know. Not until this morning when Des and I were doing damage to some doughnuts. I always think best when I'm having a sugar rush. And here's what I came up with: You knew that crazy old Pete was your uncle. That he was worth millions. You weren't supposed to know. Claudia didn't, but you did. How, did Glynis tell you?"

"John J. did," Eric replied. "Grandfather wanted me to know the truth, one man to another, so he wrote a letter to me before he died. Gave it to his lawyer, Glynis's dad, and instructed him to hand it to me on my twenty-first birthday. It was our secret. Strictly a guy thing. Grandfather never wanted Claudia to know. She was a girl, therefore he regarded her as a delicate flower." Eric let out a harsh laugh. "Not a keen judge of character, old John J."

"Why now, Eric? What made you decide to kill Pete now?"

"That's all Claudia's fault," Eric answered bitterly. "She's determined to seize power over the family pursestrings. And believe me, Mitch, the day Claudia gets Mom declared crazy is the day she puts Four Chimneys Farm out of business. She hates us. *That's* why the twisted bitch wants control—so she can plow us under. *That's* why we came up with this plan. She has her plan, we had ours."

"Small difference," Mitch argued, hearing the whirring of a helicopter in the distance. "Hers doesn't involve killing anyone."

"Doesn't it? She wants to take away Mother's control over her own life. Isn't that as bad as having her killed? So what if the old girl likes her brandy? So what if she hoards candy bars? You're supposed to make allowances for the people you love, not destroy them. Besides, this has never been about Mother. It's about how Claudia wants to ruin us. We *had* to fight her."

Many more vehicles pulled up outside now. Doors slammed. Voices shouted. Boots pounded on the pavement. The hostage unit from Meriden. They sounded like an invading army. As Mitch lay there on the church floor in terrified silence, blood pounding in his ears, he wondered if they would try to negotiate with Eric. Or would they just blow him away? So far, Mitch's cell phone had remained silent. No one had called yet to establish contact.

Danielle started toward the windows for a look, the floorboards creaking under her feet.

"Stay away from those windows!" Eric cried out, his knife blade nearly pricking Mitch's skin. "Are you nuts?"

She halted in her tracks. "I-I'm sorry. Just wanted to see. . . ."

"Sit back down, you idiot!"

Danielle returned to her pew, cowering.

Ordinarily, Mitch might have felt pity for her. But he was well past the point of extending any human kindness to Danielle Vickers. "Your farm matters that much to you?" he asked Eric.

Eric blinked at him in surprise. "Well, yeah. Small farming's our mission. We bring something vital into people's lives. We connect them to the land. If we lose the farm that connection will be gone forever. And we'll go under by next winter without help. We need more land, more sheep, more money. Lots more. Mother won't loan it to us. She's into the whole Yankee self-reliance thing."

"And the banks won't extend us another penny," Danielle added woefully, her eyes searching Mitch's for understanding. "We've devoted our adult lives to Four Chimneys Farm, Mitch. We can't go under. We just can't."

"By taking the Gullwing we squared away our cash flow problems until green market season," Eric explained. "By eliminating Pete we've added nearly twenty million dollars to the family piggy bank."

"You make it all sound like sensible financial planning," Mitch said in disbelief.

"We were responding to Claudia's provocation," Danielle insisted. "If she hadn't been so greedy, none of this would have happened. It's all her fault."

"Guy Tolliver's death was her fault, too?"

"Tolly was nothing more than a sleazy opportunist," Eric said disgustedly. "He didn't deserve to inherit the family's art collection. "That's ours."

Mitch considered their words for a moment as the helicopter drew nearer and the edge of that knife remained poised to sever his jugular vein. How long would he last if Eric used it? How many minutes before his life would bleed right out of him—five, ten? "Did it ever occur to you two that Claudia might be genuinely concerned about Poochie's health? She refuses to see a doctor. If Social Services launches a mental competency investigation then she'll be forced to see one. What if *that's* why Claudia is doing this?"

"Not possible," Eric responded. "You don't know my sister like I do."

"Here's what I know," Mitch said. "I know that you've never been the happy, smiling people who you appeared to be. You've fooled pretty much everyone in Dorset. You sure fooled me. Danielle, that way you cozied up to Mark was really smooth. Plus you are truly gifted at dishing up vicious, untrue family gossip. First you convinced me that Claudia drove Mark away by being such a greedy bitch. Then you told Des he might have stolen the Gullwing to get back at her. None of which was real. Mark is just a middle-aged guy going through a rough patch. It's *you* who planted the idea that he left her over her so-called power grab. Which I'm still not convinced was ever any such thing. I think Claudia loves Poochie and is trying to do right by her. You convinced people otherwise. But let me ask you something stupid—if you guys were so desperate for money why not just kill Poochie from the get-go?"

"She's my mother," Eric said simply. "I could never kill her."

So he'd been wrong about that part. So had Des. Not that it mattered anymore. Staying alive mattered. Seeing Des again mattered. "But you *could* savagely kill Pete and Tolly," he pressed on, fighting the fear in his voice. "And be damned calculating about it, too. You made it seem as if someone not too bright had done both killings. First by planting Pete's haul at the Kershaw place. Then by making Tolly's death look like a clumsily staged suicide. Although that didn't exactly stick. People like Des have a lot of experience with this kind of thing."

"Maybe they do," Eric admitted. "But they're under enormous

pressure to crack a case like this. If you hadn't shown up here I guarantee you they would have dragged the Kershaw brothers away today and interrogated them day and night until one of them signed a confession."

"Des doesn't do things that way."

"She's just the resident trooper. It would be out of her hands."

Eric wasn't totally off base, but Mitch wouldn't admit it to him. "I'll concede that you successfully drew the law's attention away from yourselves. You even have a back-up fall guy waiting in the wings." He turned his attention back to Danielle. "Last night at the Mucky Duck you told me Mark withdrew his last five grand so he could run off with you. Was that for real?"

"I let Mark believe it was," she answered in a tiny voice. "He thinks that . . . that we're involved."

"He's not alone. When I saw how you looked I figured you and he had just had a tumble upstairs on his office sofa."

She shot a nervous glance at Eric. "That's never happened."

"Of course not," Mitch said. "The reason you looked that way was because you'd just dragged Tolly's body into the woods and poured lye down his throat."

"It's true," she admitted. "We took care of him as soon as we left Claudia's house. Poochie didn't make it easy for us, returning to Claudia's for dinner the way she did. That was why we had to carry him down to the woods."

"Meanwhile, Mark makes for a great suspect. He's a family insider, broke, emotionally troubled. I can see why you'd point the law right at him."

"Not exactly," Eric said darkly.

"What do you mean, not exactly?"

"That wasn't our intention. We had long-term plans for Mark."

"I don't understand, what did you? . . ." Mitch's voice caught in his throat. "My God, you weren't done, were you? You were going to kill *her*. That's it, isn't it? Claudia was next."

CHAPTER 26

BEYOND THE FREEZERS THERE was a doorway.

As she passed through it, Des left behind those last rays of daylight streaming down through the cellar doors and encountered utter darkness. She had no idea where any light switches were. And she wasn't about to grope around for one. Those wide-planked floorboards over her head had shrunk and swelled across so many generations of seasons that she could see cracks of daylight between them. If she turned on a light Eric and Danielle might see it between the floorboards. She couldn't take that chance.

She waved her flashlight beam ahead of her, pointing it downward at the concrete floor. She was in the furnace room. It was a mammoth furnace compared to the one in her own cellar, as was the oil tank next to it. Across the furnace room was another, narrower doorway. And one, two, three concrete steps up to the low, vast expanse of the cellar. She scoped it out with her flashlight. Could not see to the other side of it, where the cloakroom stairs were. Only clutter. A narrow path wove through all of the junk that was crowded in down there beneath a honeycomb of electrical conduits and copper water pipes.

Des gathered herself, the damp cellar floor ice cold against her stocking feet, her ears ringing in the heavy silence. It was so quiet she could hear mice skitter along next to the foundation. And it reeked of mold. This was not good. Des happened to be super-allergic to mold. The merest whiff could set her off. But she couldn't, mustn't sneeze. Sneezing was out of the question. Don't even think about it.

She proceeded, moving slowly and carefully. She had to stay in a crouch. If she straightened to her full height her head would smack into one of those pipes. Which would make a serious thud. She could not afford that.

As she crept her way along, Des suddenly heard the floorboards creak directly over her head. She froze, her stomach muscles fluttering involuntarily. Eric and Danielle were right there, inches away from her. Mitch was right there. She could even hear their muffled voices. Couldn't make out what they were saying.

She moved forward, her head down, silent as a cat now. Even the slightest noise might alert them to the fact that she was down there. And there was no telling what Eric might do. She couldn't, mustn't make a sound. And yet already she was starting to sniffle. And now, God, she could feel it coming on. *She was going to sneeze.* And couldn't stop it. But she absolutely had to. She squeezed her nose between her thumb and forefinger, squeezed it so hard her eyes watered. A strangled, volcanic sob erupted deep down in her throat. Briefly, she felt as if she might choke. But then the sneeze passed. Wiping her eyes, she kept on going, using her flashlight sparingly.

She encountered stacks of aluminum folding tables. These were used for special events like the big white elephant sale that the church held every July, when its front lawn became a veritable bazaar of used toasters and television sets. Now the path snaked among piles of cardboard boxes that were marked XMAS. These held those electric candles that were positioned so charmingly in every one of the church's windows during the holiday season—those exceedingly delicate electric candles with their fragile little glass bulbs. Des edged her way even more carefully now. Because she did not want to nudge one of these boxes. If she broke a bulb it would sound like a grenade going off. She inched her way slowly between them, flashing her light from pile to pile, careful, careful . . .

So careful she let out a gasp when she ran smack dab into Mary and Joseph. And the infant Jesus. All of them life-sized. All of them right there before her.

She was so startled her elbow jostled one of those very boxes of electric candles. A box that was perched on top of a pile. And was now teetering from that pile and about to fall four feet to the concrete floor. She lunged for it and caught it just before it fell, its contents rattling faintly. But it did not crash.

Sighing hugely, she returned the box securely to the top of the pile and had herself another look at what she was looking at: It was the wooden figures from the beautiful creche that the church erected on its front lawn every Christmas. Sure, there were the three kings ahead of her in the flashlight's beam. And the shepherds. And the three-sided manger. She took it all in as she crouched there, listening to the hammering of her heart.

Now she heard something else. Rustling behind her. And footsteps approaching softly. She whirled, her SIG drawn. Two sets of eyes gleamed at her in the flashlight's beam. Soave and Yolie were coming up behind her, crouched low.

"What do you think you're doing?" she whispered, holstering her weapon.

"We couldn't let you go in alone," Soave whispered in response.

"If we go for the shot," Yolie explained, her mouth to Des's ear, "we can bring it from three different angles."

"Plus Yolie's way better than you," Soave added, mouth to her other ear.

This much was true. Des was no slouch, but Yolie was one of the top three gunners in the whole state. If it did come to throwing shots from up in the balcony, she'd be mighty valuable. Firing downward was just about the most difficult shot you could attempt. No matter how much you compensated, you still had a natural tendency to come in high.

"Both of you should go back right now," Des whispered insistently.

"And you should shut up," Yolie whispered back.

"But what about proper procedure?"

"Girl, we could care less about procedure."

"We care about you," Soave agreed.

Des mouthed the words, "Thank you." And warned them to watch out for Jesus, Mary and Joseph.

They didn't have the slightest idea what she was talking about but they both nodded their heads. Then the three of them pressed on.

CHAPTER 27

"MY SWEET BITCH OF a sister was planning to hang herself to-night," Eric revealed, his lip curling at Mitch unpleasantly. "Who wouldn't buy that? Just think of the mess she's made of her life. Mark inherits what's hers, and Danielle has him comfortably under her thumb. With proper handling, Mark would have kept us afloat for several years."

"By which time Poochie would die of natural causes and all of your money worries would be over," Mitch said, glancing up at Danielle. She looked pale and frightened in the front pew.

"Exactly." Eric merely looked determined as he knelt over Mitch, that knife held to his throat. It trembled slightly in his hand.

"And Bement? How did he figure into this?"

"He doesn't," Eric replied. "The kid could care less about money. All he thinks about is the Kershaw girl."

"Eric, you sure were right about one thing," Mitch concluded, pinned there on the floor with his hands lashed beneath him, his shoulders throbbing. "Madness runs in the family. You're insane. You both are. And now you're totally screwed. You should give yourselves up. Because they'll never agree to your demands. You have no chance of getting away. None."

"You're wrong, Mitch. Everything's going to be okay. But what's *taking* them so long?"

"The snipers have to get in position," Mitch explained, fighting off the overwhelming impulse to panic. He had to keep talking. As long as he was talking he could hang on. But how much longer? "Those guys, they're amazing. They can zone-in on a freckle from a half-mile away. I imagine they'll set up on the neighboring rooftops."

Eric glanced around at the windows, his eyes bulging with alarm. There were so many windows. So many different vantage points. He scrambled back behind Mitch, hugging him to his chest as a human shield. "They wouldn't shoot up a church," he argued.

"Won't have to. You asked for a car to take us to the airport. As soon as we walk out the front door they'll shoot you dead in your tracks. You won't even know what hit you."

"Don't try to rile me, Mitch. They'll agree to our terms. We'll be fine."

"You two will never be fine," Mitch said stubbornly. "You don't trust each other."

"Of course we do," Danielle objected. "You're wrong, Mitch."

"Really? Then why did Eric tell me he thinks you're fed up with him? I think he's terrified that you really *are* having an affair with Mark."

"I love my husband. I'd never do any such thing."

"Eric doesn't believe that, Danielle. He was afraid you'd try to pin this all on him and run off with Mark. It's the classic double-cross. Think *Out of the Past*. Think *The Killing,* which it might interest you to know was directed by a young unknown named Stanley Kubrick."

Danielle shook her head at him. "I don't know what any of this means."

"It means your boy has been fitting you for a pair of hot pink Jimmy Choos."

"Now I *really* don't know what you mean. But you're wrong about us, Mitch. We're together. We've always been together."

"I'm not buying that, Danielle. You see, I've just spent quality time with someone who knows the *real* Eric. And she told me his so-called mission in life is all one big, pesticide-free scam. That he's strictly about himself."

"What are you talking about now?" Eric demanded angrily. "*Who* are you talking about?"

"A girl who deserved to be treated a whole lot better than you treated her," Mitch answered, feeling the man's entire body tense up. "You talked a lot about yourself in bed, Eric. You talked too much."

Danielle peered at her husband warily. "Eric, what is he? . . ."

"N-Nothing, hon." Eric's voice suddenly cracked like an adolescent schoolboy's. "A perfectly innocent situation. Just this girl who was hung up on me years and years ago."

"*Which* girl?"

"Allison Mapes," Mitch informed her.

"She's the little teenager who used to go to the green markets with you."

"Right, I-I was mentoring her."

Mitch let out a hoot. "He was putting it to her for months and months, Danielle. She told me he couldn't get enough of her."

Danielle gaped at Eric in horror. "You were cheating on me with that *child?*"

"If it makes you feel any better," Mitch continued, "I was plenty surprised myself. Eric's such a do-gooder. Up at dawn every morning. He works hard. He cares about the land and the—"

"Oh, shut up!" Danielle screamed. "Just . . . shut . . . up!" She'd begun rocking back and forth in the pew, hugging herself tightly as tears streamed down her cheeks. "She was a *child,* you pervert. She was . . . my God, how old was she?"

"Fourteen," Mitch answered as he lay there in Eric's vise-like grip. "That does constitute statutory rape. And he could still go to jail for it if Allison wanted to press charges. Mind you, that's the least of your legal worries right now."

"Bastard!" Danielle spat, rocking back and forth like a distraught mourner.

"Hon, I'm not proud about that chapter of my life," Eric confessed tonelessly. "But I've healed myself. We're talking about something that happened a long, long time ago. It's been over for years."

"He's right about that," Mitch conceded. "Allison's good and through with him—mostly because Eric wasn't straight with her.

Kept bragging about how rich he'd be one day. How he'd divorce you and marry her. But as soon as he'd had his fill he dumped her. Nearly destroyed her, too. She's doing a lot better these days. Not great, but okay."

"You seem to know an awful lot about her," Eric muttered sourly.

"Well, yeah. We just spent the night together."

"You did what?"

"Don't tell me you're jealous, Eric," Mitch pleaded. "Because then I'll start wondering whether you were hoping to take up with her again after you made your big score. And I'm not sure I can handle any more weirdness right now."

"That wasn't going to happen," Eric told Danielle earnestly. "Don't listen to him, okay? He's strictly playing with your mind. You can see that, can't you?"

Danielle stared at him dumbly. She seemed dazed, as if she'd just staggered away from a head-on collision with a bus. "How could you *do* that to me?"

"He's a ruthless, scheming murderer, Danielle," Mitch pointed out. "Everything about his life is a total lie. What made you think he'd be honest with *you*?"

"We're in this together," she said hopelessly.

"You're wrong, Danielle. Eric betrayed you with Allison. And he figured you were betraying him with Mark. This may not be the ideal time to mention it, but you two have some serious problems with your marriage."

"If you don't shut your big mouth," warned Eric, biting off the words angrily, "I swear I will slit your throat right now!"

"Eric, you're almost enough to turn me off of do-gooders entirely. But not quite, because I'll let you in on a little secret—I believe in people." Mitch gazed up toward the balcony now, smiling hugely. "I believe we do the right thing most of the time. I have to believe that, Eric. Because if it's not true, then where are we? We're . . . well, we're you."

"Hon, d-don't *listen* to this guy!" sputtered Eric, who was now quivering with rage. "This will be okay. We can still get away."

"And do what?" Mitch persisted, goading him, inflaming him still further. "Forget about your farm. Your so-called mission is history. Where will you go now? You don't trust each other, so you'll pretty much have to stay together twenty-four, seven. And won't that suck. It means no more nubile teenaged girls for you, Eric. Just plain old Danielle, morning, noon and—"

"I *told* you to shut up!" Eric screamed, an animal roar coming from his throat as he punched Mitch in the ear with all of his might, pitching Mitch over to the floor with a hard slam.

Now Mitch's head was ringing.

And Danielle was sobbing, "No, Eric! No!"

As Eric kept screaming, "I *told* you! I *told* you!" His eyes blazing at Mitch like a wild man's. Now the wild man was on top of Mitch, pummeling him in the head with left-hand punches. "I *told* you!" Danielle screaming at him to stop. And now he had that Leatherman raised high overhead in his right hand. "Say good-bye, you fat son of a bitch! Because I am going to stick this in your eye! So help me I'll! . . ."

Chapter 28

That chopper was a blessing.

As it moved in closer overhead, the whirring of its rotor blades masked the sounds they couldn't help making no matter how hard they tried to be silent.

First, there was that old stairway up to the cloakroom. Its wooden treads went *snap, crackle, pop* even though they tippy-toed. Then there was the door at the top of the stairs. Des got to it first, Soave and Yolie right behind her as she turned the thumb latch. She eased the bolt *slo-o-owly* open but there was still an audible click. And those door hinges hadn't been oiled since Hoover was in the White House. They squeaked and groaned as she eased the door open, flooding the stairway with bright daylight.

As Des paused there in the empty cloakroom, blinking in the sunlight, she could hear a steady murmur of conversation inside the sanctuary. No raised voices. No footsteps.

They were okay.

Her SIG drawn, she inched her way across the cloakroom toward the foyer itself. There were two stairways up to the balcony, one on each side of the foyer. She had to find out whether those foyer doors were open or closed. If they were closed then the three of them could split up now, unseen by anyone inside the sanctuary. If they were open then they'd have to take the same stairway up and fan out once they reached the balcony. That would make their job harder because they'd be exposed that much longer—should Eric or Danielle chance to look up. Not an impossible job. Just a riskier one. Because if they didn't have the element of surprise on their side then they had nothing.

Only a disaster waiting to happen.

Soave and Yolie remained behind her in the cloakroom, their SIGs drawn, as she poked her head through the cloakroom door-way into the foyer itself and . . .

The foyer doors were closed.

She took a deep breath and darted her way across the building, making not a sound. When she reached the far balcony stairs she paused, glancing back toward Soave and Yolie. They were in position now to climb the stairs next to the cloakroom. Yolie pointed to her own weapon to remind Des that she'd take the shot if there was one to take. Des nodded.

Then they climbed.

Happily, the balcony stairs were carpeted. Des crept her way up, up to the church's wraparound balcony, staying low to the floor as she came out right alongside the organ. From her crouch there at the top of the aisle she couldn't make out Mitch or the killers down there. But she could certainly hear them—the acoustics were so amazing that the clarity of their voices startled her. Mitch seemed to be doing all of the talking. Big surprise there. Some noise about a young director named Stanley Kubrick. Why on earth was he talking about Kubrick at a time like this? Because he was Mitch Berger, that's why. Not that Danielle seemed to have the slightest idea what he was going on about. Des couldn't blame her. Because now her doughboy was talking about hot pink Jimmy Choos.

Soave and Yolie were crouched low across the balcony from Des. Meanwhile, through the balcony windows, she could see a whole herd of cube vans parked outside. The hostage unit had arrived.

Yolie slithered her way on her stomach between two rows of seats until she reached the balcony's center aisle. When she got there she nodded to Des. Now all three of them began inching forward on their stomachs, snaking their way row by row down to the lip of the balcony for an actual look at the situation. Slowly, Des raised her head over the top of the protective facing and . . .

It wasn't pretty. Danielle was no problem. She was seated in the front row of pews, her back to the balcony. The problem was in front of her on the floor, where Mitch and Eric lay propped against the dais, Eric behind Mitch. *Under* Mitch, really. He was employing him as a human shield. And Mitch made for one hell of a shield. Hardly any of the thinner man's body was exposed. Nothing but his arms. His left was wrapped around Mitch's chest. In his right hand Eric held a knife to Mitch's throat.

Mitch's cell phone lay next to them on the floor, as did his smashed tape recorder.

Mitch was still doing the talking. Going on about Allison Mapes now. How she'd spent the night with him last night. *Say what?* How she'd told him that she and Eric had been lovers back when Allison was a tender teen. Which sure came as news to Danielle, who seemed totally blown away.

Eric was trying to reassure her: "Don't listen to him, okay? He's strictly playing with your mind. You can see that, can't you?"

Des sure could. Mitch was trying to turn them against each other. But Danielle didn't care. She was too pissed at Eric.

"How could you *do* that to me?" she wanted to know.

"He's a ruthless, scheming murderer, Danielle," Mitch explained. "Everything about his life is a total lie. What made you think he'd be honest with *you?*"

"We're in this together," she responded.

Now Mitch was telling her how wrong she was. That she couldn't trust Eric. That the two of them had serious marital problems. Des could have sworn the fool was purposely trying to rile Eric. And it was working.

"If you don't shut your big mouth," Eric snarled at him, "I swear I will slit your throat right now!"

Des continued to lie there on the balcony floor, powerless. There was nothing they could do—not with the way Eric was using Mitch as body armor. Des was not taking this horrible realization well. Her breathing was shallow and quick, her hand clammy around the SIG. That was the man she loved down there. She was practically ready to dive right off the balcony. But all she could do was exchange a signal with Yolie and Soave to wait. And watch.

And quietly go nuts—because with each passing second Des was becoming convinced that Mitch Berger had a death wish.

"I believe we do the right thing most of the time," he was lecturing this deranged murderer who held a knife to his jugular vein. "I have to believe that, Eric. Because if it's not true, then where are we? We're . . . well, we're you."

Des had to stop herself from screaming: *What in God's name are you doing?*

As he lay there in Eric's clutches, Mitch told her. His round face was turned upwards toward the balcony and he was *smiling*. It was a blissful smile. A smile that told her he knew something that Eric didn't know:

Mitch knew that Des was up there.

How? Didn't matter. All that mattered was he knew.

Now an enraged Eric was sputtering at Danielle to ignore Mitch, insisting they could still get away.

As Mitch kept pushing and pushing: "Where will go now? You don't trust each other, so you'll have to stay together twenty-four, seven. And won't that suck. It means no more nubile teenaged girls for you, Eric. Just plain old Danielle, morning, noon and—"

"I *told* you to shut up!" roared Eric, punching Mitch in the head, driving him into the floor.

Danielle cried out, "No, Eric! No!"

But it was no use. The organic farmer was a man possessed. "I *told* you! I *told* you!" he screamed as he pummeled Mitch in the head again and again. "I *told* you!" And now he was over Mitch, raising that knife high up over his head. "Say good-bye, you fat son of a bitch, because I am going to stick this in your eye! So help me I'll . . ."

Yolie did not hesitate, did not waver, did not miss.

She pumped three shots right into Eric Vickers with her semiautomatic. The first went into the center of his back. The second into his neck. The third blew out the back of his head. So rapid and precise was her gunfire that, for a brief moment the meat sack formerly known as Eric Vickers was still suspended there above Mitch, clutching that knife overhead.

Until he collapsed on top of Mitch in a dead heap.

Danielle fell to the floor before him, screaming.

Soave sprinted down the stairs and cuffed her as Yolie threw open the church's front doors to give the all-clear sign. Des was the slowest to make it down the stairs. Her knees didn't seem to be working too well.

As for Mitch, he didn't seem the least bit fazed, despite the knife-point hostage ordeal, the punches to his head, Eric getting shot to death. The man's blood was all over him. And yet, the very first thing Mitch said to her after he'd struggled out from under Eric's body was, "What took you so long, slats? I was running out of things to say."

Des stared at him, dumfounded. "You knew I was up there," she said hoarsely, as a pair of uniforms led the stricken Danielle outside. "How, Mitch?"

"Because you're *you*. I knew you'd never wait for that hostage unit to get here." He removed his bloodied jacket and calmly tossed it aside, grinning at Soave and Yolie. "But I wasn't counting on backup. Thanks large."

"No prob," Yolie said. "Wherever my baby girl goes, I go."

"I never believed this was possible, Berger," Soave said, shaking his head. "But if anyone on earth could do it, you were the man for the job."

"What job, Lieutenant?"

"You actually talked that man to death."

"Hey, you go with your strengths." Mitch pulled a clean, folded handkerchief from his back pocket and held it out to Des. "Here, you'll be needing this. That cellar's mold city."

He knew her better than she knew herself—which sometimes irked the hell out of her. Right now, as Des proceeded to sneeze her head off, it just made her feel cherished.

"Des, I want you to know that Allison slept on the couch last night."

"Of course she did," Des snuffled.

"And Quirt peed in her sneaker."

"That's my man."

"Oh, and one other thing. It was Claudia who was next, not Poochie. They were going to make it look like a suicide. I'm sorry to say I don't have that on tape. He broke my recorder."

"Danielle will give it up," Soave said confidently. "A full confession's her only chance."

"School me on something, boyfriend," Des said. "You knew those Bilco doors were unlocked?"

"I did."

"And that there was a stairway into the cloakroom?"

"I didn't. But I assumed you'd figure something out."

"Mitch, what if I hadn't?"

"The thought never crossed my mind. I believe in you."

"But that's total lunacy!"

"Des, it's not any such thing." With his eyes he told her what it was.

She gazed back at him, swallowing. "I swear, I don't know whether to hug you or hit you."

She hugged him. And even though he'd been acting all gallant and cool, she knew he was plenty shaken. Because when Mitch hugged her back he held on tighter than she'd ever been held by anyone in her life. He was still holding on when they came in to take care of Eric's body.

Epilogue

(two days later)

The old lighthouse out on Big Sister was kept padlocked shut. Mitch had one of the keys. Des held the kerosene lantern for him while he used it in the darkness of midnight, hearing the forlorn foghorn from the lighthouse across the river at Saybrook Point. The hinges creaked mightily when he swung the lighthouse's massive steel door open. Inside, the spiral staircase up to the lantern room resembled a six-story-high corkscrew.

"We won't be able to see a thing in this fog," Des pointed out, remaining there in the doorway with the light. "Visibility's less than a quarter-mile."

"There's something up there I want to show you," Mitch said as he began to climb the twisting cast-iron stairs. "It's a surprise, okay?"

Des didn't budge. "Mitch, I hate surprises."

"I know this. Just come on, will you?"

Reluctantly, she joined him, their footsteps echoing in the narrow enclosed cylinder.

It was the first evening they'd managed to spend together since Yolie Snipes shot Eric Vickers dead on the floor of the Congo Church. Danielle had been arraigned in New London Superior Court on two counts of murder in the first degree. She was being held without bond and, as Soave had predicted, was talking her head off. Blaming it all on Eric. The news of her arrest had served as a major wake-up call for Mark Widdifield. That very same day he paid a visit to Claudia at their cottage. Stayed for dinner and never left. The two of them were trying to work things out, Mitch had heard. Claudia was also spending more time with Poochie. Her famous mother was lonely and adrift without Guy Tolliver in her life. Plus she still wasn't allowed to drive. So it was Claudia who was now chauffeuring her around Dorset. Claudia who was helping her shop for a vintage Mercedes to replace her fabulous, long-gone Gullwing. Claudia who was bringing her around to the idea that someone ought to catalog her art collection. There was even talk that she'd convinced Poochie to get a physical exam, but Mitch was fairly certain this was merely idle gossip. Likewise the rumor that young Bement was going to take over operation of Four Chimneys Farm.

Mitch's literary agent had started reading Justine's manuscript and couldn't put it down. Called Mitch immediately to tell him that he wasn't crazy—*She'll Do Ya* was indeed great. And that he wanted to represent her. Justine had shrieked with girlish delight when Mitch phoned her with the news.

Actually, Justine was the one person in town who wasn't shocked by what Eric and Danielle had done. "Well, what did you expect?" she said to Mitch. "All people are liars. Except for you. You're okay, even if you are stuck in a hopeless relationship."

Mitch didn't know what she meant by that last comment.

When he stopped by McGee's Diner to see how Allison Mapes was coping, Mitch discovered that she'd cleared out of Dorset a few hours after Eric was shot. Taken off for Daytona Beach, Florida, with Stevie and Donnie Kershaw. She'd told Dick McGee that the three of them planned to find work down there and never come back. Which didn't sit very well with Milo. The snarly little swamp Yankee seemed like a broken man when Mitch encountered him at the A&P. So downcast he didn't even bother to be nasty. Rut Peck told Mitch that the little guy was positively devastated by his boys leaving him.

Maybe, Mitch reflected, the little guy should have been nicer to them.

Mitch was huffing and puffing by the time they'd climbed their way up to the old lighthouse's lantern room. Once upon a time, twin thousand-watt lamps had been positioned up here to warn seafarers of the treacherous rocks. Now there was only an empty, glass-walled chamber with amazing views in every direction. On a clear night, the lights from Long Island's north shore were clearly visible across the Sound. Tonight, Mitch could barely make out the lighthouse at Saybrook Point. He'd already been up here twice today. Once to sweep up. Once to lug everything up here and arrange it just so. The bottle of Moët & Chandon in its ice bucket. The long-stemmed glasses. The dozen roses in a vase, candles that he'd positioned everywhere. There was a blanket for them to sit on.

"What's all this now?" Des wondered as she watched him light the candles, one by one. "We holding a séance?"

"No, I've got something for you."

She flashed her hugest smile at him. "Is it your magic feather?"

"You *really* like that feather, don't you?"

"Baby, what *is* this?"

"Have a seat, will you?"

"Okay . . ." She arranged her long, taut self on the blanket. "Now what?"

Mitch swallowed hard and plunged ahead. "I've been thinking that when I talked about us getting, you know, *married,* I didn't exactly go about it the right way. I didn't tell you how much you mean to me. I didn't tell you that I can't possibly live the rest of my life without you. And I didn't give you *this.*" He handed her the small box that was in his jacket pocket.

It was not a fancy ring. The diamond was small. It was not a new one either. The gold had a burnished glow.

"It was my grandmother's. I had my mom send it to me."

"Baby, baby . . ." she gasped. "I thought you gave Maisie your grandmother's engagement ring."

"You're the detective. See if you can work it out."

Des nodded her head sagely. "You had two grandmothers."

"This one was Sadie Mandelbaum's. I'm sorry I bungled this whole thing the way I did. I should have made it more special. I can be a bit socially challenged, in case you haven't noticed."

"Mitch, this is all so incredibly sweet of you, but that was never the issue. *You* were never the issue. It was all about me needing to get some things straight in my own mind. And I have. And the answer is yes, in case you're wondering. Soon as you want."

"I'm sorry, what did you just say?"

She frowned at him. "Are you okay?"

"Absolutely. Just feeling a little dizzy all of a sudden. Must be that climb up here. So, wow, I'm going to be Mr. Des Mitry."

"Tell you what—you can keep your own name."

Beaming, he worked the cork out of the champagne and filled their glasses. They drank, her pale green eyes shining at him in the candlelight.

"Do you have a where in mind?" she asked.

"Anywhere is fine by me, just as long as it's not the inside of the Congo church. Deal?"

"Deal. Shall we shake on it?"

He leaned over and grazed her lips with his. "Oh, I'm absolutely positive we can do better than that."

Des left Mitch's little island in the Sound shortly after dawn, utterly sleep deprived and caring not one bit. She felt positively giddy as she piloted her cruiser up Old Shore Road toward home. Didn't feel the road beneath her at all. All she could feel was Sadie Mandelbaum's ring around her finger.

She was so dreamy that she didn't notice someone sitting in the sedan parked across the street from her house. Didn't even notice the car there.

She put the coffee on as soon as she walked in. Changed into her sweats, then woke up Bella, who was snoring away in her room like a lumberjack. They were planning to check out that Dumpster behind the Rustic Inn this morning.

"We're on dawn patrol, girl," she sang out. "Ready for your coffee?"

Bella groaned, blinking at her.

"I'll take that as a yes."

Des headed toward the kitchen to get it. That was when her doorbell rang.

It was so early in the morning that she couldn't imagine who it could be. Which was pretty amazing, considering how big a believer Des was in self-preservation. And yet no survival instinct warned her that here was trouble. No inner voice said, *"Something's got to go wrong because I'm feeling way too good."* She was simply caught there, flat-footed, when she yanked open that door.

And standing there before her, wearing a charcoal gray flannel suit and a smile, was the single most beautiful black man she had ever seen in her life.

The air went right out of her body as soon as she saw him. Her knees wobbled, stomach clenched. "H-Hello, Brandon . . ." she stammered, barely getting the words out.

"Right back at you, Desi," he said in that rich burgundy voice of his. "We need to talk. It's important. May I come in?"